CHRISTINA JAMES was born in Spalding and sets her novels in the evocative Fenland countryside of South Lincolnshire. She works as a bookseller, researcher and teacher. She has a lifelong fascination with crime fiction and its history. She is also a well-established non-fiction writer, under a separate name.

CHASING
HARES

CHRISTINA JAMES

SALT

CROMER

PUBLISHED BY SALT PUBLISHING 2019

2 4 6 8 10 9 7 5 3 1

First published in Great Britain in 2019 by
Salt Publishing Ltd
12 Norwich Road, Cromer NR27 0AX United Kingdom

www.saltpublishing.com

Salt Publishing Limited Reg. No. 5293401

A CIP catalogue record for this book is available from the British Library

ISBN 978 1 78463 189 5 (Paperback edition)
ISBN 978 1 78463 190 1 (Electronic edition)

Typeset in Neacademia by Salt Publishing

Printed and bound in Great Britain by Clays Ltd, Elcograf S.p.A

For Madelaine and Marc, for their magnificent support
for all the Yates novels; and to Anthony and Marcus
for supplying me with the location and several brilliant
ideas for Chasing Hares – not to mention contributing
more than a little to some of the characters!

PART ONE

PART ONE

CHAPTER 1

DS JULIET ARMSTRONG turned off the A1175 and parked her car at the top of Campain's Lane. She leaned forward to peer at the surrounding countryside. The day was dull and bleak, the fields swathed in ribbons of mist. It was November, practically winter. Juliet hated the winter, yet was fascinated by the last gasp of the Fenland autumn. During this brief period, the quintessential soul of the Fens seemed to be laid bare, providing a glimpse of what made this secretive, primeval place tick; but possibly, she thought, just for people like herself who had not been born and bred here. Most of the local folk she knew had no time to think about the passing seasons and what they might mean. Perhaps they didn't need to: such knowledge flowed through their blood.

Despite its proximity to Spalding, she rarely visited Deeping St Nicholas. It was a strange settlement, home to barely 2,000 people, yet, with its length of approaching seven miles, it had the distinction of being the longest village in the country, largely because its dwellings were spaced well apart and straggled along the main road – in today's terminology, a 'ribbon development', though the term hadn't been coined when they were built. Its inhabitants were almost all involved in agriculture, most in a humble capacity. The village could boast none of the architectural distinction or aristocratic history of its siblings, Market Deeping and Deeping St James.

Campain's Lane was a long road, home to a considerable

number of properties. There were some between-the-wars council houses and a collection of other dwellings, most recently built but interspersed with the occasional Victorian cottage. The new houses included a modern terrace, one of the residents of which, a Mrs Lovell, had called the station to say that she thought she'd seen some men out hare coursing in the surrounding fields. Juliet had been on her way back from a meeting in Bourne when the message came through and phoned the station to suggest that she return the long way back to Spalding to take a look. Her boss, DI Tim Yates, had agreed, on the strict condition that she didn't approach potential transgressors if she saw them, but called for a squad car. Juliet, who was still undergoing treatment for the slash wound to her face inflicted the previous year by Susie Fovargue – now a notorious convicted female serial killer – readily agreed.

The landscape was not entirely obscured by the mists, but they prevented Juliet from getting a panoramic view at any given moment. The fields, when she could see them, were of deepest chocolate brown and neatly ploughed. There was no sign of human activity. All she could discern was a sizeable flock of rooks pecking enthusiastically at the furrows. She decided she would just wait for ten minutes or so: if there had been a hare coursing party out earlier, they'd either got what they'd come for or moved on to another area and would be unlikely to return.

Hare coursing had become the major scourge of the South Lincs police force in recent years; they'd had little success in catching the perpetrators, much to the disgust of animal rights groups. The problem was that the Fens were not only vast, but very sparsely populated. Surveillance was difficult, because no-one knew where the men who took part would show up next or indeed where they had come from: the scant information available indicated they weren't residents of the county. The 'sport' was despicable, cruel and pointless. Ostensibly, its aim was to discover and celebrate champion hare coursing dogs and breed from them, but the dogs were almost as likely to become casualties as the hares. The real motivation was greed: illicit prize money of several thousand pounds might be offered, together with valuable trophies of the kind presented at greyhound tracks. Champion dogs could also be sold for more thousands or put out to stud for large fees.

Juliet stayed longer than she'd intended before she decided to give up and turned the ignition key. As she did so, the building of rooks – fifty or so of them – flapped squawking to the skies. Juliet was surprised: she'd made more noise when parking the car than starting it up again and the birds certainly hadn't been disturbed by her arrival. It was likely that something – or someone – else had spooked them. Her eyes swept the landscape again, but she could see nothing new. She lowered the car window and listened carefully.

She heard it immediately: an eerie howling, as if an animal were in great pain. She wondered if there had indeed been coursing earlier and the hare had been abandoned to its injuries. She knew that hares could scream if frightened or captured. She'd never heard of a hare being left wounded by coursing, though: the dogs invariably 'ragged' them until they were dead. She also knew that an injured wild animal that had broken free of its captors would be more likely to slink away soundlessly, either to die or to recover, than draw attention to itself.

She listened intently, stretching her neck out of the window. Eventually she heard the noise again, fainter this time, as if the animal were losing strength. She scanned the fields once more. Not a soul in sight. Although the atmosphere produced by the mist and the uncanny howling gave her the creeps, she couldn't bear to turn her back on a creature in pain. Glancing round at the deserted landscape, she persuaded herself it would be safe enough to investigate.

She climbed out of her car and opened the boot to remove a torque wrench, which she slid into her pocket before walking briskly and purposefully down the road in the direction the noise was coming from. She glanced across at the houses as she passed them; again, no sign of life. Although it was a very dull day, half dark in the early afternoon, no lights were shining behind their windows.

She'd just passed the last house when she saw it: a dead hare, severely mauled, which had been tossed so carelessly into the ditch that its body was resting near the top of the bank. So Mrs Lovell had been right: they had been out coursing today. She bent down to get a closer view. The sounds she had heard could not have come from this animal; the corpse was already glassy-eyed, the body stiffening. She looked around her again, in some alarm. She would walk just a few steps further, then go back to the station and report the incident, get someone else to investigate.

CHAPTER 2

H E HAD DECIDED to call it Holyrood. It was a classy name, and his researches told him there'd once been a big house in Spalding of that name. The original Holyrood House had been demolished in the 1950s, long enough ago for the name to sound historical and only vaguely familiar to the older locals.

His Holyrood, which was built between the wars, had been called Soldier's Nook when he bought it, a name which he detested for its undertones of pokiness and sentimentality. This house was neither. The island had previously been referred to by no memorable name: people had simply called it the "The Island" or "Little London Island". That wouldn't do, either. He wanted something distinctive and unhomely, perhaps a bit mysterious. Holyrood House and Holyrood Island fitted the bill exactly.

The island almost wasn't one: at first sight it appeared to be a small isthmus protruding into the River Welland, a Rorschach-blob extension of the riverbank itself. Only closer inspection would reveal that it was a proper island, linked to the bank by a sturdy bridge which had so mossed over that it looked like part of the bank. A strong pair of black wrought-iron gates guarded this, the sole entrance. Often, they gaped open: Gordon Bemrose only left them closed when he was trying to impress.

The size of the island was deceptive: from the adjacent

bridge it seemed very small, but once present on its turf visitors were always surprised by how substantial it was. That it was pear-shaped was partly responsible for the illusion: the bulbous part of the pear lay furthest from the bridge. In total, including the straggly bit on the bridge side, it was perhaps one third of a mile long.

The big house had been built on the widest part of the island, facing downstream. It was an imposing rather than a magnificent building: a between-the-wars edifice typical of the combined high spec and questionable aesthetic of the era. Its windows were made of metal. Some had been moulded round the curiously curved corners of the house, so they looked out on two sides. It was built entirely of red brick, but the two upper storeys had been rendered and were painted white.

To the rear was a large garden, laid out so that it was divided equally between a vegetable patch, a shrubbery and a lawn surrounded by borders which in the summer attacked the eye with short neat flowers in brilliant jewelled colours. Low box hedges marked out the divisions and a thicker row of box set the boundary of the garden itself. Beyond was a dirt road which served both the house itself and the terrace of four cottages on the other side of it. They had recently been rendered and painted white to match the house. The date 1795 was picked out in black below the eaves of the end cottage.

The front doors of the cottages opened straight on to the dirt track, but at their rear each had a tiny garden. The gardens ended abruptly in a sheer drop to the river.

For almost ten years, Gordon Bemrose had owned most of the island and the big house, as well as two of the cottages, which had been bought as they were vacated by the previous owners. At the time of the sale the remaining two cottages were still inhabited by owner-occupiers, an elderly gentleman and an elderly lady, both of whom were at first determined to stay put. Gordon had plied them with blandishments, including purchase prices way above what the properties were worth and offers of help in finding more congenial accommodation. When this hadn't worked, he'd turned on the screws. Under the terms of their freehold, they were allowed access to their homes via the road past his property and the dirt track. Although he couldn't overturn this completely, he'd managed to obtain a court order restricting their ingress and egress to specific (inconvenient) times of the day. Mr Hicks, the old man, decided to throw in the towel quite quickly after the order was served, taking the money which was still on offer to buy himself a nice flat in a sheltered accommodation complex. Mrs Shennan, the old lady, had toughed it out until the end, closely monitored by Gordon. Ostensibly being a good neighbour by keeping a 'filial' eye on her, he reported her to social services every time she showed any sign of forgetfulness. Eventually, a social worker, someone who happened to be an acquaintance of Gordon's, arrived to conduct a series of tests and proclaim her unfit to continue living alone. Unlike Mr Hicks, she wasn't paid the generous price Gordon had originally offered, but instead a more modest sum based on the valuation supplied by a local estate agent. Despite some rather sticky negotiations with Mrs Shennan's niece's solicitor, the sale had gone through at this price and Mrs Shennan was obliged to accept a place at Matmore Grange, a colourless and rather grim old person's residential home a couple of miles away. She died less than six months after moving there.

That had been three months ago. Gordon Bemrose still cursed the old lady who had for years held up his plans. Her cottage was in a state of advanced neglect when he took possession of it. It had been touch and go whether he could get all the necessary repairs completed in time for the crime mystery activity weekend.

The crime mystery weekend had been Gordon's brainchild, not to say his obsession, for several years. Having tried several other business ventures of various hues, he had hit on this as the most congenial future way of supporting the island and its properties and maintaining himself. He didn't envisage it would entail too much hard graft.

His was by no means a new idea, a fact of which he was fully aware. He had conducted a great deal of research into such events and, with the help of the ubiquitous internet-delivered customer scoring system that even the smallest company seemed to use nowadays, believed he'd identified the features that worked and those that didn't. He'd gone on to invent ways of delivering an experience like no other, a privilege for which he felt he would be able to charge quite handsomely.

In his promotional brochure, he identified three 'Unique Selling Points' to support the introductory event: the location itself, which needed little artificial help from himself to inculcate an ambience of gloom and mystery; his motley but surprisingly useful relatives, two of whom he could rope in to assist him without incurring additional financial outlay; and a third, which he tantalisingly proclaimed should be kept secret until well into the weekend when the actual event took place.

Gordon Bemrose was up early on the Friday morning. After a skimpy breakfast, he mentally ran through the catalogue of jobs he needed to complete before his guests began to arrive in the afternoon. He went outside and was gratified to see the late autumn Fenland mists had come swirling round like good fairies, providing plenty of 'atmosphere'.

He walked round the back of the house and went to stand on the little jetty, sniffing the damp air appreciatively. He was pleased to notice that visibility was so poor that the bridge which linked London Road to Cowbit Road was practically invisible, swathed in thick ribbons of grey-white mist, even though it was less than fifty yards from where he stood. Perfect!

Snapping out of his reverie, he climbed up the bank from the jetty and cast a sharp eye in the direction of the cottages. The cleaners were just arriving. He'd go over to inspect their work later. Right now, he was waiting for Anton, his nephew, to arrive.

CHAPTER 3

ANTON GREENWEAL MIGHT be petulant and self-opinionated, but he was good at his chosen profession - acting. He was also inseparable from Percy Forsyth-Jones, his partner, which worked in everyone's favour. Percy, who dropped the Jones except for billboard credits, was much more down-to-earth than Anton, and while it was undeniable that he always had an eye to the main chance, he managed to combine this with that genuine love for mankind that somehow had eluded Anton. He was only ever rattled when someone referred to him by his real name, which was Norman Potts.

A couple of years ago Anton had made the leap from being a minor celebrity to a household name by appearing on a TV reality show. Fortunately for Gordon Bemrose, fame had gone to his head and he'd taken out a mortgage on an old manor house at Metheringham. By now, it would certainly have been repossessed had Gordon not been there to bail Anton out. Anton was paying back the money with interest, but erratically, so Gordon felt perfectly justified in demanding his services free of charge for the crime weekend. That Percy would be bound to turn up as well was a bonus: Percy was himself a more than passable actor and, since Gordon hadn't requested his presence, there would be no need to pay him, either.

Anton and Percy were the only two professional actors who would be taking part in the festivities. Gordon had toyed with the idea of hiring others, but he'd blenched when he found out how much they'd expect to charge. Instead, his two leading men would be supported by the cream of the local amateur dramatic society, led by their producer, Montagu Sykes. Sykes's chosen actors would each receive a small honorarium.

Gordon glanced at his watch and cursed under his breath. Where the hell had they got to? Anton had written the play they were to stage, or, to be more correct, he'd made extensive adaptations to an existing melodrama, but there were still important changes of Gordon's own devising to be made before the amateurs arrived.

Turning the corner of his house so that he was approaching the front door again, he saw a big shiny black motorcycle parked by the door. He'd never seen it before – it was clearly very new – but he knew instinctively that it was Anton's. No wonder Anton was always in arrears with his repayments. Gordon hurried into the house.

Isobel Lawrence, his housekeeper, had not arrived when Gordon was assembling his makeshift breakfast, but she was there now, busy making French toast for Anton and Percy.

"There you are!" said Gordon irritably, addressing his nephew and his friend. "I've been waiting for you. Do you have time for breakfast? There's still a lot to do."

"Hello, Uncle Gordon," said Anton airily. "We won't be long. Man cannot live on bread alone, you know."

"No, the bread needs the elegant additions of egg dip and some exquisite compote, such as only Mrs Lawrence can rustle up," added Percy, fluttering his dark eyelashes in the housekeeper's direction. She was a no-nonsense lady, but she still smiled as she bent her head over the frying pan.

"Yes, well, when you're ready, I'll be outside fixing the

lights," said Gordon shortly. "Make sure you come and find me – don't loiter about in here."

He went outside again quickly, ignoring the stream of further quips that followed in his wake.

The outside lights had caused him a lot of soul-searching. On the one hand, he would have preferred the island to be plunged into inky blackness after dark, to make it authentically eerie and menacing. The few yellow streetlights were far too brash to be atmospheric, and he would certainly want to switch them off – which he would be able to do, because luckily they weren't on the local council's grid. Nevertheless, reluctantly he had to accept that he'd have to provide some other kind of lighting; otherwise, guests following up on the clues might trip and hurt themselves or even fall into the river. The last thing he needed was for his introductory event to be plagued with health and safety issues. Floodlights could be bought and fitted with filters to obtain a ghostly look, but the cost, when he investigated, proved prohibitive. He'd finally settled on strings of white fairy lights looped between the buildings and the trees. They looked tasteful, provided an adequate but subdued amount of light, and, crucially, were not expensive, particularly if he fitted them himself.

Somehow the long skeins of lights, although newly purchased, had become knotted together. By the time he'd disentangled them and propped his ladder against the house wall ready to start installing them, Anton and Percy had reappeared.

He was about to press-gang them into light-fitting duties when there came the sound of a vehicle clattering over the bridge. Anton and Percy turned to watch as it loomed through the mist. When he could see the driver, Percy began to wave wildly. "It's Patti!" he cried. Anton was less demonstrative, but he still greeted the gaunt blonde woman who stepped out of the car with a hug and a perfunctory kiss. Percy elbowed him out of the way and enveloped her in a crushing embrace. She emerged laughing.

"Let me go," she said, "or I'll be no use for anything!"

Gordon Bemrose appeared at her elbow.

"Hello, Patricia," he said. "You've come earlier than I asked – unlike your cousin, who of course was late – but it's champion to see you."

"Hello, Uncle Gordon," she said, dodging a peck on the cheek. She eyed him levelly, then glanced at her cousin, who was regarding her with some curiosity.

"You must have taken the day off work for this," Anton said.

"Yes. That's why I'm early. I might as well make the most of it."

"So how did our esteemed uncle manage to cajole you into giving up one of your precious leave days?"

Patti looked uncomfortable.

"Oh, for goodness sake, Anton," said Gordon quickly. "Not everyone thinks like you do! Let's go inside, shall we?"

CHAPTER 4

HOLYROOD HOUSE CRIME Weekend could take bookings for up to ten guests, two to sleep in each of the cottages and two in the extension on the east side of the house. Guests choosing one of the cottages could either sleep in the same room or opt for separate bedrooms – each cottage had a modest 'master bedroom' and a smaller single bedroom, which had been furnished respectively with a double bed and a single bed. There was a tiny bathroom in each house for its occupants to share. The en suite accommodation in the extension consisted of a double bedroom and bathroom only. As guests in the cottages could also take advantage of their own sitting-room and kitchen, Gordon decided they should pay a premium. He would have to charge a little less for the room in the extension.

He'd let that room first, to the only guests who had come to inspect beforehand. They were a mixed-race couple called Margarett and Colin Franklin. Gordon hadn't particularly taken to them – although he did not consider himself to be in the least racially prejudiced, the way they pronounced their names annoyed him. Margarett – an absurd spelling! – placed the stress on the final syllable of her name, while Colin stressed the first syllable of his, presumably in imitation of General Colin Powell. Gordon thought this affected and he didn't see why people like the Franklins should feel entitled to airs and graces. They seemed a very working-class couple and, quite frankly, not the sort of people who would enjoy the weekend.

Still, he supposed their money was as good as anyone else's; but it hadn't surprised him when they'd chosen the cheaper room in the extension. Colin had assured Gordon that this had nothing to do with the price: it was because the cottages were just too close to the edge of the island for Margarett to feel comfortable with the idea of staying in one of them; she had a fear of water. Gordon thought this was a piece of nonsense: the whole island was so close to the river that if she was genuinely scared of it she'd have been better off choosing an event somewhere else altogether, though of course he had not said so.

He'd just taken Patti into the kitchen, with Anton and Percy trailing behind her, when the telephone rang.

"I'd better answer it," said Gordon. "Why don't you all go into the sitting-room? Isobel will bring you some coffee."

"Oh, will she?" said Isobel crossly. "As if 'she' hasn't got enough to do already."

"It's all right, I'll get it," said Patti quickly.

"No, you go through, I need to take this call," Gordon snapped. "If necessary, I'll bring the bloody coffee myself. Just give me a minute."

Isobel sighed and put the kettle on.

"Hello?" said Gordon tentatively, when she was the only other person left in the kitchen with him. "Oh, good morning, Mrs Dack." He sounded relieved. "How are you? We're very much looking forward to meeting you here later today. And your husband."

"That's just it," said the voice at the other end of the phone. "It won't be him."

"I beg your pardon?" said Gordon. It was no concern of his if the woman decided to bring someone other than her husband, but how she'd managed to achieve this after having already booked the husband in was intriguing.

"He won't be with me. It will just be me. Reggie can't come. The same goes for Jackson. Lizzie will be on her own."

"Who?" Gordon asked. Then he remembered that Mrs Dack had booked two couples into adjacent cottages. As far as he could recollect, the other couple's name was Fox.

"Jackson - Lizzie's husband - can't come either. He and Reggie have some unexpected business. So it will only be the two of us - myself and Lizzie. We'd like just to share one of the cottages now, so Reggie's told me to ask you how much of our deposit money we'll get back."

Gordon's brow darkened.

"Well, I hardly think I can be expected to give you a refund at this late stage," he said. "There's no chance of finding replacement guests now."

"Reggie says if you take that line, none of us will come. You keep the deposit and we stay at home. See?"

The woman was behaving outrageously. Gordon carried out a quick mental calculation. The deposit he'd asked for was practically half the full fee - which itself was discounted as an introductory offer. The rest of the fee was payable prior to departure. Because of Gordon's shameless exploitation of anyone who 'owed' him, the overheads mainly consisted of food, drink and paying the cleaners; hot water; and laundry after the event. The cleaners were a lost cause - they'd already started work and Gordon knew if he suggested they should now work shorter hours than he'd promised they'd probably walk out en masse. Some of the laundry costs would be saved, of course; so could the cost of most of the food for two people, provided it didn't perish before it could be used. On balance, he'd be just as well off if the Dacks and Foxes didn't come. But then, would he be able to run the event successfully with only six people? And the whole point of the introductory offer was to generate publicity and, hopefully, to build up loyal custom for the future. He didn't want this Dack woman bad-mouthing him everywhere she went.

"Hello? Mr Bemrose? Are you still there?"

"Yes, I'm sorry Mrs Dack, I got distracted. I suppose your husband and Mr Fox are disappointed at not being able to come?"

"Oh, very disappointed, but you know how it is: business always has to come first."

"Quite. And it's good of you and Mrs Fox to be prepared to come without them. I expect you're disappointed about it, too," he added, back-pedalling as fast as he could.

"Oh I wouldn't say . . . " there was a noise at the other end of the phone. Mrs Dack made a strangled sound and then started coughing.

"Yes, of course we're disappointed," she continued eventually. "But Lizzie and I don't want to leave you in the lurch."

"That's very good of you," Gordon said again. "Well, under the circumstances, and seeing that this is an introductory offer, I suppose we can stretch a point."

"Meaning?" said Mrs Dack sharply.

"Meaning that if you and Mrs Fox share one cottage there will be no further charge. Your husbands' deposits will cover the outstanding amount owed."

"Oh, thank you, Mr Bemrose."

"My pleasure," said Gordon heavily. "Goodbye for now,

Mrs Dack. We shall look forward to meeting you and Mrs Fox later today."

Isobel Lawrence looked at him curiously as she loaded mugs on to a tray.

"Everything all right?" she asked.

"I suppose so. Two of the guests aren't coming now, so we won't need one of the cottages, unless I can persuade the Franklins to upgrade to a cottage. I'd rather not have them in the house if I can avoid it."

"How soon can you find out?"

"I'll try calling them now. They probably won't have set off yet."

"Where do they live?"

"In Kent, I think. Broadstairs or somewhere like that."

"It's quite a way. Must be four hours' drive at least. If they're planning to stop somewhere for lunch, they've probably already left home."

"I can still give it a try," said Gordon, opening the folder that contained the booking forms for all his guests. "Damn! They haven't given me a mobile number." He seized the phone and rapidly keyed in the landline number Colin Franklin had provided. It rang eight times and went to message. Sighing, Gordon pressed the red button.

"No joy," he said. "Have them make up all the cottages anyway, will you? I'll try to persuade the Franklins to take the one that's come free when they get here."

"Fine. Here's the coffee – will you take it through?"

"Thanks for making it. I do appreciate it."

Isobel Lawrence feigned shock.

"Are you quite sure you're all right?"

CHAPTER FIVE

T HE PLAY REHEARSAL and Patti's run-through took up more of Gordon Bemrose's time than he had expected. It had been his intention merely to give Anton some directions about how he wanted to change the melodrama and then carry on with his work, but Anton and Percy, flexing their professional muscles, said he'd have to pay much more attention to detail than that.

"After all," Anton had said, "who knows who might be coming to watch? One of the guests might be a film director or a television producer in mufti. Then where would we be, if we hadn't got it right? We must polish every line and action until they're perfect."

"Quite," said Percy, fluttering his eyelashes at Gordon. He'd turned to Patti, but she hadn't been any help: she seemed to be decidedly amused by the whole thing.

It transpired that what Anton actually meant was that he and Percy should hone their own parts to perfection. Since Montagu Sykes and his small troupe of thespians had yet to arrive, Gordon and Patti had to stand in for all the other parts. Gordon became increasingly exasperated.

"Do we really have to go over it again?" he growled, as Anton burnished one of his exits for the sixth time. "This really isn't my thing."

"Nearly there!" Anton sang out. "Besides, you surprise me, uncle. I've always thought you were a natural."

"A natural *what?*" Gordon demanded testily.

"Actor. A natural actor. You've disabused me now. For years I've assumed that you were putting on an act most of the time."

Gordon lowered at him. Eventually they arrived at the end of the play.

"Right," said Gordon. "Don't go away, you two. I want you to stay to support Patti. You may need to help her out this evening."

"I'm always ready to help Patti," said Percy, with a smirk.

"Naturally," Anton added, "but in this instance I don't quite see how. I don't know anything about mucking with dead bodies. The very thought makes me feel quite squeamish."

"My job isn't just about dead bodies . . . ." Patti began.

"No, but it is on this occasion," Gordon cut in. "What I want should be a doddle for you – just give a talk about your work and an elementary introduction to forensic science, so when we start providing the guests with clues they'll have an idea of what to look for."

"So how do we fit into that?" Anton demanded.

"Perhaps you just want us to stand about in the back-ground, looking sinister," said Percy. He contorted his features into a hideous expression. Anton and Patti collapsed into giggles.

"Don't be ridiculous. Just help Patti out if she gets stuck – she's not as used to being in the limelight as you two are."

"Well . . . " Percy began. He was cut short by Anton, who was looking out of the window. Several figures were passing by.

"Oh, my God," he shrieked. "It's that Sykes creature. I'd almost forgotten you wanted us to share the stage with him."

"You'd better be nice to him," said Gordon. "You can't put on the play without him and his colleagues, and they're only getting fifty quid each."

"That's not a surprise, is it? Do you ever pay anyone properly for their services to this establishment?" Gordon didn't answer him. After an uncomfortable pause, Anton continued. "Anyway, now that they're here, I suppose we'll have to run through the whole thing again."

"You won't be needing me this time, though, will you?" said Gordon, taking the opportunity to escape. As he left the room, he shouted over his shoulder to Patti, "If anyone wants me, I'll be outside. And don't let those two offend Mr Sykes and his lot."

"Charming!" Anton called after him.

Gordon Bemrose was still fiddling with the outside lights when he heard the rumble of a vehicle trundling over the mossy bridge. He scowled at his watch. It wasn't yet 3 p.m. The guests had been instructed to arrive between 4 p.m. and 5 p.m.

He was mollified when he saw that the Franklins were the new arrivals. He hooked the chain of fairy lights he was holding over a bush and edged his way down his ladder to greet them. He was wary of ladders at the best of times and certainly hadn't enjoyed having to negotiate this one in the mist, which was now thickening into a proper fog. It was all he could do to see where he was putting his feet.

Once at the foot of the ladder, he turned back to observe his handiwork and was gratified that the lights he'd already installed were glimmering spookily through the mist.

Colin Franklin jumped out of his car and bustled up to him, hand outstretched.

"Mr Bemrose, good afternoon!" he shouted, a little too loudly. His wife was following at a distance, delicately picking her way across the gravel. Eyes downcast, she remained silent.

"Hello, Mr Franklin. Just the man I'm looking for."

"Oh? Any particular reason?" Franklin's open smile was evaporating.

"Well, yes, as a matter of fact: I have a proposition to put to you."

"Really?"

"Yes. You see, one of the guest cottages has come vacant. I know you said the reason you'd chosen to stay in the house wasn't financial but I . . . well, I thought you might be interested in taking the cottage now. At no extra charge, of course."

Franklin directed a searching look at his wife, who shook her head.

"That's very nice of you, Mr Bemrose, but what we said when we came to inspect was true: Margarett doesn't fancy the cottages. She'll be more comfortable staying in the house."

Gordon shrugged.

"Suit yourself," he said off-handedly. "Come inside, anyway. We can't go into the sitting-room because the actors are in there doing their stuff, but I'm sure Mrs Lawrence will be pleased to welcome you into the kitchen."

CHAPTER SIX

A VA DACK AND Lizzie Fox, each escorted by her husband, had been treated to lunch in a passable Italian restaurant at the heart of the town. Their husbands had then continued on their journey, leaving Ava and Lizzie to kill time by exploring Spalding until the hour appointed for tea at Holyrood House arrived. Their tour round the town had been short and sweet: they'd been vaguely amused by the old-fashioned pork butcher's shop and bought a few knick-knacks in the bookshop before Ava announced that her feet were killing her – they were cramped into four-inch-high stilettos – and that she was bored with toting round her suitcase, even though it was on wheels. Together they tottered into the White Horse for a couple of stiff gins.

"Don't know about 'White Horse'. Bit of a 'one-horse' dump, this, isn't it?" said Ava, within earshot of the barman.

"Yes, I can't think what Jackson and Reggie see in this area."

They both giggled.

"Oh, I think you've got some idea," said Ava. "Anyway, this Holyrood place sounds quite smart. I'm sure we'll have a good time there."

"We'll make it our business to. I'm not playing the martyr to Jackson's little hobbies – I've told him that already."

Ava laughed again.

"If his lark is successful, it's nailed on you'll do well out of it. Jackson's much more generous to you than Reggie is to me."

"It doesn't come naturally, believe me. He needs plenty of encouragement. Perhaps you're a bit too soft where Reggie's concerned."

"Soft!" shrieked Ava, whose face had been getting redder as the gin worked its magic. "That's a good one: I must tell Reggie you said that." She looked at her watch. "It's gone 3.30," she said. "It should be all right to turn up at Holyrood now." She rapped on the table to attract the barman's attention.

"Excuse me," she shouted across at him in a loud voice. "Get us a taxi, will you?"

"What do you think this is?" he shouted back. "A fucking hotel?"

"Well, if you're going to be like that ... "

"It's all right, madam, I'll phone for a taxi," he replied, mindful of the two farmers seated in the window, both regulars, who were regarding him with curiosity and some disapproval. "We can do without your sort in here," he muttered under his breath.

The taxi arrived within two minutes.

"That was quick!" said Lizzie.

"I don't suppose there's much for him to do round here," said Ava, haltingly negotiating a dignified exit in her stilettos.

"It's not that far," said the driver, when he'd stowed their luggage and they'd climbed into the car. "You could walk it. Still, I suppose you're a bit hampered by those cases."

Ava shut her eyes to rest them a little. She had almost drifted off to sleep when she was jerked awake as the taxi rattled over the bridge to Holyrood.

"We're here!" said the driver. "Rum place if you ask me,"

he added. "They say a soldier lived here at one time. He was tried for murder and got off."

"Really?" said Lizzie, her eyes round. "Well, we've come for a murder weekend. Perhaps it's based on that."

"Happen you're right," he replied, losing interest. "That'll be five pounds, please."

"How much?" said Ava. "We've only been in this car a couple of minutes."

"Minimum fare. I said you could have walked it."

She snapped open her handbag with an ill grace and carefully extracted a five-pound note from her purse, rubbing it between her thumb and forefinger to make sure two weren't stuck together.

"Ta," said the driver. "I'll fetch the bags out."

He'd placed their suitcases on the gravel by the time they'd emerged from the car. He climbed back in, reversing swiftly. The sound of his departing engine persisted for some seconds after he had disappeared from view. The mist had lifted a little, but it was mixed with the dusk now.

Gordon Bemrose immediately appeared. He hurried towards them, beaming, and shook hands vigorously.

"Mrs Dack and Mrs Fox, I take it?" he said.

Ava looked around her disconsolately, spotting the Ford Focus that Colin Franklin had parked close by.

"Has someone already arrived?" she enquired, consulting her watch. "According to me, it's still only ten minutes to four. I thought you said to arrive at four o'clock?"

"Mr and Mrs Franklin are already here. They've had a long drive, so it was difficult for them to judge exactly when they'd get here. The time wasn't meant to be set in stone, in any case. You're here to enjoy yourselves, not be dictated to." He gave a short laugh that came out rather forced, which Ava noticed. She'd sobered up since stepping out into the cold fresh air. She glared at him.

"Me and Lizzie's been hanging about for a couple of hours now. If we'd of known, we would of come earlier."

"Well, you're here now. Come in and meet Mrs Lawrence. She'll give you some tea. We'll have proper afternoon tea when the other guests have arrived. Here, let me take your cases."

Gordon had just seen the cases. He was astonished at their size and even more surprised when he tried to pick one of them up. In less than forty-eight hours, these two ladies would have departed. How much had they brought with them to use during that short space of time?

"They're on wheels," said Ava patiently, as if speaking to a child.

"What? Oh, so they are. But I'll doubt they'll run very well over this gravel. I'll just take this one now - I'll come back for the other. Follow me, please."

Ava raised her eyebrows at Lizzie when Gordon turned his back. They strutted after him, Lizzie grimacing with every step, conscious of what the gravel was doing to the heels of her shoes. At the porch she removed one to examine it.

"Look at that," she said. "It's shaved the leather off the heel. I could feel it happening!"

"Well, I wouldn't worry about it if I was you," said Ava sarcastically. "You can always ask Jackson to buy you another pair."

CHAPTER 7

SONIA AND RICHARD Renwick and Dora Westerman
arrived at Holyrood House together. The Renwicks had
seen Dora struggling along London Road with an old-fashioned suitcase (emphatically not one of the wheeled variety)
and Richard had stopped to offer her a lift. He wasn't surprised to learn they were all bound for the same destination:
he'd looked up the island on Google maps and knew there
were few other residences beyond the place where he had
spotted Dora.

Dora was a mousy-haired, middle-aged woman who had
told Gordon she was prepared to share the end cottage with
someone she didn't know if it meant saving money. She
hadn't even insisted on occupying the double bedroom: when
Gordon received an inquiry from a literature student who also
wanted to share, she'd cheerfully offered to take the small back
bedroom in return for a further slight reduction in the fee.

Gordon had had no option but to agree to this, as the literature student, whose name was Amelia Baker, had proved to
be quite tricky. She'd e-mailed him to say she was a postgraduate studying modern crime fiction and suggested he might like
to offer her a scholarship place on the crime weekend. She'd
even attached a PDF of a letter from her tutor supporting
this request. Gordon hadn't understood what she meant by
'scholarship place', but he suspected it meant consenting to
some scheme that would leave him out of pocket. He'd called

the tutor, who had explained that the university would contribute to the fee, but only if Gordon agreed to match what it paid – in other words, to foot half of Amelia's bill himself.

Calculating that Amelia was unlikely to be a good bet in terms of repeat business, Gordon had dug his heels in and refused, explaining as politely as he could that he'd already set an introductory price for the weekend and couldn't afford to pare it down further. To his surprise, the tutor had suddenly capitulated, saying that Amelia was such a promising student that he'd pay the rest of her bill himself. Gordon must, however, complete a form saying he'd waived half the fee.

To Gordon, himself an experienced wheeler-dealer, all this sounded extremely dodgy, but his conscience wasn't unduly troubled and he indicated it wouldn't be a problem. He mentioned that there was a room free in one of the cottages, if Amelia didn't mind sharing the cottage with a lady she didn't know. The tutor handed communications back to Amelia herself at this point. She said she'd be happy to share, but only if she could have the room with the double bed. She explained that she suffered from restless leg syndrome and would be in danger of falling out of a single bed and hurting herself. Gordon had never heard of this condition, but didn't waste much time thinking about it. The shared cottage arrangement was duly organised to please both Dora Westerman and Amelia Baker, which meant more cash in the till – all he cared about.

"It's very good of you to stop for me," said Dora to Richard Renwick, hauling her case on to the back seat of the car beside her. "It's further than I thought from the station."

"You've *walked* from the station?" said Sonia incredulously. She'd looked up Spalding herself and formed a rough idea of the lay-out and relative distances between amenities. Competitive by nature, she'd thought that a knowledge of the local terrain might help when it came to solving the mock-crime that lay at the heart of the weekend's activities. "It must be at least two miles from here."

"Needs must," said Dora, with an enigmatic smile.

"I'm sure you didn't know how far it was when you set off," said Richard kindly. "Distances can be deceptive in these rural areas."

"It doesn't take much intelligence to research the local transport," snapped Sonia. "There are buses and taxis, aren't there?"

She was annoyed with Richard for picking Dora up when she'd been on the point of winning a heated argument. Ducking out of it like that when he was losing was so typical of him.

To Richard, Dora seemed harmless enough. She was one of those women who had allowed herself to tumble into obscure middle age by failing either to assert herself or invest much time in her appearance.

Sonia, herself probably only a few years younger than Dora but very much better preserved and turned out, recognised in Dora the type of woman she most despised: frumpy, unattached and with doormat tendencies. Sonia hoped this weekend wasn't going to turn into a bore. She had no wish to listen to the vapid prattlings of a woman who looked as if she had never risen above some lowly clerical capacity, if indeed she'd managed to hold down a job at all.

Richard, observing Dora in his driving mirror, formed rather a different view. He noticed how sharp her eyes were, even though they were set in a somewhat podgy face. They were rather fine eyes and did not dart about disconcertingly like Sonia's. Dora allowed them to rest unhurriedly on a person or object, as if assessing what that person or thing really stood for: as if she could bore down into the essence of someone.

Dora saw him watching her and met his gaze steadily. He looked away. He guessed that she'd already picked up on the tensions between him and Sonia. It was embarrassing.

Richard was a struggling television script writer who had enjoyed his sole success fourteen years previously and had been trying to make a living out of writing ever since. Sonia ran a beauty salon which provided most of their income. For many years she'd been content to support Richard, thinking he was bound to hit the jackpot eventually, but now her confidence in him was ebbing away. It wasn't – exactly – that she doubted him as a writer, but she certainly wished he would write something more commercial. Their children were in their early teens and would soon need help with paying for university; and she was tired of footing all the bills.

They were both aware they'd "grown apart", as they'd been forced to admit recently after one of their flare-ups. In both cases the term was a euphemism for the fact that they'd lost their respect for each other. Sonia had begun to perceive Richard as a pretentious sponger; and he'd been horrified at her suffocating demands to give his work more vulgar appeal. A pressure-cooker relationship had developed which had finally imploded with a vicious row about something trivial. Sonia would have kicked Richard out then and there if her mother hadn't been staying with them at the time. Sensible in a bathetic sort of way, Sonia's mother had suggested that all they needed was to "establish some common interests" and everything would be fine; she had offered to pay for them to spend a couple of nights away from the children. It was more for the sake of the children than any sense of conviction that it might really bring them closer together that they'd booked the last cottage available for the Holyrood crime weekend. Richard had expressed indifference about the nature of any activity that would take him away from his writing and told Sonia to arrange whatever suited her. Sonia had chosen the crime weekend for two reasons: she hoped it might provide Richard with the inspiration to write a down-to-earth drama that might actually sell; and, more tentatively, she wondered whether, if Gordon's venture were successful, he might be interested in letting her set up a spa franchise as an additional Holyrood attraction. Whether or not she and Richard stayed together, if he was never going to earn more money she would have to take the initiative to improve her means.

CHAPTER 8

JULIET HAD WALKED only a few steps past the corpse of the hare when she saw it: a beautiful dog, muscular yet slender, that had been tied to a fence post with such a short piece of rope that it couldn't sit down. It whimpered when it saw her and shrank from her nervously as she approached.

"It's all right, boy, I won't hurt you," she said. As she edged closer to it, she saw that one of its front legs was sticking out from its body at an ugly angle. The leg was clearly broken. As she bent to inspect it, she saw to her horror that it wasn't a clean break: the leg was damaged in two or three places. Shards of bone could be seen poking through the skin.

The dog backed away from her, pushing itself as flat against the fence as it could go. She saw it was in danger of strangling itself with the rope. Not accustomed to handling animals, she was unsure how to help it. Her instinct was to cut the rope immediately, though she was afraid the dog might either run off or turn on her; but on inspecting its damaged leg again, she realised that it would be incapable of escaping.

She moved again so she was level with it and gave its head a few tentative strokes. The dog nuzzled her hand. She didn't think it would try to bite her. It was a beautiful creature, honey-coloured with a long, narrow face and drooping, fluffy ears. She had a vague idea it might be an Afghan hound, although she thought they were usually much hairier than this dog.

Her mobile rang. The sound of the ringtone made the dog nervous and it tried to back away again.

"It's all right," Juliet said, taking hold of the rope collar to soothe it. She managed to manipulate the phone with one hand.

"Juliet?" It was Tim's voice. "Where the hell are you? You should have been back here half an hour ago. I told you to call for back-up if you found anything."

"I'm sorry, Tim. I hung around for a while and was about to come back to the station when I heard a strange noise. I think there *has* been some hare coursing here today. I've found an injured dog tied up in the lane – probably abandoned by the coursers. There's a dead hare, as well."

"Are you alone?"

"Yes. There are houses nearby, but no sign of the people who live there. I think I'm safe enough – the coursers are unlikely to return."

"What makes you say that?"

"They've left the dog. If they'd wanted to help it, they'd have taken it with them. Besides, the hare's dead. The death of the quarry marks the end of one of their jaunts, doesn't it?"

"Usually it does. But I'm not happy about you being out there by yourself. Come back now."

"What about the dog?"

"I'll send a vet to look at it. Or the RSPCA."

"I'm not going to leave it, Tim. I can't. It's already been betrayed and its leg is very badly damaged. And the rope that fastens it to the fence is so short that it will kill itself if it tries to lie down."

Tim sighed.

"All right. Stay where you are and I'll send someone out to you. You're still in Campain's Lane?"

"Yes, the far end of it, beyond all the houses."

"There's a vet who lives in Pinchbeck who helps out with the police dogs sometimes. I'll give him a try. I'll send Chakrabati and Tandy out to you, as well. Call me if you see anyone approaching – anyone at all. There should be someone with you in fifteen minutes or so."

The mist was getting thicker. It was turning into a proper fog now, wet enough to dampen Juliet's hair. The dog was wetter than she was and shivering pitifully. She had a blanket in the car, but she didn't want to leave the animal even for a couple of minutes to retrieve it. She knew it was important to keep him calm now, if she could manage it. She took off her coat and draped it over him. He staggered under the weight of it before regaining his balance. He nuzzled her hand again.

"You're beautiful," she said to him softly. "You don't need to worry – we'll soon have you somewhere safe. You'll be better in no time."

She looked down at his leg and fervently hoped this was true. Could the vet save it – would he even be prepared to try? She knew that racehorses were shot if they broke their legs. She'd seen three-legged dogs sometimes, but usually it was one of the hindlegs that had been amputated.

Now she was not wearing a coat the cold attacked her mercilessly. She felt very alone, and desolate. She thought of calling Jake to hear a friendly voice and decided against it. He'd be even more annoyed than Tim at the risk she was taking. She wondered if Jake liked dogs.

She heard footsteps in the lane. She tensed immediately,

straining all her senses. They were lightly-shod footsteps, not those of a man wearing boots.

A woman appeared out of the mist. She was short and thin and enveloped in a scarlet mac which almost reached her ankles.

"Hello?" she said, when she saw Juliet. "Are you the policewoman?"

"I'm DS Armstrong. Not exactly a policewoman, but near enough."

"They rang me back. The police at Spalding station, I mean. They said a female officer was investigating after my call. I saw the car in the lane and thought I'd come down to take a look."

"You're Mrs Lovell?"

The woman nodded.

"Yours is one of the houses in the terrace, isn't it? I couldn't see any lights on when I came past."

"I must have been out the back. Is that one of their dogs? The hare coursers, I mean?"

"I don't know, but I'm guessing so. Did you notice what their dogs looked like when you saw them?"

"No. They shot by in a flash, the dogs all barking and jumping over each other." She eyed the dog warily. "It doesn't look in a very good way, does it?"

"He's been badly injured. There's a vet coming out to him. That's why I'm waiting with him."

Mrs Lovell let out a phlegmy cackle.

"Why do you find that amusing?" said Juliet crossly. The woman was supposed to be interested in animal welfare.

"That ain't a he," she said, straightening her face. "You

don't know much about dogs, do you? Have a closer look. No accoutrements. She's a bitch you've got there."

Juliet would have resented the woman's scorn if she hadn't been so cold. Her teeth were chattering.

The woman touched her on the arm.

"Tell you what," she said, "while you're waiting for the vet, why don't I bring you a cup of tea?"

CHAPTER 9

AFTERNOON TEA AT Holyrood House turned out to be quite a strained affair. The Franklins had already taken possession of their room but only Colin put in an appearance at the hour appointed for tea, claiming that Margarett was tired after the journey. Mrs Lawrence asked him if he would like to take her some tea and a slice of cake. Eagerly he agreed, adding that he wanted 'to keep an eye on her'. Mrs Lawrence cut two slices of cake and arranged them on a plate. She produced a tray on which she had assembled two teacups and saucers and another spare plate, placing the plate with the slices on top of it. From a large pot she poured tea into the two cups.

"I don't have spare milk jugs or sugar bowls. Help yourself to both while you're here," she said tartly.

Colin splashed milk into both cups of tea and, gripping the tray carefully with both hands, vanished in the direction of the extension.

Ava, who had noted with deep misgivings that he was of mixed race, decided to disapprove.

"Anti-social is what I call that," she said. "If they can't join in at the beginning of the weekend, what's it going to be like later on? It's downright rude not to make an effort!"

Richard Renwick felt compelled to take a more balanced view.

"We have no reason to doubt that Mrs Franklin's not

feeling too good," he said mildly. "She'll be better company later if we let her get some rest now."

Sonia Renwick had been about to make a comment similar to Ava's, but didn't want to associate herself with such a woman. Richard's attempt to smooth things over annoyed her, but she couldn't be seen to contradict him in front of such vulgarity. She sighed and pursed her lips.

"I wonder what's happened to Miss Baker?" said Dora Westerman, who had chosen to sit by herself in a corner by the window that looked out over the river; up to this point, she'd been calmly staring out at the water. "She said she would be here in time for tea."

"Is she a friend of yours?" asked Lizzie Fox.

"Never met her in my life, but we've spoken on the phone, about the practical arrangements. We're sharing one of the cottages."

"I wouldn't want to share with someone I didn't know," said Lizzie. "Asking for trouble, probably."

Dora Westerman flicked her a glance of contempt which was quickly recomposed into something softer.

"Needs must," she said firmly. Richard Renwick regarded her with some curiosity. It was the same expression she'd used when they'd been in the car. Did Dora attach any particular importance to it?

"Has there been word from Miss Baker?" Sonia asked Mrs Lawrence. She wasn't remotely interested in the woman, but thought it was time she said something. "Do you know anything about her?"

"She's not been in touch today, but I can't say I'm too worried. There are likely to have been delays with all this fog we're getting. All I know about her is that she's a literature student. A postgraduate, I believe; studying crime fiction. Now, do help yourselves, everyone. There are scones and cake. I've poured the tea."

"My God," groaned Richard Renwick, passing the back of his hand across his forehead.

"Are you all right, Mr Renwick?" Isobel Lawrence was concerned.

"I suppose so. But since when were the terms 'literature' and 'crime fiction' considered bedfellows? Are we now so decadent we believe in encouraging young people to dissect pulp novels?"

"Don't be such a snob, Richard," said Sonia, trying to smile but failing to conceal her acid tone. "The girl will be studying authors who've made their fortune. Surely that's a good thing?"

"We don't know that she's a girl," said Isobel Lawrence. "She could be a mature student."

"True, but she did sound quite young," said Dora Westerman reasonably.

Ava Dack raised her eyebrows at Lizzie Fox.

"What do you do, Mr Renwick?" she asked. "To earn a living, I mean."

"I'm a scriptwriter."

"For the telly? How exciting!"

"Not for television. For the theatre. West End, mainly," said Richard carelessly.

"It's some time since one of Richard's plays was produced in London," said Sonia. "Or anywhere, come to that. I'm the main breadwinner. I own a beauty parlour."

"Oh, how exciting! Do you do massages? My back is killing me after walking round that little town in these shoes," said Lizzie.

"I could if . . . "

"Sonia's here to take the weekend off and relax," Richard interceded quickly. He was aware of Sonia's plan to inveigle her business into Holyrood and didn't altogether disapprove of it, but it was typical of her to show her hand too soon!

Gordon came into the room at that moment, accompanied by Anton, Percy and Patti. A self-assured man with greasy black hair sporting what looked like a fake moustache was following Patti.

"Are the rehearsals going well?" Isobel Lawrence asked.

"Swimmingly," said Percy. "Couldn't be better."

"I wouldn't say that," said Anton, throwing a meaningful glance in the self-assured man's direction. "Professionals are always taking a bit of a risk when they agree to perform with amateurs. But I daresay that between us we'll muddle through."

The self-assured man was not fazed by this comment.

"There are professionals and professionals," he pronounced gnomically, "and there again, there are amateurs and amateurs." He glanced around the room triumphantly, as if he had expressed himself so compellingly that there could be no disputing he was correct.

"Allow me to introduce my team," said Gordon, sweeping the room with his equivocal eyes. "This is my nephew, Anton Greenweal . . . "

"Not *the* Anton Greenweal!" Ava Dack squealed. "The one from the telly – the Island Castaway bloke!"

"Your fame precedes you!" said Percy sotto voce to Anton. He enjoyed Anton's little moue of discontent. Anton believed himself to be an artiste of the top rank. He was unlikely to relish the adulation of this woman.

"Yes, the very same Anton Greenweal," Gordon beamed. Turning to his nephew, he added in a quieter tone, "We must remember not to hide your light under a bushel, Anton. I'll make much more of your talents when I'm billing future events."

Richard Renwick groaned again. Sonia jabbed him with her elbow.

"And who are these other two gentlemen?" she purred. "Should we recognise their names as well?"

"Oh, I doubt it," said Gordon airily, "this is Percy Forsyth-Jones, who is also a professional actor, but not at all well-known. And Montagu Sykes, who runs the local amateur acting group. They've kindly agreed to help out."

"Well, that damns us both with faint praise," said Percy to Montagu Sykes, giving him a broad wink. Sykes was clearly rattled by Gordon's introduction, but when Percy suggested they were colleagues he shrugged and managed a faint smile.

Gordon waved his hand expansively at the cakes and scones.

"Tuck in everyone, and enjoy yourselves," he said.

"We've finished our tea now," said Ava meaningfully. "I think it's the done thing to polish off afternoon tea with a glass of champagne, isn't it?"

Gordon glared at her.

"I don't . . . "

Isobel Lawrence cut in.

"You're quite right," she said. "Though I'm afraid we can't run to champagne. I've got a couple of bottles of Prosecco on the chill for that very purpose."

"Prosecco'll do," said Ava. "It goes down the hatch just

the same, don't it?" She was appealing to Dora Westerman for support.

Dora bowed her head.

"Not for me," she said. "I've had elegant sufficient with the tea."

Ava shared another of her looks with Lizzie.

"All the more for the rest of us then."

"Should I take Mr and Mrs Franklin a glass each?" Isobel Lawrence asked Gordon.

"Why aren't they in here?" Gordon clearly hadn't missed them before she'd spoken.

"They're in their room. Mrs Franklin was feeling a bit under the weather."

"I shouldn't bother in that case," said Gordon. He was annoyed with himself for having missed the Franklins. Now he counted the number of guests present: only five of them.

"There's someone else missing," he said.

"Yes, it's Amelia Baker, she hasn't arrived yet," said Isobel Lawrence.

Sonia Renwick bestowed a patronising smile on Patti.

"Are you an amateur actress?" she enquired.

"No, I'm . . . ."

Gordon Bemrose couldn't resist indulging in another promotional fanfare.

"This is Patricia Gardner, also a relation of mine. She's a pretty brilliant forensic scientist. She's even more essential to the weekend's activities than Anton is."

Even Anton couldn't help smiling at such blatant showmanship. Patti herself was horrified at being so brutally pushed into the limelight. How had she managed to let herself in for this?

CHAPTER 10

G IASH CHAKRABATI AND Verity Tandy arrived in their squad car just as the vet emerged from his Land Rover. Verity hastened to meet Juliet. She had accompanied Juliet to the hospital the previous year after her face had been slashed by Susie Fovargue, reinforcing the strong bond between them that already existed. Each had regard for the other's high standards and professionalism. And Verity understood that Juliet would brook no coddling; it was essential to tread carefully when offering her sympathy.

Juliet had her hands round a thick white mug of tea, but was still shivering uncontrollably. She was dressed in a tweed skirt and cashmere jumper – adequate clothes for working inside, but not warm enough for standing around in a mist-shrouded fen in November.

"Juliet! Are you all right? You look frozen. Where's your coat?"

"I'm fine, just a bit cold, that's all." Juliet gestured towards the dog. "She needs the coat!"

Verity hadn't noticed the dog; as she turned to look, her face crumpled. She loved animals.

"Oh, my God! Poor dog! Who could have done that to it? But your coat – it'll be ruined!"

"I expect it will clean. If not, I'll claim damages!"

Juliet tried to laugh, but her teeth were chattering too much.

"We've got a foil blanket in the car. You should carry one."

"I do. I didn't want to walk back up the lane and leave the dog."

"I'll fetch it for you." Verity turned and bumped into Giash, who had taken one look at Juliet and immediately headed back to the squad car for the blanket. He slid it out of its cover.

"Put this round you, DS Armstrong. At least you have a warm drink - where did that come from?"

"The woman who reported the hare coursing made it for me. Her name's Mrs Lovell. She's gone back to her house now. She says she doesn't want to be caught 'busybodying'."

"Unfortunately, that's how most people feel about hare coursers. It's not surprising, really. They're a rough bunch. Reprisals aren't unknown when people report them."

"I thought most of them weren't local?"

"A lot of them don't come from round here. But some do - they must do - who would ever be able to suss out an area like this without local help? Besides, there are always plenty of yobbos willing to earn a quick few quid by roughing someone up or making life unpleasant for them - breaking their windows, say, or daubing excrement on their front doors."

"Ugh! I sometimes wonder whether civilisation really is improving or going backwards."

"Well, as far as hare coursing's concerned, the answer is probably neither. It's been a so-called 'sport' in this area for centuries. Like bull fighting in Spain, except that coursing's illegal now."

"I just don't understand it. What pleasure can they get from seeing that beautiful creature lying dead in the ditch over there? And look at the dog!"

The vet's name was Philip Trawford. Juliet had met him previously on a few occasions. He was a small, spry man close to retirement age. He knelt to examine the dog's leg, speaking gently to the animal as he did so. She accepted his attentions quite calmly but yelped with pain when he touched her foreleg. He let go of it carefully and came to speak with them.

"DS Armstrong," he said. "I don't know if you remember me? Philip Trawford. I won't shake hands, as I've just been examining the dog. She must have been a fine creature before she was injured."

"Mr Trawford, thank you for getting here so quickly. Of course I remember you. This is PC Tandy and PC Chakrabati. What's the verdict? Can you save her leg?"

"If you want my honest opinion, I think that's unlikely."

"Oh my God," said Verity again. "Does that mean she'll have to be put down?"

"Not necessarily. The leg can be amputated with a reasonable chance of success. Dogs can manage on three legs, though it's easier for them to balance without a hindleg than a foreleg. It all depends on how they cope after amputation. Some dogs just give up the struggle. But she's quite young and very strong. There's every chance she could learn to adapt."

"Will it be expensive?" asked Juliet. "I doubt if we'll be allowed to use police funds to pay for it."

"The dog needs treatment urgently. There are various charities that can help with funds, but they usually like to approve costs in advance. I'm prepared to take a chance on operating on her for free. If the police or one of the charities wants to make a contribution afterwards, that's a bonus and will be gratefully accepted."

"That's very kind of you. I will try to help raise some of the money."

"That's ok. It's not unheard of for my practice to treat bona fide strays without charging. However, the real issue you're up against is that someone must be prepared to give her a home. That's what many of the charities will also tell you before they commit funds. Finding a home for a three-legged dog that may need extra daily care and is almost certainly going to generate higher than average vets' bills isn't going to be easy. And the brutal truth is that if this dog doesn't have a home to go to, there's no point in my operating. I'm sorry if that sounds cruel."

Verity turned away, her face torn by distress and anger.

"It sounds understandable, if cruel," said Juliet, trying to be rational. "It isn't really you who are being cruel, it's the owners who let the dog injure itself in this way. I suppose there's no chance of making them pay, if we can track them down?"

The vet gave a short dry laugh.

"You're the police officer, not me! I don't know if you can take out an injunction on someone to make them pay for a wounded animal. What I do know is you'd have to catch them first. What are the chances that this dog's been chipped? If she hasn't, there's no proof of ownership."

"Can you check whether she's been chipped?"

"If I take her to the surgery, certainly. But people who use dogs for illegal activities usually leave as light a footprint as possible. If the owners of this dog thought they could be traced, I doubt she'd have been abandoned here alive. She'd be lying dead somewhere you wouldn't find her, with a bullet in her head."

Juliet shuddered.

"It's sickening!" she said fiercely. "I hope to God we catch the bastards."

"Indeed," said Philip Trawford, "but at present the dog is our most pressing concern. What do you want me to do with her?"

"She isn't going to be put down!" said Juliet. "She deserves at least the chance of a happy life. Will you really operate on her for free?"

"If no money can be raised to help pay for her treatment, then certainly. Provided she has a home to go to when she's recovered."

"I will guarantee that she'll have a home," said Juliet. "If no-one else wants her, I'll gladly take her myself."

"That's very noble of you, as long as you're sure what you're proposing to take on." Philip Trawford scrutinised Juliet's face. She returned his stare without flinching, conscious that he must be noticing her scar. Whatever else he saw there seemed to satisfy him.

"PC Chakrabati, I'm going to give the dog an injection to sedate her. When it's taken effect, do you think you could help me carry her to my vehicle?"

"Sure," said Giash. He looked at the dog. Apart from her shattered leg, she was quite beautiful.

"She's a lovely dog," he said. "I don't recognise the breed, though. Do you know what it is?"

"She's a Saluki," said Philip Trawford. "They're ancient hunting dogs. I believe they were already being used for hunting in prehistoric times."

CHAPTER 11

After Gordon Bemrose had finished parading the skills of his 'staff', Mrs Lawrence appeared with the Prosecco and a trayful of small fluted glasses.

"Not for me," said Dora Westerman. "I enjoyed my tea, thank you, but it really is too early for me to start drinking."

"I won't have any, either," said Patti. "Nice idea, though."

Clearly performing the necessary mathematical calculation, Mrs Lawrence poured modest amounts into eight of the glasses, using up exactly one of the bottles of Prosecco in the process. As she handed round the wine, Ava Dack eyed the unopened bottle.

"You've forgotten to pour one for yourself," she said. "Shall I open the other bottle?"

"I'm on duty," said Mrs Lawrence firmly. "I think we should save the other bottle in case Mr and Mrs Franklin decide to join us. Miss Baker should be arriving at any moment, too."

"Agreed," said Gordon, taking one of the thimblefuls of wine and downing it in one. He hadn't authorised Mrs Lawrence to splash out on the Prosecco – was unaware she had bought it – so as far as he was concerned agreeing with her suggestion was a form of damage limitation. "When you've all finished your drinks, I'll show you to your quarters. I'm sure you'll be wanting to unpack before dinner."

Anton sidled up to him, ostensibly to help himself to a

glass of the wine, but actually to nail his uncle about an idea that had been buzzing in his mind all afternoon.

"Could I just have a quick word?" he said.

Gordon was immediately suspicious. It sounded as if Anton was going to ask for a favour. If it was more money he was after, he could whistle for it. He glanced around the room. He could see that both Dora Westerman and Richard Renwick were watching them. Having just praised his nephew to the skies, he realised that snubbing him now would damage his own credibility.

"Of course," he said. "Shall we go into the hall for a bit of privacy?"

"We're fine here," said Anton, taking full advantage of being observed. "It's only a small thing. Percy and I were wondering if we could have the spare cottage, now that you don't need it for your guests."

"What's wrong with the room I've given you?"

"Nothing. It's just a bit small, that's all. Cramps our style. We'll work better if we can relax properly; we're not at our best when we're prowling like a couple of caged tigers," Anton added winningly, but with just the touch of a threat.

Gordon looked across at Percy; his antennae were clearly attuned to their conversation. Percy raised his glass and smiled. Gordon felt constrained to smile back. He sighed. Now that the Franklins had turned it down, he hadn't wanted to go to the expense of having that cottage cleaned again when the weekend was over, but Anton had put him on the spot.

"Very well," he said, "you and Percy can move in, but only after I've got the others settled."

"In case they think they've been relegated to the staff quarters?" Anton enquired mischievously.

"I've said you can have the cottage. If I were you, I'd quit while I was winning. And a word of thanks might not go amiss."

"Thank you, dear Uncle," said Anton, putting down his glass and patting his uncle's cheek. It was a gesture calculated to infuriate – and it succeeded. Gordon twisted away from him.

"That was nice," said Sonia Renwick, placing her empty glass on the tray. She took Richard's glass from him and put it on the tray, too, surprising him with this small act of courtesy. As if duty bound to match it, he gathered up Ava's and Lizzie's empty glasses from the occasional table on which they'd plonked them. At this point, Montagu Sykes decided to hand his glass to Richard, too. Richard took it with seeming good grace while marvelling at the cheek of the man. Isobel Lawrence put the other bottle of Prosecco on the sideboard and picked up the tray, carrying it across to Anton, who had re-joined Percy and was busy whispering to him.

"Can I have your glasses, too, gents?" she said.

"What now?" asked Montagu Sykes, when Ava and Lizzie, the Renwicks and Dora Westerman, led by Gordon, had all filed out of the room as instructed.

Anton looked at his watch.

"When did you say the rest of your group were planning to get here?" he asked. "I know we've only given them minor roles, but I must say they're cutting it a bit fine. We don't want our performance to be fouled up because they don't know what they're doing."

Montagu Sykes also consulted his watch.

"I asked them to be here at five, so they're probably all on their way now. I can try calling them if you like. I have all their numbers on my mobile."

Patti noticed his peeved tone and cut in quickly.

"I'm sure they won't want to let anyone down. You three could help me by listening to another run-through of my talk, if you've got a few minutes to spare. I could do with a bit more advice on voice projection."

"I'm sure Percy and Montagu would love to help you," said Anton. "If you'll excuse me, there are a few things I want to do, now we're moving into one of the cottages. I'll be back by five, don't worry."

"You're a born speaker," Percy said to Patti. "I thought you were great when you rehearsed earlier. I think it's very unlikely that either Mr Sykes or myself can have anything to teach you, but if it'll make you feel better, I'll be more than happy to listen to your talk again." He appealed to Montagu Sykes with a questioning look.

"What? Oh, yeah, sure, good idea," said Sykes, who obviously felt out of his element. He was finding the whole set-up weird. He wouldn't be surprised if this crime weekend malarkey was a front for something more sinister.

Mrs Lawrence came back into the room.

"That's strange!" she said. "I thought I'd left the other bottle of Prosecco standing there. I suppose I've already put it back in the fridge. I must be going mad."

"I don't think your sanity can be in any doubt, Isobel. You did leave it there – I saw it myself – and you haven't been back into this room since you went out with the tray. I think it's unlikely you'll find it in the fridge."

"I'm not sure I understand you," said Mrs Lawrence, but in a gentle tone. As a rule, she allowed only Gordon to call her 'Isobel' and then only when they were alone, but Percy was a very nice young man and he'd become a kind of confidant. "Do you know where it is?"

"I'm afraid I have no idea: I'd tell you if I did. But I'd stake my dinner on the likelihood that someone's 'borrowed' it."

CHAPTER 12

"WE REALLY OUGHT to join the others soon," said Colin Franklin to Margarett. More than an hour previously, she had kicked off her shoes and had since been lying on her back on their bed with her eyes closed. She'd drunk the tea he'd brought for her but left the cake untouched.

"How long is it since I took the Panadol?" she asked.

"Not long enough ago for another dose yet. I'd lay off them now, if I were you. Then you can take a sleeping pill before you go to bed."

"I suppose you're right," she said dully.

Without warning, his patience snapped.

"Do try to pull yourself together, Margarett. We've paid good money for this weekend. We might as well try to enjoy it."

"That's an odd thing to say under the circumstances. Insensitive, even."

"Oh, insensitive now, am I? Let me tell you I've already been mustering up as much sensitivity as I can to explain your absence to the other people here. We're supposed to be blending into the background, aren't we? Fat chance of that if you insist on staying in your bedroom all day. Before we came, we agreed we'd join in the activities. It's a whodunnit weekend, or had you forgotten? And since you care so much about people's feelings, what effect do you think it will have on the others if you don't participate? You want to fuck up their weekend by being a misery?"

Margarett opened her eyes and sat up. Wearily she swung her legs over the side of the bed and wriggled her feet into her shoes.

"All right, Colin, you win," she said. "I'll come out to meet them. Do they seem nice? The sort of people we could get on with?"

Colin shrugged.

"Difficult to say. I've hardly met them myself. There are two ladies a bit older than us as well as another lady, who's on her own. And quite a smart couple. I'd say they're younger than we are."

"You mean there are only *five* others? I thought the weekend was organised for ten."

"Maybe some people haven't arrived yet. I could hardly ask, could I?"

"I don't see why not, in a casual sort of way. What are they all doing now, anyway?"

"They *were* having afternoon tea." Colin gestured at the empty teacups and the cake. "That's probably over now. Let's have a look at the programme."

He got up from the only chair in the room and opened the plastic folder that had been placed on the vanity unit.

"4 p.m. to 5 p.m. Afternoon tea, after which guests to be shown to their cottages. 5 p.m. to 7 p.m. Free time. Guests are invited to walk round the island or spend time getting to know each other in the sitting-room while the players put the finishing touches to their performance. 7.00 p.m. Guests are invited to change for dinner if they wish (smart casual). Pre-dinner drinks will be served until 7.30 p.m."

"Ha!" exclaimed Margarett, reviving a little.

"'Ha' what?" asked Colin, bewildered and still annoyed by her previous apathy.

"Not much time for a drink if you've got to fit that and changing for dinner into the same half hour, is there? You'll get one drink at the most. Typical of Gordon Bemrose to be so tight."

Relieved by this show of spirit, Colin laughed and took her hand.

"You're right, but it's one drink more than you'll be having, isn't it? Unless you've changed your ways since we arrived here."

Margarett smiled palely as she disengaged her hand.

"That's not the point. As you said, other people have come here to enjoy themselves. Anyway, it doesn't sound as if we've missed anything much yet." She shuffled off the bed and stood up. "Perhaps it is a good idea to try to meet some of the others now, if any of them are in the sitting-room. It won't be as unnerving as coping with them all at once at dinner."

He gave her elbow an encouraging squeeze.

"That's more like it," he said. "And believe me, we can make this work."

Colin assumed correctly that the sitting-room was where he'd earlier collected their tea. It was quite a long way from their bedroom: the annexe which they occupied was connected to the house by a sliding door which opened on to a long corridor. The sitting-room was at the far end of the corridor, next to what was rather grandly called the 'ballroom'. Several other rooms led off the corridor, including the kitchen. The kitchen door was open and as they passed they could see

Isobel Lawrence preparing a salad. She looked up and gave them a guarded smile.

"I'll be with you in a minute," she said, "if you'd like to go through."

Colin had been leading the way, but when they reached the sitting-room he paused and motioned to Margarett to precede him as he opened the door.

She entered the room a little nervously, hoping that it wouldn't be too packed with other guests. She was always ill-at-ease with strangers.

It was dark now, but the curtains had been left open. The blackness beyond them was unrelieved by any glimmer of light. The room itself was lit only by two small candle-shaped electric lamps fixed on the wall on either side of the fireplace. As her eyes acclimatised themselves to the poor light, Margarett could make out two figures standing on the hearthrug. She thought they sprang apart when they heard her coming, but she might have imagined that.

She cleared her throat.

"It's quite dim in here," she said in a wavering voice. "Do you mind if we switch on some more lights?"

Colin had already located a bank of light switches near the door. He snapped them all on, one after another.

"God, that's a bit bright!" came a young female voice. "Can you turn some of them off again?"

"Sorry!" said Colin. "Is that better?" He rapidly flicked three of the switches again, leaving only the light fixed in the central ceiling rose burning. It threw a harsh orange glare across the room.

"Can we manage something a little more restful to the eye?" enquired the other person, a man.

Colin resented his tone.

"Help yourself," he said gruffly, gesturing at the bank of switches. "You're probably much more sensitive than I am."

Margarett shot him a look, but he studiously refused to meet her eye. He plonked himself down on one of the fireside chairs arranged around the small coffee table and appraised their new acquaintances.

The girl – or young woman, he supposed he should call her – was quite short and rather plump. She had thick dark wavy hair, some of which had been looped into a kind of loose plait at the back of her head. The rest hung down below her shoulders. Her eyebrows were heavy and dark and the eyes beneath them large and also dark. Her smooth olive skin was her best feature, aside from her surprisingly small mouth and cupid's-bow lips. 'Sulky but sexy' was how he would sum her up.

The man, by contrast, was very tall. He was good-looking and aware of it. He also had thick dark hair, worn longer than most men would contemplate, but his was swept back in a series of ostentatious waves that showed off his fine forehead. He strode over to the lighting panel and fiddled about with the switches, trying out several different combinations before he hit on one that pleased him. He then approached the fireside chair where Colin was lounging and stretched out a slim, perfectly-manicured hand.

"Dr Victor le Grange," he said. "It is a great pleasure to meet you."

"Oh," said Colin. He took the proffered hand and pumped it up and down a few times. Words had deserted him. Dr Victor le Grange did not seem to mind or show much curiosity about Colin's own identity.

"And this is Ms Amelia Baker," he added, pointing at the

young woman with outstretched arm. "A very talented young lady, if I may say so."

Colin could only stare and splutter some incoherency. Margarett felt sorry for the girl for having been thrust to the forefront in this way – she knew that she herself would have hated it – and tried to shoot Amelia Baker a sympathetic smile. However, when she dared to look the young woman full in the face, she saw that Amelia was revelling in Dr le Grange's introductory description.

"You here for the crime weekend?" Colin managed eventually. He knew it was an inane comment and wasn't surprised when Amelia giggled. "Well, I suppose you must be," he continued, answering his own question.

"I am not staying," said Dr le Grange, with great emphasis. "I just came to escort Ms Baker."

"I'm Margarett Franklin and this is Colin. It's nice to meet you," said Margarett to Amelia, coming to Colin's rescue. "And it will be lovely for us all to enjoy the company of a young person this weekend. I hope you won't mind – I'm afraid we're all a lot older than you."

"Oh, I'm here to watch the rest of you as much as anything," Amelia Baker said. "It doesn't matter to me how old you are."

Margarett looked down at her shoes. It was one of her coping mechanisms when she felt a panic attack threatening. Colin recognised it immediately.

"Why don't you come and sit over here, love?" he said.

Margarett hesitated.

"You don't have to if you don't want to," Amelia Baker said, "just because he told you to."

Margarett could hardly believe her ears. Quickly she moved

across to where Colin was sitting and took the chair next to his. She had expected an excruciatingly awkward silence to follow, but Dr le Grange and Amelia Baker simply resumed their positions on the hearthrug – though Margarett was sure they were no longer standing as closely together as they had been – and continued their conversation in a whisper, having turned their backs to the Franklins.

"It's very dark outside," she remarked to Colin, just for something to say.

"Yes, but right for the weekend," he replied. "Atmospheric, or something." He smiled at her and took her hand.

Mrs Lawrence came in, bearing a tray on which she had set a decanter of sherry and four glasses.

"I hope this will be all right for you," she said in a perturbed voice. "There should have been some Prosecco, but it disappeared."

Dr le Grange smiled indulgently.

"Really?" he said. "Was that part of the proceedings?"

"Sorry?" she said. "What proceedings?"

"Oh, please ignore me if you wish," he replied, his tone suggesting this would be a novel circumstance for him. "I was just attempting to be humorous. I thought perhaps the 'disappearance' of the Prosecco was part of the weekend's entertainment – to get everyone warmed up, as it were."

Mrs Lawrence set her mouth. She had enough to do without pandering to this show-off. He wasn't even one of the proper guests.

"I doubt it very much. Anyway, all I have now is sherry. You're welcome to have some if you think you'll be ok driving afterwards. I assume you're planning on leaving shortly?"

Dr le Grange looked at his watch but otherwise didn't attempt to answer her.

"Sherry!" exclaimed Amelia Baker. "How quaint! Do you know, I don't think I've ever tasted any."

"Really?" said Mrs Lawrence, her tone a mixture of disbelief and frank lack of interest. "Well, you can try some now, if you want. You might like to get used to it before the pre-dinner drinks are served, because it will be sherry again then."

"How very Agatha Christie!" said Dr le Grange. "I assume that is the intention?"

"I wouldn't know about that," said Mrs Lawrence severely. She cast a glance in the direction of the Franklins. "Mr and Mrs Franklin, would you care for some sherry?"

"Not for me, thank you," said Colin. "And Margarett doesn't drink." Margaret let go of his hand and raised her head.

"It's true I don't usually drink," she said slowly, "but I think I will have just a small glass. To get me warmed up for the rest of the evening."

Amelia Baker smirked at Colin, but his wife's words had so astonished him that he was now quite heedless of the younger woman's presence.

CHAPTER 13

JAKE FIDLER LOOKED at his watch for the tenth time in ten minutes. He was worried. Juliet might be unpredictable in some ways – he'd learnt never to take her for granted – but she was scrupulous about keeping their dates and always called him if she'd promised to. He treated her with similar respect. Each of their jobs was demanding in its own way, but both tried not to let work get in the way of their developing relationship. They always told each other as soon as possible if something unexpected cropped up.

Juliet had promised to meet Jake for a drink at the Red Lion. It had to be early because he was doing one of his night duty stints at the children's home. He must be back there at 7.30 at the latest and Juliet was well aware of this. While he was not in much doubt that seeing her was more important to him than seeing him was to her, Juliet was not the sort of person to destroy his pleasure on a whim. He could only hope that she'd merely been held up by something that prevented her from contacting him. Since she'd been attacked by Susie Fovargue, any unexplained departure from their plans made him fear the worst.

For the third time he took out his mobile. He was torn between putting his mind at rest by speaking to her and risking her wrath by 'fussing'. Juliet hated anyone keeping tabs on her and she most emphatically didn't want him to perceive her as vulnerable. Moreover, Jake had a particular reason for wanting this evening to start off on the right foot. If he could summon up the courage, he had a proposition that he wanted to put to her. He would lose the opportunity if he infuriated her by 'smothering' her.

His hand toyed with the phone. Juliet *was* vulnerable, even if he always went along with the pretence that she could take care of herself. The series of operations she'd had to undergo on her face had weakened her, and he knew she was afraid that if she sustained another injury in the same place the final plastic surgery that had been planned might no longer be possible. He would call her on some pretext, just to make sure that she wasn't in danger.

The phone erupted into life in his hand, making him jump. He was relieved to see Juliet's number come flashing up on his screen.

"Juliet? Has something happened?"

"Hello, Jake," she said. "Don't sound so worried. Something has happened, but not to me. At least, not directly to me," she added in a less assured voice. "I'm sorry, I don't think I can make it tonight now. Can we meet tomorrow?"

"Only if you come to the home. I'm on duty much of the weekend."

"Sure, I can do that. There's something I want to ask you." He detected the same note of diffidence again.

"You've intrigued me now," he said. "But you don't need to sound worried, either. There's not much that I would refuse you. Unless you want me to break the law, that is." They both laughed. "Can't you just give me a clue?" he added. "Otherwise, I shan't sleep tonight."

There was a long silence.

"Juliet?"

"I was wondering," she said, then halted again. "I was just wondering . . . how do you feel about dogs?"

"Dogs?" Jake repeated, puzzled. "What sort of dogs?"

"Salukis, as a matter of fact. Or one Saluki, I should say."

"I've never heard of them, but that's not saying much. I grew up with a cocker spaniel, but otherwise I don't know much about varieties of dog. Is it a well-known breed?"

"I don't think so. I hadn't heard of them until today. It's a kind of hunting dog. Very beautiful."

"I didn't know you liked dogs."

"I like all animals. I've just never had the opportunity to get to know a dog before."

"And now you have? Is that why you were delayed?"

"Yes," said Juliet slowly.

Jake laughed again.

"What's funny?" she asked, immediately defensive.

"Are you going to tell me about this . . . er . . . Saluki? It's not usually so difficult to get you to tell a story, but today it feels as if I'm trying to draw hens' teeth. Is there something special about this dog? How did you come across it?"

"I'm sorry, Jake, I realise I'm being infuriating! I've just been trying to weigh up all the possibilities, that's all. Yes, there is something special about this dog. I found her abandoned in a remote lane near Deeping St Nicholas. A woman who lives there reported she'd seen some men out hare coursing – there's been a spate of it recently."

"You think the dog was being used to chase hares?"

"Almost certainly."

"Then why was it abandoned? I thought the whole point of hare coursing was that the dogs are valuable – they make their owners a lot of money."

"That's true. But not when they've been injured. Injuries among the dogs aren't uncommon, according to the vet. The hare twists and turns, continually changing course in its desperate attempt to throw off the dogs. It can move fast and change direction more rapidly than they can, making it perilous for them. They often suffer the canine equivalent of a twisted ankle, but this dog's injuries are far worse than that. The vet thinks she may have fallen awkwardly; perhaps the other dogs piled into her. Her leg's broken in several places, and not cleanly. There's little hope that the vet can avoid amputating it."

"And you're thinking of adopting this dog?"

"It's kind of been forced on me. The vet said he would operate for free if I could give her a good home. Otherwise there'd be little point, as she would have to be destroyed anyway."

"Do you really want a three-legged dog that's possibly been brutalised by mishandling?"

"She isn't brutalised – she's very gentle. And – I know this will sound silly – but I feel I've got a bond with her. I'd like to give her a few years of happy life, even if with one front leg missing."

"Jesus, Juliet – you didn't say it was one of its *front* legs! Will it be able to cope?"

"It's a she, not an it. The vet says that young, strong dogs can adapt and walk with a missing foreleg. I'm prepared to give it a go."

"I'm not going to try to talk you out of it. But just be aware that you'll be very upset if she can't adjust and you have to have her put down anyway."

There was a long silence.

"And how do I come into it?" Jake continued. "Apart from accompanying you both on very slow walks, I mean?"

Juliet laughed despite herself.

"Well, that would be nice, but unfortunately I'll need more help than that. The problem is that I'm not allowed to keep animals in my flat – not dogs, anyway. One or two of my neighbours have cats. And I'm going into hospital again soon. I wondered if she could live with you at the children's home? I'll pay for her upkeep, of course, and I'll come to take her out every day except when I'm away. The children do have some animals, don't they?"

"Yes, but while I've been working there we haven't had a dog. We had a cat that died in unfortunate circumstances, as you'll remember, and we've got a couple of rabbits and some guinea pigs. In theory we could take a dog – there's nothing in the rules to say we shouldn't have one. But as you know, some of our children are deeply disturbed. We supervise their contact with caged animals very carefully. A dog would present more of a challenge – especially a disabled dog. We can't watch them all the time; they could be quite unkind to it."

"I suppose it was a stupid idea."

Juliet sounded crushed. Jake's heart went out to her. Her predicament emboldened him to broach the subject that had been preoccupying him for the past few days.

"I think there may be a solution. There's something that I've been meaning to ask you for a little while . . . "

"Go on," said Juliet in such a strangled voice that, unexpectedly, Jake found himself laughing again.

"There's no need to sound so suspicious. It isn't a proposal of marriage."

"Oh," said Juliet flatly.

"Though that can be arranged if you fancy the idea," Jake added mischievously.

"Don't be silly. Tell me what it is."

"I really think we need to meet to discuss it. You say you can come to the home tomorrow?"

"Yes," said Juliet, "and I'll know how Sally is by then, too."

"Who's Sally?"

"Sally the Saluki," Juliet replied. "That's what I thought we'd call her."

Jake might have laughed yet again, if Juliet's use of the word 'we' had not filled him with such joy.

CHAPTER 11

AVA DACK KICKED off her stilettos and flopped into a chair, tucking her legs up beneath her. The cottage that she and Lizzie now occupied was the best-furnished of the four – though she was not to know this. She was quite pleased with it, however. The furniture in the 'parlour' (Gordon Bemrose's appellation) consisted of a two-seater leather Chesterfield with matching armchairs and an oblong coffee table. The room was of modest size, so rather crowded by the larger items, but not so much that it seemed oppressive. The walls had recently been painted white and there was a fresh reed diffuser on the mantelshelf. The overall effect was cheerful, clean and slightly 'olde worlde'. Ava didn't mind this if all the amenities were in working order. Having experimented with the gas fire and checked there was plenty of hot water, she had established she could be comfortable here and afford to relax. The main disappointment was that the fridge contained nothing but half a pint of milk.

Lizzie Fox removed her own shoes more carefully and took the chair opposite.

"What shall we do now, then?" she asked. "Do you fancy going back to the sitting-room in the main house to mix with the others?"

"Plenty of time for that later," Ava replied. "It's annoying there's nothing to drink in the fridge, but I doubted there would be. I took my own steps to remedy the situation!"

She rummaged in her designer tote bag and pulled out a bottle of Prosecco with a triumphant flourish.

"It's still cool enough to drink! I thought it would be."

"Oh, really, Ava, did you take that just now?" said Lizzie, at the same time scandalised and laughing. "Technically, it's stealing!"

"Technically it isn't. We've paid for this do and we deserve to be treated right. If they're mean with the drinks, they can expect people to take matters into their own hands. I assume there are some glasses in the kitchen, even if there isn't anything to put in them?"

"I'll check," said Lizzie, massaging her feet before she stood up again. "God, this tiled floor feels good on my toes. I can't believe how far we walked today."

"It looks cold to me," said Ava doubtfully. "Still, at least there's a hearthrug." She pulled her feet out from under her and plonked them on it, scrunching her toes into the pile. "Hmm, it looks Persian, but I reckon it's a knock-off. Still, it isn't bad."

Lizzie had disappeared into the kitchen.

"I've found some glasses," she called out. "Just tumblers, though."

"They'll do. Bring us a couple, will you?"

Lizzie returned with the two tumblers. They were made of recycled glass.

"I don't like this stuff much," said Ava, pointing to the opaque surfaces. "But never mind." She twisted the wire on the bottle of Prosecco until it snapped. The cork shot to the ceiling and wine exploded from the bottle.

"Stick that glass under here, Lizzie, quick," said Ava urgently. "Phew. I thought we'd lost it there." She filled the glasses until bubbles rose from their brims, waited for them to subside and topped up. "Here!" she said. "Cheers!"

"Cheers!" Lizzie repeated. She took a large swig from her glass and pulled a face. "Ugh!" she said.

"What's the matter?" Ava was glugging her wine fast. She wanted to concentrate on the lift it was giving her.

"Don't you think it tastes funny?" Lizzie asked.

Ava drained the last of the liquid from her glass. She held the wine in her mouth for a few moments before swallowing it.

"Tastes funny? No, I can't say that it does. It's just the same as the stuff we had after tea, as far as I can see. It's quite cheap booze, I'll give you that." She picked up the bottle again and refilled her glass. "I take it you don't want any more?" she said, hovering over Lizzie's glass, which was still half full.

"Oh, I wouldn't say that," said Lizzie, taking another deep swig from the glass and setting it down next to Ava's. "If this is all we're going to get until 'pre-dinner drinks', I'll have to make do. It'll probably grow on me."

"Well, that shouldn't be too hard," said Ava, topping up Lizzie's glass and pouring what remained of the wine into her own. "We've finished it now."

"It's going to be a bit of a problem, though, isn't it? As the weekend wears on, I mean," said Lizzie disconsolately.

"What is?"

"Getting enough to drink, if they're only going to dole out the vino in penny measures. There isn't a shop for miles. We're going to be stuck here on this bloody island for forty-eight hours, practically forced to be teetotal!"

"I wouldn't worry about that!" Ava said airily. "I've already thought about it." She rummaged in the tote bag again and pulled out a bottle of gin, waving it aloft. "And," she added in a conspiratorial whisper, "when that's finished, there's another in my suitcase!"

"Oh, Ava!" Lizzie giggled. "You really do amaze me, sometimes!"

"I'm glad . . . " Ava frowned.

"What's the matter?"

"Can't you hear it? My phone's ringing. Just when I was beginning to enjoy myself."

"It's probably only Reggie."

"It's bound to be Reggie. And he's bound to want something. He never calls when he's with his mates otherwise."

"Where is your phone? I can hear it now, but it sounds a bit muffled."

"It's in this damned handbag," said Ava, yanking the bag on to her knee and stirring the contents vigorously. "I can't think why I bought it. Everything always falls to the bottom." She began to pull things out of the bag, scattering purse, tissues, keys, a packet of mints and various lipsticks across the coffee table. Finally, she extracted the phone and held it to her ear.

"It's stopped ringing now," said Lizzie. "Will you ring him back?"

"No. He'll try again soon enough if it's something he really wants. I'll leave it here so I don't miss him next time," said Ava, putting the phone down on the table. She scooped up all the other items and tipped them into the bag.

"Now," she said, "I think you may be right about the Prosecco. It has left a bit of a funny taste in my mouth. How about a small snifter to perk up the taste-buds a bit?"

She seized the bottle of gin and broke the seal on the cap.

CHAPTER 15

SONIA AND RICHARD Renwick had also installed themselves in their parlour. Theirs was one of the two cottages Gordon Bemrose originally bought with Holyrood House. It had been in a reasonable state of repair, so he hadn't done much work on it. The wallpaper was dingy and old-fashioned and the furniture, although not scratched or worn, was of cheap 1970s vintage. The room was dominated by a massive all-in-one television cabinet and sideboard fitted with drawers on one side of the TV and a cupboard on the other; it also incorporated a fancy overhead structure of shelves bearing white vases in strange shapes and other knick-knacks. It was made of light-coloured, thickly-varnished wood which gleamed dully in the half-light. It had been placed along the back wall of the room. The only other piece of furniture, the three-seater settee which faced it, was pushed up hard against the windowsill. The fireplace had been built outwards in red brick, probably at the same time as the furniture was purchased, to create two ledge-like outcrops, one of which could be used as a makeshift table by the person sitting on the fire side of the settee.

Richard Renwick had immediately occupied this seat and placed his laptop on the outcrop next to it. Looking around for a socket in which to plug his power supply, he could discover only the one to which the standard lamp had been connected. He unplugged the lamp and plunged the room into darkness. Sonia, who was seated at the other end of the settee and had started flicking through some health and beauty magazines, gave a yelp of indignation.

"God! What did you do that for?"

"Sorry," said Richard. "There isn't another socket. Would you mind switching on the main light?"

Sonia sighed. She half-stood to reach the light switch, snatched at it and sat down again. The room became suffused in an orange glare.

"Ugh," she said. She looked up at the light. "Who in their right mind could have fitted those lamp-shades?"

Richard followed her line of sight. A chunky wooden light fitting was affixed to the ceiling. It had three arms, each of which was topped by a light bulb screened – if that was the right word – by a squat orange lampshade. The effect was hideous.

"Turn it off if it annoys you so much," said Richard curtly. "I'll put the lamp on again and make do without charging the laptop until the battery runs down."

"There's no need to be so stroppy," said Sonia. "You don't mean to tell me you like this garish light?"

"Of course I don't like it, but I'm prepared to put up with it for a couple of days. I didn't choose this place and I certainly foresaw there would be inconveniences."

"You should have picked somewhere yourself, then," she retorted. "I don't recall getting much help from you when we were deciding on where to come this weekend."

Richard didn't reply. He hunched himself over his laptop, logged on and started scrolling through some text. Sonia returned to her magazine, but the altercation had upset her. She'd resolved to try to make the jaunt work for them and hadn't wanted it to start so badly. She began reading an article on South American massage techniques but couldn't concentrate on it. After a couple of minutes, she looked up again.

"What are you working on, anyway?" she enquired with studied gentleness.

"I've just been reworking a bit of 'The Oddballs'."

"That play you started writing a few years ago?" said Sonia, more tautly.

"Yes," said Richard in a self-satisfied tone. "There were a couple of things not quite right about it, but I think I've fixed them now. Or can do, anyway."

"Is it still set in the early 1960s?" She managed to keep her voice neutral.

"Yes. It's such an interesting period. A time of change. A time when women were beginning to take a true interest in their appearance for the first time after the war, but to explore emancipation at the same time, see how far they could go with blokes in that direction."

Sonia sighed.

"Is the heroine still a busty blonde? A bit like Marilyn Monroe?"

"She's whatever the leading actress makes of her," said Richard airily. "But I do envisage her as a blonde, yes."

Sonia jumped to her feet and flung the magazine to the floor.

"For Christ's sake, Richard, what is the matter with you? I honestly think you need to see a shrink! That play is nothing but a plagiarised version of The Misfits. I've told you that, your agent's told you that and every theatre director you've had the effrontery to send it to has told you the same thing. Why can't you let it go and write something more original?"

"Something more saleable, you mean?"

"That as well. Is there any point in slogging away at a script that's never going to be performed?"

"How do you know that?"

"Because a) it's a pale copy of something Arthur Miller did more than fifty years ago and b) the themes might have been fresh and new then but they're tired and hackneyed now. No-one's interested in female emancipation any more. Women have achieved an equal place in society, or damned near. Some people think the pendulum's swinging the other way – that it's men who are being emasculated by controlling females now. Why don't you write about that?"

"Because I don't fucking want to." Richard was shouting now. "Not that it would be too difficult in my case. I've had plenty of experience of a fucking female control freak. Writing about it would be a piece of cake."

"If you're referring to me, I'll take it as a compliment. If it weren't for me, you'd have had to take a job as a hack reporter or trainee teacher a long time ago. Who do you think keeps you, not just in food, but in all the poncy writer's clothes you like to strut about in? Just suppose that I wanted to take time off – not twelve years, like you, but, say, six months – to do something I really wanted to do? What would you do then? Write about that, if you understand our relationship as well as you say you do." Sonia's voice had risen to a shriek. She was choking back the tears now, tears of frustration and self-pity, and, at the back of her mind, that persistently nagging message that the weekend wasn't supposed to be like this.

"All right," said Richard, icy now. "If that's what you want, that's what I'll do and to hell with any attempt to write something decent. You won't like how you come out of it, though, and serve you right, you cow!"

Sonia sank to her knees on the flagged floor and dissolved into a paroxysm of sobbing. She didn't hear the tapping noise at first.

"Listen!" said Richard, holding up his hand. "What's that?"

"I don't know what you're talking about," said Sonia, wiping away her tears with the knuckles of both hands. Despite herself, she sat up on her heels and strained her ears.

The tapping came again, more insistent now.

"Hello?" came a woman's voice. "Is everything all right?"

"It's that Miss Westerman," Richard whispered. "She's in the cottage next door. She must have heard us through the wall." More loudly, he called back. "Yes, all is well here, Miss Westerman. Have you settled in yourself?"

"Up to a point," Dora Westerman replied. "I shall feel more at ease when Miss Baker gets here."

"Oh, hasn't she arrived yet?"

"No, I don't think so." She paused. "Are you sure you're both all right?"

"We're fine," Richard said. "Sonia's just been helping me by reading aloud some of the lines of my next play. She's good, isn't she?"

"Very good. A natural, you could say." Did he detect a dryness in Dora Westerman's reply?

"But we're sorry to have disturbed you. We'll make sure we keep our voices down in future."

He and Sonia both listened in silence for a couple of minutes, but the dialogue through the wall had clearly been closed down. Richard looked at Sonia, still kneeling on the floor, her eye make-up smudged, her face blotchy from crying, and was assailed by a rare pang of guilt. He shuffled along the settee until he was seated opposite her and reached out for one of her hands.

"We'll have to be careful while we're here," he said quietly. "No mad passionate sex. Otherwise the neighbours will complain."

Sonia stared at him for a moment and then erupted into peals of laughter. Richard also started laughing, though less spontaneously. Were they making up after their quarrel, he wondered, or were they simply hysterically incompatible?

CHAPTER 16

DORA WESTERMAN TURNED away from the wall she shared with the Renwicks and sat down on the brand-new spindly two-seater – it could hardly be dignified with the name 'sofa'. Like the cottage occupied by Ava Dack and Lizzie Fox, hers had been redecorated and newly furnished throughout, but it had been the last of Gordon Bemrose's renovation projects and by the time he'd managed to get hold of this property he had been running out of both funds and enthusiasm. The furniture was cheap and cheerful. All the items were small, fabricated by a manufacturer determined to get the most from every piece of wood and square of fabric. As they were new, the effect was quite pleasing: there was certainly more free space than the other cottages could boast. Dora suspected that shabbiness would set in quite quickly – and not the comforting shabbiness conveyed by worn leather and fine old polished wood, but the dingy and dismal scruffiness that was the stuff of poverty. Not unlike how it had been before, in fact.

She was content with how it looked now. She had expected her parlour to be peopled with ghosts, but it was hard to see anything shadowy or frightening in a room that resembled the 'after' picture in a DIY-on-a-budget magazine.

Dora looked down at her hands. She'd never worn a wedding-ring, but the only finger on which the ruby and amethyst ring fitted was the third finger of her left hand. She'd felt a little strange when she slipped it on to that finger at first, but it was pretty much all she possessed in the way of family heirlooms. Not to wear it would be a betrayal; to have it altered for another finger would be sacrilege.

She looked at the innocuous little clock standing on the mantelpiece. She didn't know why she was so anxious for Amelia Baker to arrive – she hadn't particularly taken to the young woman when they'd spoken on the phone – but the girl's absence made her fidgety. The cottage would be incomplete without her. Dora disliked spaces and gaps. She knew they could let in danger.

Her suitcase was still in the tiny hallway where Gordon had dumped it when he'd opened the cottage door and given her the key. She'd had to fight her horror of going upstairs – she'd have preferred to have been accompanied – but there now seemed every chance that Amelia Baker wouldn't arrive in time for dinner and Dora felt she must exchange her well-worn skirt and cardigan for a dress, even though the dress was also of a certain vintage. She also didn't want Amelia, should she arrive in the next half hour or so, to assume that the suitcase was sitting there waiting for her to lug it upstairs. Dora had no intention of exploiting Amelia's youth.

She stood up and eyed the suitcase again. The cottage was light and bright; there was nothing to be afraid of. She crossed the room, seized the suitcase and turned on the hall light. The stairs were flooded with a harsh glare; looking up, Dora saw a naked lightbulb hanging from the top of the stairwell. No shadows here; no dust; no decay.

She grabbed the handle of the suitcase and laboriously hauled it, one step at a time, up the short flight of stairs, alternately holding the rail set into the wall with her left hand

and using both hands to move the suitcase to the next step, her feet in their sensible lace-ups with block heels planted firmly on each step as she went.

Instinctively she didn't turn right into the 'master bedroom', but into the tiny second bedroom on the left. She was grateful to Amelia for agreeing to this arrangement. The small room suited her much better: in a way it was familiar, although from it, also, all traces of the past had been expunged. It contained a very short bed (Dora suspected it was a child's bed, but she was short enough not to worry) and a narrow white-painted chest of drawers with an oval white-framed mirror suspended above it. That was all. She hunted briefly for a wash-stand, before remembering that of course the box room had been turned into a bathroom. She heaved the case on to the bed and, hesitating only for a second, went to inspect.

The bathroom was a miracle of ingenious design. Half of it was taken up by a shower fitted over a hip-bath, of the kind you found in small boats; a toilet and hand-basin were wedged side by side in the remaining space. There was just enough room for someone to stand inside the door and close it. Dora wasn't keen on showers, so she grudgingly acknowledged that the hip bath was an excellent compromise. A full-size bath would have been impossible.

Dora shut the bathroom door carefully and fastened it – it was a sliding door fitted with a hooked latch as a lock – and used the lavatory. Afterwards she washed her hands carefully, having unwrapped the small cake of soap on the hand-basin. She dried them with equal care on the miniature towel on the hook beside it. She looked at her watch.

She tried to tell herself that she had little time, that she really must unpack and change for dinner now, but she knew

81

this wasn't true. She must force herself to bite the bullet: otherwise she would be uneasy all weekend, and probably no further opportunity would present itself. She emerged from the bathroom, slid the door to again, and, descending the single step to the landing, turned to her left as she did so. It was hardly even a question of being brave.

The master bedroom door was right in front of her. It had been painted pale blue. It was just a door, a door that had seen better days, perhaps, or even a replacement door: the blue paint might equally cover the scars of age or a sheet of modern hardboard. The doorknob was the same, however: a round wooden knob with a circle of glass set in the middle of it. Astonishing, she thought: the only thing in the whole house that she had so far managed to recognise. She seized the doorknob and turned it.

CHAPTER 17

"YOU REALLY DON'T have anything to worry about," said Percy, as Patti concluded the second rehearsal of her talk. "That was brilliant. Besides, it's more of a demonstration than a lecture. They'll be anxious to find clues in what you're saying, rather than criticising your delivery. And the slides are a nice touch. Nothing like some photographs of genuine gore to get them going."

"Does the talk really contain clues to the mystery? Is it aligned to the play?" asked Montagu Sykes, impressed.

"Well, sort of," said Percy, always loath to pass up a compliment.

"Not really. Well, not directly," Patti added, afraid she might seem disloyal to Percy. She knew he was her best ally and, although Percy was everybody's friend, which meant he was a little shallow, she was more comfortable with relying on him for support than her narcissistic cousin. She and Anton (or Anthony, as he was then) had never got on as children and she knew the uneasy camaraderie that prevailed between them now was only skin-deep.

Montagu Sykes looked puzzled rather than disappointed. He was having difficulty in weighing up any of the people who were running the event at Holyrood. Even the two professional actors were unlike other actors that he knew (though his experience was limited) and seemed to him to have an alternative but impenetrably-hidden agenda. He was relieved when one of the double doors swung open and Mrs Lawrence came in with a gaggle of his fellow amateurs at her back.

"Christ! It's cold in here," said Avril, not one to mince her words. "And I'm starving. Are we getting something to eat?"

"There will be a light collation after your performance," said Mrs Lawrence, at her most prim. She'd taken an instant dislike to Avril, who had short blonde hair embellished with a green fringe. She couldn't imagine what role this woman might take in the play and hoped that at least she'd be wearing a wig.

"What's all that food I saw on the way in, then?" asked Avril belligerently.

"You may have caught a glimpse of some of the preparations for the guests' dinner," said Mrs Lawrence with a certain hauteur. "They'll be dining at seven-thirty. My understanding is that you'll be rehearsing while they eat."

Avril looked at Montagu Sykes, rolled her eyes and blew a raspberry. He turned away, embarrassed. His new Holyrood acquaintances might be odd, but they weren't common. It was unfortunate that Avril had come in first. She was accompanied by several middle-aged (well, one was quite elderly) men, all members of his amateur theatrical society and, to be honest, none of them very good at acting; but at least they knew how to behave.

"Hello, Harold," he beamed at one of them. Harold White was a portly man currently engaged in a tussle with his overcoat. "And Archie, George and Paddy. Good to see you. Come over and meet Percy Forsyth-Jones."

Archie, the elderly man, who was a little unsteady on his feet, tottered up to Percy and held out his hand, scrutinising him at the same time. He had a lazy eye that had never been corrected, so he was leering rather horribly when he fixed his attention on Percy's face.

"Pleased to meet you," he said. "Percy, you say your name is? Percy what?"

"Percy Forsyth," said Percy, shaking the proffered hand vigorously.

"Funny," said Archie, still staring as he retracted his hand. "I thought you was a local lad. Someone I used to know. Wally Potts's son, that's it. Norman Potts. Is he a relation of yours? You look just like him."

Percy flushed scarlet and turned his head away. Patti was trying not to laugh. That Norman Potts was Percy's real name was a secret known only to a few friends – and, of course, those who had known him as a child, before the dawn of his ambition to become an actor. Any reference to it was the only thing that ever seriously rattled Percy. She put her hand on his arm.

"Let's go and find Anton, see what he's up to while they get themselves sorted out," she said. "Mr Sykes, you don't need Percy and Anton immediately, do you?"

"No," said Montagu Sykes tartly. He was mortified that two of his colleagues had now proved socially inept. "We ought to rehearse our roles separately once more before we put the whole thing together."

"But we've been doing that for weeks, ain't we?" said Avril. "I thought we was going to do something different now. Like acting with Anton Greenweal." She rolled her eyes again. "What a dish! He's the only reason I've come."

It was Percy's turn to smirk. If Anton knew this girl 'fancied' him he'd pass out on the spot.

"Yes," said Montagu Sykes weakly. "Mr Greenweal was

with us this afternoon and will be back shortly. Before he comes, we need to acclimatise ourselves to this stage and practise our parts in this room, because we haven't been here before. Then Mr Greenweal and Mr Forsyth will go through the whole lot with us. Chop! Chop!" he added with more vigour. "We haven't got long."

"Shall we come back in fifteen minutes?" asked Patti.

"Perhaps better make it half an hour," said Sykes, watching with consternation as one of the men tried to re-open the door he'd just come through, noisily pushing it the wrong way. "Are you all right over there, George?"

"Yes," said George. "I'm just looking for the toilet."

"We'll show you where it is on our way out," said Patti, leaping nimbly from the stage. Percy Forsyth followed her.

They had almost reached the door, before which George was still hovering, when Mrs Lawrence came in again. The door bumped into George, who was a tall, powerfully built man, and caught him on the forehead.

"Oh, I'm so sorry," said Mrs Lawrence. "Are you all right?"

"I expect so," said George, rubbing his head. "But I really do need the toilet."

"Come on," said Patti, leading him out into the corridor.

"Can we help you, Mrs Lawrence?" Percy asked pleasantly, equilibrium restored.

"I'm not sure you can, but I do hope so. You don't know where Gordon – Mr Bemrose – is, do you? I can't find him anywhere."

"He's not been in here with us. He's probably still in one of the cottages," said Percy.

"I don't think he is. The last person he took across was

Miss Westerman, and I saw him shutting her door behind him when I took out some rubbish."

"That can't have been very long ago. I'm sure he'll turn up soon."

"Well, I hope he doesn't take too long, because the red wine's still locked in the wine cabinet. I need to uncork it soon to let it breathe. The white's already in the fridge."

"God, that is a bit of a catastrophe!" Percy exclaimed. "Anton won't drink white wine. And he won't want to drink red wine if it isn't chambré."

"Well, he'll have to do without, then," said Mrs Lawrence, with asperity. "The wine wasn't bought for him anyway."

"Why don't I do a quick tour of the island?" said Percy. "I bet I'll be able to find Gordon. He's probably tinkering with those lights he's been hanging up."

"You're an angel," said Mrs Lawrence, opening the door wider so she could get past George and Patti, who had just returned. "Oh!" she exclaimed, as a very buxom young woman came barging through the middle of them.

"Sorry!" said the young woman, without sounding contrite. "I'm a bit bothered. I'm late. Hiya, Avril!" she shouted across the room, her red face brightening.

"Well!" said Mrs Lawrence, smoothing her hair, although the girl hadn't touched it.

"Come on," said Percy to Mrs Lawrence, "let's leave them to it. I'm going to have a look round for Gordon," he added to Patti, "he can't have gone very far."

"Do you want me to come with you?"

"No, you go and see Anton. He'll be getting the jitters now. He always does before a performance."

"Even this kind of performance?" said Patti, gesturing at

the thespians, who were now gathered in an untidy huddle round Montagu Sykes.

"I can't think what you mean!" said Percy. "But, actually, if Anton could see this lot it would make him even worse. He can't stand anything that threatens his professional integrity."

Patti tried not to show her disdain for his words.

"All right," she said, "I'll go and look after my gifted but sensitive cousin. Do you know where he is?"

"He'll be in the top cottage – the one nearest the river. He persuaded Gordon to let us have one of the cottages when those two . . . ladies' . . . husbands didn't turn up."

CHAPTER 18

PATTI PICKED HER way along the gritty footpath, flinching at the thought of what it might be doing to her high-heeled shoes. Compared to the creations displayed on Ava Dack's and Lizzie Fox's feet they were modest to the point of frumpiness but were still the only smart pair of shoes she possessed and had been a guilty purchase, swallowing money she knew she should have spent elsewhere. If she damaged them, she wouldn't have the funds to replace them.

She regretted having changed into this outfit so early: she'd thought they'd have little time after the guests started arriving, but, on the contrary, time seemed to be hanging heavy on everyone's hands – everyone's except the amateur actors', that was. They were going to have their work cut out to produce even a passable sketch, let alone perform to the standard that Anton was expecting. She wouldn't tell him what a motley lot they were unless he asked her directly. She had no wish to endure one of her cousin's famous sulks.

The air was still damp with fog and a raw chill had descended with the darkness. Patti hadn't bothered to go upstairs to fetch her coat, reasoning that it could hardly be a three-minute walk to Anton's cottage – another decision she now had cause to rue. She realised she should have asked Mrs Lawrence for a torch: her way was vaguely lit by Gordon's strings of fairy lights, but she could hardly see the gravelled path or which way it turned. She headed in the general direction of the cottages. Some of their windows were emitting a dull orange glow, a series of grudging little beacons that sullenly matched her mood.

She had drawn level with the first cottage – it was the one she thought Dora Westerman was occupying – when she heard a strange noise. It seemed to be coming from the patch of rough land at the side of the cottage. She stood still and listened. She could hear nothing, although she waited for several seconds, and was just about to move on when she heard it again. It was a little further away this time. It didn't sound human: it was the kind of keening that a wounded animal makes, suffering yet not comprehending. Patti dug her nails into the palms of her hands. She hoped it wasn't a dog – she had been afraid of dogs ever since one had jumped up and put its paws on her shoulders when she was two years old. She glanced across at the waste ground, but an unrelieved expanse of blackness stared back at her: there were no windows facing out that way and the solitary outside lamp Gordon had installed was sited opposite the middle two cottages; in any case, it shed nothing more than a dim circumference of light on the area immediately surrounding its base. Patti listened again; she was no longer standing still, but already hurrying away from the pitch black of the waste land, too frightened to loiter longer. She could hear nothing, now. She'd ask Anton to walk back to the big house with her when the time came to return. If they could both hear something then, at least she wouldn't have to investigate on her own. Despite her fear, she managed a small smile. Would Anton be any braver than she was, she wondered? She doubted it. Lincolnshire yellow-bellies, the pair of them!

Anton's cottage still had its original front door and

doorbell. The latter was a convex disk of brass fitted with a clapper. Patti recognised the type: it was a mechanical bell, the clapper operated by a contraption on the inside of the door which included a key for winding it up when it ran down. Her grandmother's house had had such a bell and she'd been fascinated by it as a child. A little breathless, she pressed the button in the middle of Anton's doorbell. It made a choked whirring noise: either it needed rewinding or the clapper was stuck.

She pressed it again, nevertheless. She didn't like to bang on the door: it might alarm some of the guests or they might embarrass her by coming out of their cottages. It made the same noise again, but this time she thought she could hear someone moving towards her from the inside of the house.

Anton flung open the door. The tiny hallway was in darkness; harsh orange light was pouring from the room beyond.

"Oh, it's you!" he said. "What do you want?"

"Charmed, I'm sure. Percy thought you'd like me to keep you company for a while. Can I come in?"

"You may."

Anton stood to one side. Patti stepped into the hall and shut the door briskly behind her. She'd just remembered the thing in the wild patch again. She followed Anton into the light.

"Mind my feet," he said. "They're bare. I took my shoes off to give them a bit of a rest before this evening and I stubbed my big toe on that bloody great fender thing. I've just taken my sock off to look at it. It's probably broken. It needs a splint or something." He lifted up his foot with a piteous expression on his face.

Patti had no intention of examining Anton's feet. Ignoring

the gesture, she sank down on to one of two hideous green chairs near the fender. They were made of unpleasantly fake leather and were slippery to sit on.

"I doubt if it's broken," she said. "But if it is, there's nothing you can do about it except wait for it to heal. That's all a doctor would tell you to do – they don't put splints on toes."

"You always were a know-all," said Anton, but his tone was teasing rather than unpleasant, and he softened the comment with a smile. "Where is Percy?"

"He's looking for Uncle Gordon."

Anton frowned.

"Waste of time, that is. He'll show up when he's ready. He's good at making himself scarce when he feels like it. I don't know why Percy's bothering."

"He's bothering on your account. Mrs Lawrence says there'll be no red wine at dinner if we can't find him."

The frown was replaced by a grin. He tutted.

"I'm disappointed Percy thinks so badly of me. He may be correct if he's assuming I won't want to do without red wine; but knowing our dear uncle's hit-and-miss approach to hospitality, I have taken precautions."

Anton hobbled to the side-cupboard fixed on the wall to one side of the fireplace and yanked it open.

"Ta-da!" he sang.

Patti stood up to get a better view. She observed several bottles lined up in the cupboard. Anton lifted one of them out carefully and stroked its label.

"Claret," he said , "and good stuff, too. Shall we open this one now?"

Patti laughed, feeling suddenly light-hearted.

"Better not!" she said. "We've both got a long evening ahead of us."

"You only need to have one glass. Percy'll be along in a minute. He'll swig more than his share, you can guarantee."

"All right, then. If there are any glasses," she added.

"There weren't – not wine-glasses, anyway, only tumblers. But I've brought some of mine. I can't stand drinking wine out of the wrong type of glass."

He fished in the back of the cupboard and drew out three slender-stemmed glasses, placing them on the round tray that was sitting on the brickwork to one side of the fender. He took a corkscrew from the tray and inserted it expertly into the bottle, extracting the cork cleanly with a single twist.

"Might as well get Percy's glass out as well. It'll save me having to put my weight on this foot later."

"I'm afraid you're going to have to put your weight on it for quite some time this evening," said Patti. Secretly, she was touched that he'd thought to bring a glass for her, too. "Steady on! That's plenty for me," she added. Obediently, Anton stopped pouring. Turning the bottle once, he caught the single drip thus captured and added it to the contents of the glass. He then poured for himself, filling his own glass to the brim, and sat down in the other ugly chair.

"Your health!" he said, raising the glass. "And I suppose I should say, to this weekend! I'm sure we'll manage to laugh about it afterwards. Or find it amusing to reminisce about, anyway."

"Hmnn," said Patti, sipping her wine, which was indeed excellent – much costlier than any she might have bought, she thought. "I'm inclined to share your views about the weekend. What I don't understand is why you agreed to take part in it in the first place. I'm sure producers are queueing up to give you acting jobs. How did Gordon talk you into doing this buckshee?"

"I was about to ask you the same question. But how do you know Percy and I aren't getting paid for it?"

"I'll be very surprised if you are. I'm not, that's for sure. And, like you, I've noticed a certain predictability about Uncle Gordon. He doesn't like parting with his cash, and he has strong views on the favours members of his family ought to feel they owe him."

"Is that why you're here? Family piety?"

"Not exactly," said Patti, realising too late that she should have been more reticent. She hadn't wanted anyone to know about her predicament.

"Well, I'll tell you why I'm doing it. You know I bought a house last year?"

"Yes. Out towards Metheringham, isn't it?"

"Yes. Gordon lent me some of the deposit. It's a great house, but it needed more work than we'd expected – Percy and I, that is. And obviously we couldn't skimp. The upshot is that I agreed to pay him back in one year and I haven't managed it. So now the bastard wants to start charging me interest. It was part of the deal."

"How much interest?"

"Twenty per cent."

"How much do you still owe him? How soon can you pay it off?"

Anton squirmed slightly in his seat.

"I haven't paid any of it off, yet. And it's sixty thousand pounds. Anyway, he offered to defer the interest for a while if I helped him out with this circus."

Patti took a bolder slug of her wine before throwing back her head in laughter.

"I don't see what's so funny about it," said Anton, offended. "It's practically blackmail!"

"I'm not laughing at you! It *is* blackmail! And he's trapped me in just the same way."

"Little Goody-Two Shoes!" exclaimed Anton. "You! I'm astonished! I wouldn't have thought you were the type to get into debt."

Patti was suddenly serious.

"It isn't my debt," she said. "Listen, Anton, I'll tell you about it, but you must promise not to tell anyone else. Not even Percy. Can you manage that?"

"Of course," said Anton, perhaps too fast to inspire confidence. He leaned forward conspiratorially. "Now, do tell me what it is. I wish I'd known about it before. Perhaps between us we can get our own back on the fucker."

"I'm afraid I won't be trying to retaliate. And you must keep your word about this. If anyone were to find out, Mother would be heartbroken."

"Auntie Marjorie? What's she got to do with it? And I'm sure she can stand up to Gordon. She's always been one to give as good as she gets."

"I think it's probably quite a long time since you last saw her. She isn't well – she hasn't been well for a couple of years now. She's become quite forgetful and she's easily persuaded. I'm worried that she's got Alzheimer's, or some other form of dementia, but she won't agree to be tested. She's too afraid."

"I can understand that. Has Gordon found out about it? Is she the one who's being blackmailed?"

"He didn't find out about it – I told him. I didn't have

any choice, because somehow Mother managed to register for a credit card with a £10,000 limit on it. And she'd spent the whole £10,000 and racked up a lot of interest before I found out. I had to pay it off before the interest spiralled even more and I didn't have that sort of money."

"So you borrowed it from Gordon? Under the same terms?"

"From what you say, yes. He's given me a year to pay it back before he charges interest. The year isn't up yet and I think I should just about be able to do it. But he put it to me that under the circumstances I couldn't refuse to help him out this weekend."

"Surely he didn't threaten to expose her to the rest of the family? Or her friends?"

"Not in so many words. He didn't spell it out to me; he just made it quite clear I'd regret it if I didn't agree."

"The louse! But I think you can get debts cancelled if they've been run up by someone with impaired faculties."

"You can, sometimes. But think what that would do to Mother. She'd have to undergo the tests, for one thing; and if the case went to court, the publicity would kill her."

"Do you know, Patti," said Anton earnestly, as he topped up her glass before she could stop him, "you really are an angel! No-one could expect you to do that – it's amazingly generous of you. But," he added in a darker tone as he refilled his own glass, "we shan't let him get away with it. Whatever you say, we're going to teach that conniving shit a lesson."

CHAPTER 19

M ONTAGU SYKES WAS cold, yet sweating, if that were possible. He rubbed his forehead with his sleeves and lifted his arms aloft like a conductor about to motion to the orchestra to rise. The purpose of the gesture was to gather his whole troupe into the symbolic embrace of authority – or, lowering his sights a little, at least to get them all to face in the same direction and listen to him while he was speaking. Although over the past few weeks they'd practised most of their parts during their regular meetings in the church hall, this was the first time they'd tried to put the whole thing together. Montagu was an optimist by nature, but even he had had a few misgivings about how successfully they could pull it off; after his arrival at Holyrood House, these had swollen into giant doubts.

Anton's assessment of Montagu's acting when Anton and Percy had rehearsed with him that afternoon had been un-settling . . . and only partially allayed by Percy's kinder comments. The audience would forgive the bumbling old men, who were mostly just playing themselves – even though there were more of them than the script demanded – but what was really troubling him was how Avril could perform even passably as Elaine. It wasn't just that her acting talent was modest – although Anton had muttered some disconcerting threats about what he would do if he didn't get a decent leading lady – it was her failure to comprehend what it meant to be lady*like*.

He was well aware of the fact that he had made the situation worse by spelling this out to Avril. He was almost certain she had decided to retaliate by accentuating her Lincolnshire accent and exaggerating her bad manners even more. He was beginning to wish he'd never got involved with the Holyrood House set-up in the first place.

"Now, everyone, pay attention!" Montagu ordered, desperation making him bossy. "It would help Avril if you weren't all talking among yourselves when she's trying to rehearse. Do you think you could just watch quietly, maybe give her a tip or two when she's finished?"

"A *tip?*" Avril screeched. "From one of them? No, ta very much."

"There's no need to be rude . . . " George began.

"It's just first-night nerves, George," said Montagu. "We all know what it's like. Now, Avril, from the top!"

"I've given it my best shot already," she grumbled. "I might do better if my first man was 'ere supporting me. Not to mention that I'm fuckin' 'ungry!"

"I'm sure that nice lady we saw earlier would give us some biscuits," said Montagu, casting around him for a messenger. Most of the cast had begun to ignore him again, but George was still loitering nearby. "George, do you think you could ask her?"

"Me?" George said, pointing to his own chest as if Montagu had asked him to stick a knife in it. "Why me?"

"Oh, because she . . . " Montagu didn't get any further, because Percy came bursting through the door at that point.

"Has anyone seen Gordon?" he asked.

"Are you still looking for him?" said Montagu peevishly.

"Is that why you and Mr Greenweal have yet to grace us with your presence?"

"Who is this Gordon, anyway?" Avril demanded, her hands on her hips. "We don't even know 'im."

"I met him this afternoon," said Montagu nervously. "He's the proprietor of this place."

"Oh, really? Well, someone ought to tell 'im that if you want people to do sumfink for peanuts, they at least want feeding. I'll tell 'im myself if you like."

"I wish you could," said Percy. "He took the guests to their houses after afternoon tea and no-one's seen him since. I've scoured the whole island. He's not in any of the cottages or the rooms in this house and as far as I can make out he's nowhere outside, either, though it is very dark out there."

"What a nuisance," said Montagu, without much conviction. "But if you've looked everywhere possible, do you think we could borrow you for a few minutes? And Mr Greenweal as well? You did say you'd be back here half an hour ago." He tapped his watch reproachfully.

"What? Oh yes, all right. Sorry," said Percy. "I'll go and get Anton."

"And while you're about it, could you get some food brought in 'ere?" Avril flung at him, her voice rising to a crescendo, "because if I don't get sumfing to eat soon, I'm going 'ome."

Percy tried not to show his consternation. Privately he thought this might be a very good idea, now he could see from the script Avril was holding that she'd been cast as Elaine. Goodness knew what Anton would say! But the troupe seemed to be one woman short already; he guessed they'd just have to plough on with who was there now.

"Right you are," he said. "I'll pop in to see Mrs Lawrence on my way out to our cottage."

"Does that let me off the hook, then?" asked George.

"Yes, George, you go and sit down." Montagu Sykes clapped his hands. "All right, everyone, let's take a little break now. We'll start again when Mr Forsyth-Jones comes back with Mr Greenweal."

"Mr Forsyth-Jones, my foot!" said Archie in a loud voice. "That's Wally Potts's lad. Now I've seen him again, I'm convinced of it."

CHAPTER 20

After her conversation with Jake, Juliet had spent a miserable two hours sitting at her kitchen table. Since she'd been attacked, she'd made a big effort to discipline herself not to take work home, but this evening she was deliberately trying to complete a routine report to make the time pass. She kept glancing at her watch. The vet had told her not to call him until at least 9 p.m. – the dog wouldn't have recovered from the anaesthetic before then. She couldn't help feeling irritated by the length of time the operation was taking, though she knew this was both ungrateful and illogical. It was good of Philip Trawford to give up his evening to operate on Sally, especially as he wasn't going to be paid for it, and Juliet knew more than she'd ever wanted to about how much time surgery took – her operations had lasted many hours longer.

She stroked the scar on her face. It was still quite deep, but no longer lurid. The plastic surgery had been as successful as was possible: the surgeon had said the next operation would be the last one he'd be able to perform to reduce the scar further. Juliet was no longer self-conscious about it; she hadn't exactly come to terms with it, but she had learned to live with it. It helped that the people she cared about and saw most – Tim and Katrin, her other work colleagues, and Jake – genuinely didn't seem to notice it. The only change in their attitude towards her was the at times suffocating protectiveness towards her some had assumed. Everyone except Katrin and Verity, that was: only they understood that Juliet passionately resented being pigeonholed as victim.

The hours would have passed more quickly if Jake had been with her. She hadn't thought much about missing their date – it had only been for a quick drink, anyway – but she was feeling lonely without him. With a pang of conscience, she played back their conversation in her head and knew that she'd been . . . not exactly offhand with him, but she'd certainly not given him the impression that seeing him today had been important to her. That he was important to her.

How important was he? She'd asked herself this question many times over the past few months. She invariably enjoyed his company – she must remember to tell him that – and she liked him as much as anyone she had ever met. Did it go deeper than that? She needed to find out. She knew she couldn't keep him dangling on a string for much longer; had in fact no wish to do that.

The sex had been . . .

Her mobile rang. Annoyingly, it was just outside her reach – by the time she had stood up and moved along the table the caller had rung off. She picked it up and recognised Philip Trawford's number. She seized the phone and called him back.

"Mr Trawford? It's DS Armstrong. Juliet Armstrong."

"Ah, good evening. I just tried to call you. I wanted you to know the operation appears to have been a success. It didn't take as long as I expected. I'm just on my way out now – I should still be in time to take my wife to a dinner."

"How is Sally – the dog, I mean? You had to amputate?"

"Yes, I'm afraid that was inevitable. I told you I thought it would be. She's all right – she's quite heavily sedated. You can come and see her tomorrow, if you like. We'll be keeping her here for a few days. I'll make sure I'm here if you come early. If you'll excuse me, I must run now!"

"You mean you're leaving her in the surgery on her own while you go out?" Juliet was horrified.

Philip Trawford let out a small chuckle.

"The surgery is adjoining my house but, yes, she will be left on her own overnight. Please don't worry – she'll be fine. I'll ask my son to look in on her a couple of times and I'll check her out when I come back. It's quite normal to leave animals on their own after they've had a general anaesthetic; but if I think she's restless or in pain, I shall stay with her overnight, of course."

"Oh!" said Juliet. "Thank you."

"Well, I'll see you tomorrow morning, then, shall I?" Philip Trawford's bonhomie had evaporated. He sounded tired and a little cross.

"Yes. Thank you," she said again, tepidly.

"Don't mention it!" He rang off precipitately. Too late, she remembered that she really hadn't thanked him properly for all his work. She didn't like to think of Sally on her own in a strange place. She knew she wouldn't sleep well.

She decided to call Jake again.

"Hello?" he sounded distracted.

"Jake, it's me. I've just called to say that Sally's ok."

"Who?" Jake was puzzled.

"Sally. The dog I told you about earlier. Do you remember?"

"What? Oh, yes. That's good. I'm sorry, Juliet, I'm trying to get the kids to bed and there's a bit of a skirmish going on at the moment. I'll call you back."

"No need," said Juliet, cutting the call short.

CHAPTER 21

P ERCY KNOCKED TENTATIVELY on the kitchen door. It was open, but something about the set of Mrs Lawrence's back told him she wasn't in the best of moods. She was busy gouging balls out of a melon with a weird instrument fitted with a sharp little cup at either end.

"Yes?" she said discouragingly.

"It's me - Percy - Isobel," said Percy, turning on all his charm, in a tone that suggested, 'you wouldn't be speaking like that if you knew.'

"Yes," said Mrs Lawrence flatly. "I know it's you. What do you want?"

"You couldn't rustle up a few sandwiches for the actors, could you? They're starving and the hunger's not improving their performance. And believe me, they'll need all the help they can get tonight!"

"Yes, well, you invited them."

"It was Gordon, actually."

"All right, Gordon invited them. I know I wasn't consulted; and no-one mentioned anything about feeding them."

"I know - I'm sorry. It was an oversight. I can help if you like."

Percy wandered into the kitchen and casually opened the fridge door. This had the effect he was after.

"Don't you go poking in there! Go away and do whatever

you have to do. I'll make some sandwiches when I've finished this. It'll have to be cheese."

"Cheese is great, thanks. And perhaps a bit of the cake left over from tea?"

"I'll think about it. Have you found Gordon yet?"

"No. I've given up on him for now. I can't believe Gordon won't show when he's supposed to. It's a pity about the red wine, but we'll just have to uncork when he gets here. I'm on my way to fetch Anton. The hams are a bit lost without us."

"Gordon's supposed to have 'shown' already; but you're probably right. Who are the hams? Oh, the amateurs, you mean. That's a bit unkind, isn't it?"

"Sorry!" said Percy. "I'll leave you to it. And thanks for making the sandwiches."

He didn't return to the main entrance but headed instead for the side door that led from the annexe into the part of the garden nearest the cottages. As he passed the Franklins' room, he could hear them talking in low voices, but he was unable to make out what they were saying.

Percy was wearing a black Emporium Armani sweatshirt and black skinny jeans. It was what he always wore – he had six other sweatshirts and pairs of jeans that were practically identical. Coats didn't interest him all that much, but he did possess a black leather bomber jacket. Offhand, he couldn't re-member where he'd left it, so, like Patti half an hour earlier, he went out into the darkness wearing no outdoor clothes. Also like Patti, he reasoned that it wouldn't take long to reach the cottage; he'd hardly catch hypothermia in a couple of minutes.

The route he took was more direct than Patti's because it didn't involve traversing the side of the house and approaching the cottages from the road, as she had done. If he could pick his way across the scrubby bit of garden, the front door of the end cottage was almost directly opposite, on the river side of the streetlight. Glancing across at the other cottages, as she had done, he saw they all appeared to be occupied. There were lights shining in all the windows – bright lights in his and Anton's and one of the others, more subdued lights in the other two.

Beyond the last cottage it was pitch black; there were no lamps there and Gordon's strings of fairy lights didn't stretch that far. Percy couldn't remember what that area looked like during the day; he suspected it was just another untidy patch of scrub. As he gazed at it, he thought he saw a flicker of something pale in the blackness. He turned away – the fog was still swirling in thin ribbons and he thought it was playing tricks on him. He shuddered, however – he'd heard some tale of a mad soldier who'd lived in one of the cottages and he had a vivid imagination. Gripping both his forearms with his hands to keep warm, he hastened across the road and had almost reached the front door he temporarily called his own when he heard a strange sound.

He turned and looked back at the waste land. Was something pale fluttering there, or was it just the fog? He hesitated. He didn't feel like investigating, but maybe he should? He temporised: he didn't have much time, because he'd promised to return Anton to the players as fast as he could. He took the final two steps to the door and pressed the bell, which whirred unmusically.

Anton opened the door, the half-finished bottle of wine in one hand.

"You took your time! Patti's here. We're just having a quick drink to fortify ourselves. Want some?"

"What? Oh, yes please! But we'll need to be quick."

Anton stepped back to let him into the little house.

"What's the matter with you? You look as if you've seen a ghost."

"I've seen something – in that funny patch of land at the end of the terrace. Something swirly and pale."

"It's probably Gordon dressed up in a sheet, to give the place a bit of atmosphere," said Anton, leading Percy into the parlour.

Patti, who had drunk only about a third of her glass of wine – she was determined not to be befuddled when she was speaking – was suddenly alert.

"What did you just say, Percy?" she asked.

"I said I thought I saw something white fluttering on the land at the end of this row of cottages."

"Did you hear anything?"

"Like what? Woo-ooo-ooo!" trilled Anton. "Evil spirits!"

"Stop it!" said Patti, smiling. "I'm serious."

"Why do you ask?" said Percy.

"Because I thought I heard something coming from that direction myself. It was like an animal's cry."

"How long ago?"

"When I was on my way here. Half an hour ago, tops!"

"I did hear something like that; I thought I must be imagining it. Maybe we should stop by there on our way back to the house. There may be something lying there hurt or trapped."

"I'm no good with wild animals," said Anton, filling a glass and handing it to Percy, then pouring the rest of the wine into his own. "Especially hurt ones. I'm just too delicate to be able to take it."

"Patti and I will protect you," Percy replied, grinning broadly at Patti. "Or you can stay here and we'll go on our own."

"There's no need to mock. I'll come with you, if you lead the way. I wouldn't know where to look, for one thing."

"All right," said Percy. "Find a torch, will you? And are there any spare coats here? I should have brought mine."

"There are a couple of cheap waterproofs hanging in the hall," said Anton. "Gordon must have put them there for guests. Not the sort of thing I'd be seen dead in myself."

"Great, that's one each for me and Patti, then. I assume you've got a coat of your own?"

"I've brought my Musto parka. But I don't want to get it messed up."

"You won't," said Percy. "We're only going to look. If it is an animal and it's injured, we'll get help."

CHAPTER 22

AMELIA BAKER AND Victor le Grange had just arrived at the cottage Amelia was sharing with Dora Westerman, having made a quick tour of the island first. Mrs Lawrence had given Amelia a key, but no-one had been available to show them to the cottage, so she wasn't entirely sure she'd got the right one; however, she remembered that Dora had described it as the end house, furthest from the river.

"Be quick!" said Victor le Grange, peering furtively at the next house in the terrace. "I don't want anyone to see me!" Someone looked out of its window and their eyes met as he spoke.

Amelia thrust the key into the lock. She had to waggle it a few times before it yielded, but she managed to open the door. Le Grange pushed past her and hopped inside.

"Excuse me!" he said. "I could hear some people coming out of one of the other cottages."

Amelia frowned as she stepped inside herself, closing the door behind her.

"That's fine," she whispered, "But don't forget we're not alone here."

"Hello!" came a tremulous voice from above them. "Who is that?"

"Is that the old biddy?" le Grange enquired.

"Shhh!" said Amelia. "Don't upset her! We need to keep on the right side of her."

"Hello!" came the voice again, sounding even more fearful. "Is anybody down there?"

Amelia cleared her throat.

"It's only me, Miss Westerman," she trilled in a bell-like voice. "Amelia. I've just arrived!"

"Oh, I'm so glad you're here. I was wondering . . . " Dora had emerged from the master bedroom and was standing at the top of the stairs. "Hello," she said again. "I didn't realise you had someone with you."

"This is my tutor, Miss Westerman. Dr le Grange. He was kind enough to give me a lift. He won't be staying for very long."

Dora Westerman descended slowly. When she arrived at the foot of the stairs, there was barely room for the three of them to stand in the tiny hall without touching each other.

"We'd better go into the parlour," she said. "Don't you think?"

Anton, after spending some time foraging in the kitchen, re-appeared triumphantly brandishing a small plastic torch. Percy drained his glass and put it down.

"Excellent!" he said. "Let's go."

Anton passed him the torch and went upstairs, returning with his parka, which was wrapped in a dry cleaner's polythene sleeve. He removed the sleeve with care and slid his arms into the parka, admiring the effect in the mirror over the fireplace as he pulled the zip to his neck. Meanwhile, Patti and Percy had bundled themselves into the cheap cagoules.

"Right!" said Percy. "We're all set!"

He opened the door.

"What was that?" he said.

"I didn't hear anything," said Anton, who was still in the parlour. "Was it the same noise you heard before?"

"Yes!" said Percy.

"No, I don't think so," said Patti. "I think that was one of the other cottage doors slamming."

"Well, we're going to have to be very quick," said Anton hurriedly. "That Montagu Sykes will be wondering what has happened to us."

CHAPTER 23

"ARE YOU ALL right?" Ava Dack called up the stairs. She listened as Lizzie flushed the lavatory chain yet again. "Lizzie! Are you all right? Answer me!"

Lizzie Fox appeared at the top of the stairs. She had removed her tight-fitting floral fuchsia-coloured dress and was standing there in her bra and pants. Her underwear was scarlet trimmed with black lace. Despite her concern for her friend, Ada noted the set included a skimpy suspender belt and wondered why. There was little point in subjecting yourself to the discomforts of such a garment unless you had someone to show it off to. Perhaps Jackson had enjoyed watching Lizzie put it on that morning, the dirty old goat. If so, Ava had no doubt that Lizzie would have extracted something from him in return. She observed with satisfaction that the tops of Lizzie's legs were quite flabby. It had always been a bone of contention that Lizzie was so much slimmer than she was.

"I think I'm going to be ok now," said Lizzie. Her face was pinched and her cheeks a dirty white: all the colour had leached – or been scrubbed – from them. Lizzie's eye make-up was smeared all round her eye sockets and mascara was running in rivulets down to her mouth. She began to shiver violently, her teeth chattering audibly.

"You need to put some clothes on," said Ava, not wasting more time on sympathy now her scare that Lizzie might be seriously ill had proved ill-founded. "And wash your face. And clean your teeth – that always makes me feel better when I've had one too many. I thought you could hold your gin better than that," she added reflectively.

Lizzie was incensed. She put her hands on her hips, assuming the stance of a jaded chorus-girl.

"I didn't have 'one too many'," she said indignantly. "There was something wrong with that Prosecco. I told you it tasted queer."

"It didn't do me any harm," Ava pointed out.

"No, but you've always had the constitution of an ox."

"Just as well, if I've got to look after you. Anyway, let's not argue. Do you think you're going to be fit to join in this evening?"

"I'll come to the talk and see how I cope. I might not want any dinner." Lizzie put her hand to her throat. It felt bruised on the outside, raspingly red-raw inside.

"Drink some water," commanded Ava. "You'll feel better if you do. You won't be able to drink any more tonight if we can't get some food down you," she added, wheedlingly. Ava disliked drinking on her own. "Listen! Is that my mobile again?"

"I can't hear anything," said Lizzie. She disappeared back into the bedroom.

Ava hurried back into the parlour and snatched her phone from the coffee-table.

"Hello?"

"Hello, Ava, ducks, is Lizzie there? She's not picking up."

"Oh, hi, Jackson. Lizzie's getting changed for dinner. Do you want me to fetch her?"

"No, don't disturb her. Ask her to give me a bell later, will you? I've got to meet someone now. See a man about a dog." Jackson spluttered a throaty laugh.

"It could be quite late. Tonight's evening do goes on a long time."

"Doesn't matter. I won't be in bed before midnight."

"I'll tell her. Is Reggie with you?"

"No, he just popped out," said Jackson smoothly. "You girls having a nice time?"

"So-so," said Ava. "It's a bit of a weird set-up here. What about you two?"

"*You* know what doing business at weekends is like. It's a bloody pain in the arse. We'd much rather be with you. Both of us."

"Huh!" said Ava. "You reckon?" If Jackson was anything like Reggie, the more he protested he wasn't enjoying himself, the more he probably was.

"Sure," said Jackson. "Now, if you'll excuse me, I've gotta go. Don't forget to tell Lizzie."

"I won't," said Ava. "Shall I give her your love?"

"You do that, sweetie."

Ava put down the phone. As she did so, she glimpsed her reflection in the mirror. Her pony-tail needed tying back again and her make-up could do with a refresher. Her dress was crumpled, too. She couldn't let herself down by showing up looking like that.

She returned to the hall and had just begun to mount the stairs when Lizzie came rushing out of the smaller bedroom and shut herself into the bathroom again. The unlovely sounds of more barfing followed.

Richard Renwick had decided there was no need to change his clothes. He undoubtedly looked smarter than any of the other men he'd encountered at Holyrood and he thought it unlikely they'd be transformed at dinner. He considered it a courtesy to the others not to try to upstage them any more than he could help – though he did feel a grudging admiration for Percy's careless but Armani-buttressed look.

Sonia thought differently. She was determined to make a good impression on Gordon and show him how classy she was. She'd disappeared upstairs about twenty minutes before. Richard could hear occasional sounds as she made her preparations: the creaking and shuddering of the pipes when she ran her bath; the thrum of the hairdryer; the squeak of the floorboards as she moved about the bedroom; the sound of something dropping to the floor followed by a sudden "Fuck!" as she put on her make-up.

Richard was taking advantage of her absence to revisit his typescript. The earlier altercation between him and Sonia was typical, their recent past punctuated with similar episodes. Going over the script again, however, he sustained an unaccustomed – and unwelcome – pang of doubt. Perhaps the play was a bit cliché-ridden, perhaps not even very relevant to today, as Sonia asserted. Maybe he would have to face up to the tragedy that its time had come and gone – though that didn't mean he had to turn himself into a hack, as Sonia was suggesting, he thought fiercely. But perhaps he could be a bit more flexible about what he was willing to write: brilliant authors had sometimes triumphed in the most unpromising of genres, after all.

The squeaking of the floorboards redoubled. It alerted him to the fact that Sonia was pacing the few feet between the bed and the cheval mirror. It was a ritual she always completed at home when she'd finished her toilette. Richard logged off and closed the lid of his laptop as a precaution against sparking another row. Sonia was coming down the stairs now, quite slowly, he guessed because she was wearing very high heels.

She came into the room and stood in front of him, not parading, exactly, but certainly conscious of the effect she was creating. She was wearing a strappy dress of black velvet. It wasn't too tight, but it showed off her excellent figure, clinging in all the right places. Her face was expertly made up and her blonde hair blow-dried into a shining bob.

Richard was transfixed. He stood up and took her hand.

"Sonia," he said, "you look beautiful."

CHAPTER 24

PERCY HAD ASSUMED the lead. Patti was following him, with Anton lagging a few steps behind. Percy was holding the torch. He didn't turn it on until they'd passed the last of the cottages.

He stood at the edge of the waste land and waved the torch about. It provided only a modest circle of light, which Percy caused to dance over the rough ground, illuminating nothing more singular than some broken ranks of sodden brambles and a few patches of balding grass that were waging battle with the mud.

"There's nothing here," said Percy, palpably relieved. "Let's get back to Mr Sykes and his crew."

"Just a minute!" said Patti, clutching his arm. "What's that?" She pointed towards the furthest of the brambles. Something white was flapping on the ground there, even though no wind was blowing.

"It's just an old cattle feed sack, or something like that," said Percy. He turned away quickly, but Patti didn't move with him. She let go of his arm and watched the white shape carefully.

"It's shifting upwards," she said. "I think it's someone trying to stand up."

"I don't like this!" Anton said in a loud whisper. "I've far too vivid an imagination for these sorts of tricks! Should I go and fetch more help?"

"You stay where you are for now," said Percy. "If we need more help, we'll tell you." He turned to Patti. "Take the torch. I'm going to go over and see what it is. Shine the torch in front of me as I go. Run if I tell you to!"

"Ok," said Patti, "but wouldn't you be better off keeping the torch? It's not exactly a weapon, but it's better than nothing!"

"That cheapo thing? My fists will be more effective if I'm attacked, which is why I want to keep them both free."

"Oh!" wailed Anton. "This is turning into a nightmare!"

"Shut up, Anton," said Percy grimly. "Otherwise I'll make you go over there, posh coat and all."

Patti held the torch steady as Percy picked his way over the mud. By the time he reached the thing, it was standing at its full height. It looked like a roll of carpet that had been wrapped in heavy-duty plastic, but it was clearly alive.

Percy suddenly clutched at the plastic and began pulling at it. He took something from his pocket.

"What's he doing? What is that?" Anton asked. Percy's reprimand had shamed him into standing next to Patti.

"I think it's a penknife. He's cutting something – maybe a piece of rope."

Patti had swung the torch away from Percy to reply to Anton.

"Can you shine the light back here again?" Percy called urgently.

"Sorry," Patti shouted. "Are you all right?"

"I think so – nearly done. We'll be coming across in a second."

Patti caught Percy in a dot of light again. He'd discarded all the plastic. It lay in a heap to one side of him. She could see now that he was supporting someone on his shoulder. He started walking towards them, half carrying the other person. He was within a few feet of them when Anton exclaimed, "My God! I think that's Gordon!"

Margarett Franklin was awaking from a troubled sleep. Her shoulder was stiff and her mouth felt dry. She couldn't remember lying down again and didn't know how long she'd slept. There was a slight throbbing in her head which she attributed to the sherry. She shouldn't have drunk it, especially in the frame of mind she'd been in at the time.

The door clicked to almost soundlessly. She sat up. Colin had just entered the room. With immense care he was easing the door-handle back into position. He was wearing a cheap-looking cagoule.

"Colin?" said Margarett, waking sharply. "Where have you been?"

"I just went outside for a quick breather," said Colin, unzipping the jacket and hanging it on the hook attached to the door. "I was beginning to feel a bit groggy in here."

"Where did you go?"

"Just for a walk round the house. There wasn't anywhere else to go, was there, unless I'd crossed the bridge back on to the main road. But I didn't fancy that and the gate's been closed now, in any case."

"Did you see anyone?"

"No. We ought to get ready for dinner. What are you going to wear?"

"I've brought my blue dress."

"Good – I like you in that. I think I'll just change my shirt."

Margarett slid off the bed.

"You'll need to change your shoes, too. Look at them! They're filthy."

"So they are. I didn't notice. It's dark out there – I couldn't see where I was walking."

"Did you bring some others?"

"Yes – well, trainers. Let me help you with that," he added, as Margarett tried to reach the zipper on the back of her dress.

"What did you think of that girl – the one we met in the sitting-room?"

"Bit of a stuck-up madam. And clearly having it off with the teacher bloke."

"I thought the same. He could get into trouble for that, though, couldn't he?"

Colin shrugged.

"None of our business," he said.

CHAPTER 25

GORDON WAS LEANING heavily on Percy when they reached Patti and Anton. Although he was a relatively short man - Percy was several inches taller - he had a muscular, compact body. Percy was staggering under his weight.

"Take his other arm," Percy said to Anton, trying to catch his breath.

Anton did as he was told, though he could see Gordon was very muddy. He feared sorely for the Musto.

"Is he conscious?" Patti asked.

"Just about. Gordon, can you hear us? You need to stay conscious if you can."

"Fknmmnnyou," said Gordon, his voice muffled not only by the state he was in but because his head was turned in to Percy's chest.

Patti pointed the torch obliquely, so that she could see Gordon's face without shining it into his eyes.

"You've got a nasty cut over one eyebrow," she said. "You'll need to see a doctor. There's quite a lot of blood, but head wounds always bleed like that. It's not necessarily anything to worry about."

"Eugh!" screeched Anton. "I didn't know he was bleeding!" He tried to twist out of the three-man tableau into which Percy had forced him.

"Hold him firmly!" said Percy. "If you're worried about

ruining your blasted coat, I'm sure Gordon will buy you another one."

"Fkmmnhouse!" Gordon growled.

"What was that?" asked Pattie, bending her ear close to her uncle's mouth.

Gordon raised his head and regarded her balefully. His bloodshot eyes glared through a mask of dried blood and mud. He looked like a bull that had been cornered and wounded by the matador.

"I said get me into the fucking house. And before that I said of course I can fucking hear you. Why are we standing about out here in the dark?"

"Your gratitude does you credit, dear Uncle," said Anton.

Gordon fixed him with a poisonous scowl, but had no energy for more talk.

"He's got a point," said Patti. "We need to get him inside and warm him up. He should be in bed with a hot drink. And we'll ask the doctor to come out."

Gordon made a superhuman effort.

"I'm not going to bed! And I don't want a hot drink or a fucking quack. A decent Scotch'll see me through. And I'm not going to miss this evening's kick-off. I want some clean clothes, that's all."

He paused and took a deep breath. He coughed several times, a sinister, ragged cough that seemed to come from deep within his chest. He leaned forward and spat on to the ground before he could speak again. Anton turned away his head in disgust.

"And I hope you've been rehearsing properly with Montagu Sykes and his bunch. That play has got to be good."

"If the play doesn't work out it won't be our fault," said Anton meaningfully.

Together Percy and Anton hauled Gordon into the house, entering through the side door that Percy had used earlier. They passed the Franklins' room and staggered into the main part of the house, eventually lowering Gordon on to the wooden bench that stood outside the kitchen door.

Mrs Lawrence emerged, wiping her hands on a towel.

"Good God!" she exclaimed. "What's happened to you? Did someone hit you?"

It occurred to Patti that none of them had thought to ask Gordon how he'd sustained his injuries. Percy had been too busy saving him and Anton not particularly interested. She herself had assumed Gordon had fallen while continuing with his obsessive odd jobs – trying to hang some more lights, in all probability. Now, as Percy and Anton helped him into the kitchen and she looked at him again, she saw that the cut above his eye had probably been delivered by a punch – a stray or perhaps not-so-accidental left hook? Her opinion that he'd been the victim of an attack changed from a suspicion to a certainty when Gordon became evasive about answering.

"I don't know what it was – or who it was," he said, his tone of voice forbidding further speculation. "One moment I was clearing up some plastic, the next I was down on the ground. I think I must have passed out for a few minutes."

"The plastic was tied with rope," Percy pointed out.

"Yes, it was," Gordon agreed. "I don't know how I managed to get tangled up in it. Isn't it time you got ready?"

"I'm on first," said Patti. "I'll go up to my room for a final run-through while Anton and Percy rehearse with the other actors. I'll have to change these shoes, too. Pity – I don't have any other nice ones."

Mrs Lawrence looked at the shoes. The heels were caked with mud but the uppers were clean and didn't appear to be scratched.

"Those'll clean," she said. "Leave them with me. You can leave Gordon with me, too. I'll wash his face and see to that cut." She turned to Gordon. "If you're sure you want to go ahead this evening, we'll try to help you, though you'll look pretty evil. But there's one condition: you've got to see the doctor in the morning."

Gordon cackled. Already he was regaining his aplomb.

"I don't mind if I look evil. Fits the part, doesn't it? Talking of which," he turned to Anton and Percy, "don't forget my little surprise."

"We haven't forgotten," said Anton, as he prepared to walk away, exasperated. "And don't you forget about my parka. I want it to be cleaned professionally. And if they can't shift these marks," – he pointed to some dark stains on the left sleeve – "I expect you to do the decent thing."

"What's that, then? I'll give you a tenner to get one off Spalding market tomorrow."

Anton kept on walking. He didn't reply.

"Really, Uncle Gordon, you don't have to tease him like that. He's put a lot of effort into this for you, after all."

"Who says I'm joking?" said Gordon. "I wouldn't mind if he had more money than sense, but the fact is he's got no money *and* no sense. You can't expect me to sympathise."

CHAPTER 26

A NTON CAME OUT of the kitchen and shut the door
firmly behind him. No-one must see Gordon until he
had cleaned himself up properly.

"Hi!" said a voice just behind him. Anton's heart leapt.
Gordon's contretemps had made him jumpy and the passageway was darker than he had remembered. He didn't recognise the voice: the speaker was male and so near to him he
could feel warm breath on his face. He turned round quickly.
Montagu Sykes greeted him with a Heepish smile.

"Where've you been?" he asked. "Been looking all over for
you, we have."

"I'm so sorry," said Anton, assuming a cloak of hauteur,
"I've been otherwise engaged."

"Is that so? Well, do you have a bit of time to spare for
us now?"

"Of course," said Anton, instantly *noblesse oblige*. "Kindly
lead the way."

He didn't notice the odd look that Sykes shot at him or
reflect that he was supposed to understand the geography of
the house much better than Sykes himself.

Sykes returned to the ballroom with Anton in his wake.
Once inside, Anton was dismayed to notice the chaos that
had invaded the room. The several old men present had
moved some of the chairs that had been laid out and placed
them in a semi-circle round a radiator. Two other chairs had

been jammed together to create a makeshift table on which two of them were playing a game of gin-rummy while the others looked on. A sandwich platter had been pushed to the floor on one side; it was decked with crumbs and some half-chewed crusts which had apparently defeated someone's false teeth. Plates and half-empty teacups were strewn across both stage and floor. Two beefy girls had perched themselves on the edge of the stage and were scrolling on their mobiles. One was frowning intently; the other smoked a cigarette and was making no bones about using the stage as an ashtray.

"My God!" groaned Anton.

Montagu Sykes took in the scene.

"They're just taking a little break," he said. "We had to wait, you see. It won't take a jiffy to get them back into acting mode."

"Really?" said Anton, arching his brows. "Hey," he shouted at the girl who was smoking, "you'll have to put that out. You can't smoke in here."

"Who says?" she flung back feistily, blowing a smoke ring at the ceiling. When she'd again lowered her head, she met Anton's eyes steadily, intent on sending him a look of defiance. Her demeanour changed in a trice.

"Oh my God!" she said, levering herself off the stage with an inelegant thud. "It's you, isn't it? Anton Greenweal! I only come today because of you. I seen your programme lots of times." She ran up to Anton and planted a smoky kiss on his cheek. He had barely time to recoil before she dropped a bombshell.

"I can't believe I'm your leading lady! It's like a dream come true!" She rolled her eyes and flicked her elbow at his arm.

"Who knows what it might lead to, eh?" She glanced down at his trousers. "Ooh, sorry!" she added.

Anton looked down at his trousers, too. A thick wedge of dropped ash had settled in the fold of one of the turn-ups on his chinos, where it was glowing menacingly. Avril fell to her knees and swiped at it several times with her hand.

"There, that's out now. It's left a little mark, but nothing to worry about. It'll prob'ly wash. Looks as if you was right about the cigarette." She hauled herself to her feet again, grinning, and ground the cigarette into the parquet with her heel.

Anton took a step back, shaking his trouser leg vigorously as he did so. Normally such an assault on his attire would have enraged him; but if he had heard aright, a comment the woman had made a few seconds earlier had plunged him into a much worse crisis.

"Did you say you were my leading lady?" he gasped. "You mean, you're playing Elaine?"

"'Sright," said the girl. She stuck out her hand. "Avril's me name. I couldn't believe me luck when Monty said it would be me."

Anton turned to Montagu Sykes in silent but stricken appeal. Sykes nodded encouragingly.

Anton took stock of the situation and realised there was no way out: the performance would be starting in less than two hours and he'd be obliged to act with either this girl or the other one. Glancing across at the latter, he saw there was little to choose between them, but there was more likelihood that Avril would have learnt her lines. She would have to do. He gave everyone a green smile, his stomach lurching, and touched Avril's hand gingerly. It was fleshy and sticky and adorned with many rings.

"Well, that's all sorted, then," he said, trying to keep the shrill of hysteria out of his voice. "We'd better make a start. Can something be done about all of this?" He waved his arms in several directions in an attempt to encompass the debris in a few swift movements.

"Of course," said Sykes smoothly. He clapped his hands. "Come along now, everybody. Chop, chop! Mr Greenweal's ready for us. Don't let's keep him waiting. We need to do a spot of tidying before we start. Everyone, collect up the cups and plates and stack them on the tray. George, can you please put those chairs back where they were?"

"I was just winning," grumbled George.

"Too bad," said Sykes unsympathetically. "You need to remember why you're here, George."

"Yes, well I've got that Freddy off to a T now," said George. "I don't need no more rehearsals."

"And I've backed George to win," one of the other old men said belligerently.

Montagu Sykes consulted his watch.

"Well, ok, maybe you could finish your game, then." He looked at Anton. "Perhaps we should just focus on some of the scenes between Mortimer and Elaine now, as time is short? Get you two used to working together."

"Oh, *yes!*" said Avril, punching the air.

"Whatever you say," said Anton, his face ashen. The evening had got off to a bad start with Gordon's accident, but that was as nothing compared to the ignominy of being expected to act with this girl. This whole 'troupe', in fact. Gordon owed him, big time. That Gordon had agreed to delay the repayment period on his loan didn't even begin to cut it.

CHAPTER 27

IT WAS TIME for the guests to assemble for pre-dinner drinks in the sitting-room that overlooked the river. Sonia Renwick was first to enter the room. Her eyes raked it.

"Oh, are we the first?" she said, simperingly shrugging her shoulders and accompanying the words with a little-girl giggle that sat uneasily on her sophisticated cocktail dress.

Richard trailed in her wake. He was wearing the same smart casual clothes he had worn at afternoon tea. He appraised his wife with baleful cynicism; he knew that she'd wanted to arrive before the others in the hope that Gordon would be there to welcome his guests, so she could bend his ear undisturbed about her spa project. Intent on her cause, she'd broken her usual rule of bursting in upon such a gathering at the last minute with the intention of creating what she called 'an éclat'.

Mrs Lawrence, stooping slightly, was standing at the table, her back to the door, methodically pouring out half-glasses of sherry. She turned as the Renwicks effected their entrance and pointedly stared at the clock on the wall.

"Goodness, you are early!" Her smile was unconvincing. Events had not gone her way this evening: she'd been annoyed by having had to make sandwiches for the thespians and decidedly unnerved by Gordon's contretemps. Now she was worried that the meagre reserves of sherry wouldn't stretch the full half-hour. She recovered her aplomb quickly; no point in taking it out on the Renwicks. "But you both look so nice! We're grateful to you for taking so much trouble, I'm sure. Would you like a drink, or will you wait for the others?"

The last question was articulated in such a way that they could be in no doubt about the correct answer.

"Oh, we're happy to wait," said Richard. Sonia nodded and moved across to the fireplace, where she arranged herself in a semi-seductive pose.

Dora Westerman came next. Sonia absorbed every detail of her toilette before presenting her with an encouraging nod. It was clear that Dora had made an effort: her coarse grey hair had been pinned up with a tortoiseshell slide and she'd changed into a shirt-waister dress patterned in swirling blues and greys; however, the dress had seen better days and she was still wearing her stout lace-up shoes. She was just the kind of woman next to whom Sonia liked to be standing at parties: it enabled her to shine, her modesty uncompromised. Such women removed the need to draw attention to your own attractiveness.

"Miss Westerman, good evening," said Mrs Lawrence cordially, having now snapped out of her gloomy mood. From what she'd seen of the guests so far, Dora Westerman was her favourite by some distance. "Would you like a drink?"

"Oh, not for me, thank you," said Dora, waving her hand. Isobel Lawrence noticed that she was wearing rather a nice amethyst ring on her wedding finger. Surely she wasn't engaged to be married to someone? "Not unless you have some fruit juice. Or water, of course."

Isobel Lawrence frowned. That decidedly was not the right answer! Her stocks of fruit juice were intended for breakfast only . . . and she didn't want to leave the sherry unguarded in case guests started helping themselves to more generous quantities than she could spare.

"I'll fetch some water shortly," she said, "when everyone else has arrived."

"Oh, thank you, that would be wonderful," said Dora, recognising the snub for what it was. She retreated to the corner where she'd been sitting earlier and looked out upon the river. The fog had lifted and she could see the water shimmering black against the soft glow emitted by Gordon's fairy lights.

"Dear me," said Mrs Lawrence, bustling across to her. "I've forgotten to draw the curtains. There's no hope of keeping the heat in if we leave them open, is there? Would you mind just moving again for a few seconds? I'm so sorry to disturb you!"

"Let me do it," said Richard Renwick, who had been pacing aimlessly around the perimeter of the room and at this moment was close to Dora's chair. He'd been trying to think up some original characters for the commercial work he'd now promised Sonia he would attempt. The trouble with all the guests at Holyrood, he had been thinking, was that they were so uniformly boring. From a writer's perspective, there wasn't an ounce of inspiration in any of them.

"I wouldn't dream of it!" said Mrs Lawrence. She reached the chair herself as he spoke. Dora stood up awkwardly to allow her to get closer to the silk rope that operated the curtain rail. Richard noticed that Dora was still gazing at the water, as if expecting to see something materialise from its depths.

"Hi, everyone!" Ava called out, teetering into the room in another pair of vertiginous heels. They appeared to be made of gold. She darted in a beeline for the sherry and filled to the brim one of the glasses that Mrs Lawrence had yet to reach.

"Cheers, everyone!" she said, stumbling slightly as she turned to face the others. Richard wondered how she had managed to pour her podgy figure into the skimpy sequinned two-piece she was sporting. He guessed that the evening would be a push-over for Sonia: there was no other woman present on the island blessed with the remotest capability of making herself look elegant – unless you counted Mrs Lawrence. But she was only the housekeeper.

"Good evening, Mrs Dack," said Isobel Lawrence severely, as she hurried back to her post. "Do let me help you with that," she added, as Ava skidded on the parquet. She held out her hand for the glass. Ava steadied herself and responded by downing its contents in two or three gulps, handing it back empty.

"Got a little catching up to do, don't I?" she said, grinning at Isobel.

"Actually, we haven't started yet," said Isobel Lawrence frostily.

"A drink would be nice now, though," said Richard, moving across to the table and picking up two of the poured half-glassfuls. He took one to Sonia. "Isn't your friend going to join us?"

Ava was preoccupied with watching Mrs Lawrence prepare her refill. She willed her to replenish the glass to the brim but wasn't surprised to see it receive an even more niggardly measure than the others. She took the drink and eyed Richard glassily.

"Eh?" she said.

Richard tried again.

"I asked about your friend. Will she be coming along later?"

"Who, Lizzie? Well, I damn well hope so, but at the minute she's likely throwing her guts up again. Been sick almost non-stop since we 'ad tea, she 'as."

"My God," said Richard, "I hope it's not something catching." It would be just his luck to be laid up for weeks with a debilitating and persistent bug because he'd been fool enough to agree to this jaunt.

"Oh dear, I'm sorry to hear that," said Mrs Lawrence. "Do you think she needs to see a doctor? Because there's one coming . . . " She pulled herself up without saying more. Richard regarded her curiously, but he remained silent.

"Lizzie?" asked Ava, delivering the word with a cross between a guffaw and a shriek. "Not 'er! Got the constitution of a ox, just like me, she 'as. She'll be right as rain soon. 'Ere in time for dinner, I shouldn't wonder." She winked at Richard. "Probably overdid it a little on the gin."

Richard gave her a blank look while Isobel Lawrence pursed her lips. The woman's vulgarity would have been even more annoying had she not been desperate to close the conversation down before someone picked up on her comment about the doctor. As if in answer to her prayer, at that point Margarett and Colin entered the room together. Margarett looked nice in a royal blue dress - M & S, Sonia and Mrs Lawrence both guessed, but probably from one of its more exclusive ranges. Colin was wearing a knitted jerkin, unzipped, and open-necked shirt and slacks. Not exactly ideal evening attire, even if the dress code had been described as 'informal', but he looked neat enough – until Isobel Lawrence glanced down at his shoes. She was aghast at the state they were in; he'd clearly been outside in the mud and although he'd apparently made some attempt to clean them up, by doing so had probably created a worse mess. The uppers were smeared with dirt and the toecaps were beginning to take on that strange salty white hue that disfigures leather when it's been properly soaked. She daren't begin to think of the state of the soles; she could only hope that he'd made a better job of removing the mud from them. It was on the tip of her tongue to remonstrate, but now was not the moment. If any guests happened not to enjoy the weekend, she would give Gordon no opportunity to land failure at her door. She'd have to choose a discreet couple of seconds.

"Would you like a drink?" she said, smiling sweetly, because she guessed that Margarett would refuse. Margarett was looking round her nervously. She found both the Renwicks and Ava intimidating: she'd already deduced that the Renwicks were posh and Ava was rich. The sight of Dora sitting by the window comforted her a little.

"Yes, please," said Colin. "What about you, love?" Like Isobel, he expected her to decline the drink.

"What? Oh, yes, please."

"*Really?*" said Colin, raising his eyebrows.

"Yes, *really*," she said, defiant now. "I said yes, didn't I? I enjoyed the one I had earlier. Perhaps I'm discovering what I've been missing all these years."

"Good for you, darling," said Ava, taking the opportunity to sashay back to the table for a refill. "Nothing to beat a little drinkie on a miserable night like this."

"I hope it's not going to be *too* miserable," said Isobel, reluctantly pouring a tablespoon or so of sherry into Ava's glass. "We want you to enjoy yourselves."

"I'm sure we shall," purred Sonia. She raised her glass. "Good health, everyone! And here's to a fascinating weekend."

Margarett took the glass that Colin handed her and joined in the toast. "I think I'll go and sit over there with that lady," she said to Colin. "She looks comfortable."

"All right, love, you do that. I'll just . . . "

"Mr Franklin, a word," Isobel Lawrence cut in, as Margarett walked away from him. "I'm sure it's just an oversight, but had you noticed there is mud on your shoes? I daresay you went out for a little constitutional and forgot."

Colin looked down at his feet.

"Oh Gawd," he said. "Yes, you're right, I did go out. And Margarett told me about the shoes. I cleaned them up as best I could, but I didn't mean to slip them on again. My fault entirely – I'll go and change them now. Trainers do you?"

"If *clean* trainers are the only option, of course they must suffice," said Isobel rather pompously. "I wouldn't mention it, but the parquet . . . "

"No, no, you're quite right to say – I'll be back in a jiffy." He looked across at Margarett anxiously. She was already talking to Dora Westerman. She seemed to be ok.

"Well," said Richard, looking at his watch, "it's seven-fifteen now. Who hasn't come yet? There don't seem to be very many of us."

"There aren't," said Sonia. "When will Mr Bemrose be here? I've been looking forward to having a chat with him."

Richard raised his eyes heavenwards. Experimentally, he'd allowed himself to feel proud of her; but he might have known she'd introduce all that vulgar business stuff into the conversation again as soon as she could.

Isobel Lawrence tried to hide her perturbation.

"He might not be able to make it for drinks," she said. "I'm afraid he's a little . . . indisposed."

Richard was truly alarmed now.

"He hasn't got the same bug as Mrs Dack's friend, has he? Because, if he has, that means it's infectious. Maybe you should call the weekend off, rearrange it some other time."

Sonia shot him a viperish look.

"We mustn't be cowardly about it before we know what's wrong," she said.

"Oh, it's nothing like that," said Isobel Lawrence brightly. "He's just taken a little tumble, that's all."

"Don't tell me he's fallen off that ladder of his," said Richard, raising his tone to one of manful bonhomie to counteract Sonia's jibe. "I was watching him balancing on it earlier. Positively dangerous, the way he was leaning out over the river, especially in the fog. We're not that fussy about where he puts his fairy lights. He didn't fall into the river, did he?"

"Oh, no, I don't think so," said Isobel. "Really, it's just a trivial thing – a small fall – but it's shaken him up a bit and he needs a shower. That's all." For the second time in ten minutes, she found herself casting around for a new topic to move on to. This time it was Dora Westerman who came to her aid.

"There's Miss Baker," she called across the room.

"I'm sorry, I didn't quite catch that. What did you say?" said Isobel, bestowing her friendliest of smiles.

"Miss Baker. She isn't here, either." It was on the tip of Dora's tongue to suggest that Amelia Baker's gentleman friend might not yet have departed, but she thought better of it. She didn't want to get the girl into trouble and she certainly didn't want to spend the night alone in that cottage.

"Well, she was a late arrival," said Isobel indifferently. Amelia Baker was the least of her concerns. "Perhaps she's still changing or putting her things away. She'll probably get here in time for dinner. Talking of which, I need to put the starters out now, if you'll all excuse me. Do help yourselves to more drinks." She spread her arms expansively, as if presiding over the bar at The Ritz.

Ava was back at the table before Isobel had left the room. She held up the sherry bottle. A drain of the wine remained, which she poured into her own glass, shaking the bottle to make sure she had extracted the last drop.

"Anyone else want any more?" she asked, indicating the four half-glasses that were still untouched. Richard Renwick and the three other women present all shook their heads.

"In that case, I'll just polish off this little lot," said Ava, with great satisfaction. "It would be a shame to let it go stale."

CHAPTER 28

ROUNDING THE CORNER next to the kitchen door, Percy saw Anton standing under the dim kitchen porch lamp. He was taking a deep drag of his cigarette: the tip of the fag projected a series of scarlet pinpricks into the feeble light. Percy had almost reached him when he looked up.

"Hi, Percy." His tone epitomised melancholy.

"What's up, Anton? You all right?"

"What do you think? Have you seen that girl who's supposed to be playing Elaine?"

Percy tried not to grin.

"I have, as a matter of fact. But cheer up: you only have to play opposite her once, and the audience isn't for real."

"Just because Gordon won't pay out a few quid to get someone decent! And who knows about the audience? Never trust an audience not to do the unexpected, has always been my motto. What if one of the bastards posts something on Twitter or such?"

"They won't," said Percy soothingly. "But if you're really worried, we can ask the 'guests' not to film or take photos. We can say we're entitled to a royalty if any shots get into the media. That should put the wind up 'em."

"Hmm," said Anton. "I suppose it's worth a try. Where have you been, anyway?"

"I saw Gordon upstairs first; left him to take a shower. He

said he'd lost his watch. I thought I'd go out and have a bit of a recce, see if I could find it."

"I doubt it was worth the trouble. He probably won it in a cracker! Did you find it?"

"Oh, we are snippy this evening, aren't we? Do try to snap out of it. And no, I didn't find it, as it happens. Probably not very wise to try in the dark. I'll have another go tomorrow." Percy consulted his own watch. "It's time for dinner, isn't it? You need to put that fag out and come inside."

"Dinner? That's another of Gordon's farces. Why he wants us in there eating with his 'guests' when the play's so bloody ragged is beyond me."

"Oh, come off it, Anton, you know exactly why he wants you there. You're a minor celebrity and he wants to capitalise on it as much as possible. He knows you'll have them eating out of your hand – or drooling over it, anyway!"

Anton pulled a face. "Your imagery is disgusting," he said.

"Sorry! If you really want to get out of dinner, I'm sure it can be arranged. Do you want me to go and ask Gordon if you can carry on rehearsing instead?"

"No, I don't – thank you very much. The play's beyond redemption. Another hour or so isn't going to help. Besides, the hammies aren't invited to dinner, which is a very good reason for me to be there. It'll keep me out of the clutches of that appalling girl for a while . . . and I can anaesthetise my feelings a bit, too. You did get Gordon to hand over the key to the wine cupboard before he went for his shower, didn't you?"

"Isobel did; I confess I might have forgotten about it. You'd better pace yourself, though. It won't improve the performance if you're pissed!"

"There's no need for you to lecture me. I assume you won't be averse . . . "

"Good evening, gents!"

Anton gave an exaggerated start. Colin Franklin had suddenly appeared, as if from thin air. Anton scowled at him.

"Hello," said Percy in a strained approximation to friendliness. "What brings you here? It's Colin, isn't it?"

"Yes, that's right. Well remembered! Mrs Lawrence sent me back to change my shoes. I had mud on the ones I was wearing."

Anton scrutinised Colin's footwear disdainfully. The man was wearing trainers.

"If you've just come across the grass, you'll be lucky if those aren't messed up, too."

Colin lifted first one leg, then the other, to examine the soles of his Nikes.

"They seem to be fine. I wasn't thinking, really: I had to fetch these from the car and I thought I might as well change into them while I was there. As you say, it was a bit stupid of me, but no harm done."

There was an awkward silence.

"Well, I'd best be going in – Margarett will be wondering where I am. I'll see you at dinner."

"Sure," said Percy. Anton tossed the briefest of nods in Colin's direction.

"I don't like that bloke," said Anton, almost before Colin was out of earshot.

"I don't see why not. Gordon's managed to gather a very strange set of people here, I grant you, but he seems to me to be one of the more straightforward. I wouldn't have thought a crime mystery weekend would be his cup of tea, though."

"Precisely," said Anton. "You can bet that whatever the reason he's come here, it isn't so he can solve Gordon's crap fake crime. He's got some other motive. He's an impostor. I'm convinced of it."

Percy collapsed into a fit of giggles. He had to lean against the door jamb for support.

"I don't see what's so bloody funny," said Anton.

"You are," said Percy, erupting again. "That's the funniest thing you've said for ages." Percy jerked his head in the direction of the sitting-room. "Which one of that lot do you really think are interested in a 'crap fake crime'?"

"It's '*is* interested'," said Anton petulantly. "And quite honestly I don't get the joke."

CHAPTER 29

ISOBEL LAWRENCE WAS adding a few finishing touches to the dining table when there was a light tap at the door.

"Anybody there?" enquired a familiar rough voice. By the time she'd raised her head, Fred Sharman had poked his own round the door. Having announced himself, he strode right into the room. He was wearing his trademark tweed jacket and waterproof trousers tucked into waders. He removed his cloth cap and shoved it under his arm.

"Hello, Fred," said Isobel in a worried voice. "I didn't know you were coming." She'd spotted his waders but couldn't gather the energy to remonstrate with him.

"Yeah, Gordon asked me ter drop by," he said. "'Bout ter-morrer, like."

Fred ran the water taxi service that offered rides on the river to tourists. The season had ended now, but Gordon had persuaded Fred to take the guests on a little jaunt up the river the following morning, before the main activities of the day began. It was to add a bit of local colour, he had explained, and to enable him to plant in their minds a few clues – and the odd red herring – before they started on solving the whodunnit.

"I'm afraid Gordon's had a slight accident. Nothing serious, but it's shaken him up," said Isobel. "He's resting just now. Can I help?"

Fred plucked the cap out again and stood twisting it in both hands. He had a strange expression on his face which Isobel, who knew him well, couldn't fathom.

"I s'pose so," he said. "Don't need to know too much – just 'ow many passengers there is and what time I've to get 'ere."

Isobel straightened her back and fished in her apron pocket for the piece of paper Gordon had given her listing times for meals. "Breakfast 8.00 a.m. – 9.30 a.m.," she read to herself. "They'll have finished breakfast by half-past nine," she announced to Fred in a louder voice. "Best to give them a few minutes to themselves afterwards, I guess. Can you come at ten?"

"Yep!" said Fred. "And 'ow many is there?"

"There are eight guests," said Isobel. "There are a few other people here for the weekend, too, if they want to come. Gordon's nephew and his friend. And his niece. And Gordon himself, of course. How many can you take?"

"Up to twenty including meself," said Fred. "Don't sound as if there'll be a problem. Tell 'em I'll be leaving at ten sharp. Got other things to do termorrer after, I 'ave."

"I'm sure Gordon's very grateful . . . "

Fred Sharman silenced her with a ferocious grimace.

"Ha!" he said bitterly. "Not that one. Don't know what gratitude is, 'e don't. Everybody always owes 'im. That's 'ow 'e works."

"Well, if you give me your invoice tomorrow, I'll make sure it's paid promptly."

"Invoice?" said Fred, raising his eyes ceilingwards. "Don't make me laugh!"

Isobel was about to pursue the point when Montagu Sykes appeared in the doorway.

"Excuse me for interrupting," he said. "I knew everyone would be sitting down to dinner soon, so I've seized my chance. I wonder if we might just borrow a sherry decanter? To make the scene with the old ladies more realistic. I meant to bring one and somehow I've forgotten it."

"I'll see what . . ."

"'Allo, Monty," Fred cut in.

"Fred! What are you doing here? Not interested in the crime weekend, are you?"

"Yer can fuckin' say that again. Sorry," Fred added, as he was confronted with Isobel's suddenly frozen face. "Been roped in to tekkin' 'the guests' on a river trip, I 'ave. Come ter think of it, they should of asked you, too. Don't fancy it, do yer?"

Isobel threw Montagu a quizzical look. "I'm something of a local historian," he said to her in a confidential voice. "I've done the commentary for some of Fred's parties, as they've been going along the river. Told them about the buildings as we pass, how the river was used for commerce in the past, that sort of thing. Do you think there'd be any interest in that among your people?"

"I'm sure there would be," said Isobel, "but we'd have to ask Gordon."

"Twenty-five pounds an hour 'e charges," said Fred threateningly. "Unless Gordon's got something on 'im, so's to wriggle out of it."

Montagu Sykes looked uncomfortable.

"I'd be happy to waive the fee on this occasion," he said. "We'll practically all be friends by tomorrow."

Isobel looked angry.

"I'm sure Gordon will be more than happy to pay your

fee," she said. "It'll only be for a couple of hours, won't it? I'll tell him I've arranged it."

"On your 'ead be it," said Fred. "Well, I'll be pushin' off now. I'll see you termorrer."

"You came in the boat?" asked Isobel.

"Yep. Summat's up with the car."

"Well, take care. It's dark out there this evening. Make sure you don't slip."

"Not me!" said Fred. "Cheerio, then."

Isobel turned back to the table.

"Er . . . hmm!"

Montagu Sykes alerted her to the fact that he was still standing there. She'd forgotten about him and his wretched decanter. There was something creepy about the man, even if she had just engaged his services for tomorrow morning. He was too ingratiating – or too persistent. She couldn't decide.

"I'll be with you in a minute, Mr Sykes. You want me to find a decanter, don't you? For the two old ladies in the play?"

"If you would be so kind."

"Come back to the kitchen with me. Incidentally," said Isobel, pausing again, "who's playing the two old ladies? There don't seem to be any mature women in your group."

"Vicky's playing one of them. She's very versatile – she can age forty odd years, no trouble at all. And Paddy will be the other one. A brilliant pantomime dame, Paddy is. You should have seen him in Mother Goose."

"You mean, one of the old ladies will be a chap *in drag?*"

"Yes," said Montagu Sykes. "A small troupe like ours often has to improvise – and I flatter myself we're pretty good at it!"

"Goodness!" said Isobel Lawrence. She wondered what Gordon would think of it; not to mention Anton.

She began to rummage in the cupboards over the sink.

"I can't find a decanter at the moment," she said. "There's a hip flask here. Will that do?"

"I suppose we can improvise. We already seem to be doing a lot of that."

CHAPTER 30

THOSE WHO HAD attended the drinks party were now assembling for dinner. They had yet to be joined by Gordon Bemrose or either of their missing fellow guests. They entered the dining-room in single file: Dora Westerman, Sonia then Richard Renwick, Colin then Margarett Franklin and Ava Dack. Anton and Percy wandered in behind them. Patti joined the group as they were taking their seats.

"Does it matter where I sit?" she asked Isobel Lawrence, who had just finished setting out dishes of melon balls exquisitely decorated with crystallised fruits. Gordon's sole instruction when Isobel had asked for directions about the menus was that the food should resemble the fare served at country house parties between the wars – sumptuous, plentiful . . . and very British. "The sort of grub you might read about in an Agatha Christie novel," he'd added expansively. He'd then abandoned Isobel to accomplish this with his somewhat less than sumptuous and plentiful catering budget.

"Please, sit where you like," she said to Patti, indicating the four empty seats. "I think we may be several people short for dinner tonight."

Patti scanned the faces of each of her fellow diners.

"I'm not surprised Gordon hasn't made it," she said. "I think he took a nastier knock than he let on to us. Who else is missing? Your friend?" she added, smiling at Ava Dack.

"Lizzie's got a stomach bug," said Ava. "She said she'd come if she felt better. I suppose I should have gone back to check on 'er," she added, obviously intending to do no such thing.

"And there's Miss Baker. She isn't here yet," said Dora Westerman. She was beginning to irritate Richard Renwick by continually drawing attention to that girl's absence. As far as he was concerned, they were better off without a young woman who saw fit to waste her time studying pulp fiction under the pretence that it was a scholarly occupation.

"Someone should probably check on *her*," said Isobel. "She hasn't joined in much yet. I do hope she's all right." Like Dora, she suspected that Amelia Baker was still canoodling somewhere with the rather odious academic who'd brought her to Holyrood. She took a less charitable view of the liaison than Dora; if she caught Dr le Grange trying to freeload for the weekend, she would have him kicked out.

As if on cue, Amelia Baker came bursting through the door.

"I'm sorry, am I late?" she exclaimed. "I've only just found that folder thing."

She was wearing a diaphanous black blouse in a sheer silky material, its high neck a mock-nod to modesty, belying the fact that both her bra and her navel were on clear display. Her entrance roused her fellow diners from the ennui that had been afflicting them. Most reacted with more or less concealed disgust. Anton averted his eyes from the small roll of fat around Amelia's stomach: if the girl must make an exhibition of herself, she should take care to cultivate the appropriate physique. Sonia and Mrs Lawrence, while neither knew the other's opinion, silently united in labelling her a tart. Ava, on the other hand, spiking a hard stare with unmistakeable envy, lamented the long-gone years when she could cut a similar figure. Richard Renwick recognised that the outfit was in poor taste and not to be compared with Sonia's much classier look, but allowed himself the indulgence of giving it the odd glance of surreptitious appreciation. Percy, who wasn't too fussy about the aesthetics of female dress, enjoyed basking in everyone else's shock. Only Dora Westerman and Patti showed no reaction to Amelia's toilette. Amelia sensed their friendliness. Dora was seated at the far end of the table, sandwiched between the two Renwicks, so approaching her was impossible; but the chair next to Patti's was free. Amelia took it.

There was a strained silence.

"Well, you could cut the air with a knife, couldn't you?" said Percy, with a mischievous wink at Sonia. She instantly averted her head.

"I think you are the last to arrive," said Isobel to Amelia, with more than a touch of the disapproving headmistress. "Perhaps you'd all like to start eating now, since Gordon isn't here to give you a formal welcome."

"Aren't you forgetting something?" said Ava, with peremptory rudeness.

Isobel raked the table with her eyes.

"I don't think so," she said.

"I think Mrs Dack means she'd like some wine," said Percy helpfully. "Would you like me to serve it?" He stood up.

"That's kind of you, but I can manage," said Isobel. "Do sit down again." She moved to the sideboard, where a bottle of white wine was standing in a terracotta cooler. Next to it a lone bottle of burgundy had been opened to allow it to 'breathe'. It hadn't been her intention to serve wine with the starter; she thought it bad form, as well as an unnecessary expense. She knew how to behave, however, and proceeded to wait on the guests silver-service fashion, pouring from the left.

"How's the play coming on?" asked Richard Renwick, falsely jovial.

Anton sighed heavily and took a gulp of wine. Percy kicked him fiercely under the table.

"It's an amazing piece of fun," he said. "I think you'll enjoy it."

"Golden age stuff, is it?" Richard continued.

"I suppose you could call it that. It's loosely based on *Arsenic and Old Lace*. Of course, we can't stage the whole play: it's far too long."

"Not really golden age, then, is it?" said Amelia, with unexpected pedantry.

"What do you mean?" Richard was instantly ruffled. He'd been tact itself so far and even tried to oil the works of the somewhat stilted conversations that had taken place, but he was damned if he would be lectured on drama by this ill-bred little . . .

"I remember when I first saw the film," cut in Dora, her expression turning dreamy. "Cary Grant was the star. He was *such* a good actor. I can't remember who played Elaine, his girlfriend. Some starlet, I suppose. They all tended to pale into insignificance beside him, didn't they?" She beamed around the table, inviting the others to agree. Sonia and Amelia both stared at their plates.

"Surely you're not old enough to remember when that film came out?" said Percy gallantly. "It must have been during the war."

"Not quite old enough. I didn't see it at the cinema. It was one of the films they used to show on television in the 1960s. On Sunday afternoons."

"You were lucky if you 'ad a telly then," said Ava. "We didn't."

"Oh, it wasn't mine; it belonged to my aunt. We used to come and . . . see her . . . she . . . "

"Miss Westerman, are you all right?" said Patti with some urgency. The older lady looked as if she might be about to faint. She was certainly holding back tears.

"Aaah . . . yes," said Dora uncertainly. "I do apologise." She dabbed at her eyes with her paper napkin. "I was just overcome for a short while. It was remembering my aunt, you see. We were very close."

CHAPTER 31

THE CHICKEN FRICASSEE was delicious. Isobel Lawrence, returning to the dining-room to gather plates, was showered with compliments from all sides of the table.

"You really must let me have the recipe," said Sonia Renwick.

"It came from an old 1930s cookery book." Isobel was gratified that her efforts had been appreciated. Her asperity was dissolving: she was visibly more relaxed, even though she was watching the emptying wine bottles with misgiving. She told herself it wasn't her problem: if Gordon had to buy more wine tomorrow, so be it. "I had to adapt it a little, naturally."

Everyone had cleared their plates except Anton. He'd accepted only a small portion and toyed with it while the others were eating. It wasn't because he didn't like the food, but he was acutely conscious of how ephemeral his hold on fame would be if his figure started to bulk up . . . and only too aware of his own weakness for sweet things.

"I hope the pudding's authentic, too," he said as Isobel took his plate.

"It certainly is: it's rum baba," Isobel announced, confident now her choice would be a triumph.

"Does that come from the 1930s?" Ava demanded truculently. She'd become louder and more belligerent as the meal had progressed.

"I think you'll find it was a society hostess favourite of

the period, but it's much older than that. It has French and Russian antecedents and dates back at least to the eighteenth century – the cultures of the two countries were more intertwined than they are now."

Everyone gazed in astonishment at Dora Westerman, whose voice had suddenly grown depth and authority. Ava stared at her fishily, meaning to send a withering look that was sabotaged by an unexpectedly loud belch.

"Oh, pardon me!" she tittered, putting her hand to her mouth.

Patti was watching Dora. She'd clearly amused herself with her burst of erudition, but was slipping back quickly into her former nondescript diffidence. Not wanting to stare too long, Patti was about to look away when Dora's face was contorted by another strange transformation. Her eyes were glinting and she set her mouth in a straight line. Dora was no longer a self-effacing rather dowdy old lady. She had become formidable. She was glaring at something beyond the table.

Patti was sitting with her back to the door, but she now became aware of a slight movement behind her. She turned to see Gordon Bemrose standing in the doorway.

Gordon was impeccably turned out in a white open-necked shirt and dark blue jacket. His crinkly hair, still damp from the shower, had been combed back from his face. Despite his sartorial efforts, he looked ghastly. Both sides of his face were scratched and bruised. He was holding his arm in a makeshift sling. He put out his other hand to steady himself by gripping the empty dining chair next to Patti's. She saw his knuckles were skinned and bloody. He managed a slight smile.

"Banquo's ghost," said Richard Renwick quietly to his wife. She smiled back.

"Evening everyone," Gordon said. "Sorry I'm late. Something came up." He waved his bandaged arm, widening the smile to a feeble grin, and, pulling out the chair, sat down rather heavily. Dora continued to hold him in her gaze. He flicked several glances at her but did not maintain steady eye contact. "Do you know," he said, "it's a long time since I heard that story. About the rum baba, I mean. Someone else told it to me once. No-one that mattered, I suppose: otherwise I would remember who it was." He chuckled mirthlessly. Dora's eyes dropped to her lap.

"Uncle Gordon, are you sure you're all right? Wouldn't it be better to go back to bed now and wait to see what the doctor says tomorrow?"

"I haven't been in bed," said Gordon, shaking off the arm Patti had placed on his sleeve. "And I don't need a doctor. I've told you that already. I'm not going to miss tonight's fun. No question. The boys and I have got a little trick up our sleeves, haven't we, lads?" He nodded across the table to Anton and Percy. Anton raised his eyebrows disdainfully.

"Only if you're up to it, Gordon," said Percy.

"I'm sure they can improvise without you," said Richard Renwick. "They seem to be very talented."

"Oh, they can improvise all right," said Gordon. "Bursting with talent, they are. What I'm talking about *is* improvising. We don't want to change it again."

"Well, if you're determined to join in this evening, you'd better at least eat some dinner," said Isobel Lawrence. "I've saved some chicken fricassee for you."

"I don't want it," said Gordon, roughly; then, in a gentler tone, "but I will have one of them rum babas. Steeped in history, as we've heard. A very fitting start to the evening." He was staring at Dora now; she resolutely ignored him, fixing her full attention on her hands, which were folded in her lap.

Isobel Lawrence sighed and brushed past him, bearing away the pile of dirty plates.

"Rum baba," he said to her, turning so no-one but Patti could hear. "Quite an extravagance!"

"They're made with cake flavouring, not the real thing," she hissed back. She stalked off to the kitchen.

"A drop of wine, Mr Bemrose?" said a voice at his elbow. He turned his head sharply to find Sonia Renwick standing beside him, the bottle poised over his glass. "I feel sure red will be your preference. As it is mine!" Her laughter tinkled through the tension. Gordon took in her svelte dress and sleek hairdo and found himself feeling appreciative.

"You're right there," he said, passing across the glass from his table setting. "Just a splash, though. Mustn't forget I'm working!" He chuckled thinly; she padded it out a bit with her own silvery laugh. "I'm always interested in work," she said. "I know you have many irons in the fire and, I'm sure, some fascinating tales you could tell. Why don't I pull up a chair so we can chat for a few minutes? I expect it will take Mrs Lawrence a while to sort things out in the kitchen."

At the other end of the table Richard Renwick groaned and dropped his forehead into his hands.

"Are you all right, squire?" said Colin Franklin anxiously. "It doesn't seem too healthy round here, does it?"

CHAPTER 32

PATTI STOOD ON the raised dais in front of the stage and surveyed her audience. Two rows of chairs had been set out. Gordon had seated himself ostentatiously in the middle of the first row, even bringing his chair forward so that he could have touched her if he'd reached out to her. Patti found his proximity oppressive. She was glad that she'd asked for a lectern; glad also that she'd decided to base her talk around a series of video clips and slides. Despite welcoming Percy's encouraging comments after her run-through and even Anton's more measured praise, she knew she was not a natural speaker. Almost as great a problem as her own shyness was her lack of knowledge of the guests' expertise and capabilities. Now she'd met them, she doubted any of them had more than a superficial understanding of what forensic science was about; nevertheless, Dora's display of learning during dinner had unnerved her. Patti knew that pitching any talk to the correct level of its listeners was crucial for success, but did this disparate group of people have anything in common except their (frankly, incomprehensible) willingness to pay Gordon to provide dubious entertainment on his tiny island as the bleak Fenland autumn segued into winter?

Anton and Percy had taken the chairs that flanked Gordon's. Patti knew they'd done it to support her, even though they, too, seemed uncomfortably close. She'd noted they'd been too quick for Sonia Renwick, who had evidently wanted to sit next to Gordon herself. Patti had heard snatches of Sonia's and Gordon's conversation at dinner. She had been amused, despite her apprehensiveness about the talk. Evidently Sonia had some kind of business proposition she wanted to run past Gordon, who'd responded entirely in character by immediately launching into a description of something he called "speculative percentage gains". Patti had no idea what these might be, but she was certain they'd be of material benefit to Gordon, probably at Sonia's expense. The scales had not fallen from Sonia's eyes yet, however – probably nothing short of a financial sting would wake her up from her business reverie – and she'd seated herself immediately behind him, her husband beside her. Amelia Baker was sitting on Richard Renwick's left, at the end of the second row, and Margaret and Colin Franklin occupied the two chairs to Sonia's right. Some adroit flattery on Percy's part had persuaded Ava Dack to take the seat next to his, where he could keep tabs on her; and the seat to Ava's left was empty. Dora Westerman had chosen to leave the seat next to Anton vacant and settled herself at the end of the first row. Now that Gordon had moved his chair forward, Dora's line of sight between herself and him was uninterrupted. She stared at him uncompromisingly.

Montagu Sykes's group of players had disappeared into the area behind the stage and the two makeshift changing rooms beyond it to prepare themselves for their performance, but Montagu himself was already attired in his costume and, having asked Patti if he might stay to listen, was standing by the wall to one side of the rows of seats, making himself as self-consciously unobtrusive as a tall, moustachioed man dressed in a 1940s New York policeman's uniform possibly could. Isobel Lawrence had joined the group belatedly and was also standing, having positioned herself on the opposite side of the room to Sykes.

Patti checked that her slides had been uploaded and tested the internet connection on her laptop. Using the web for clips was a risky strategy, but the short films she wanted to show were accessible only through her police account and not downloadable. She cleared her throat. Having thought back to her own introduction to forensics when she was at college, she'd decided to employ a similar Q & A approach to get the session started.

"Good evening," she said. "I hope you enjoyed your dinner as much as I enjoyed mine." There was a general murmur of approval. Isobel Lawrence preened discreetly.

"Now," Patti continued, "let's move on to the more serious part of the evening. Shortly we're going to be entertained by a play about murder; but first I'm going to give you a quick guide to forensics. Nothing too daunting; but both the talk and the play will help you when you begin solving your own mystery tomorrow."

She paused to look at her listeners. Everyone except Ava Dack was watching her intently. Ava had fallen asleep with her mouth open. Patti anticipated the snore that was rumbling up from Ava's chest by trying to raise her voice loud enough to drown it out. She hadn't taken to Ava, but still she felt embarrassed by the vulnerability to which the woman's drunkenness had exposed her.

"Would anyone like to give us a definition of what forensic science means?"

"My guess is it means whatever you want it to mean," said Richard Renwick smoothly. "I'm no expert, but I believe that the techniques in use are frequently discredited. They become superseded by other techniques that get discredited in their turn. Heaven help the poor innocent bloke who falls foul of the latest flavour-of-the-month theory, in other words."

Patti's face fell.

"Clever Dick!" Colin Franklin called out. Margarett dug him in the ribs with her elbow. Sonia looked annoyed. Everyone else laughed.

Patti was grateful to Colin. His interjection helped her to recover her poise.

"That's not far wrong," she said, addressing Richard after she'd smiled at Colin, "even though you have started right in the middle. Like other sciences, forensics is continually pushing back the boundaries and of course that means over time some of the measures used are no longer deemed reliable. Part of the problem is its very public nature – as the name indicates, forensics is a science – or, more accurately, a group of sciences – practised in public. Rather like the law itself, it builds up a body of knowledge and assumptions *in public*."

"That's a bit deep for me," Margarett whispered to Colin. Gordon heard her.

"Cut the cackle, Patti, love," he said. "You've only got half an hour."

"All right," said Patti, her face reddening angrily. "I was just going to spend a few minutes talking about how forensic science has developed over the past hundred years, before I show you some short clips on well-known procedures. But if you'd rather watch the films with no introduction, that's fine by me."

"I'm sure we'd all like . . . " began Richard Renwick.

The swing doors burst open with a bang. Lizzie Fox came catapulting through them and collapsed on the floor beyond.

Isobel Lawrence was the first to reach her. She crouched beside her as Lizzie slowly heaved herself to her knees. Lizzie let out a long, low moan - whether of pain or fear was hard to interpret.

"Mrs Fox!" said Isobel. "Are you all right?"

"I've cut my knee!" The words came out in disjointed half-sobs.

"Surely not! The floor's . . ."

"Hold on to me and try to stand up, love," said Colin Franklin, who'd quietly crossed the room before the others could work out what was happening.

Unceremoniously, Lizzie pushed Isobel away and clung to Colin's arm, which he'd stooped down to offer her. He hauled her to her feet. Her skin-tight red lycra dress was torn at the hem and her tights were ripped to shreds. A mess of blood and mud was disfiguring her right knee. She was wearing only one peep-toed red stiletto shoe. The toes of her unshod right foot looked as if they had been scraped along gravel and were also bleeding.

"You're right, you 'ave cut yourself," said Colin.

"What a mess!" exclaimed Isobel. "Someone bring a chair."

Dora stood up and moved her bag to the seat next to Gordon's. Percy seized the chair she'd just vacated and came hurrying over with it.

"What the f . . . deuce is going on now?" demanded Gordon, himself only able to rise to his feet with difficulty. Patti came down from her dais and took hold of his arm. He stared at her hand crossly, then thought better of shaking her off. He limped across to the injured woman, leaning on Patti as he went. Margarett Franklin and Sonia Renwick followed them.

"You'll have to excuse me," Anton said faintly, leaning

back in his chair and closing his eyes. "I can't stand the sight of blood. I shall be absolutely no good for my performance unless I keep calm."

"I can't say I'm all that keen on blood myself," said Richard Renwick, looking round him for an excuse to get no closer to the victim. His eye fell on Dora, who had now taken the chair next to Gordon's; she immediately stared fixedly at her hands. "Miss Westerman, are you all right?" He walked over to her with as much dignity as he could muster. She looked up at him as he approached, her dark eyes twinkling with irony.

"I'm quite all right, thank you, Mr Renwick," she said. "Please don't worry about me. Miss Baker will look after me."

Richard hadn't noticed that Amelia Baker had moved to sit beside Dora. He turned away and took in the group that had surrounded Lizzie. There were quite enough of them without his butting in; between them they might suffocate the woman.

"In that case, I'll just take a little turn outside. I'm not feeling too good myself."

It was clear that Lizzie really was shaken up, but not so much that she wasn't enjoying the attention.

"Can you tell us what happened?" said Patti. "Try to keep calm. Take your time."

Lizzie took a deep breath and then exhaled. Her breath smelt foul. Patti and Isobel Lawrence, who were standing closest to her, both turned their heads away.

"I was beginning to feel better," said Lizzie, "and I'd promised Ava I wouldn't miss this evening, so I put on me dress and shoes and I was just coming across here when I saw a man."

"A man! What sort of a man?" asked Gordon quickly. "I

161

mean, was it someone you knew?" he added. Patti gave him a curious look.

"No, I'd never clapped eyes on him before. He was evil-looking, though. I could see he meant harm."

"Why do you say that?" asked Patti.

"He just looked . . . furious," said Lizzie. "And he started running towards me. I was that frightened. Then I tripped." The words were coming out between sobs again.

"Well, it wasn't any of the men with us. They're all here," said Sonia. "Unless it was one of the old actors."

"It wasn't an old man," said Lizzie. "An old man wouldn't scare me."

"Perhaps it was just someone who turned into the island by mistake," said Percy. "It must happen sometimes." He looked at Gordon for corroboration and was surprised to see the beads of sweat standing out on his forehead.

"Na," said Colin. "I shut the gates when I went out for me shoes. You said the gate was closed at night and I wasn't taking any chances. Our car might not be up to much, but it's all we've got. The insurance wouldn't buy us a new one."

"I've lost *my* shoe," Lizzie wailed. "It was a Christian Labootin!"

"It's probably still out there," said Mrs Lawrence briskly. "We'll find it in the morning. I'm going to fetch something to put on those cuts. Would you like a glass of water?"

"She don't need a glass of water. What she wants is a good, stiff drink. Then she'll be right as rain."

Ava's large, pale head reared like a sea monster over Patti's shoulder. Isobel Lawrence looked enquiringly at Gordon.

"There's some brandy in the drinks cupboard," he muttered grudgingly.

"I'll get it," said Percy. "Anybody else like some? I think we've all had a bit of a shock."

"Well, I wouldn't say no," said Ava.

"I don't think any of us doubted that," said Sonia acidly.

"I'd like some, too." Amelia Baker's voice came trilling across the room.

"Good for you," said Percy, then, turning back to the others. "Go on! No one's driving, so we don't need to worry about the police . . . Talking of which, where has Montagu Sykes disappeared to? He was standing there a few minutes ago."

CHAPTER 33

J ULIET WAS LYING on her sofa, where she had fallen
into an uneasy doze. Although still half awake, she was
dreaming of mutilated animals. Dogs and hares filed silently
past her, a procession of misery, their abject eyes imploring her
to act. Beyond them, a man with a gun was hunkered down.
Juliet was straining to see his face, but ribbons of mist were
obscuring it from view and each time the man's head floated
back into sight it had changed shape. First it was long and pale,
the eyes unnaturally elongated; then the face flattened and
shortened and sprouted two hideous cauliflower ears. The ears
were still there next time it appeared, but were now affixed
to the bald bullet head of an all-in wrestler. All the faces were
horrible, all their expressions leering threat. The man cocked
the gun. Juliet ran towards him, her arms outstretched, trying
to save the line of animals that kept on coming. She screamed
as he leapt at her, jangling a little bell in her ear.

She sat up. Groggily, she reached for the phone.

"Hello?" Her voice was panicky: her first thought was that
Philip Trawford had rung to tell her Sally had died.

"Juliet, it's me; are you ok?"

"Oh, Jake, thank God," she said.

"What's wrong?"

"Nothing's wrong. I thought you must be the vet – that
perhaps Sally didn't make it. I've been having a horrible dream
. . ."

"That dog's certainly gripped your imagination, hasn't it?"

She thought she detected criticism in his tone and prickled immediately.

"I'm sorry if you don't like it . . . "

"Juliet, darling Juliet, it's not about what I like. I just don't want you to keep on punishing yourself about everything. You've done the best you can for that dog and so has the vet. If the dog doesn't survive, neither of you will be to blame."

"No, I know. I'm sorry if I snapped at you."

"That's all right. That's why I called."

"What, to be snapped at?" Juliet managed a small laugh.

"No, to try to improve your mood. I guessed you'd be brooding."

She disliked his choice of words, but bit back another angry retort.

"Anyway," Jake continued, "do try to get a decent night's sleep. You're still coming tomorrow, aren't you?"

"Yes," said Juliet, "after I've called in at the vet's."

"Ok. If you want to go back again later, I might be able to come with you."

"Really? I thought you had to work all weekend."

"I can get someone to cover for me for an hour or so."

"Thanks! That'd be great."

"Promise me you'll go to bed now. And don't stay awake all night just in case the vet calls you."

"All right, I promise."

"Goodnight, then."

"Goodnight."

As she put the phone down, Juliet wondered if she enjoyed being taken care of like this. Try as she might to appreciate it, she still found it mildly irritating; but perhaps she'd feel worse if Jake didn't show so much interest?

She sighed as she pushed herself off the sofa and headed towards her bedroom.

CHAPTER 34

PERCY RETURNED BEARING a tray on which he'd set a bottle of brandy and several jacquard glasses. The audience had re-grouped. Dora and Amelia were still sitting together. Ava had returned to her old seat and Lizzie, two large sticking plasters on her knee, had hobbled across to join her. Colin and Margarett were standing close to the window, apparently engaged in a low-key disagreement. Sonia was sitting alone, ostentatiously scrolling through her mobile, her brows knotted impatiently. Amelia turned round from her first row seat and met Sonia's eye just as she was looking up.

"Where's your husband?" she asked.

"How should I know?" Sonia snapped back tautly. "This whole thing's a shambles."

"I'm inclined to agree with you," said Anton, appearing from the back of the room, where he'd been engaged in what was evidently an unsatisfactory discussion with Patti and Gordon. "I think we should get on with the show now. Then we can all bugger off to bed."

The other players filed in as he spoke, Avril leading them. She was a very sturdy Elaine, dressed in a negligee that was bursting at the seams and somewhat incongruously fastened at the bust with a giant kilt-pin. She was followed by Paddy, who presented them with the spectacle of a lumpy Aunt Abby in a long black dress with a detachable whiteish jabot round his neck. The dress didn't quite reach his ankles, showing his trouser bottoms when he walked.

"I'm up for it if you are," said Avril to Anton, making calves' eyes. She took a few steps towards him, her breasts wobbling dangerously under the flimsy material of the negligee.

Anton turned away, muttering "Jesus!" under his breath. Gordon broke free of Patti, who was still helping him to walk and rushed towards him despite his limp.

"You can't start yet!" he said. "Patti's got to do some more. Otherwise there won't be enough grounding for tomorrow. I'm sorry we've had a hold-up, but there it is."

"I've told you, Uncle Gordon," said Patti, "I've prepared some photocopied notes to give them the basics. You can't expect them to take it all in if I just talk, in any case. Let me hand these out now. I'll ask the guests to read them by mid-morning tomorrow. If they've got any questions, they can talk to me after the boat trip."

"Sounds like a good idea to me . . . " Anton began,

"Well, no-one asked you, did..?"

"Now, now, children, no squabbling," Percy cut in smoothly. "Why don't you have a glass of brandy before you do anything else?" He turned the bottle round on the tray. "I don't think the label'll bear much scrutiny, but it'll warm your cockles just as much as any other plonk."

"Less of your wit," said Gordon, eyeing the bottle. "Just go easy on that, too."

"You know I don't drink before a performance," said Anton haughtily.

"And I don't want none, neither," said Avril, aping him. "Say," she added, giving him a playful punch, "when are you going to grab me by the fanny?"

"When am I going to *what?*" said Anton, springing back a few steps in horror. Not even the most talented actor could have feigned the look on his face. Patti tried not to giggle.

"That's what it says in the play-book," said Avril, flourishing her script. She raised her voice. "Mortimer grabs her by the fanny!"

"Well, really!" said Sonia with disgust. "Just what is this play about?"

"It's perfectly respectable," said Dora calmly, "apart from that one stage direction. The playwright is American. Americans have a different view of things."

Ava let out a dirty laugh which was cut short by a loud belch.

"We're wasting time," said Gordon, "what does everyone think about Patti's suggestion? Are you happy with the notes?"

"If we're going to . . . " Amelia began. The unfinished sentence vibrated into a scream as the room was plunged into darkness. "I don't like the dark!" she wailed.

"Neither do I," said Margarett. She put her hands out in front of her and waved them around until she found Colin's arm.

"What the fuck..?" said Gordon.

"It's a blown fuse – or a power cut," said Percy. "Don't worry, there's a little light on my key fob. It'll help me see well enough to fetch some torches. You've got some in the kitchen, haven't you? Where are the fuse boxes?"

"They're in the cellar," said Gordon. Then, immediately afterwards, "Don't you go down there! I'll do it myself."

"Please yourself . . . " Percy began.

"I think you should let Percy do it, Uncle Gordon," said Patti. "You're still a bit shaky on your feet."

Someone switched on a torch.

"Here," said Anton, passing it to Percy. "I've still got the torch I brought from the cottage."

"Give me that!" said Gordon, snatching it from Percy before he could grasp it properly. "I've said I'll go."

"Why don't you let me go?" said Colin, stepping forward to make himself visible. "I'm neutral!" He switched on his mobile's torch. "I can use this."

"Somebody had better do something quickly," said Sonia, flicking on the torch on her mobile. "Richard's outside some-where – and maybe Montagu Sykes is, too - stumbling around in the dark. They might fall into the river or anything."

"Why don't you go outside to look for them while I go down into the cellar?" Percy said to Colin. "You're obviously a practical bloke and you've got the lie of the land now – you went out for a walk earlier, didn't you?"

"No-one's going down into the cellar except me!" Gordon almost screamed the words.

"Oh, for God's sake," said Patti, her patience snapping. "If you're determined to do it, I'll come with you, just to help you keep your balance."

"All right," said Gordon. "but you'll stay at the bottom of the steps. There's a lot of stuff in there. I don't want you falling over something and hurting yourself."

Patti almost laughed.

"I think I'm a bit nimbler on my feet than you give me credit for," she said. "But fair enough – if you don't want me to come right in with you, I'll wait. Just let me help you down the steps. Percy, if you come with us as far as the kitchen, you can help me find some more torches. I'll take one and you can bring the others back here."

Percy sighed.

"Thank God we've got all that sorted out," he said.

Colin was standing next to him.

"Right, I'll push off, then," he said. "Don't worry if I don't come back soon. I might be gone some time." He grinned.

Margarett appeared suddenly at his elbow. She grabbed his arm.

"Please don't go," she said. "I don't want you to. You know how scared I am of the water."

"Don't be silly, love," said Colin, gently disengaging her fingers. "You know I'm not afraid of the water, but I promise not to go too near the river anyway. We've all got to pull together here if we don't want this weekend to turn into a disaster. In half an hour, we'll probably be watching the play and laughing about all this."

CHAPTER 35

COLIN FELT LESS happy about venturing out into the darkness than he'd suggested to Margarett. He thought Gordon's fairy lights were naff, but they had at least offered some feeble illumination when he'd been outside before. Now he thought about it, it was probably Gordon's tinkering with the electricity that had caused a power surge and plunged them all into darkness.

The fog had returned with a vengeance: the light from his mobile's torch barely penetrated the gloom. It could cut only a dim circle in the murk. Colin had to shine it down at his feet to see the path. He decided to head towards the cottages first: he could think of no reason why Richard Renwick and Montagu Sykes would have gone towards the bridge. He wondered if they were together. They'd left the house separately, but they could have met each other and stopped for a chat, or to enjoy a cigarette together. It was a bit of a long shot – he didn't even know if either of them smoked – but there had to be some reason why both had gone out for a short break and neither had returned.

Despite his bravado, he felt afraid. Like others of the party at Holyrood House, he was suspicious of Gordon's so-called accident. Gordon had offered several feeble explanations, but the evidence pointed clearly to his having been beaten up. But by whom? And was whoever it was still lurking in the foggy darkness? Something told him not to call out to the missing men – the same instinct that told him to make as little noise as possible and shine his light low to avoid being noticed. He came to the end of the path that skirted the house.

He knew exactly the spot he had reached: it was where the track in front of the row of cottages began. He turned left into it and carried on walking slowly. He moved the torch sideways to his right until he could make out the garden gate of the first cottage – the one allocated to Dora Westerman and Amelia Baker. He hesitated. Should he try to enter the house, see if either of the men he was seeking were there? But Amelia had probably locked the door when she left and there was no need to get carried away. Try to think logically, he told himself. If they'd gone into one of the cottages it would surely be the one in which Richard and Sonia were staying. He wasn't absolutely certain, but he thought it was the next one along. He edged his way to the second garden gate.

Unlike the gate he'd passed, this one had been pushed open. He shone the torch at it, trying to slant it so the light would reach as far as possible. It stopped short of the front door of the cottage. Colin stepped into the garden, moving the light forward. This time it reached the doorstep. One more stride and Colin could shine the light on the door itself. It was firmly closed, but that didn't mean it would be locked. The house was in darkness, but Richard and Montagu might still be inside.

Colin was still very nervous. He was a down-to-earth man, but at this moment he was assailed with an irrational dread: a conviction that something horrible was lingering in the air.

"Pull yourself together, man," he muttered, as he took more tentative steps towards the cottage.

"Aaeerr!" The sound was unearthly. The moan of an animal in pain?

Colin cleared his throat.

"Is there somebody there?" he said as firmly as he could. He shone the torch to the right of the door and picked up the outline of a shoe.

"Who are you?" he demanded more belligerently. "What are you doing here?"

The noises were more intelligible the second time.

"Haerr. Help!"

Against his better judgment, Colin stepped off the path and moved forward again, pointing the torch steadily at the ground. Now he could make out the form of a man lying at the edge of the grass. The man had hunched himself into the recovery position, but now he rolled over on to his back, slowly and awkwardly, as if in pain. Colin shone the torch full in his face. Slowly the man pressed the back of his hand across his eyes, as if even that slight movement caused anguish.

"Push the light away!"

Colin did as he was asked, but he didn't turn off the torch. In normal circumstances, he would have crouched down to ask the man how badly he was hurt, but his instinct told him not to compromise his own safety. He couldn't shake off his conviction that something evil was lurking nearby. Perhaps this man was out to trick him and would grab him if he got too close.

"Who are you?" he asked again. He'd shone the torch on the man's shoes. They were town shoes, rathy spivvy, he thought, but despite the mud caking the soles and most of the uppers he could see they were expensive.

The man didn't reply. He remained supine on the ground, still shielding his eyes.

"Look, I want to help you. Can you sit up?" said Colin.

The man removed his hand from his face and clawed at the ground with both hands. After a lot of scrabbling, he managed to haul himself into a sitting position and, shuffling backwards, leant his back against the boundary wall of the small garden. Colin played the torch gently over him. His lip was badly swollen and he had a head wound which was still bleeding. He touched it with his index finger, which was now covered in mud.

"I wouldn't do that if I was you," said Colin. "Tetanus and all that."

The man attempted a smile. He caught his swollen lip against his teeth and grimaced.

"This is all a bit . . . . too . . . Agatha Christie," he said, issuing the words haltingly and with obvious suffering. The sentence struck a chord in Colin's recent memory.

"You're the lecturer guy, aren't you?" he said. "Amelia Baker's BF!"

CHAPTER 36

G ORDON WAS HOBBLING along the corridor. Percy and Patti stood on either side to support him until they reached the kitchen. Gordon half-fell on to a stool while Percy opened and shut cupboard doors, looking for more torches.

"What are you doing now? Isobel said the spare torches are in the cupboard under the sink," said Gordon irritably.

"Sorry, I'm sure," said Percy. His renowned good humour was wearing thin.

"Percy's only trying to help," said Patti. "We both are."

"Here they are," said Percy, his geniality returning. "Two more torches like the one we found in the cottage. And a storm lantern, too – one that runs on a battery, by the look of it." He pressed a switch. The kitchen burst into light. "How about that? It's better than Skegness illuminations! Why don't you take that down into the cellar with you?"

"This torch I've got is fine," Gordon cut in before he'd finished speaking. "I always take a torch when I go down there. It's easier to hold."

"But surely there are electric lights there usually?"

"Only in parts of it," said Gordon defensively. "The torch is fine."

"Gordon has a torch," said Patti. "You take these two and the lantern into the ballroom. Let the others get the benefit of them."

"Exactly," said Gordon, as if he'd had the same thought

already. He heaved himself off the stool and stood up shakily.

"Are you sure you're fit for this?" said Percy. "I don't understand why you're so determined to put yourself through it when I can so easily help."

"Enough! It's my cellar," said Gordon, "and my house. Can we get on with it now?"

"Thanks, Percy," said Patti, briefly touching his arm as he passed her. He disappeared into the corridor. Patti watched the shadows on the corridor walls dance briefly before he was gone. She regretted the loss of the lantern: she knew the cellar would be pitch black. Patti prided herself on her ability to maintain a level head, but she was apprehensive about the string of unfortunate events that were bedevilling the first evening of the weekend. What was it that Tim used to say all those aeons ago when she'd been his girlfriend? "I don't believe in coincidences." Unfortunate coincidences were much more to be suspected than lucky ones.

"Take your time," she said to Gordon.

He rose to his feet as smartly as he could.

"I'm ready."

"You keep the torch for now, while I support you. You'll have to leave it with me when we get to the cellar."

"I won't be able to do that, will I? I'll need it to look at the fuse box. You won't mind waiting in the dark for a few minutes, will you?"

Too late, Patti realised she hadn't been thinking clearly. She should have asked Percy to give her one of the spare torches; she'd been too focused on the altercation about the storm lantern to realise that she and Gordon needed a torch each.

"I can't say I'm mad about the idea. I don't like damp, enclosed places without windows."

"Go on! In your job, you must see them all the time."

"Sometimes. But I'm not alone then and we use very powerful lights."

"I'll be as quick as I can; and you won't be alone: I'll be there." Gordon had begun to recover some of his customary chutzpah.

"I've never thought of you as a knight in shining armour," said Patti. Gordon chuckled. "Let's get on with it, then."

She took hold of his arm above the elbow, but he still stumbled when he tried to walk.

"Put your arm round my neck," she said. She placed both her own arms around his waist, almost staggering under his weight. Gordon was not tall, but he was very sturdy. Now that Percy was no longer there to share the burden, she realised how heavy he was.

They meandered the length of the corridor, veering from one side to the other until they approached the entrance to the cellar, which was almost opposite Colin and Margarett Franklin's room. As they drew nearer, Patti thought she heard the quiet click of a door being closed very carefully.

"What was that?" she said.

"What was what?"

"I thought I heard a door closing, in a controlled sort of way."

"Well, I didn't hear anything. It's unlikely, isn't it? We know where both the Franklins are and it's doubtful anyone else would be coming down here, because they wouldn't be able to see a fucking thing, let alone 'control' closing doors. Here, hold this torch for me while I find the key."

Patti took the torch while Gordon fumbled in several of his pockets, eventually fishing out a large bunch of keys.

"Shine it on the keyhole, will you?"

Patti played the light from the torch over the lower half of the door. The handle was set very low, the keyhole immediately beneath it and covered with a metal plate.

"It's awkward," said Patti. "I think I'd better kneel down and slide back the plate so you can get the key in easily. Or you could give me the key: I'll put it in the lock and turn it. I'll give the bunch of keys back to you when the door's open."

Gordon was clearly not keen on this idea, but his attempt to go down on one knee himself ended in failure.

"Christ!" he said, straightening up again and leaning heavily on Patti's back as he did so. "Here, you do it, then." He thrust the bunch of keys at her. She grasped them by the one he was holding and stuck it in the lock. It turned easily.

CHAPTER 37

"**A**MELIA BAKER'S *what?*" repeated Victor le Grange testily. Colin had managed to haul him to his feet and deposit him on the shallow wall that fronted the cottage, where he sat with his shoulders hunched, clinging to the gatepost. Although he was still shaken, he was making a rapid recovery. Colin guessed that he'd mentally magnified his injuries through fear.

"BF. Boy Friend," said Colin succinctly.

"I'm certainly not that . . . " le Grange spluttered.

"Come off it, mate. Even my wife spotted it – and she's one of nature's innocents. There's no need to pretend to us, anyway: we've got other things to think about."

"Yes. What exactly is going on in this place? They're supposed to be holding a crime weekend, aren't they? It's got a bit too realistic for my liking."

"It hadn't occurred to me that this could all be part of the fun," said Colin. He stopped to consider for a moment. "Nah," he said. "Nice idea, but the power-cut isn't helping things along and Gordon really has been hurt; so have you, by the look of you. Even Gordon wouldn't think of staging real accidents to liven up his event. Far too risky."

"You mean Gordon Bemrose? What's the matter with him? No-one could find him when I was having a drink with you earlier."

"He turned up eventually. Someone had jumped him – or

at least, we think they had; he won't admit it. Is that what happened to you?"

"I don't remember. I thought I heard something and then I tripped. I must have been out cold for a while and then you showed up." Le Grange rubbed the back of his head. "My head's sore, so it looks as if someone did 'jump me', as you put it. What are you doing out here, anyway, especially as you say there's been a power-cut?"

"I'm looking for two other geezers who came outside for a few minutes and haven't come back to the house. You haven't seen anyone, have you?"

"As you point out, it's pitch black – the lights went out just before I came outside. I haven't seen anyone except you – and you've got a torch."

"But you got a sense of someone else out here?"

"I wouldn't say that. I literally didn't know what hit me – still don't. I think it's unlikely I managed to knock myself over the back of the head, though."

"So do I," said Colin grimly. "If you're up to it, I'm going to take you across to the house now. You'll be safer with the others."

"I shouldn't think I'll be very welcome . . . "

"Don't worry about that. Their evening's so fucked up they aren't going to worry about a gate-crasher. There's a load of fake actors over there, too. You should blend in."

"Well, really, I . . . " Le Grange was bristling again. Colin's patience was wearing thin.

"If I was you, mate, I'd forget the airs and graces. Just think yourself lucky I found you – it could have been a lot worse. Let's get you inside double-quick so I can come back out here to look for the other two blokes." He pulled le Grange off the wall. "Put your arm round my shoulder. That's right. Ready to go now? I'll have to hold the phone with my other hand, so that's all the support I can give you."

Le Grange winced and was wheezing a little, but still Colin set a briskish pace. He was very worried about Renwick and Sykes now. Where could they have gone, if not to one of the cottages or the area around them? The car park and a smallish garden were on the other side of the house: he would try there next. The only place left to search for them after that was the jetty; but it was a steep drop down to the river and the path would be treacherous in the dark.

Colin shuddered. He wouldn't call himself an imaginative man, but he knew the river already held bitter secrets. Others had plunged into its dark and dangerous depths; perhaps Renwick and Sykes had joined them.

He became aware that Victor le Grange was speaking again.

"What did you say? Sorry, I wasn't listening."

"I said, 'Did he fall or was he pushed?'" Le Grange repeated the words with some emphasis.

"What are you talking about?" said Colin, at once frightened and annoyed.

"Gordon. You said Gordon had had an accident. I asked you whether you think he fell or was pushed."

"Oh," said Colin, the tension easing a little. "Good question. I don't know. Like I said, he claims there was no-one else involved, but it seems unlikely."

"Yes. Gives the impression of being quite a dodgy character, doesn't he?"

You can say that again, Colin thought. Aloud he said, "Well, no-one's perfect, are they? I guess we've all got something to hide, yourself included." The words hung meaningfully in the air. He and le Grange trudged the final few steps to the house in silence.

They entered the house via the passageway that led past Colin and Margarett's room, the door to the cellar and the kitchen. Le Grange shook Colin off before they entered the ballroom and hobbled in unaided. Everyone in the room had crowded round an electric storm lantern, their faces ghostly in the white light.

Amelia Baker half stood when she saw le Grange. She seemed embarrassed – almost horrified – to see him.

"Victor . . . Dr le Grange . . . " she began. He flapped her away with his hand and sank down into a chair.

Margarett came running to Colin as soon as she spotted him.

"Thank God you're back," she said. "You've been gone for ages! I've been really worried about you."

Colin looked at his watch.

"I don't think I have been gone 'for ages'," he said. "Barely a quarter of an hour, in fact. I need to get back out there: I still haven't found Renwick and Sykes."

"Let someone else go this time."

Colin looked round the circle of faces, most of which were fixed on Victor le Grange, keen to hear his story.

Immediately dismissing the idea of sending any of the women outside into the darkness, he said, "Who would you suggest? There isn't another proper man here unless you count Percy; and someone has to stop you lot from getting hysterical."

Margarett let go of his arm. He put his hand on hers.

"Sorry, love," he said more gently. "This whole thing's

getting to me, too. I don't want to go out there again but I'm going to have to. It's nearly an hour since Sykes and Renwick went out. They may be trapped and if it's somewhere exposed they won't survive, not on a night like this."

"Promise me you'll be careful."

"Of course."

"Why is he still here?" she added, tipping her head towards le Grange, a flicker of amusement crossing her face despite herself.

"He can explain that," said Colin. "I bet he comes up with a good story." He bent to kiss her. "I'll see you later. If I haven't found them in the next half-hour, we'll call the police."

She nodded, though her eyes had widened with fear.

"Don't go near the river, Colin. You won't, will you?"

"No," he said, mentally chiding himself for the lie. The riverbank was the next place he had decided to search.

CHAPTER 38

" . . . AND then I realised I had Amelia's phone in my pocket, from when she'd lent it to me to call my wife while we were driving, and I knew she'd need it. So I thought I'd give it back to her before I left," Victor le Grange was saying.

He wasn't giving as good an account of himself as Colin had predicted. Dora Westerman, for one, wasn't convinced.

"Why didn't you just leave it in the cottage? Amelia would have found it."

"I . . . I thought about that, but then the lights went out. I didn't know how long the power-cut was going to last. I guess I wasn't thinking straight."

"You may have been thinking 'straighter' than you'd have had us believe until now," said Anton. sarcastically. "How long are we going to carry on huddling here? If Gordon hasn't fixed the lights in the next ten minutes, I vote we call out the emergency services."

"Which ones?" Percy asked. "Police, Fire or Ambulance? Which of them do you think would take responsibility for a power-cut?"

"Well, an electrician, then," said Anton lamely.

"We do have call-out insurance for electricity. I think the number to ring's on the notice-board in the kitchen," said Isobel Lawrence.

"Right, I'll go and find it and call them on my mobile."

"You'll be lucky," said Sonia Renwick. "I've been trying to

call Richard for the last half hour. I can't get a signal."

"Perhaps it's just your phone that's died," said Percy. "I'll try mine. No, I can't get a signal, either: it must be something to do with the fog."

"Mine in't working, either," said Avril. "This could get exciting: we might 'ave to stay the night!" She sidled up to Anton. "I could help you to keep warm."

Percy laughed as Anton backed away, furious.

"No-one's going to have to stay the night except those of us who already have rooms here," he said. "Someone will miss you and turn up for you, even if you can't tell them you need fetching."

"Who's that, then?" said Avril. "We come in a taxi – a people carrier – and I told me mam I'd be spending the night with *her*." She gave the other girl a push.

"Yeah, and I said I'd be spending it with Avril," said the other girl.

"Why'd you do that?"

Avril shrugged. "Just keepin' our options open."

"What about you gents?" asked Percy, nodding across at the gaggle of old men who had gathered together to one side of the storm lantern. "Won't your missuses wonder where you are?"

"We're all widowers," said Charlie. "That's how we met – well, not Bert, like, he's a confirmed bachelor, you might say. But we all met at a do for single retired blokes. Some of us thought it would be a laugh to have a go at amateur theatricals. Bert knew Monty and said he was setting up an acting club. He's a widower, too, but younger than us. He agreed to give us a go."

"Yeah, and me and Vicky joined as part of our community

service. Judge said it would give us a 'social conscious'," said Avril.

"Oh my God," Anton groaned.

"Oh," said Percy, momentarily lost for words. "That's interesting." It explained why the membership of Sykes's troupe was so . . . unbalanced. "Well," he added, "we're crossing our bridges before we come to them now. We still don't know that Gordon won't be able to fix the fuse. I don't want to crowd him out – let's wait a few more minutes and if nothing happens I'll go down to the cellar to help him, whether he wants me to or not."

"What are we supposed to do meantime?" Lizzie asked. "Play games?"

"That's not a bad idea, if we can think of something suitable. How about consequences? We can play it in the dark and it doesn't need any props. But perhaps you can think of something that raises the bar a little higher than that."

"Did someone mention the bar?" enquired Ava, struggling out of a fitful doze. "I'd like a gin and tonic, please."

CHAPTER 39

GORDON HAD TAKEN the torch and limped off into the further reaches of the cellar. Patti watched the small tunnel of light thrown by the torch disappear with him. She sat down on the bottom cellar step and waited, trying to think of anything but the dark and the rodents that were bound to inhabit this dungeon.

The whole crime weekend episode had been such a farce that participating in it might even have helped her: she'd long been aware that she was floundering, unhappy and no longer in control of her life. The pressure Gordon had put on her by saying he would expose her mother for the debts she had run up - effectively, he was blackmailing Patti and she was only too aware that as an employee of the police force she should have reported him - was the last and nastiest in a series of unpleasant events that had been snagging her life ever since she had broken up with Tim. She was deeply ashamed that she'd allowed the misery she'd felt then and the unhappiness that still gutted her to cloud her sense of purpose and, at times, even her judgement. She had to be strict with herself when remembering the facts of how they'd broken up: most people who knew they'd been an item assumed it was because Tim had met Katrin and it was tempting not to disabuse them, to allow them to keep on thinking that Patti was the wronged party. In truth, they had been drifting apart for some time when both had agreed to a three months' trial separation, Patti perhaps with less conviction than Tim himself. She'd hoped the spark between them could be re-kindled; Tim's decision that it couldn't, brutally analytical, perhaps, but also scrupulously fair – he'd kept his promise to meet to discuss when the three months were over – had left Patti distraught but in no doubt that Tim had not abandoned her for someone else. That had been in the spring, and she knew he hadn't met Katrin until towards the end of the same year.

She ought to request a transfer, make more effort to meet new people, especially outside work. Her mother's fragile state was a tie, but distance-wise Patti could certainly cope with working for the North Lincs or Norfolk police forces. Or she could look for another kind of job – lecturing, perhaps. She ought to explore the options, see what kinds of change she could make to her career. She'd have a more balanced private life if she could avoid working such unsocial hours; she'd be a more relaxed person if she didn't have to spend her days examining crime scenes and cadavers.

The lights flickered on briefly – long enough for her to be able to see something pale and greasy scurrying away into the darkness before the cellar was plunged into gloom once again. Patti drew up her legs and bumped herself up a couple of steps.

"Gordon!" she called out. "Gordon! Can you hear me? You almost fixed it then!" She stood and went back down the steps to the floor. She gazed into the blackness.

"Gordon?"

"What the fuck?" his voice came back, gruff and urgent. "I . . . " Whatever Gordon had been going to say was choked off abruptly. Then came a great crashing noise, the single large boom of something slamming to the ground. Patti called out to him, trying to keep her voiced steady.

"Gordon! Whatever you say, I'm coming in to find you. Can you try to point the torch towards the entrance?"

There was no reply. Spreading her arms wide, she touched the walls on either side of the stairs to get her bearings and crouched to sweep the ground in front of her with her hands. To her left she caught her fingers on something cold and cylindrical, probably a paint tin. There appeared to be no obstacles immediately in front of her. She considered moving forward on her hands and knees, but, shuddering, remembered the rat: as long as she didn't trip, walking upright would be safer. She moved along slowly, taking small steps like a blind person, kicking forwards with her feet, her arms outstretched.

She'd taken several shaky paces when she saw a tiny glow of light. She headed towards it, moving more quickly but still cautiously, her arms pointing forwards like divining rods, her feet kicking front and sideways like a horse trying to evade obstacles on its stable floor.

She had almost reached the place where the light was coming from. She could see the torch on the floor, pointing towards her, its light dimmer than she'd remembered. She prayed fervently that the battery wasn't dying. Ahead of her she could dimly perceive what at first seemed to be a bundle of clothes lying across some oil drums. She moved closer to the bundle until she could make out, not a formless collection of rags, but the outline of a man stretched full-length along the barrels, his eyes staring up at her. His expression was so wracked with fear and pain that it took her some moments to recognise him. Gordon was lying there, unmoving – so still that she was convinced that either he had had a seizure or was dead.

Patti put her hand to where she should find a pulse in Gordon's neck. It was beating quite strongly, but to her horror her fingers came away sticky with blood. She peeled back the collar of his shirt and saw an ugly gash gaping there. It didn't look like an injury that had been caused by falling: it was almost certainly a knife wound.

Had Gordon been attacked? She became instantly aware of how vulnerable she herself was. She had just come from the only entrance to the cellar: if Gordon had been assaulted, his attacker must still be there in the cellar with them. Without a source of light, they'd be sitting ducks. She had to save the torch.

It was there at her feet, rolling slightly because she'd just kicked it. Panicking, she crouched to retrieve it, scrabbling at the filthy floor. It rolled away from her, but she leapt forward and grabbed it. As she did so, Gordon sat up.

"What the fuck?" he said again, rubbing his head and feeling gingerly at his collar. "Fuck!" he repeated.

"Be careful how you touch your neck," Patti said. "You've got quite a nasty cut there! You don't want to get an infection in it."

"How'd I manage to fall?" asked Gordon, the false guile-lessness of his tone putting Patti on lie alert immediately. "Clumsy bugger, aren't I?"

"More than clumsy," Patti replied. "You must be a genius at self-harm. You couldn't have got that cut just from falling. Someone attacked you. They must still be down here with us right now." She picked up the torch and shone it round the walls.

"Don't do that!" said Gordon urgently. "You're making me dizzy," he added lamely. "Nonsense: there isn't anyone down here with us. You're letting your imagination run away you!"

"What's that over there?" Patti was shining the torch at a black bin liner that had been slung in the far corner of the cellar. Whatever it contained was both angular and bulky. She noticed the unpleasant smell that pervaded the cellar was stronger here than it had been on the staircase.

"It's nothing," said Gordon. "Just some old junk. This cellar's full of rubbish – we must get it cleared out. Now, give me that torch – I almost fixed the fuse then. I just need one more go at it. Then let's get out of here."

"You need medical attention . . . "

"Now, don't start that again," said Gordon. "Give me the torch."

Patti handed over the torch. She stood behind him while he crouched near to the floor. Her eyes were accustoming themselves to the dimness now. She could make out the black bulk of the fuse box showing up in relief against the wall.

"Kneel down beside me," Gordon said peremptorily.

She did as he asked, squirming as the gritty dirt caked her knees.

"Now take the torch and shine it exactly here." He took her hand and guided it to the place he meant. She watched as he fiddled with the fuse box. Suddenly the lights came on again. This time, they didn't flicker out.

"Job's a good 'un," said Gordon. "Now, let's go. We can still save the evening."

Patti stood up and brushed the dirt from her knees. She cast a long backward look at the bin liner; she was convinced it contained something unpleasant and, judging from Gordon's evasiveness about it, probably illegal.

"Don't worry about that, Patti," he said now, putting his hand in the small of her back and giving her a push. "Let's get back upstairs. If you want to come back some time and help me clean out the cellar, you'll be very welcome. Now, move it!"

His abruptness annoyed her – she was used to Gordon's uncouthness, but he was rarely downright hostile. As she was as anxious as he was to leave the cellar, she made no protest. She led the way back to the staircase, Gordon following close behind her. She'd almost forgotten he'd been injured again until they reached the foot of the steps and he stumbled. She grabbed his upper arm and held on to it.

"Take it easy," she said. "There isn't room for us to walk up the steps beside each other, so I'm going to let you go first. I'll hold you round the waist so you don't fall. All right?"

"Yeah," said Gordon grudgingly.

He teetered on the final step as Patti hung on to him. She gave a final glance over her shoulder at the cellar. It was illuminated only by a single low-wattage light-bulb – the apparent brightness earlier had been deceptive, just a contrast to the pitch black that had preceded it. The room was nowhere near as untidy as Gordon had claimed. It had been fitted with a series of steel shelves, fastened together like the bookcases in a library. Some held recognisable tools and other pieces of equipment, but most were stacked with bulky packages shrouded in plastic or covered with tarpaulins. At the far end of the cellar, close by the bin bag on the floor, there was a shallow alcove. She thought she could see the outline of a figure standing in the alcove, casting its shadow on to the steel shelving beyond it.

"There *is* someone there!" she exclaimed.

"Don't talk wet," said Gordon. "Your imagination will get you into trouble one of these fine days. Now, are you going to help me get up them stairs, or not?"

CHAPTER 40

COLIN HALF SCRAMBLED, half fell down the river bank towards the jetty. His shoes were so clogged with mud that his feet were like those of birds he'd seen on TV that'd been trapped in resinous effluent and had to be chipped free.

The fog was denser on this side of the house. He couldn't see the jetty or the river; he was relying on memory to tell him where they were. He recalled that Dora Westerman had been sitting exactly opposite the jetty at the drinks party, staring out of the window, before Isobel Lawrence closed the curtains. He judged where to start his clamber down the bank from what he'd identified as the same window, but as the decline grew steeper he wasn't so certain about it. Surely the ground must have been flattened out more than this to build the jetty?

Over the tops of his trainers in mud, he stopped suddenly, waving his arms urgently to stop himself falling down in the mire, as his ears picked up a noise. He listened intently. Muffled though it was by the fog and issuing from an indeterminate distance, he heard it again: it was not the night playing tricks on him. He was listening to the gentle phut-phut of an outboard motor. Was it coming towards him or moving further away?

Turning his head towards the direction the noise was coming from, he caught a glimpse of the jetty through the fog, its white paint shimmering. It was well below him and about three metres to his right. There was a narrow path leading from it up to the house. He waded through the mud to the path – which was also muddy, but more stable than the ground surrounding it – and tried to kick the worst of the muck from his shoes. He turned on his torch, but the fog merely sent the light bouncing back into his face.

He wondered who had been in the boat. Surely not Renwick and Sykes? It was hard to believe they would have abandoned the rest of the group to go off on some impetuous jaunt. Colin couldn't imagine they could be complicit in anything – Renwick clearly affected superiority to everyone else staying at Holyrood and as a ham actor Sykes was likely to be even more the butt of his contempt than the others. Whoever it was had gone, anyway: he could no longer detect the sound of the outboard motor. It seemed pointless to carry on down to the jetty: he'd probably have more luck searching the cottages, if Isobel Lawrence would allow him to borrow the duplicate keys.

He tried playing the torch over the area of the jetty one more time and was rewarded by being able to penetrate a gap in the swirling fog. The jetty itself was empty, but as he was turning away he saw something move to the left of it. He took a few steps forward. The movement was more frenzied now: it took him a while to work out what he was watching, until he realised that it was two large boots drumming up and down, just short of the jetty itself. He hurried down the path, sliding as he went, until he was level with the boots and could see they belonged to Montagu Sykes, who, still resplendent in his 1940s NYPD uniform (now considerably muddied) had been roped back-to-back with Richard Renwick. Both men had duct tape over their mouths.

Pitching himself into the mud again, Colin clambered across to them and ripped the tape from their faces, wiping his fingers on his trousers with some distaste after he'd performed the service for Sykes, who'd chewed half way through the gag, coating it unpleasantly with saliva.

"Untie us, will you?" Sykes spluttered, spitting out a piece of plastic. Richard Renwick remained mute. Colin bent to examine the rope. It was wound round them quite loosely, but their hands were fastened behind their backs with plastic ties.

"I'm going to untie the rope first," he said, "then I'll have to cut the ties on your hands. I have a penknife. I'll warn you before I do it." He could see the plastic digging into Sykes's pudgy flesh. They'd need to keep very still while he released them. Still Richard Renwick didn't speak.

"You all right?" asked Colin, moving round so that he could look at Renwick's face.

"I'm just . . . bloody . . . cold," he said, almost unable to get out the words. "Can you be a bit quicker about it?"

Colin took in Renwick's sleek casual clothes and bit back a retort about dressing suitably for the weather. Sykes's NYPD uniform was much warmer. Colin nodded.

"Tell you what, I'll cut through the rope as well. Hold still, both of you. There, that's saved some time. Now for the plastic ties on your hands. You're going to have to hold very still. I'll do you first." He jerked his head towards Richard.

Richard's hands were long and narrow, his fingers slim and tapering. Colin cut through his restraints with relative ease.

"Now stand up and shake your arms and legs about. Get the circulation going." Richard did as he was told, stumbling slightly as he executed a weird sort of dance. Montagu Sykes let out a chuckle.

"Hold still, damn you!" said Colin through gritted teeth.

"Ow!" yelped Sykes.

"Sorry, mate I think I've just nicked you a bit. I did tell you not to move. There you go, anyway."

Sykes shook his arm vigorously before standing up shakily. He sucked at the heel of his hand.

"Now, let's get both of you inside," said Colin. "Then you can tell us what happened. The path's just there. Can you see it?" He shone his torch at the ground. Sykes and Renwick crossed to the path and started climbing the slope to the house. They had almost reached the house itself when lights appeared in several windows.

"That's a bonus!" said Colin. "They've got the electricity working!" He looked at his watch. "It's not nine o'clock yet. There's still some evening left." Although he knew that the two men must have been assaulted as well as Victor le Grange, now that he'd found them his forebodings had all but vanished; in fact, he felt elated at the success of his efforts, as if he'd cheated something very evil. He had to remind himself that it was a different kind of evil he'd come here to address.

"Well, I hope no one's expecting me to join in any more fun and games," said Richard Renwick grimly. "First I'm going to call the police. Then I need a hot bath. After that, if I feel up to it, I'm going to suggest to Sonia that we drive home."

Montagu Sykes was still sucking his injured hand.

"I'm still up for the performance, if everyone agrees. In for a penny, in for a pound."

He had just stepped under an outside light. It cast a

greenish hue over his features, but Colin could see his expression quite clearly.

"I suppose there's that about it," he said, amused. "Presumably you won't get paid if you don't perform? And the same will go for the rest of your lot, too!"

Richard Renwick expelled a huge sigh of exasperation and quickened his pace. He disappeared round the side of the house, his arms crossed, hugging his biceps with his hands to get warm.

CHAPTER 41

Richard Renwick stumbled into the ball-room, the sudden warmth making him feel faint and nauseous. Montagu Sykes followed him, carrying aloft his peaked cap emblazoned with the letters NYPD. Colin arrived shortly afterwards. He'd paused to lock both the kitchen door and the door to the extension. If someone was still out there, it would stop them creeping up on the crime weekend gathering unannounced.

"Evening, all," said Sykes. The cold had had an even more curious effect on him than on Renwick: he'd suddenly become unpleasantly elated.

"Spare us the feeble jokes," said Richard Renwick through gritted teeth. Hanging on to the back of a chair, he surveyed the scene in front of him. If Sykes had hoped to burst upon the community and cause a stir, he'd been sadly disappointed. The others were all gathered in a circle around someone seated in a chair. Peering dizzily through the palisade of human forms, he saw that the seated man was Gordon Bemrose. Patti Gardner was standing beside him; Isobel Lawrence was kneeling on the floor, dabbing at his neck with a powerful astringent. Richard could smell it from where he was standing; it did nothing to assuage his nausea.

Patti turned when she heard Montagu Sykes's voice and caught Richard's eye.

"What in God's name has been going on here now?" he

demanded. Beyond the knot of people he'd just noticed Victor le Grange slumped on the floor by a radiator, up to his armpits in a sleeping bag. The silly girl who was 'studying' crime fiction was bending over him.

"Richard!" said Sonia, appearing from the far side of the main group and hurrying to his side. "Thank goodness you're back – I've been worried about you!"

"Really?" said Renwick sardonically. If Sonia was trying to create some intimacy between them, she couldn't have chosen a worse time. His anger was not directed at her in particular: he simply felt furious with everyone. If he hadn't been so alarmingly queasy he would have given her a good verbal lashing.

"Yes, really," she replied coldly, immediately catching and matching his tone. She took a step away from him. He backed down immediately.

"Sorry," he said. "I'm not feeling too good. I didn't mean to take it out on you. What's the matter with him?" he gestured at Gordon Bemrose.

"He says he fell again when he was down in the cellar," Sonia answered in a friendlier voice. "He's got a nasty wound on his neck."

"Was that before or after he fixed the lights?"

"I don't know. Does it make any difference? What's more interesting is that the forensics woman clearly doesn't believe him. She thinks someone attacked him. Where have you been?"

"Sykes and I were walking towards the jetty – we heard a noise coming from there. Sykes missed his footing and I fell over him. It may be that something was left there for him to trip over. Whatever . . . I don't know. What I do know is that there was someone out there who didn't want us to see what they were doing. Before we could get back on our feet, our hands had been bound behind our backs and we were roped together. We'd been there quite some time when Colin Franklin found us. I'm absolutely bloody frozen."

Sonia put out her hand and felt his cheek. To her it seemed feverishly warm, as if he was going down with flu. He caught her hand in his own and held it for a couple of seconds.

"Why didn't you shout for help?" she said, gently disengaging it.

"Whoever it was gagged us, too. Look, Sonia, I don't want to spoil the weekend, but don't you think it's time we admitted this isn't going to work?"

"What do you mean?" she asked, her face suddenly white. Richard Renwick smiled.

"Don't read too much into that. I just mean this bloody weekend. I don't know what this lot are up to – they must be crooks or charlatans or both – but I don't want anything more to do with it. When I first came back in here, I was intending to call the police, but I'm not sure I can face it now. There'll be a huge fuss and we'll have to give statements and there'll be no chance of getting away. Why don't you let me have a quick shower and just take you home?"

"Home?" Sonia repeated. "But we planned to . . . "

"I know," said Richard, "and your mother paid for it, too. And on the face of it, it was a good idea, despite my lukewarm response. But you can't want to stay here for almost another forty-eight hours. I'm not against continuing with our weekend away, but I don't want to do it here. Let's go home for now and I'll find a nice hotel to take you to first thing tomorrow. We're unlikely to be able to get in anywhere tonight."

Sonia glanced across at Gordon, who was listening. He bestowed on her his best smile. Although she'd still had no opportunity to talk to him, her dream of the beauty salon franchise was instantly rekindled.

"I don't know . . . " she said. "I don't want to go home again so soon. Mother will certainly think we've fallen out. Why don't you go for your shower now and see how you feel afterwards?"

Richard shivered involuntarily.

"Look, Sonia, Sykes and I were assaulted. Whoever it was could very well still be out there. Come to think of it, I'm not wild about the idea of returning to that cottage on my own."

Colin Franklin, who had been pounced on by Margarett as soon as she saw him - she was now clinging to his arm - was still hovering. He'd also been listening to the Renwicks' conversation.

"I think you're right, mate, about going outside again on your own. But don't break up the party - we've been looking forward to it and as there's only eight of us - if you two drop out now I can't see how we can go on. Why don't you take a shower in our room? I've got a spare jumper you can have - and some clean jeans."

Despite her anxiety, Sonia almost laughed aloud at the expressions that crossed Richard's face. It was fortunate that Colin didn't know her husband: she hoped that he couldn't interpret correctly Richard's look of mixed disbelief and utter distaste at the idea of wearing Colin's clothes, closely followed by something like shame at his own ingratitude and a rather ineffectual attempt to seem pleased.

"I don't think I could let you do that . . . " he began falteringly.

Percy came to his rescue.

"It's good of you, Colin, but we all need to get back to normal now. As you say, we don't want to spoil the weekend. I'll come with you to the cottage while you take a shower. Then I suggest we all get on with what we were supposed to be doing after dinner."

Anton sighed audibly. Percy glared at him.

"What about you?" Percy turned to Montagu Sykes. "Do you need a shower, as well?"

Sykes glanced down at the mud on his NYPD uniform. It was caked on in places, but already drying. He peeled a large chunk of dirt from his trousers and flicked it on the floor.

"I think I'm ok. I just need a good brush down. We don't have a spare uniform, so I'm going to have to keep this on anyway. And I didn't get cold like Richard did. But my hand's stinging – Colin caught it with his penknife when he was cutting us free."

"Good. You stay here, then. We'll be as quick as we can. I'm sure Gordon can entertain everyone with a drink while they're waiting for us, can't you, dear uncle?" he added, raising his voice with the final sentence. And, in an aside, he added to Sykes, "if you've still got that hip flask on you, give it to me and I'll put some brandy in it. You can use it as antiseptic!" He winked. Sykes handed over the flask surreptitiously.

"I'm not *your* uncle," said Gordon sulkily. He'd clearly been enjoying all the attention he'd been getting, but he hadn't banked on taking another hit on his pocket.

"It's a good idea, though . . . uncle," added Patti mischievously.

"Touché!" Anton giggled. It was the first thing anyone had said to make him smile all evening.

"What have we got, Isobel?"

"Just about everything . . ."

"Well, let's stick to beer and wine, shall we?" said Gordon quickly. "We don't want everyone to get plastered."

CHAPTER 42

JULIET WAS IN bed. She desperately wanted to call the vet to see how Sally was, but she knew she should not disturb him again. He'd promised to let her know if the Saluki gave cause for concern and pestering him would be counter-productive. She wouldn't call Jake again because he was on duty; besides, she'd be seeing him the next day and she didn't want to pre-empt whatever it was he was going to tell her.

She dozed uneasily for a while. She wasn't in a deep sleep but not fully awake, either. Once again, her thoughts flooded with grotesque images of damaged animals. Suddenly, she was wide awake again. She turned on the light and sat up in bed, wiping a sheen of hot sweat from her forehead and glancing at her alarm clock. It was only a little after ten: she couldn't have been sleeping for more than a few minutes.

She got out of bed to search for a book, but couldn't find one she wanted to read. Wandering into the kitchen, her eyes fell on her laptop. It was one of her strictest rules that she never turned it on this late in the evening, but, as it was obvious she wouldn't be able to sleep, she decided to do some research into hare coursing – particularly the methods other police forces used to catch the perpetrators.

Juliet braced herself for the horrific images she knew she would find. She discovered there were more instances of hare coursing in Northern Ireland than anywhere else in the UK, but in mainland Britain East Anglia was hardest hit. The best clue that coursing was taking place was when clusters of large vehicles, unfamiliar to the neighbourhood, were spotted in stubble fields – so perhaps the woman who lived in Campain's Lane had been aware of this. Police forces often used helicopters to apprehend the perpetrators, but most forces only had one helicopter at their disposal and these were needed for other activities: observing motorway congestion, assisting with police chases and even crowd control. She was surprised to read of a growing trend for hare coursers to operate at night to evade detection. She'd heard of 'lamping', but thought it was mainly about after-dark rabbit-, fox- and badger-hunting. Apparently, lampers also chased hares and deer – as well as hoping to evade detection, they got more of a kick out of it because it required more 'skill'. Helicopters were less use at night: they disturbed local residents and powerful lights were needed to pick out suspects on the ground. Some forces used drones – she must find out more about how that worked. She made some notes. Suddenly, she felt very tired again. Perhaps she'd be able to sleep now.

CHAPTER 43

A GAINST ALL ODDS, everyone had settled down, some more willingly than others. Reluctantly, the players abandoned their drinks as Montagu Sykes herded them backstage to change into their costumes, while the guests, most of whom, except Colin Franklin, were drinking wine, were permitted to recharge their glasses before Isobel Lawrence spirited the unopened bottles away.

Glancing back at Amelia Baker, who was now seated immediately behind her, Sonia Renwick noted that she was surreptitiously holding Victor le Grange's hand. "Silly little fool," she thought to herself. "He'll probably be coming here with another girl next time."

Margarett and Colin Franklin had resumed their former seats at the end of the front row, but – deliberately or not – Margarett's chair had been pushed a little distance from her husband's. Appraising them with some shrewdness, Sonia decided they must have an ulterior motive for signing up to the weekend; two people less likely to want to sit through a crime extravaganza would be difficult to imagine. She smiled at the thought: she and Richard were hardly crime buffs, either. Suddenly she was conscious he was staring at her, and frowning. It had been with some difficulty that she'd managed to persuade him to drop his plan of precipitate departure from Holyrood.

"What are you thinking about?" he demanded. "You might

like to share the joke. I don't see that there's much amusing about our present situation."

"I was just thinking how strange . . . "

There was a clattering noise to her left, as Ava Dack's chair tilted forwards and Ava herself fell gracelessly to the floor. Richard sprang to his feet to help her. With his aid, Ava hauled herself to her feet and stood swaying unsteadily on her high heels.

"Are you all right?" he asked solicitously.

Ava gave him a shove with her elbow.

"'Course I'm all right!" she snapped belligerently. "It's these cheap old rickety chairs. It's impossible to get comfy on them." Out of the corner of his eye, Richard noticed a wine-glass rolling on the floor. There was no sign that its contents had been spilt: they must have been consumed already.

Lizzie Fox stood up and restored the chair to its place beside her own.

"Sit down, Ava, and stop making such a fuss," she commanded. Ava, surprised, did as she was told. A moue of distaste, fleeting but intense, passed over Dora Westerman's face as she pulled her skirt well down over her knees.

"Can we have some hush now?" Gordon enquired crossly, glaring balefully along the row. "The play is about to start." Patti Gardner, sitting beside him, reflected that it appeared not to occur to him that he owed Ava a duty of care while she was on his premises. Still, it was understandable: she couldn't be bothered to check on Ava, either. The woman had seized every opportunity to make herself as obnoxious as possible.

"It's a skit on *Arsenic and Old Lace*, isn't it?" Victor le Grange asked, tapping the back of Gordon's chair to attract his attention. The gesture irritated Gordon.

"Sort of," he snapped back. "But don't spoil it for everyone. There's a twist to it, in any case."

"Shush," Colin hissed, as the curtain rose.

PART TWO

CHAPTER 44

A LATE, GREY dawn edged itself sluggishly into Saturday morning. Patti, who had been drifting in and out of a restless doze, sat up in bed suddenly and clutched at her alarm clock, stabbing at the button on her bedside lamp at the same time. 7.45 a.m. She had overslept, but not by much. Her sense of relief was quickly eclipsed by the thundering headache that clobbered her, closely followed by a deep feeling of unease about the previous evening. She could summon only a vague recollection of the sequence of events after the play had begun. She supposed she must have had too much to drink: like everyone else, she had consumed alcohol several times during the course of the evening, though at well-spaced intervals and without accepting more than one drink on any single occasion. Still, she wasn't used to it.

She heaved her legs over the edge of the bed and stood up cautiously. Immediately, the hammering in her head grew worse and the furniture in the room lurched dizzily, her line of vision finally coming to rest at a forty-five degree angle that persuaded her she would have to tilt her body in the same direction to attempt to walk.

The hammering surged, a red pain searing up out of her guts and bullying her into flopping down on the floor like a rag doll. A wave of nausea swept over her. She grabbed at a length of cloth lying beside her and vomited into it copiously, the bile scorching her throat as she half-choked on it. When the spasms had ceased, she screwed up the cloth to trap its vile contents, realising too late that she was holding the ruins of the dress she had discarded the night before when she'd tumbled into bed. She was consumed with self-loathing.

Pushing the hideous bundle away from her, she made another attempt to stand, levering herself up from the divan as she held on to the bedside table for support. This time she managed to stay upright. After some seconds' spinning, the room settled down. Gingerly, Patti let go of the table and straightened her back until she was standing free of all supports.

There was a washbasin set into the wall on the other side of the room. Placing one foot slowly in front of the other, Patti set herself the target of reaching it, flinging out one arm to grab at its rim as she completed the task in eight faltering paces. The colour of the basin – a hideous orange/tan relic from the seventies – prompted more vomiting, but now she was retching on nothing. The first bout of sickness must have emptied her stomach completely.

With exaggerated care, as if working in slow motion, she cleaned the basin. Her toothbrush was standing in a tumbler beside the taps. She couldn't locate the toothpaste, so instead groped for the brush and scoured her teeth briskly with clear water, swallowing as much as she could in the process. She rinsed the basin again and filled it with cold water, splashing her face several times before she plunged her whole head into it, submerging it as far as it would go. She held her face under water for as long as she could before springing up again, gasping for air and shivering, her scalp prickling from the chill.

The headache still hovered, but the symptoms had diminished: it was more like a conventional hangover than the raging beast that had first assailed her. No doubt her faculties were still impaired, but at least she felt able to make a decision about what to do next. She could go back to bed and plead illness. There was no compulsion on her to join the boat trip that morning – as Gordon's forensic specialist, she was next needed to supervise the guests as they solved their crime after lunch.

She glanced across at the bed. The sight filled her with distaste: the sheets were rumpled and damp. She herself smelt rankly of stale sweat. And she had no tea-making facilities in the room – she could kill for a cuppa. It would be better to shower and dress and join the others for breakfast - even though the thought of food turned her stomach – and plead that she had work to do while the others went for their ride down the river. Yes, that was what she would do.

She had silently resented the fact that Gordon had given her one of the only two rooms at Holyrood House with no en-suite bathroom – the other was occupied by Isobel Lawrence when she stayed the night – because instinctively she'd known it was an intended slight. Gordon was telling them both they were mere women, though in his eyes Isobel probably carried the double slur of being both a woman and a servant. It was typical of Gordon that he hadn't thought to offer Patti the other upstairs en-suite room when Anton had made his pitch for the cottage.

She bitterly regretted not having asked for it now. Putting on her bathrobe and navigating the way to the bathroom seemed like a major expedition and she was not confident she wouldn't throw up again en route.

She scanned the room for her bathrobe and couldn't see it. Out of impatience and because she couldn't face the journey back across the bedroom, she seized a towel from the neatly-folded heap that had been placed on the chair next to the basin and wrapped it round herself. She staggered to the door, clutching the towel with one hand and steadying herself against the wall with the other.

Opening the bedroom door cautiously, she peered out into a greyish darkness as the black of night was relieved by the first vestiges of the winter dawn creeping in at the upstairs windows; the curtains remained undrawn. The corridor was deserted: there was no sign of anyone stirring and no smell of the morning's breakfast wafting up the stairs. The doors both to Gordon's room, halfway along the dog-leg that led from her corridor, and Isobel Lawrence's bedroom, next to her own, were firmly closed. Feeling grateful for this small mercy, Patti walked as briskly along the corridor as she could and took possession of the bathroom, sliding the bolt carefully so the action made little sound.

Too late, she remembered that she'd left her toilet bag in her bedroom. She couldn't face making the journey back to the bedroom again and risk being seen, perhaps having someone collar the bathroom ahead of her; she'd use whatever toiletries she could find.

The bathroom had been refitted since her last visit to the house. It was now tiled ceiling to floor in tall, narrow biscuit-coloured tiles which, if not of genuine marble, presented a passable imitation. Two deep, round double sinks had been fixed in the wall beneath the window, replacing the single, more modest, cracked and stained 1970s model she remembered. Of the former bathroom, only the old-fashioned, claw-footed bath – older than the house itself, a trophy that Gordon had picked up from a country auction – remained in place. Somewhat incongruously, a shower unit had been fitted to the wall at its tap end, and a solid plastic guard installed to protect the floor – also newly tiled – from spills.

An elongated cupboard with sliding doors nestled below the twin basins. Crouching down, Patti slid open the doors and was rewarded when this action triggered obligingly brilliant illumination from a set of internal lights, exposing clearly the contents of the cupboard. A large, dark-red sponge-bag, flashily embroidered with the initials 'GB' in gold and black, sat uncompromisingly at the front of the shelf. The thought of raiding Gordon's sponge-bag filled her with disgust, but, having pushed it to one side, Patti discovered some unopened bottles of shower gel and shampoo. She delved into the cupboard and pulled out one of each. As she did so, she heard a clatter and felt something bounce off her bare foot. Looking down, she saw that she'd dislodged a knife. It was about six inches long, black-handled, with a fierce narrow blade. It was a strange thing to find in a bathroom cupboard, but Patti didn't give that much thought. She picked it up by the handle and shoved it back again.

She was gratified to find she was able to stand up straight now without courting either vertigo or nausea; even her headache seemed to be ebbing rapidly. She yearned to sink herself into the luxury of a deep bath, but she knew there wasn't enough time. Instead, she climbed into the empty bath and turned on the shower, masochistically enduring its assaults of too-hot, too-cold water until she had mastered its temperature gauge.

CHAPTER 45

MUCH TO HER surprise, Juliet was disentangling herself from a deep sleep. After several false starts, she'd been overcome by exhaustion around midnight and had slipped into a profound, dreamless slumber. As a result, when she awoke, she was better refreshed and feeling more energetic than she'd expected.

Immediately desperate for the day to start, she sprang from her bed and yanked open the curtains. Outside, the street was wet and dark, lit by a few modest streetlamps and, dimly, the prospect of a stuttering dawn. Yesterday's grim fog appeared to have lifted, however. She held her watch up to the window. It was 7.45 a.m. She was astonished that she'd slept so long. In less than an hour she'd be able to see the Saluki again. She assumed the dog had had a peaceful night; she knew she wouldn't have slept through the call if the vet had contacted her.

Ten minutes later, she had showered and washed her hair and was addressing the perennial problem of how to dry the latter quickly without unleashing a dense halo of frizzy curls. She dressed quickly in old jeans, shirt and jumper, and, with a belated brief nod to her 'date' with Jake, added a bright blue-and-green silk scarf. She had little appetite for breakfast, but, as she'd barely eaten the night before, she forced herself to down a meagre slice of bread and jam with her cup of tea.

Juliet checked her watch again. It wasn't yet 8.15, but the

vet's surgery was a good fifteen minutes away and she thought he'd probably not mind if she was a few minutes early. Shoving her phone into her handbag, she hurried out of the flat. In less than a minute, she was in her car.

CHAPTER 46

DETECTIVE INSPECTOR TIM Yates was in a reasonably good mood. It was Saturday morning, he was up bright and early and he was looking forward to spending the day with his wife and daughter. Although at the back of his mind he suspected the hare-coursing episode might turn into something very ugly and far-reaching, at present he was enjoying one of those relatively rare periods when he and his team seemed to be on top of their workload.

Today, he and Katrin planned to take Sophia, their five-year-old daughter, to the German Christmas market. After that, they'd treat her to lunch in a café and then, if she wasn't too tired, they'd walk round the town to see the Christmas illuminations. Spalding couldn't compete with Blackpool – or even Skegness – but the town council made a pretty good stab at putting on some nice Christmas lights.

With self-conscious virtue, Tim had started making breakfast while the rest of his small family were getting up. He whistled as he moved noisily about the kitchen assembling cereal packets, bowls and cups and saucers in a jumble in the middle of the table. Sometimes he thought he'd enjoy being a house-husband. Now that Katrin had gained her Masters in Criminology, perhaps she'd like to become the breadwinner for a while. He'd put the question to her at some convenient moment when they were alone; not today, obviously.

There came the sound of a light footfall tripping rapidly

down the stairs. His daughter burst into the room.

"Hello, Daddy!" she said. "Do you like my sweatshirt?"

She paraded around the kitchen to show it off. It was mainly navy-blue but appliquéd with several unicorns in violent shades of pink and mauve.

"Lovely!" he said, catching hold of her briefly to give her a kiss as she sped up to him. "What would you like for breakfast?"

CHAPTER 47

PATTI EMERGED FROM the shower feeling a little refreshed. Folding the now-damp towel around her, she returned to her room. She dressed carefully in tailored trousers and a formal shirt. She'd damaged her high-heeled shoes on the previous day but would in any case not have risked more giddiness by wearing them. Instead, she put on a pair of patent-leather loafers.

She combed and blow-dried her hair, achieving a neat coif without really trying. She applied a modest amount of make-up and, after a quick scrutiny of her face in the mirror, decided she was ready to face the world.

As she descended the stairs warning alarms began to go off in her head. It was eerily quiet. Everywhere was in darkness and there was still no smell of breakfast cooking. She reached the kitchen first. The door was closed, yet, when she opened it, she wasn't greeted by Mrs Lawrence bustling at the stove. The room was cold and smelt of spilled alcohol. On a table in the corner, the crockery and cutlery from last night's dinner had been neatly stacked; it was clean, presumably left out to cater for today's round of repasts. The island in the middle of the kitchen still bore several dozen dirty cups and glasses, however, as well as other debris from the post-dinner activities. Shuddering, Patti noted some used swabs of cotton wool tossed among the glassware. They must have been discarded after Gordon's and Victor le Grange's wounds had been washed, but she doubted Isobel Lawrence was capable of such a slovenly act.

Feeling her stomach begin to rebel, she turned away from the mess. She was coming out of the kitchen, having not switched on the lights, when she heard movement in the corridor beyond. Instinctively, she shrank back into the kitchen. Listening carefully, she heard a door close quietly. She didn't think it was the door that led outside from the extension – she'd heard the sound follow on too swiftly after the footsteps, and that door was stiff – it banged unless the person who opened it hung on meticulously until it closed again.

Whoever it was had therefore gone into the dining-room, the cellar or the room occupied by the Franklins. The most logical explanation was that Colin Franklin had gone out for an early morning stroll and was just returning, but Patti could not dispel the sensation of menace. Inexplicably, she was terrified: she sensed something evil lurking, even though she knew her fear was illogical. She'd seen enough hysterical women – and men – in her time to be able to despise her own cowardliness; yet she was also a believer in the power of instinct.

She hastened to the sitting-room. The heavy curtains still covered the windows. She flung them back quickly: the room was deserted. There was no sign that anyone had been there after the drinks reception the previous evening. There was a stale-ish smell.

The ballroom lay beyond the sitting-room. She was reluctant to enter it – she had a vague memory that some of the players had been invited to stay the night rather than brave the fog when their taxi failed to arrive – but her hesitation stemmed rather from the dread of encountering more unsavoury detritus than respect for occupants who might still be sleeping. She doubted her stomach could withstand the shambles she could all too easily imagine.

She heard a noise behind her. Spinning round, she found herself being greeted by Percy. He gave her a broad grin, rubbing his head ruefully. As usual, he was dressed in head-to-toe Armani. Patti could have hugged him.

"Quite a night, wasn't it?" he said. "How are you?"

"Yes," she said. "A bit dazed, that's all. To be honest, I can't remember much about last night."

"Join the club!"

"But where *is* everyone? I haven't even seen Mrs Lawrence yet."

Percy shrugged.

"I don't know. I've only just got up myself. Anton's still sleeping like a baby."

"I'm surprised, after all the fuss he was making."

"Well, you know Anton. Never one to pass up the chance of extracting drama from a situation."

"Am I right in thinking that some of Mr Sykes's players stayed the night, or did I imagine that?"

"No, you're absolutely right. They all stayed, in fact. The landlines weren't working after the power cut and no-one could get a signal on their mobile, so when their people carrier didn't show up Gordon suggested they could doss down for the night. They didn't need asking twice."

"The girls as well?"

"Yep. But I don't think you need to worry about those two: they can take care of themselves. Anton certainly thinks so. He may have been hamming it up a bit last night, but I can tell you he made sure our door was locked and bolted before we went to bed. That Avril scared the living daylights out of him."

"What shall we do now?" Patti asked. She was annoyed with herself for sounding so helpless, but she was at a loss to know how to deal with a houseful of people who refused to wake up.

"Do?" said Percy. "You can do whatever you like. Personally, I don't intend to do very much until I've had some breakfast."

"But if the players have been sleeping in the theatre, it's going to need tidying up, isn't it? And they'll all need showers."

"I don't see why we need to offer them showers: they can all go home now, as soon as they like. They aren't part of today's activities, are they? I suppose we'll have to offer them breakfast. Then they can bugger off. Gordon's probably got some cleaners coming in. They can tidy the place up."

"Well, I'm glad you're being so laid-back about it, Percy, but I'm worried. No-one's appeared except you and me and the crime buffs should be eating their breakfast now. Will you help me find out what's going on?"

Percy sighed theatrically.

"I suppose so," he said.

CHAPTER 48

JULIET WAS ABOUT to ring Mr Trawford's doorbell when the door was flung open. A curly-haired youth stood in front of her, holding a half-eaten slice of toast and marmalade.

"Oh!" he said indistinctly through a large mouthful. "I thought you were one of my mates. Have you come to see my Dad?"

"If that's ok," said Juliet. "I'm a bit earlier than I said I'd be."

"Yours the dog in the surgery, is it? I looked in on her a few times last night."

"Thank you. I . . . "

"Hello," said Philip Trawford, appearing from behind his son. The boy ducked past him and disappeared. "Do you want to come in for a moment, while I get the key to the surgery?"

Juliet stepped into the hallway. Philip Trawford disappeared into a room leading off the hall, returning immediately with a bunch of keys. He opened the front door again.

"There's a way through from the house but it'll be easier to use the outside door at this time of day," he explained. "Kids and stuff in the kitchen."

"Have you seen her yet?" Juliet demanded. She realised that she sounded more accusing than she'd intended. Philip Trawford laughed.

"Yes, indeed, I've seen her," he said. "You don't need

to worry – I haven't been shirking my responsibilities again."

Juliet felt her face flush, but she wasn't to be deflected

"How is she?"

"Very groggy from the anaesthetic still. Not able to stand yet, which is just as well, as she'll need to have her wits about her to achieve any kind of balance. But, all things considered, I think she's come through it quite well."

"Thank you!" said Juliet, involuntarily clasping her hands together.

"It's early days yet, mind you. And you certainly won't be able to take her away with you. She'll have to stay here for a while."

"Oh, I didn't expect to take her today – in fact, I can't. Animals aren't allowed in my flat."

Philip Trawford ceased smiling immediately.

"But you said you'd be able to give her a home!"

"Don't worry, I shall be able to. I'm on my way to see a friend when I leave here and I'm certain he'll be able to help me. And even if I can't cover the cost of the operation, you must let me pay for her board while she's with you."

Philip Trawford's heart went out to her. He encountered people who were besotted with their pets every day of the week, but he'd rarely met someone as earnestly in love with a wounded stray as Juliet was.

"We can discuss that later. If you've got any spare cash, it might be better if you look for a tripod trainer."

"A *what?*"

He was unlocking the surgery door.

"I'll tell you later. Come and see her now. You'll do her good."

Juliet felt a surge of pleasure. The dog's recovery would put purpose back into her life.

Sally the Saluki was lying in an animal crate in the middle of the surgery floor. Juliet hurried into the room and knelt beside the cage. The dog wasn't sleeping: her eyes were open and she turned her head towards Juliet when she heard her. A broad bandage encircled her upper abdomen. Below it, a lone foreleg was stretched out straight. She didn't try to stand.

"Her eyes look very dark."

"That's the anaesthetic. It'll wear off soon."

The dog attempted a couple of feeble wags of its tail. Juliet was delighted.

"I think she recognises me. May I touch her?"

"Yes, but don't startle her. She'll be feeling confused. And her previous owners probably weren't very gentle."

He opened the cage at the top.

"Talk to her before you put your hand near her. And let her smell it first."

"Hello, Sally," Juliet murmured. "It's only me – do you remember, from yesterday? I'm going to look after you now. Would you like a little stroke?"

She lowered her hand slowly to the dog's nose. The dog sniffed it and wagged her tail once more.

"That's right," said Juliet, lightly touching one of her silky ears. "We're going to be friends, aren't we? Good friends."

Sally wagged her tail yet again and closed her eyes.

"That's remarkable," said Philip Trawford. "I think she trusts you already."

Juliet withdrew her hand from the cage with as much care as she had introduced it.

"Let her sleep now," she said. "I'll come back later, if I may."

"Sure. There's a surgery later this morning but I'll be here this afternoon as well. Just ring the doorbell again if the surgery isn't open."

"What were you saying about tripods? It sounds like something to do with cameras."

The vet laughed.

"It's the technical name for a three-legged animal – or a three-legged anything, I suppose. There are people who teach animals with amputated limbs – dogs, especially – on how to cope with their disabilities. You'll have to watch out for charlatans, though. If you're interested, I can probably help find someone reputable."

A sudden thought struck Juliet.

"Is she psychologically damaged? Like a person would be if they lost a limb, I mean?"

"Good question. And it's one I've looked into. There's not much evidence one way or another, though some amputee dogs can become more assertive – like small dogs who try to assert themselves, it's probably because they're feeling vulnerable. But if this dog has behavioural problems, they're more likely to be associated with her past life. She's a trained killer, after all."

Juliet didn't reply. She preferred to think that it was Sally's reluctance to join in the hare coursing that had caused her to be so badly injured. The other dogs had probably set upon her.

"What about a prosthesis? Do they make them for dogs? And are they a good idea?"

"The answer is yes, and again, I don't know. A prosthesis can make the dog sore and sometimes it's better for it to learn to balance on its own three legs. On the other hand, over time there may be evidence of stress on the bones and muscle joints of the remaining legs, because they have to do more work. But we can think about all of this later. It's too early to suggest what's best for her yet."

CHAPTER 49

PERCY GRASPED THE handle of the ballroom door, turning to grin at Patti as he did so.

"Take a deep breath!" he said. "You may need it."

Patti attempted a wan smile. Her stomach had ceased its churning, but now felt sore. She was weak from lack of food and her capricious sledgehammer headache was threatening to return.

"Hey-ho!" said Percy, his voice rising shrilly. He threw open the door and plunged through it, Patti following reluctantly behind him. "Wakey-wakey, everyone!" he yelled with boisterous cheerfulness. "Rise and shine!"

Like the rest of the house, the ballroom was in darkness. The heavy velvet drapes succeeded in both excluding the light and trapping the foetid smell that hung over the room like a pall.

"Christ!" said Percy, abandoning his metrosexual twang. "Stinks in 'ere, dunnit?"

Patti covered her nose and mouth with one hand and tried to swallow the bile rising from her stomach. Deeper into the room, she could discern the bulbous shapes of people lying on the floor, some in sleeping-bags, some cocooned in untidy arrangements of blankets. A couple of them were stirring, propping themselves up on their elbows, awakened, no doubt, by Percy's raucous greeting.

"Where's the lights?" he asked. "We can't see where we're

walking. I wouldn't want to step on one of the old blighters."

"They're just round here, by the door," said Patti. "Do you want me to switch them on?"

"Wouldn't be a bad idea, would it? I can see it's goin' to take a while to get this lot on the move."

Patti groped for the row of switches and turned on the two middle ones. The room was instantly filled with harsh yellow light.

"Bloody 'ell! Turn that off! Do you want to blind us?" It was one of the old men speaking, disentangling himself from a web of grey blanket as he did so. The old man stood up shakily, straightening his shirt and jacket. "Gawd, I feel as if I've been hit by a ten-ton truck!" He kicked the blanket away from him and crouched to retrieve his shoes, which were lying nearby, carrying them over to one of the chairs at the edge of the room to put them on.

Several of the other figures lying on the floor raised their heads. There was more swearing and grumbling, accompanied by a variety of crude bodily sounds. The atmosphere grew yet more pungent.

"Eeugh!" said Percy to Patti. He turned to look at her more closely. "You all right? You've gone a bit green around the gills."

She clutched at his elbow for support.

"Sorry, I'm just not feeling too good. And this isn't helping." She gestured at the messy chaos in front of them.

"Too right it isn't! Let's get out of here as soon as we can." Gently he removed her hand from his arm and clapped both his own hands smartly together.

"Now listen, everyone! It's time to get up. Great that you could stay overnight, but we've got the day's programme to get on with now. Patti and I'll rustle up some toast for you and then we'll call some cabs to take you home. Is that ok with everyone?"

Gradually heads and faces emerged from the bundles and their owners heaved themselves into sitting positions. Patti noticed that Avril and Vicky, who'd been sleeping at the edge of the room some distance away from the others, were among the last to wake. Some of the old men began to stand up, stamping their feet to improve their circulation. George, the one who'd been putting on his shoes, made a rapid exit, presumably in search of the toilet.

One heap of bedding remained inert.

"Who's that?" said Avril, inelegantly kicking herself free of her blankets and standing to stretch. "God, my head! I've never had a 'angover as bad as this. Didn't 'ave that much to drink, neither. That booze must have been really cheap old stuff." She walked across to the heap of bedding and pushed at it gently with the toe of her shoe. "Come on now, sweetheart, you've got to get up." She flicked an amused glance at Percy. "The gentleman says so."

There was no response. She saw that the man inside the bedding had buried his face completely. Crouching down, Avril pulled at flaps of blanket until she had exposed his head. It lolled limply to one side, hitting the floor with a small thud. Avril had uncovered the once-swarthy visage of Montagu Sykes; it was now parchment-white.

Patti could see at once that Sykes was dead. She ran across to him, yanking back the blanket to his waist and held her hand to his neck. There was no pulse.

Percy realised something was wrong and hurried to join her.

"Should we try CPR?" he muttered, trying not to alarm the others.

"Too late," she said. "He's been dead quite a while – several hours, I'd guess!"

"Ugh!" said Avril, smartly stepping back several paces. "And I touched 'im!"

"That won't have done you any harm," Patti said briskly. "Stand back, everyone," – for the old men had come crowding round like sheep – "and put your shoes on if you haven't done so already."

"I'm out of here!" said Avril. "Come on, Vicky!"

From the other side of the room, Vicky regarded them dully. Obviously she had yet to take in what had happened.

"I'm afraid I'm going to have to ask you all to stay where you are," said Patti, summoning as much authority as she could and cruelly hampered by the painful hammering in her head. "If you aren't yet aware of what we've just discovered, it is that Mr Sykes appears to have passed away during the night. It's likely, of course, that his death was from natural causes, but, until we can establish that, it's what a coroner would call 'unexplained'. We'll have to call the police now and they'll be sure to want to take statements from everyone."

"Does that mean we can't go home?" Vicky demanded.

"Not yet you can't," said Patti. "It will be up to the police to say when you're free to leave. I can't imagine they'll want to keep you here longer than is necessary."

"Sykesie won't be the only one to snuff it if I don't get summat to drink soon," said one of the old men.

"We'll bring you some tea," said Patti. "Now, I'd like everyone to go to the end of the room, next the stage, and stay there."

"I need the lav," said one old man, espying George as he returned.

"Of course you must use the toilet when you need to," said Patti. "Take turns to leave the room and please don't speak to any of the guests if you see them."

"Why don't you stay here and supervise?" said Percy. "You're a lot more wised-up about what to do here than I am. I'll call the police and make the tea."

"Thanks," said Patti. "If you see Gordon or Mrs Lawrence, tell them what's happened. Not anyone else, yet. And don't let anyone come in here until the police arrive."

"Ok. Poor old Gordon – looks as if his weekend of crime's been put paid to after all, despite all our efforts to save it last night." He gave her a conspiratorial wink.

Patti was irritated by his coarseness. She knew of course that Percy's self-proclaimed status of high priest of good taste was a sham, but she hadn't expected him to stoop to such crudeness, given the circumstances. She shrugged off her distaste. She knew she had her work cut out keeping the bedraggled and now mutinous thespians under control and she needed to achieve the miracle of mind over matter with some urgency, if she wasn't going to throw up again, this time in front of them. She became aware that Percy was asking her a question.

"Do I just call 999?"

"Yes . . . No. Look, Percy, it's probably best if I make the call. I can talk to some of my colleagues at South Lincs police, explain to them what's happened to help cut down the fuss. We don't want half the cop cars in the county converging on the place for one unexplained death."

Percy shrugged.

"Up to you. You go and make the call, then, while I keep an eye on this lot. I'm still up for making the tea when you come back if you want me to."

"Thanks." Patti managed a smile. "That would be great." She fished out her phone. "Let's hope I can get a signal this morning."

"Oh, I think you will be able to. I got one earlier; and the fog's cleared now."

CHAPTER 50

JULIET HAD A pass to the electronic gates of the children's home. As she swiped it against the metal disc and the gates swung noiselessly open, she felt a sudden pang of apprehension. She'd been so absorbed in sorting out arrangements for the Saluki that she'd barely paused to think about what Jake had said to her the previous day. Now she wished she'd been more cautious. What was this proposition that he wished to make? He'd said – half in jest – that it "wasn't a proposal of marriage"; but was it something equally tying? Something that required the kind of commitment she still felt afraid to give?

The previous day's fog had lifted; although today was bone-gnawingly cold, it promised to be fine. A watery sun was trying to struggle through the clouds. The children's home looked tranquil enough, partly because no children were yet in evidence. Its long, flat playing fields ran smoothly away from the building to the river. Its playground and the two asphalt-covered tennis courts, each also fitted with a netball stand for winter play, were pristine, free for the moment from litter and discarded kit. Jake was a stickler for making the kids clear up after themselves at the end of every day.

Juliet parked her car in the small visitors' car park and walked slowly to the main door, still wrapped in thought. As she reached the door it was flung open. Jake came rushing out to envelop her in a tight embrace, planting several kisses on her mouth.

"Stop it, Jake, I can't breathe," she laughed. "How did you know I'd arrived?"

"Oh, I just happened to be in the office and picked up your car on the CCTV," said Jake, with such studied offhandness that she knew immediately he'd been watching for her. "Have you had breakfast?"

"Some," she said cautiously.

"What does that mean? Half a slice of toast and a cup of tea on your way out the door?"

Juliet laughed again. His powers of prediction were uncanny – or perhaps she herself was just very predictable?

"There's no need to scold me. I've had a lot on my mind."

"Wouldn't dream of it, but do come and have breakfast with me now. The day staff are here, so we can go straight to my sitting-room. They can cope with supervision this morning – it'll be quite a light day for them, as some of the kids are going into town with volunteers for football practice. The rest will be outside shortly."

"Thanks. A decent cup of coffee would go down well."

"My speciality, as you know. Come in quickly now, otherwise you'll be surrounded."

Juliet was a favourite with those children who were long-term residents at the home. She'd been visiting them since the child killer Grace Brackenbury had stayed there briefly two years before. Her relationship with them didn't pre-date hers with Jake, but the two had grown in parallel: she was more to the children than just 'Jake's girlfriend'.

"I like seeing them . . ."

"Yes, but not today. We have things to talk about," said

Jake earnestly. Then, in a lighter tone, "and the croissants are warming; I don't want them to burn!"

Jake's flat was both cosy and shabby. Juliet sank into the big old sofa that virtually filled the sitting-room and kicked off her shoes. She closed her eyes briefly. When she opened them she saw Jake observing her.

"What?" she said, sitting upright.

"Did you sleep last night?"

"Yes, as a matter of fact I did. It took me a while to get to sleep – I was worried about the dog – and then the next thing I knew it was morning. Why do you ask?"

"You just look a bit . . . drawn, that's all."

Juliet bit back a retort about coddling. She probably did look "drawn": worrying about Sally had been a huge emotional burden.

"I've been concerned about Sally – the dog. But I've just been at the vet's, and she's making good progress."

"That's great news." Jake drew up a small coffee table and placed on it a cafetière of coffee and a plate of fragrant croissants.

"Those smell amazing!"

"Dig in," said Jake, sitting down beside her, "and tell me about the dog."

Juliet poured out two cups of coffee and took a croissant, breaking a piece off it as she spoke.

"The vet had to amputate – I think I told you that. The operation was successful and she had a good night. When I saw her, she was still sedated, but she seemed to recognise me." Jake grinned. "Oh, it's not just a figment of my imagination," Juliet added, a little huffily. "Mr Trawford thought so, too." She popped the piece of croissant into her mouth.

"Which leg?"

"The front right one, as she is facing forwards," said Juliet indistinctly.

"What's the prognosis?"

"Apparently, many dogs cope perfectly well with three legs, even if it's one of the front legs that's missing. They're called 'tripods'. Yes, I thought it sounded funny, too. But there are special therapists that can be hired to rehabilitate them."

"And you're thinking of finding one?"

"Yes," said Juliet tersely. "Why do you ask?" She'd picked up the croissant to tear off another piece, but now she returned it to her plate.

"Don't be defensive. I'm just interested. Helping this dog means a lot to you, doesn't it?"

"It's not just about helping her. I've been thinking for a long time there's something missing in my life. We can help each other."

Jake was more than stunned by this latest pronouncement, but he tried not to show it. Untypically, Juliet seemed not to have noticed how tactless she was being. She took a bite out of the croissant and carried on talking.

"There are lots of obstacles in my way – I know that. I'll be going in for my final operation soon and I'm going to need someone to look after Sally for at least two weeks then. And I'm not allowed to keep dogs in my flat – I've told you that."

Jake was wise enough not to wind her up by telling her the next operation would put her out of action for at least a month. Instead, he asked her gently, "What are your plans, both for the flat and the dog? You tell me, Juliet. You've said you want me to help, and I'm happy to do so if I can. But I want to know how you see things first."

"How do you mean, 'see things'?"

"Well, for a start, is it your intention to keep the flat on and house the dog somewhere close? That seemed to be what you were suggesting when we spoke yesterday."

Juliet was silent. She'd taken on board that Jake had said that it probably wouldn't be possible for Sally to stay permanently at the children's home and she'd been relieved when he'd said he had an alternative suggestion. She hadn't thought further than that. She could see where this conversation was leading now.

"What are you suggesting?"

"I'm not suggesting anything, yet." Jake was trying to sound reasonable, but Juliet wasn't making it easy for him. "Does the flat mean much to you?"

"Not really. It's a place to live – and the first place I've had on my own. But it's a council box and I don't own it."

"What about the dog?"

"I've tried to explain about the dog . . . "

Jake made a calming motion with both hands.

"Yes, you have, Juliet, and I think I understand what you said about needing her. Now – I'm going to have to ask you this, so please don't fly off the handle – what about me?"

Juliet was reduced to silence again. She put down the croissant. Although she had turned away her eyes, she reached out to find Jake's hand. He took hold of hers and grasped it tightly.

"You . . . said . . . it wasn't a proposal of marriage."

"Yes, I did say that – and I meant it. But I need to know where I stand. Surely you can see that? If there's no future for us, what happens to the dog, if you can't look after it yourself? Or did you think I would be happy to be cast in the role of your perpetual platonic dog-walker?" The gentle humour in

Jake's tone took the sting out of what he was saying. Despite herself, Juliet burst out laughing.

"I don't see what's so funny . . . " Jake was reproachful now; he felt humiliated. To his surprise, Juliet flung her arms around his neck and kissed him.

"Oh, Jake, I'm not laughing at you. I'm so sorry that I've been wrapped up in myself, particularly over the past two days. I'm an idiot, but you knew that already. Of course you deserve to know where you stand! But it would make it easier for me if you told me what you were thinking of first. Since, practically speaking, Sally can't stay at my flat or here, what is your solution? I know you've thought of one because you said so yesterday."

Jake held her hand more tightly.

"Do you remember my speaking about my great-aunt?"

"Vaguely. Her name's Emily, isn't it? She was the one who helped you buy your car?"

"That's right. Her real name's Emmeline, but she doesn't like it - she calls herself Emily."

"Is she ok?"

"She'd say she is 'right as a trivet'. But she is very old - exactly how old, I'm not sure . . . she doesn't like people to know, but well into her eighties. Her husband was a diplomat and many years older than herself - she's been a widow for at least thirty years. They didn't have children."

"Where does she live?"

"In an old cottage near Fishtoft. When I say old, I mean very old - parts of it are mediaeval."

"Fishtoft? But that can't be twenty miles away. We should have been to see her."

"I frequently go to see her. I've never asked you to come,

because Emily's rather good at putting two and two together and making five. She would immediately assume that you were my fiancée – or, failing that, that either I was wasting your time or you were wasting mine."

"I see," said Juliet.

"You probably don't see – you're thinking that she's an old reactionary and you wouldn't like her, but actually she's a very astute lady. She'd certainly pick up on the imbalance in our relationship."

Juliet didn't answer.

"Anyway," Jake continued, after a pause, "she's decided that the cottage is too much for her. She's about to go into sheltered accommodation – has been trying to get somewhere for a while – and now she's been given a supervised flat. And, since I'm her sole heir, she's decided to give me the cottage now, rather than wait until she dies."

"Doesn't she need to sell it to pay for her flat?"

"No. She has a fair bit put by – how much, I don't know, but I suspect that she's giving me the place to try to avoid death duties. That and the fact that it'll deteriorate if it's not occupied. So anyway . . . " Jake suddenly became reticent.

"You thought we might live there together?" Juliet finished the sentence for him.

"I wasn't going to put it as baldly as that. I thought you might like to live there and I could stay when I'm not on duty here; and I can probably move in and put myself on days for a few weeks so I can look after the dog while you recover. But obviously it couldn't be an entirely no-ties arrangement. The house needs some work doing on it, for one thing. It would have to be a joint enterprise, with all that that implies. But I repeat, this isn't a proposal of marriage. I'm not saying I wouldn't like that, at some stage, but it's not my intention to keep it hanging over your head like the sword of Damocles."

Juliet gave him an uncertain smile.

"Anything else?"

"And you'd have to meet my aunt."

"Who will immediately expose me for the gold-digging strumpet that I am!" It was Jake's turn to laugh.

"I think it's a wonderful idea," said Juliet. "And much more than I deserve."

"That's where you're wrong," said Jake, enfolding her in another embrace.

CHAPTER 51

"WHAT DO YOU mean he was dead when you tried to wake him up? Why were you trying to wake him up anyway?"

It was after breakfast. Tim had taken the call from Patti while Katrin was helping Sophia put on her outdoor clothes. Since their split almost ten years ago it had been unusual for Patti to call him at all and, as far as he could recollect, never at the weekend unless he was on duty. It made him uneasy as well as irritable. He was acutely aware that Katrin would be able to hear the conversation from the hall. Not that he had anything to hide, but Katrin knew about his past relationship with Patti, which made talking to her or about her awkward. He'd never managed to assuage his sense of guilt about Patti, either, which made him unnecessarily terse.

"A *crime* weekend?" he echoed. "So who is the guy who died? One of the punters?"

Katrin, listening just as keenly as Tim had supposed, noted the long silence that ensued. Patti had evidently embarked on an elaborate explanation of whatever it was that was going on.

"I see. So how many people are there at the premises now?" There was a shorter pause. "About twenty? Christ! Well, they'll all have to be detained until they've given statements." Another pause. "No, I don't think I can. I'm off duty this weekend and I've got something on. If what you're surmising is correct, it's not a suspicious death. I know taking all those statements will be time-consuming, but you don't need me there to supervise. Why don't you get on to Andy Carstairs? He's working this weekend. He can come with a couple of uniforms." He held the phone away from him for a few seconds, as if about to terminate the call, and then thought better of it. "Look, I'm sorry that you've got caught up in this - I know it means you'll have a rough time today. Keep me posted, won't you, on how it goes . . . and ask Andy to give me a call as well." Patti's response must have been very brief, because Tim pressed the red button on his phone almost immediately. He went to join his wife and daughter.

"Was that Patti Gardner?" Katrin asked innocently. Tim nodded. "What did she want?"

"She's at one of those crime weekends - you know, where the 'guests' act out a whodunnit. It's being run by a relative of hers, who asked her to go and give a talk on forensics. Apparently one of the people involved snuffed it overnight."

"That kind of thing probably attracts quite elderly people - the sort who go in for cruises. I expect it'll turn out to be natural causes."

"That's what Patti thinks, though actually the person who died was neither elderly nor one of the paying guests - if that's what they call them. Apparently he was the leader of an amateur acting group who entertained them last night. The actors had to stay the night because of the fog - they couldn't get a signal to call cabs at the end of the evening."

"Where did all this happen? It doesn't sound very like Spalding."

"I agree, but it did happen here - on that island in the river near Little London. Do you know where I mean?"

"Yes, I've read about it – it's had quite a past. St Catherine's Island, I think it's called."

"Well it may have been called that once, but the chap who lives there now calls it Holyrood. His name's Gordon Bemrose – a local character; we've come across him a few times. Sails close to the law, almost a petty criminal, though we've never managed to pin much on him. I'm surprised that he's Patti's uncle, though."

Katrin smiled.

"You can hardly blame her for that. Everyone has disagreeable relatives. And if you don't mind my saying so, you were pretty abrupt with her just now. She's obviously worried about this death: otherwise she wouldn't have called you."

"I suppose you're right; but at the same time she should know better than to bother me with it."

"Well, thanks for not letting it capsize our day out. Let's get away as soon as we can – you never know what might happen later."

Tim shot her a sharp look. It was Tim's good fortune – and sometimes his misfortune – that the two women to whom he was closest, Katrin and Juliet, both at times exhibited an uncanny prescience. He hoped Katrin would be proved wrong, and that the amateur actor had simply died in an inconvenient place at an inconvenient time.

CHAPTER 52

ANDY CARSTAIRS WAS dozing at his desk, having inflicted upon himself quite a heavy Friday night. He was supposed to be compiling a dossier of recent hare-chasing crimes that had taken place both in Lincolnshire and other counties, to see if he could spot any similarities. It was a daunting task, mainly because all he could see were similarities: the perpetrators usually came from outside the county concerned, almost invariably plied their 'sport' on deserted farmland and were quick to decamp once the day's activities were concluded. There was considerable evidence of links to organised crime, but what did Tim expect him to do? Trawl through the files of all the convicted living crime bosses on record to see if there were any references to dogs? Andy didn't think so – in fact, he thought the whole exercise was a waste of time and that the only way of apprehending hare coursers was to catch them red-handed in the act. What was worse, he firmly believed this was Tim's view, too; the paper-pushing exercise was probably to fulfil some bureaucratic quota that had been wished on Tim from on high.

Andy got up from his desk and went to the window, where he stared out disconsolately at the Saturday shoppers. Christmas was coming, with its inevitable spate of petty crimes, some of them heart-rending thefts carried out by those too poor to be able to afford presents for their children. There were plenty of chancers quick to take advantage of poverty, too: from where he was standing he could see two street-sellers peddling, respectively, cheap wrapping paper and some kind of mechanical child's toy, in full sight of the cop shop, too. Still, it was the job of the coppers downstairs to tell them to move on – no longer his concern. Sighing, he turned back to his desk and leafed through the set of photocopied photographs he had accumulated, some of the remains of ripped-apart hares, others of badly-injured dogs. It made his blood boil. He was determined to help catch these bastards, even if it did mean wading through several tons of crap.

Nevertheless, when his mobile rang, he seized it with relief. A proper job, involving some action, was just what he needed to blow the cobwebs away.

"Hello? DC Carstairs?" The voice was both hesitant and familiar.

"Yes? Who's speaking?"

"It's Patricia Gardner. DI Yates asked me to call you."

Patricia Gardner? Andy had to think for a moment. The speaker clearly expected him to know who she was.

"Patti," she added. "I lead the SOCO team. Do you remember me?"

Faintly embarrassed by his own obtuseness, Andy gave her a warm reply.

"Patti! I'm sorry, I was miles away, thinking of something else. What can I do for you?"

She launched into the same explanation that she'd given Tim, though she was calmer now and managed to cut it short.

"I'm on my way!" said Andy, not trying to conceal his jubilation. The bloke probably had died of natural causes, but at least interviewing the inmates of Holyrood House would involve human interaction.

"DI Yates said you'd want to bring two uniforms with you. There are about twenty people staying here and they'll all have to be interviewed – did I mention that?"

"No," said Andy. "But good thinking – I'll find a couple on my way out. Are you all right?" he added. "You don't sound too good."

"To tell you the truth, I'm feeling a bit hung over." Andy was about to say, "Join the club", but thought better of it before Patti continued. "So is everyone here. It's a bit strange. I suppose it's possible we did all over-indulge, but it seems unlikely."

Alarm bells were already ringing in Andy's head.

"The bloke who died," he said. "Had he been 'over-indulging', too?"

CHAPTER 53

JULIET WAS FEELING anything but prescient when her mobile rang. Still in Jake's flat, she was enjoying one of those rare occasions of living entirely for the moment as they laughed and chatted. The idea of moving into his aunt's cottage had grabbed her more than Jake could have hoped for in his wildest dreams and she was happily quizzing him about when they could visit his aunt, when they would be able to inspect the house, when they would be able to move in. Jake registered her repeated use of the words "we" and "us" and exulted quietly. He was still afraid that too overt a show of his own delight might give her cold feet.

The insistent ringing of the phone intruded. Juliet looked at her watch. "It's not ten, yet – Mr Trawford said I could take you to see Sally later if you could get away, but the anaesthetic still won't have worn off completely yet. I hope she hasn't had a relapse."

"You'll have to answer it, whatever it's about," said Jake, as the phone stopped ringing. He grinned. "Or perhaps not. Let's hope it was a wrong number." The words were no sooner out of his mouth than the ringing started up again.

"This isn't about Sally," Juliet said, with a sinking heart. "It's work. Ringing off and then ringing again is one of the ways of alerting an off-duty officer that they're needed." She rummaged in her bag for the phone. "DS Armstrong," she said briskly.

"Juliet?" Andy sounded harassed.

"Yes, I've just said. What's the matter?"

"A report's come in of two deaths on Holyrood Island."

"Holyrood Island? Where's that?"

"It's the island in the crook of the Welland on the outskirts of the town. It's called St Catherine's Island on maps."

"I know where you mean. Two deaths? Do you know who's died? And does it look suspicious?"

"It certainly looks suspicious now. The deaths weren't reported together – the first one came in a few minutes ago. The circumstances were a bit odd, but there was reason to believe the guy died of natural causes. But we've just been notified of the second one and there can be no doubt he was murdered – he's got a kitchen knife stuck right between his shoulder blades."

"Any witnesses?"

"No-one's admitting to having witnessed the actual deaths. There are about twenty people on the island. We'll have to take statements from all of them."

"Twenty people? Was there some kind of do going on?"

"You could say that. A crime weekend, apparently." Andy barked out a short, sarcastic laugh, which Juliet ignored.

"Are you at the scene?"

"No. Just on my way. I'm taking Tandy and Chakrabati with me. I'd lined them up to take statements after the first death was reported."

"How do you know there are 'about twenty people' there? Could the caller be exaggerating?"

"Possibly, but I don't think so. It was Patti Gardner."

Juliet's first impulse after she'd taken in what Andy was saying had been to call Tim, but now she wasn't sure. There was a tension between him and Patti that she'd never fully understood. Patti was an acquaintance of hers rather than a friend – she'd always struck Juliet as rather dour, though she was undoubtedly good at her job; but if Patti had somehow got herself mixed up in a murder investigation, Juliet's keen sense of compassion prompted her to try not to make it worse for her by involving Tim immediately. She'd suss out the situation for herself first.

"I'm on my way."

CHAPTER 54

PATTI PRESSED THE red button on her phone and turned to the grim-faced woman beside her.

"I think you should sit down, Mrs Lawrence. You've had a terrible shock."

"I'll bring you some tea," said Percy.

"I don't want tea!" Isobel Lawrence exclaimed truculently. "I just want this nightmare to be over and done with."

Patti nodded automatically. She felt the same; she was annoyed with herself for taking charge – it could only protract the length of time she would have to stay there.

"I've called my colleagues at the police station. They'll be here very soon. Percy, I think you should still take tea to the actors. We have to try to keep them in the ballroom if we can."

Percy nodded and returned to the kitchen, from which he had emerged when Isobel Lawrence had appeared, gliding like a wraith down the stairs, her face constricted with horror, and put her hand on Patti's arm. Patti had just concluded her first call to Andy Carstairs.

Percy had listened while Mrs Lawrence explained that she had come in to find the house in darkness and decided to begin the task of waking the household by taking Gordon Bemrose a cup of tea. She'd knocked on his bedroom door and when there was no answer had decided to enter. Even in the poor light cast by the gap in the half-drawn curtains, she could see that a struggle had taken place. Various items had been knocked to the floor and the bed itself ransacked. She hadn't at first realised that Gordon was still in the room. She'd put down her tray and, seizing the overturned mattress, had tried to wrestle it back on to the bed. She'd failed to do this, but not before she had seen Gordon lying face down on the floor, a large knife wedged between his shoulder blades. Crouching down, she'd felt the body. In her opinion, Gordon had been dead for several hours: the corpse was already cold. Percy had leapt the stairs three at a time, returning almost immediately to confirm that Gordon was dead. Patti had called Andy Carstairs again, managing to catch him before he left the station with the two PCs.

While Percy was still in the kitchen, Colin Franklin came out of his room. He was bleary-eyed and had obviously just thrown on the same clothes he'd been wearing on the previous evening.

"God! Is that the time?" he said, holding his watch up to his face. "Margarett and I seem to have overslept. We'll come to breakfast as soon as we can." He looked from Isobel Lawrence to Patti and back again to Isobel.

"Is something wrong?" he asked.

There was a painful silence.

"Mr Franklin," Patti said at last. "There's been an accident. We've had to call the police. It would be very helpful if you could go back to your room and stay there until they arrive . . . and ask your wife to stay there, too."

"An accident? What sort of accident?"

"Mr Franklin . . ." Isobel Lawrence began.

"All right, all right, I hear you. Margarett and I will wait in our room until you give us a knock. I hope that whatever it is won't upset her: she's very highly strung."

"Well, really . . ." said Isobel.

"It's understandable, under the circumstances," said Patti quietly. "We haven't told him what's happened, after all."

"Is there anything I can do?" asked Isobel dully.

"You could go to the cottages, knock on the doors, and ask everyone else to stay put, too," said Patti. "Tell them the same as we've just told Colin Franklin – that there's been an accident and the police are on their way."

CHAPTER 55

ANDY CARSTAIRS ARRIVED at Holyrood House with Giash Chakrabati and Verity Tandy just as Mrs Lawrence was returning from the cottages. He noted her striking way of carrying herself - her back ramrod straight, her shoulders held back. She was immaculately dressed, too, even if her tastes were a bit old-fashioned for her age - he didn't think she could be much older than forty. She was wearing a black woollen dress with a high collar, relieved only by thin white cuffs. When she came closer, her face was ashen and mask-like: she didn't look happy, but otherwise her mood was inscrutable.

"She in mourning already?" said Giash. "If so, she's a class act."

Verity tittered and then stopped herself.

"That's not really funny," said Andy, but he was smiling, too. He composed his face into a more suitably sombre expression as he climbed out of the car. He had intended to step forward to introduce himself, but she had already quickened her pace and was beside him before he could shut the car door.

"Thank goodness you're here!" she said. "There are guests in all the cottages and more people in the house. We're trying to keep them separated, but naturally they all want to know what's going on. I'm sure they'll take instructions better from you than from us."

Her words belied a very commanding presence. Privately, Andy doubted he could do a better job.

He held out his hand.

"I'm DC Carstairs," he said. "And this is PC Tandy and PC Chakrabati. Could you tell us your name? Then perhaps you could take us to Ms Gardner, who made the original call. She's a colleague, as she probably told you."

"I'm Isobel Lawrence, the housekeeper," she said. "Not live-in. I'm just here to help Gordon with . . . or I was." She looked stricken, but there were no tears. "You'd best come into the house."

"Do we need to wear plastic over our shoes?" Verity Tandy asked.

"Probably a good idea – although from what we've been told, the place is bursting with people. Not much chance of not contaminating the scene. But if it is a murder and the killer wasn't supposed to be here, I suppose we stand a chance of isolating his DNA. Best bet will be the knife, though."

Isobel Lawrence shuddered.

"Miss Gardner's in the kitchen," she said. "I don't think she's feeling too good."

Verity produced some polythene shoe-covers from the boot of the car and she and the two policemen fitted them over their shoes. Mrs Lawrence led the way into the house, the others following.

Patti was seated at a stool with her back to the kitchen table, facing out into the corridor. Someone had placed a mug of tea on the table behind her. Her face was chalk-white. When she saw Andy, she began to shake uncontrollably.

"Steady!" He soothed. "Take it easy. We're here now. You

need to drink some of that tea." Verity sat down beside her and felt her wrist. Her pulse was rapid and fluttery.

"Where is the..?" asked Andy.

"Which one?" Isobel Lawrence cut in grimly. "You can take your pick. Gordon's upstairs in his bedroom. Mr Sykes is on the floor in the ballroom."

"We should have called for a doctor," Patti murmured.

"Why? There's no doubt that they're both dead, is there?"

"Standard procedure," said Andy, "but don't worry, DS Armstrong said she'd ask a doctor to attend. She's on her way, too."

"Have you notified DI Yates?" Giash Chakrabati asked.

"I started with him in the first place," said Patti tonelessly. "He told me that DC Carstairs was on duty."

"Wasn't that before the second body was found?" said Andy. "I'm sure he'll want to know now."

"Well, you can call him - you're in charge," said Patti, more spiritedly than she had spoken before.

Andy raised his eyebrows but said nothing. Like Juliet, he had on occasion noted the tension between Patti and Tim.

There were sounds of another car drawing up outside. Someone rapped on the door.

"I'll get it," said Giash Chakrabati. He returned in a few seconds, walking ahead of Juliet and a small, rotund man with a bald head.

"DC Carstairs," said Juliet, nodding at Andy. "This is Dr Paxton. He's the police surgeon on duty today. He'll need to see both the deceased and certify death. Just a formality, I know. Professor Salkeld is on his way, too."

"How much longer do you think . . . ?" Percy Forsyth had

been on the point of entering the kitchen. He stood framed in the doorway. "Sorry, I . . . "

"It's all right," said Patti. "If you were going to ask how much longer we need to keep everyone waiting, things are going to start moving now. The police have arrived."

Juliet hadn't noticed Patti. Too late, she realised how rude it must have looked not to acknowledge her.

"Anything I can do to help?" said Percy, addressing Giash Chakrabati. Giash looked embarrassed.

"DS Armstrong is the senior officer here."

"It's ok," said Juliet. "This is Dr Paxton. Perhaps you could take him to the deceased actor – you said the body was downstairs?" she added, turning to Andy.

"Yes. I haven't seen it myself. We arrived only just before you."

"Thanks," said Juliet. "PC Chakrabati, go with them."

"I understood there were two bodies," said Dr Paxton.

"Gordon is upstairs," said Isobel Lawrence. "In his bedroom."

"Could you show DC Carstairs the bedroom? PC Tandy, please go with them and guard the door until Dr Paxton comes."

When they'd all gone, Juliet was left on her own with Patti, as she'd intended.

"I'm sorry, Patti, I didn't register that you were sitting there when I first came in," she said. "You know, you don't look well."

"Thanks!" said Patti, attempting a wry smile. "To tell you the truth, I feel like shit. But whether it's because I had too much to drink last night, or we were all drugged with something, I'm not sure."

"Drugged?" said Juliet. "You really believe that? All of you?"

Patti shrugged.

"I know it sounds melodramatic," she said, "but there was something very strange going on here this morning - oh, I don't mean the two deaths. I got up late, but no-one else was up before me. The house was in darkness."

"Did anyone else feel ill?"

"I haven't seen any of the guests yet - I mean the people who paid to come here for the crime weekend. Oh, except one of them - Colin Franklin; he and his wife are the only ones staying in the house. As far as I could tell, there wasn't much wrong with him. The others are in the cottages at the back. The actors were sleeping in the ballroom. They all looked pretty rough when Percy and I went in to see them. And, of course, Montagu Sykes - their leader - is one of the men who died."

"You asked everyone to stay put?"

"Yes. Usual procedure - keep everyone contained until the police arrive."

"The guests are in the cottages, you say?"

"All except the Franklins. They've got a room in the extension."

"When Dr Paxton's finished signing the death certificates, we need to ask him to take samples from everyone."

"You're right, I should have thought of that. I'm sorry, I'm not thinking straight."

"You're doing fine," said Juliet. Then, more awkwardly, "I'm going to have to ask DI Yates if he wants to get involved. Is that a problem?"

"Andy already mentioned that. Why should it be a problem?" Patti was immediately on the defensive.

"No reason," said Juliet. "Well, yes, there is a reason. I shouldn't insult you by pretending – it's just that there always seems to be an atmosphere . . . a kind of tension in the room . . . when you and Tim are in it together. Nothing to do with me, I know, and I'm not trying to pry."

Patti sighed. She felt overcome with fatigue and despair.

"You're right," she said, "and I'll tell you about it some time, but not now – I don't have the strength. I did call Tim earlier, by the way, but he was on his way out for the day. He told me to get in touch with Andy."

"When was this?"

"After Percy and I discovered that Montagu Sykes had died."

"So he doesn't know about Gordon Bemrose's murder?"

"Well, not from me, certainly."

"I'll have to tell him," Juliet said again.

CHAPTER 56

TIM, KATRIN AND Sophia had arrived at the German Christmas market early. It wasn't crowded, but there were already quite a few visitors, some breakfasting on pastries or German sausage. One or two people were even braving the glühwein, although it wasn't yet ten o'clock.

"Ugh!" said Tim. "Alcohol for breakfast!"

"Glühwein's different," said Katrin. "It gets you into the spirit of Christmas. It's like having a nip of brandy before you go skiing; or drinking champagne for breakfast on Christmas morning."

Tim gave her a curious look.

"We've never had champagne for breakfast, at Christmas or any other time," he said. "In fact, the only time I've ever had alcohol that early was on the day of the royal wedding. Someone brought some bottles of Prosecco into the station."

"Well, there you are, then," said Katrin, adding mischievously, "I hope Superintendent Thornton was well out of the way; otherwise he'd have had you all on a charge for drinking on duty."

"Don't talk about Thornton," said Tim. "I don't want to think about him today. Anyway, do you want some?"

"What, glühwein?"

"Yes - since you seem to think it's the right drink for the occasion."

Katrin screwed up her nose.

"Only in theory," she said. "What I'd really like is a nice hot cappuccino."

"Done!" said Tim. "And we'll get a hot chocolate for Sophia."

"With marshmallows and cream?" said Sophia, gazing earnestly up at him.

Katrin frowned. She didn't like Sophia to eat too many sweets. Marshmallows were particularly bad – they'd wreak havoc on her teeth. Tim grinned at her conspiratorially, trying to look over Sophia's head, but aware that his daughter, beady-eyed, was watching them.

"Just this once," he said. "Because it's nearly Christmas. Marshmallows are like glühwein – they're not for every day."

Sophia was wise enough not to throw her mother a triumphant look.

Tim's mobile started to ring. He took it out of his pocket and saw that the caller was Juliet.

"I'm going to have to take this," he said. He pressed the phone to his ear and listened for a long minute.

"Shit!" he said. Katrin threw him a warning look: Sophia was solemnly listening to him. "Sorry!" he mouthed to Katrin. He crouched down to talk to Sophia.

"I'm sorry, sweetheart, I'm going to have to leave you here with Mummy. She will buy the hot chocolate."

Sophia nodded and gave him a brave smile. He could see she was close to tears and decided that more apologising would only crack her up. He stood up.

"Sorry!" he said to Katrin, standing up, wincing as his legs creaked. "We'll come here again before Christmas."

Katrin was usually understanding about the constraints of Tim's job, but there was an edge to her voice today.

"What is it?" she demanded. "You haven't had a weekend off in ages."

Tim glanced down at Sophia again. A youth carrying a tray of jumping beans had caught her attention. She was no longer listening.

"Two deaths," he said quietly. "One of them certainly murder."

CHAPTER 57

WHEN TIM ARRIVED at Holyrood House Andy took him straight into the ballroom. There was a familiar gaunt figure kneeling on the ground, in the act of zipping up a body bag.

"Professor Salkeld!" he said. "You got here quickly."

"Aye," said the Professor, locking the top of the zip into place before he looked up. "The wife fancied a look round your Christmas market. So I was on the spot when Armstrong called."

"That's funny . . . " said Tim.

"I don't see anything funny about it," said the Professor severely. "As Morag pointed out, it's the first time for weeks I've taken her out somewhere. She's none too pleased, I can tell you." Professor Salkeld habitually blamed in equal measures the person who'd died and the police dealing with the death for disturbing his routine.

"I see you're bagging this one up already," said Tim. "Any idea about the cause of death?"

"None at all, except that there are no obvious injuries. Could be natural causes, I can't say until we've done the post-mortem. I've taken photos of the body as it was shown to me, though I gather it had already been moved from its original position when I saw it. The one upstairs is a different matter – I've left him for you to look at before I make a start. Nasty mess up there," he added grimly.

"In what order would you like to do things, sir? Do you want to see DS Armstrong? Or should we start with the interviews in here?" Andy asked.

"In here?" said Tim. "Surely there's somewhere else . . ."

Andy gestured at the stage. Tim hadn't noticed the bedraggled group of what seemed to be predominantly elderly men accompanied by two young women who were sitting on the stage, watching him silently. They were surrounded by a litter of mugs and milk cartons.

"We've kept them all in here, sir. This room was being used as an impromptu dormitory – they were putting on amateur dramatics here and the weather was too bad for them to go home last night. The deceased must have died while they were all sleeping, but until we can rule out foul play we thought it best not to let them go anywhere else."

"Fair enough, thanks. I think I need to understand a bit more about this set-up before we do anything else. Where is Juliet – DS Armstrong?"

"She's in the kitchen, sir, with Ms Gardner."

Tim blenched. He'd forgotten about the call from Patti earlier in the day – or, rather, he'd put it out of his mind.

"Do you want to see them now?" Andy pursued.

"What? Oh, yes. Please. And then I'd better see the body upstairs," he added, catching Professor Salkeld's eye.

"Aye, well tell me when you're ready and I'll come with you," said the Professor. "I'm going outside for a smoke."

Thinking that Patti would be the most reliable source of information, Juliet had begun questioning her about the crime weekend and the names of everyone who had stayed at the house overnight. She'd sketched a rough plan of the house and cottages and written names against the rooms. Patti had supplied her with a copy of Gordon Bemrose's programme for the crime weekend. They were about to work through it when Tim tapped at the door and came in.

"Hello, Tim," said Juliet. "Thanks for getting here so quickly."

"Well, I won't say it's a pleasure. I was at the Christmas market with Katrin and Sophia. Hello, Patti," he added.

"Good morning, DI Yates." Patti stood up, moving away from Tim and Juliet until her back was against the sink and she could retreat no further. There was a tense silence.

"Patti was just describing the lay-out of the island to me and telling me who is staying where," said Juliet in a strained voice. You could cut the atmosphere with a knife, she thought. "And Dr Paxton is here. He's probably finished with the people in the ballroom now and gone to the cottages. He's taking blood and urine samples from everyone."

"Whatever for?"

"Patti thinks most of the people here may have been drugged last night. Apparently they felt very groggy this morning; some of them vomited."

"Interesting," said Tim. This was rapidly turning into the strangest case he'd ever worked on. "And you, Patti? How are you?"

She managed a wan smile.

"Not too bad," she said. "The last twenty-four hours have been more than weird, but I daresay I'll get over it."

"I'm sure you will!" said Tim. "Carry on talking to Juliet; I'll be back as soon as I can. Professor Salkeld is going to show me the body of the guy upstairs. Knifed, did Andy say?"

"Gordon Bemrose, the deceased man, was Patti's uncle," Juliet said gently.

"Oh. Oh, I'm sorry," said Tim. He cursed himself for forgetting this fact.

"Don't worry, we weren't close."

"Well, I'm still sorry. Look, help Juliet as much as you can, but don't push yourself." Juliet noticed that his tone had softened. So did Patti. Her lip trembled. Tim left the kitchen precipitately. Under her austere exterior, Patti had always been more emotional than he could cope with: it all came flooding back to him.

Professor Salkeld handed Tim a pair of latex gloves to put on before together they lifted the mattress off the dead man.

"This is how he was found? Tipped out of the bed with the mattress on top of him?"

"So I believe. I just had a wee look when I came up before. I thought you'd like to see the body in situ."

"Thanks. Who found him?"

"The housekeeper. She said she was bringing him tea. It's still there," he added. He pointed to a china mug of cold tea, surface coagulated with a film of milk, which had been placed on the chest of drawers. "Tough woman - she didn't drop it, as you see. Doesn't fit the stereotype of the loyal servant throwing a fit of histrionics when she discovers the corpse, does she?"

"No," said Tim. "She certainly doesn't. Did she touch anything?"

"It's your job to interview her, not mine, but she says she just lifted the mattress up and then when she saw him let it fall again. She didn't check for vital signs - but then, confronted with that, you can't blame her. It must have been clear to her he was dead."

"Any ideas about the cause of death?"

"You know I won't commit to anything yet. But it wouldn't take a genius to suggest that the knife had something to do with it. Pierced the heart, at a guess. It's going to be awkward moving the body to the lab. It won't go into a body bag in that position."

"Get an undertaker to bring a van?"

"Aye, if that's all right with you. It'll cost you."

"I'll leave it to Superintendent Thornton to worry about that. One other thing . . . "

"Yes?" The Professor raised an eyebrow quizzically.

"You'll check for barbiturates, drugs, poisons, etcetera?"

"Of course – why do you ask?"

"It appears that everyone who was here last night slept very heavily; most overslept and woke up feeling rough."

"In that case, your man here might be more help than you think. If he died soon after ingesting drugs, there'll be more traces left than in someone who managed to survive the night."

CHAPTER 58

ANDY AND GIASH Chakrabati had taken statements from the thespians, using the curtained-off area at the back of the stage that had served as a dressing-room to interview each of them individually.

"That Avril's a bright spark!" said Giash, mopping his brow. "Did you hear what she said when I asked her how much she'd had to drink?"

"Yeah – what she could lay her hands on, which hadn't been enough."

"She admitted to waking up with a splitting headache, though. I think they were all telling the truth, don't you?"

"Not sure about that. The old men seem pretty straight. I've met girls like Avril and Vicky before – they're practically congenital liars. I suppose they've been in trouble so many times it's a kind of reflex to lie, to cover their tracks."

"Do you think they could be suspects, then?"

"Everyone's a suspect until we find out who did it. But we don't even know that Montagu Sykes was murdered yet . . . and I can't see that any of this lot would have a reason for wanting to top Gordon Bemrose."

"Did you hear Avril say Anton Greenweal was staying here?"

"Yeah – not sure who he is, though. The name sounds vaguely familiar."

"He's the guy who won that reality show last year – 'King of the Island', I think it was called."

"Sorry, I don't watch that sort of thing. Avril seems to think he's taken a shine to her, though."

"She should be so lucky!"

"There's no need to get personal! She may be just his type."

"I wasn't referring to her looks; and I doubt it. One of the reasons he became famous was because he was openly gay throughout the contest: the first gay bloke to win it. His partner's here, too – he was the bloke in the corridor when the housekeeper first brought us in."

"Poor old Avril. Stars in her eyes turning to dust."

"What next?" asked Giash. "Dr Paxton's taken samples from them all. How much longer are we going to keep them here? We'll have to give them something to eat soon."

"I'll ask DI Yates. Personally, I think we should let them go. We can ask them not to leave the town without notifying us – not that any of them look as if they're about to go on a world tour."

"They need to keep their mouths shut, too. No talking to the Press."

Accompanied by Isobel Lawrence, Tim had been doing the rounds of the cottages. He'd talked to all the inmates, explained to them what had happened, asked them to keep calm and said there were refreshments on the way. He'd ordered a police catering van to bring coffee and sandwiches. He didn't want the kitchen to be used again until Forensics had examined it and bringing in commercial caterers was out of the question. He knew the Press would get wind of the deaths eventually, but he wanted them kept under wraps for as long as possible. Besides, there was every sign that Bemrose's murder was an inside job, so the fewer outsiders allowed access to the site, the better. He'd already sent for two more uniforms.

"Who else is there now?" he asked Isobel, as they headed back to the house.

"Mr and Mrs Franklin are staying in the extension. That's all the guests. Then there's Anton Greenweal, Gordon's nephew and his . . . friend, Percy Forsyth. Or Forsyth-Jones, as he calls himself professionally. And Miss Gardner, but you know about her."

"And yourself," said Tim, smiling at her.

"Yes, and me. Of course," she replied stiffly, her mouth set in a line.

Andy met them as they came through the extension door.

"Could I have a word, sir?"

"I'll wait for you further along the corridor," Isobel Lawrence said. "I assume you'd like me to introduce you to the Franklins?"

"Yes – thank you, Mrs Lawrence."

She moved out of earshot.

"It's nothing very sensitive, sir. I just thought we might let the actors go home now? We've taken statements from them all and Dr Paxton has blood and urine samples. I can't think of a reason for keeping them here, except to make sure they don't leak to the Press."

"Did they all co-operate? With the samples, fingerprinting, statements, the lot?"

"Yes. I really don't think that any . . . "

"Let's keep an open mind on that, shall we?" said Tim sharply. "But I agree with you about letting them go. We'll get some squad cars to come and take them home. I'll warn them not to gossip about what's happened here."

Andy led the way along the corridor. They were opposite the door nearest the entrance when it burst open.

"Just how much longer are you going to keep us prisoner?" A powerfully-built man emerged almost at a run, as if he was squaring up to them. "My wife suffers with her nerves. No one's been to tell us what is going on – we've been cooped up in here for hours!"

Isobel Lawrence hurried back towards them.

"This is Mr Franklin," she said.

"So I gathered," said Tim curtly. "If you and your wife wouldn't mind waiting just a little bit longer, sir, I'll come and tell you all that I can. There will be some refreshments soon, too. Have you both seen Dr Paxton?"

"Yes," said Colin Franklin belligerently. "And we did co-operate, before you ask."

Mrs Lawrence retreated again.

"Thank you. We'll be back very soon. Now, if you wouldn't mind going back inside . . . "

Colin Franklin turned on his heel and disappeared into his room, slamming the door. Tim and Andy could hear raised voices, then the sound of muffled sobbing.

"Oddly overwrought, even in the circumstances," said Tim. "What do you think?"

"The whole set-up here is odd," said Andy. "I don't know what to think."

After Tim had given the actors a stern talk about confidentiality, he returned to the Franklins. Colin Franklin's attitude had changed completely – he was meek and subdued, just as the occupants of the cottages had been. Mrs Franklin had a careworn face which had probably once been beautiful. Their relationship was difficult to gauge – she seemed to defer to him, yet most of the time he pussyfooted around her as if creeping on eggshells. Tim promised not to make them wait longer in their room than was necessary.

"Now," Tim said to Mrs Lawrence, "there's just Anton Greenweal and his friend."

"And Miss Gardner."

"And Miss Gardner, as you say. And yourself." Tim wanted to see if Isobel Lawrence would set her mouth again when he spoke of interviewing her. He wasn't disappointed.

"If you'd just introduce me to Mr Greenweal and Mr . . . er . . . Forsyth, you can leave me to find Miss Gardner on my own. We don't need a preliminary briefing with you – you've heard what I've said to the others. Next we shall be interviewing everyone properly, including you. Is there somewhere convenient – private and preferably warm, where we can conduct the interviews?"

"The sitting-room would be best. I don't know how warm it is in there yet, but the cleaning staff will be here soon . . ."

"Cleaning staff? How many?"

"Oh, I think . . . just two, today. There were four here yesterday, but . . ."

"You must call them and tell them to stay away. Don't tell them why yet. We'll have to see them eventually, to take their fingerprints, but they mustn't come here this morning."

"All right. They'll want to know if they're getting paid . . ."

"That can be sorted out later," said Tim.

CHAPTER 59

T IM HAD TO brace himself for his interview with Patti but he knew he must do it now. Along with everyone else who'd been present on the island when the deaths had occurred, she was a suspect. He doubted she'd quite taken that in.

Patti was the most reliable witness they had and she'd already given Juliet a statement of what had happened at Holyrood. Juliet had shown it to Tim and he had skimmed through it with mounting disbelief. Four separate attacks, on four people, had taken place on the island during the previous evening, but no-one had called the police. Two of the men attacked were now dead. One of them, Gordon Bemrose, the owner of the Holyrood complex, had been assaulted twice in the evening before he was murdered in the night. The leader of the amateur dramatics group, Montagu Sykes, had also died, possibly from natural causes, but to Tim such a coincidence seemed doubtful: he thought Sykes had probably been murdered, too. A third victim of the attacks, Victor le Grange, was a gate-crasher, his presence officially unexplained, though it was likely he was having an affair with the student who was one of the 'guests'. There'd been a mysterious power cut that had lasted for at least half an hour and subsequent loss of telecommunications for the rest of the evening. Almost everyone present on the island overnight had slept heavily, all waking up late, some much the worse for wear. Drink or drugs? Tim had sent the jumble of dirty cups, plates and glasses left unwashed in the kitchen for analysis and hoped they would provide more clues. Following Professor Salkeld's comments, he was less hopeful that the blood and urine tests would yield evidence; if a 'date-rape' drug had been used, it would have left little trace by the morning, except, perhaps, in the two corpses. And was the amateur actors' impromptu 'sleep-over' genuinely accidental? If not, Montagu Sykes must have been a deliberate target; otherwise, if Gordon Bemrose was the only intended victim, why risk having so many more people on the premises when he was killed?

Patti had said the whole thing felt wrong from the start, but when Juliet asked her why she'd got mixed up in it at all, particularly as she clearly disliked her uncle, her reply was evasive. She'd said that she was "just helping out". It didn't square with the robust opinions she'd held about members of her dysfunctional family when she'd been his girlfriend.

The statement Juliet had taken from Patti provided a useful short-cut to getting a handle on how events had unfolded. Tim now wanted a formal statement about Patti's own movements since she'd arrived at Holyrood. Juliet would be present, but it would still be awkward.

Patti was still seated in the kitchen. Like the inmates of the cottages, she'd been supplied with tea from the police catering van. Tim had thought about and decided not to ask her to wait in the sitting-room with the others. She'd made it clear that she'd no affinity with them and, while he had to be careful not to give her too much special treatment, he wasn't prepared to be unkind.

He entered the kitchen ahead of Juliet and was stricken by

the wary look Patti gave him. She blinked it away when she saw Juliet.

"Patti," he said gently. "This is a formal interview. You understand?"

"You mean I'm a suspect now?" She shot the question back at him, but her voice was weary – resigned rather than indignant.

"Everyone who spent last night here is technically a suspect. It's a formality. You know that. You won't mind answering a few questions about your whereabouts? Just the same ones we're asking everyone else."

"No," said Patti uninvitingly.

"Thank you. What time did you arrive yesterday?"

"Late morning. I'm not sure of the exact time. It was just after Anton and Percy. They came for breakfast, if that's any help."

"We'll check with them. I understand the guests didn't begin to arrive until late afternoon. What did you do until then?"

"I mostly worked on my talk. Gordon wanted me to take the first slot in the formal programme."

"The talk was about forensics?"

"Yes. I planned it to be quite interactive, with hand-outs and video clips. At various times, Anton, Percy and Montagu Sykes helped me with it, with voice projection and stuff. In between, I tried to be sociable. When the guests started arriving, I joined them for tea."

"You said to Juliet 'the whole thing felt wrong'. What did you mean by that? When did you start noticing things seemed strange?"

"Right from the start, I suppose. But I wasn't surprised

278

– Gordon's always been a fly-by-night. He sails – sailed – close to the law. He's had brushes with the police, some minor convictions, I'm sure you'll find them. It was obvious the crime weekend was entirely about making money. He called it an 'introductory offer', but you can bet he was making something out of it. He was doing the whole thing on a shoestring – most of the people helping weren't getting paid, or if they were, just a pittance. Anton, Percy and I certainly weren't; I'm not sure about the amateur actors. He may have offered them a small fee."

"Did you want to help him?"

"Not really," said Patti, her face shutting.

"Ok, we'll come back to that. What about the guests? What was your impression of them?"

"A pretty mixed bunch. And – what's really odd – I didn't get the feeling that anyone was much interested in the crime weekend. The activities, I mean."

"So why do you think they were there?"

Patti shrugged.

"You said the first attack on Mr Bemrose was before dinner. You were one of the people who found him and took him back to the house. About what time was that?"

"Not long before dinner – Percy had been looking for Gordon because he'd locked away the red wine. Dinner was at 7.30. My talk was supposed to precede it, but that went by the board after we found Gordon."

"So were you with Percy?"

"I was when we found him. Before that I'd been to see Anton – my cousin – in his cottage. He opened a bottle of wine and then Percy came to share it, too. Percy and I had both heard a strange noise coming from the waste land at the end of the cottages, but we didn't pay much attention to it until we were all on our way back to the house. We found Gordon there – he'd been beaten and tied up."

"Why didn't you call us?"

"Gordon wouldn't hear of any 'fuss', as he called it. He wouldn't even see a doctor. He didn't want anything to spoil his event."

"Was he frightened? Did he have any idea who'd done it?"

"He wouldn't talk about it. He did seem a bit frightened, but annoyed even more. He was taking it out on us, especially Anton."

"So you all just carried on as if nothing had happened? What about the other guests? Did they find the attack unsettling?"

"We didn't tell them about it. We all had dinner – Gordon joined late – and then we started on the evening's programme. I was on first, doing my forensics talk. He was jumpy then. He told me to hurry up. Then there was the power cut. Oh, just before that one of the guests came in late – Lizzie Fox. She'd tripped and cut her knee."

"Was she attacked, too?"

"I don't think so. I think she just fell. She arrived just before the power cut. She reckoned she'd seen someone and they'd frightened her, which was why she fell, but she'd been drinking. She could have imagined it, or made it up to disguise that she'd been tight."

"So was everyone in the ballroom when the power was cut?"

"No. Montagu Sykes had gone outside for some air. And Richard Renwick, as well."

"Sykes was the man who died in the ballroom?"

"Yes. Colin Franklin went outside to look for them, while I helped Gordon down to the cellar where the fuse-box was, because he was still a bit shaky on his feet. Colin and Percy both offered to go, but he wouldn't let them. He got quite nasty about it. Someone suggested Colin should go and look for Montagu and Richard if he wanted to do something useful."

"So was it pitch black everywhere?"

"No. We found some torches and a storm-lantern. One or two people used their mobile torches. The storm lantern was put in the ballroom. Colin had a torch and so did Gordon and I."

"Who was in the ballroom? Everyone except you and Gordon, Colin Franklin, Sykes and Renwick?"

"Victor le Grange wasn't there – but everyone thought he'd left the island by then. Except Amelia Baker – she must have known he hadn't gone."

"Patti doesn't actually know who was in the ballroom when she was with Gordon in the cellar," Juliet pointed out.

"Well, yes," said Tim irritably, "but it's le Grange I'm interested in at the moment. Where was he if he wasn't in the ballroom?"

"I assume he was in the cottage that Amelia Baker was sharing with Dora Westerman. I didn't see him until Gordon and I returned to the ballroom after he fixed the fuse."

"He'd been attacked, too?"

"Yes. But he wasn't badly hurt – I think he was just putting it on to enjoy the attention. And, I suppose, using the attack to cover up the fact that he wasn't supposed to be there."

"When was Gordon attacked again?"

"While we were in the cellar. But he wouldn't admit to it.

Said he'd fallen and hurt himself."

"But you didn't believe him?"

"He had a stab wound in his neck. Fairly superficial, but quite nasty."

"So there was someone else in the cellar besides you and Gordon?"

"I thought there was. He said there couldn't have been."

"If there was someone there, how could they have got out again? Was the door left unlocked?"

"I think so – yes, it was. It had been locked before we went in – Gordon had trouble with the key and gave it to me – but I didn't lock it when we came out again. I was too busy looking after him."

"So then what did you do?"

"I took Gordon to the ballroom and we cleaned up his wound. And then Colin Franklin came in with Montagu Sykes and Richard Renwick."

"Meaning everyone was in the ballroom then, including Victor le Grange?"

"Yes, I think so."

"And then you all just carried on as if nothing had happened?" Tim had allowed the sarcasm to creep into his voice. Juliet saw that his change in tone was not lost on Patti.

"Patti couldn't have been responsible for that decision," she said gently. "Everyone must have agreed."

"We did agree," said Patti, "though some of us were more reluctant than others. Richard Renwick wanted to go home there and then. Anton would have packed in then, too, if . . ." she paused.

"Go on," said Tim. "If what?"

"If he hadn't promised Gordon he would do it," Patti finished lamely. "Gordon was still very keen to run the weekend as planned."

"So the play went ahead? How did that go?"

"I . . . I can't remember. To tell you the truth, I don't remember much about the rest of the evening. We had some more drinks – wine and beer, and I think there was tea and coffee as well. We'd been having drinks on and off the whole evening. I didn't think I'd drunk too much . . . but I don't remember going to bed and I was certainly not well when I woke up this morning."

"And when you did get up this morning, what did you do?"

"I went to the bathroom – my room is one of the ones that doesn't have an en suite. Then back to my room to dress. Then I came downstairs. I thought it was strange that no-one was up before me, because I was late down myself."

"Did you go into Gordon Bemrose's room?"

"Certainly not!" Patti flashed anger for the first time since the interview had begun. Juliet felt relieved: it was painful to see Patti as dejected as she had been.

"Did you see anyone either while you were upstairs or on your way downstairs?"

"No. No-one. The first person I saw was Percy, while I was wondering whether to go into the ballroom or not."

"How did he seem?"

"The same as usual. Cheerful, helpful. A little bit subversive, in a nice way."

"What do you mean by that, exactly?"

"Well we had a bit of a laugh at the expense of the actors who were dossing in there. Nothing malicious."

"And you'd remembered the actors were sleeping there, even though you say your memory of the later part of the evening was hazy?"

"I . . . yes. I didn't forget everything . . ." ·

"But you did forget some crucial details, such as when and how you got to bed?"

"Yes."

"Why did you want to go into the ballroom?"

"I didn't, actually. I knew it would be pretty horrible in there. I just thought someone should do something to wake up the household. Percy offered to help."

"You had no inkling that Montagu Sykes had died?"

"No."

"But you were the one who found him?"

"That's not quite correct. His face was exposed by one of his colleagues – he'd burrowed into his sleeping-bag. But I was the first person to realise he was dead."

"Why was that?"

"it's obvious, isn't it?" said Patti impatiently. "I've got more medical knowledge than the others."

"Of course," said Tim coolly. "When did you find out Gordon Bemrose was also dead?"

"When Mrs Lawrence came downstairs. She found him. It was only a few minutes after I called you about Montagu Sykes."

Juliet shot Tim a look. He didn't meet her eye.

"Yes. I told you to call DC Carstairs."

"And I did as you said." Patti was defiant now.

"Right, that's all for now," said Tim. "Thank you for your co-operation." Even to himself, he sounded like a stuffed shirt.

"My pleasure," said Patti, with irony. "Can you tell me something?"

"Sure."

"You seriously don't think I killed Gordon, do you?"

Tim looked at her levelly.

"You know how murder investigations work, Ms Gardner. We have to treat all witnesses equally."

"Really, Tim . . . "

"But just as a matter of interest, did you have a reason for wanting him dead? Something stronger than not liking him very much, I mean?"

Patti lowered her head.

"No," she said, almost in a whisper.

Juliet was astonished. She'd heard many guilty people protest their innocence – and most had been more convincing than Patti was now.

CHAPTER 60

TIM HAD TOLD Andy Carstairs to call Ricky MacFadyen to ask him to help with the interviews. Ricky turned up half an hour later in an extremely bad mood.

"Wasn't there anyone else you could call on?" he grumbled. "I'm supposed to be off this weekend."

"So are we," Tim said, looking at Juliet. "Andy's the only one officially on duty."

"I said I'd watch the cadets' football match later today," Ricky continued. "Any chance of getting there?"

"I doubt it," said Tim. "We're dealing with two deaths here, one certainly a murder, and several assaults."

"Christ!" said Ricky. "What kind of place is this?"

"That's a good question," Tim answered wryly. "Perhaps you can help us find out."

"Does Superintendent Thornton know?"

"Not yet, but we'll have to tell him. Why do you ask?"

"He said he'd support the cadets today, too. He's going to notice if I'm not there."

"We'll tell him before the match starts," said Tim. "Andy, can you fill Ricky in on what we know? Then we can start interviewing in pairs. Juliet, you work with Andy and I'll work with Ricky. Are Tandy and Chakrabati out there on the gate?"

"Yes," said Ricky. "They're being quite discreet. You'd hardly notice them unless you tried to drive over the bridge."

"Good," said Tim. "The Press are bound to get wind of

this sooner or later, but we're not ready for them yet. And Thornton will certainly want to be involved then."

"Where should we do our interviews!" asked Andy

"This house is full of interesting little rooms. There's a sitting-room where the crime event guests are waiting. It has two little rooms leading off it. We can use those."

"There are two lots of married couples," said Juliet. "Do we interview them together or individually?"

Tim hesitated.

"Individually," he said. "It'll take longer, but it will be interesting if they don't tell the same story. We'll use Patti's account as our standard. Anyone deviating significantly from that will need questioning more closely."

"Even though Patti's also a suspect?" said Juliet.

"Yes. We have to start somewhere. And we can use discrepancies to challenge Patti, if need be, as well as the other way round. And Andy . . ." he added, as Andy was turning away.

"Yes, boss?"

"Get the cellar door sealed off with scene of crime tape, will you? We're going to have to do a thorough search down there. Ricky, I'll be with you shortly."

Andy and Ricky had barely left the kitchen when Juliet's phone began to ring.

"Hello? Oh, Jake, I'm sorry," she said, painfully aware that Tim was listening. "Oh, would you? You know I promised Mr Trawford. I'll do my best to come myself a bit later."

Tim tried to look uninterested. He succeeded better than he could have hoped to fake when his own phone also rang. He had immediately recognised the number that flashed up on the screen.

"Superintendent Thornton! I was about to call you."

Juliet could hear a very cross voice booming out.

"I didn't realise you were on duty today, sir. Of course I would have asked DC Carstairs to inform you. Perhaps he left the station before you arrived."

This elicited a further furious response.

"Two deaths, sir, one certainly murder, and some assaults – and other strange happenings, too. No, not yet. I thought you'd like to contact them yourself, sir. Dealing with the media has always been one of your strengths."

The voice lowered a few decibels, but still sounded peevish.

"Yes, I know we've just got on top of the crime figures, sir. Apart from the hare coursing, that is. I know – it's unfortunate. Yes, I'm certain that one is a murder. Yes, sir, I'll remember that."

Tim sighed as the call was terminated.

"That was Superintendent Thornton," he said unnecessarily. "He hasn't got much in common with Professor Salkeld, but there is one thing: they both seem to think that this murder's our fault, deliberately plotted to spoil their weekend."

CHAPTER 61

INTERVIEWING THE GUESTS, plus le Grange, took several hours. No-one's story deviated much from the account Patti had provided. Amelia Baker was vague about the early part of the evening, particularly on why she had arrived late, but no doubt that was because she and le Grange had been canoodling somewhere. According to her, she'd barely spoken to Gordon Bemrose during the time between her arrival and his death; they had no reason to doubt this. Victor le Grange was sketchy on detail, too, and affected to have got trapped at Holyrood by mistake after he'd dropped Amelia off. His main concern was blatantly obvious: that neither his wife nor his head of department should find out where he had been. He was obviously guilty of playing away, but that in itself made it unlikely that he was the murderer. Not only did he and Amelia have no discernible motive, they had every reason for not drawing attention to themselves. Getting mixed up in a murder enquiry would have been the last thing they wanted.

Despite the several attacks, Tim didn't think this was the work of a psychopath. Motive was therefore what the police were trying to establish, but by the end of the day they'd collected more motives than they'd bargained for. That final question they'd asked Patti had been repeated at each of the subsequent interviews, with surprising results. No less than three people – Margarett and Colin Franklin, separately, and

Dora Westerman – admitted that they detested Gordon Bemrose and were happy to see him dead.

Margarett Franklin had been the first to confess this. She'd needed no persuasion: as soon as Tim had asked the question, her bile had come tumbling out.

"We had a daughter, Colin and me. Cicely. A lovely girl. Practical, like Colin, not academic. She got a job with Gordon Bemrose, working in a pop-up shop he opened before last Christmas. We don't know what happened, but he did something to her – we don't know what. She couldn't bear it. She drowned herself. In the river here. Almost a year ago."

Cicely Franklin. Tim remembered the case now. The girl had a history of depression. Gordon Bemrose must have testified, but the coroner had deemed it an open-and-shut case – he hadn't laid the blame at any door, except – Tim racked his brains – had he suggested the parents were at fault? That Cicely was a vulnerable girl who shouldn't have been encouraged to work away from home? He'd get someone to dig out the coroner's report.

"Mrs Franklin, why did you and your husband come here? Was it to kill Gordon Bemrose?"

"No!" she cried out, her eyes wild with alarm. "We wouldn't do anything like that. We did want to harm him – to embarrass him in some way. Colin was planning a showdown later in the weekend."

"What kind of 'showdown'?"

Margarett Franklin's expression dulled. All energy visibly seeped out of her.

"I don't know. You'll have to ask him." She burst into tears.

She passed Colin on her way out, still weeping. He squared up to Tim belligerently as soon as he entered the room.

"Did you have to upset her? You can see how fragile she is!"

"I'm sorry, Mr Franklin, we . . . "

"She told you then, did she? About Cicely?"

"Yes. I remember the case now. Very sad."

"'Very sad!'" Colin Franklin mimicked. "You have no idea!"

"Your wife has told us that you came for the crime weekend because you intended to embarrass Gordon Bemrose. How did you plan to do that?"

Colin Franklin took a seat. He sat silently frowning, his arms folded.

"Mr Franklin?"

"Ok," Colin said at length. "I'll tell you the truth. Margarett thought I was going to give him a bit of a scare, drop him in it in front of the others. I had to tell her that, but I was going to top him. I was just looking for an opportunity to do it without getting caught – for her sake, not mine, I'd have swung for the bastard. But I didn't kill him. Someone else got there first."

"You realise what you've just told us still makes you a suspect?"

"Yeah. But it wasn't me. I'd like to know who it was – I'd shake him by the hand."

"Him? What makes you think it was a man?"

"Well, it wasn't a woman, was it? He was thick-set, quite strong, I'd say."

Dora Westerman was interviewed by Juliet and Andy.

"Miss Westerman, how long have you been interested in crime weekends? Have you been to one before?"

"No. I don't have the money to fritter on this sort

of thing and, to answer your question, no interest whatsoever."

"So why are you here?"

Dora Westerman's intelligent eyes glittered like a cat's after catching prey. She set her mouth in a rictus-like grin.

"It's quite simple. I came here to kill Gordon Bemrose."

"Did you kill him?"

"No. I was going to wait until further into the weekend. I was enjoying making him feel ill-at-ease. I don't think he had quite placed me, but he was certainly uncomfortable when he saw me. And I probably didn't try very hard to conceal how much I despised him."

"Why did you hate him so much?"

"My aunt lived here for many years – long before Gordon came – in the end cottage, the one I'm staying in now. I wouldn't say she was a dear old lady – she'd grown rather strange as she'd aged – but I loved her when I was young and what he put her through was inhuman. He hounded her and practically evicted her from the house, persuaded social services that she needed taking into care. She didn't last for six months after she was forced out."

CHAPTER 62

THERE WERE NO more confessions, but some of those who didn't confess were even trickier to interview than those who did. Richard and Sonia Renwick, for example. Like all the others, they were interviewed separately and each of their stories corroborated the other's to such a surprising extent that they could have been rehearsed. Both swore the crime weekend had been a gift from Sonia's mother, a break away from the kids and household cares to revive a marriage that had fallen into difficulties. It could have been any activity, or simply a weekend in a hotel doing nothing in particular. Sonia had been intrigued by the whodunnit idea; Richard, as both freely admitted, had been indifferent to what they did.

"So why did you choose Holyrood? There are plenty of other events like this one; it wasn't even tried and tested."

"I think that was part of the charm," said Sonia.

"It was cheap," said Richard.

Neither admitted to knowing Gordon Bemrose before their arrival. They vehemently asserted they had no reason to wish him ill. The weekend had got off to a bad start and they'd agreed with each other not to stay; they had been planning to leave when Sykes' and Gordon's bodies were discovered.

But obviously that Gordon had organised a duff – and at times alarming – event wasn't a reason to murder him.

"We just wanted to get the hell out of here," as Richard put it.

"Tell me about the attack," said Tim.

"Nothing much to tell, really," said Richard. Was he being evasive? "It wasn't really an attack so much as attempt to incapacitate us. Sykes and me, I mean."

"What happened?"

"It was very dark. Sykes fell part of the way down the bank . . . "

"The riverbank?"

"Yes. We thought we'd heard a noise. We went to take a look."

"You haven't explained why you were outside in the first place. As you say, it was pitch black and very cold. What tempted you out there?"

"Sykes went out for a cigarette. I joined him because Mrs Fox had rushed into the ballroom bleeding. She said she'd had a fall. I don't like blood – seeing her made me feel quite queasy. So I decided to go out for a while, get some air. I bumped into Sykes. He said he could hear a noise coming from the river and we agreed to investigate."

"Why?"

"Strange things had been happening. Everyone was jumpy. We wanted to get to the bottom of it."

"You say Mr Sykes 'seemed to fall'. What did you do when you realised?"

"I jumped down to the place where I thought he'd landed. Someone tripped me up. They didn't assault me, but I think Sykes was punched. I couldn't see him properly, but I knew he was there, sitting on the ground. Before either of us knew what was happening, we'd been roped together."

"Did you see the person who did it?"

"Obviously not."

"Do you think the person who assailed you and Mr Sykes was after him, rather than you?"

"I can't answer that; but he must have been a local man, otherwise he'd never have known how to get around this place. I can't think why anyone out here would be interested in me. I'd never set foot in this town before and I certainly don't intend to come back!"

"You hadn't met Mr Sykes before?"

"I've just said that, haven't I?"

"Not in as many words. Was there, your wife excepted, anyone here whom you'd met before yesterday afternoon?"

"No. Certainly not."

Tim had rather been looking forward to interviewing Ava Dack. He had her marked down as the sort of feisty, uncompromising woman who could add welcome fireworks to a long day of interviews. He wasn't disappointed. Ava came storming into the interview room and plonked her considerable weight on a slender, straight-backed chair. It creaked audibly. Ava's thighs, encased in shiny black tights over which she'd placed an alarmingly short black leather skirt, bulged over the sides of the velvet-upholstered seat. Her feet were shod in bright red pixie boots with kitten heels.

"Are we going to get our money back?" she demanded without preamble.

"I'm sorry, I . . . "

"We paid good money for this weekend, Lizzie and me. And it won't happen now, will it?"

Tim had thought he was unshockable, but when he realised what Ava meant he was astonished.

"Ms Dack . . . "

"It's Mrs. Mis-sus," Ava snapped back.

"Mrs Dack, I'm sorry." Tim was at his frostiest. "I have no idea whether you can expect a refund. If it's important to you, I would suggest you refer it to Mr Bemrose's solicitor. If he's not administering the estate, he'll know who is."

"Ha!" said Ava. "It'll be like getting blood out of a stone, I expect!"

"Could we concentrate on the task in hand?" said Tim. "Can you describe your movements yesterday evening?"

"I just joined in everything, like everybody else. Lizzie, too. Except she came back a bit late after we'd been to the cottage to change. She'd had a bilious attack."

"You mean she vomited?"

"If you must put it like that. We'd had a few drinks and I thought perhaps they hadn't agreed with her. But now you mention it, it could have been something else," said Ava archly.

"What do you mean by that?"

"Well, everyone was out cold this morning, wasn't they? Maybe me and Lizzie was just early victims."

"Were you ill, too?"

"Not as such, but I did feel a bit queer, like. Got the constitution of a ox, I have. I probably shrugged it off better than most."

"Why did you come here this weekend? Is this type of thing a hobby of yours?"

"No, never done anything like it before. Probably won't want to again, neither."

"So why did you come?" Tim persisted.

Surprisingly, Ava was gobsmacked.

"I . . . we . . . Lizzie and I thought it would be a bit of a laugh, I suppose," she said eventually.

"I see. How did you find out about it?"

"I think Reggie found it . . . or Jackson. No, it was Reggie His treat, he said."

"Reggie being your husband?"

"Yes, and Jackson's Lizzie's."

"Where are they both this weekend?"

Ava had recovered her aplomb. She sniggered.

"It don't pay to question them too closely. Could be up to owt, they could. I don't mean nothing illegal, like," she added as an afterthought. Tim saw she was watching him closely from under her curled eyelashes, trying to clock him, no doubt.

"I have no reason to suppose you do," he said, levelly.

CHAPTER 63

TIM AND RICKY had finished with Anton Greenweal and were about to interview Percy Forsyth. Greenweal had been sulky and a little shifty. Pushed to say why he had agreed to help out with the crime weekend when he so clearly disliked his uncle, he'd admitted that he owed Bemrose a substantial amount of money and had been put under pressure to contribute.

"What did you think he would do if you refused?"

"Not much doubt about that. The old bastard would have ratcheted up the interest."

"Would you say that could be a motive for murder?" Tim said evenly.

"Probably," Anton shot back, "for some people. Perhaps for me, even, if he'd goaded me enough. But the method – what do you people call it – the MO? The MO cuts me out. I couldn't stick a knife in someone to save my life!" He laughed theatrically, a nervous little whinny that quickly strangled itself.

"What about Mr Sykes? He wasn't stabbed."

"Oh, was Sykes murdered, too? Well, he deserved it for being such a rotten actor." Anton whinnied again. "Only joking. I had nothing against Sykes. Didn't even meet the man until yesterday. And to be frank I wasn't surprised that he and his merry little pack turned out to be so shambolic. How does the saying go? If you pay peanuts, you get monkeys!"

"Unpleasant character," said Ricky, when they'd let Anton go.

"Yes," Tim agreed, "but I doubt he's a killer. He doesn't have the backbone, whatever the 'MO'. Forsyth interests me more. I'd like to know how he sees his role in this set-up. He's Anton's boyfriend, of course, and obviously props him up emotionally. He also seems happy to play second fiddle to Anton the famous actor. But I wonder? He's full of bonhomie and strikes me as quite a resourceful sort of guy, too. Not lacking in brain, either. I think he'd be more than a match for Gordon Bemrose if he decided to take him on."

"You mean, get money out of him in some way? Or help to reduce Anton's debt? But if you're right, why kill the bloke? It's unlikely that Percy's one of the beneficiaries of his will."

"Good point . . . and the sooner we get hold of the will, the better. Hopefully it will provide a few clues. In the meantime, let's try and get as much out of Percy as we can. I've still got a feeling that he's mixed up in the deaths in some way."

Percy smiled conspiratorially at the two policemen as he entered the room, as if he were one of them and not a suspect.

"How can I help?" he asked, spreading his hands expansively as he took a seat before it was offered. "I'll do anything within my power, obviously."

"Thank you, sir. Tell us about yesterday evening," said Tim.

"Which part of it?"

"I hope we'll cover most of it eventually. But let's start with the arrival of the amateur players, shall we?"

"Ok. Sykes arrived first. The rest of his lot came later. In the meantime, he and Anton and I gave Patti some coaching."

"Coaching?"

"She was nervous about her presentation. Unnecessarily, as it happens. But she wanted to run through it with us."

"And then?"

"The other actors came. They were a rum lot – well, you've seen them, you know." Again, the conspiratorial look. "One of the girls was kicking up a fuss about being hungry so I went to ask Isobel if she'd make them some sandwiches. Isobel told me Gordon had disappeared and she needed him to come and open the red wine – he'd got it locked away somewhere. So I went to look for him. I couldn't find him, though I did hear a strange noise . . ."

"Did you go to investigate the noise?"

"Not straight away. I carried on to the cottage Anton and I were staying in and joined him and Patti there for a drink. That's when Patti said she'd heard a noise, too. So we all went to investigate."

"After you'd had a drink?"

"Yes. It didn't feel as if it was urgent; in fact, we wondered if we were imagining things – we were joking about ghosts."

"But you found Mr Bemrose, when you looked?"

"Yes. He was lying on the waste land at the end of the cottages. He'd been tied up. Someone had given him quite a pasting."

"So I understand. Was it you?"

Percy sat up straighter in his chair.

"I beg your pardon?"

"Was it you? Did you give Mr Bemrose a 'pasting'?"

For one moment Percy looked rattled. Then he smoothed his features and smiled wryly.

"Of course it wasn't me. Why would I have wanted to hurt Gordon? Any more than anyone else did, I mean."

"You tell me, Mr Forsyth. As you suggest, many people present last night may have wanted to hurt him. Not everyone got the opportunity. You were apparently alone for some time between Mrs Lawrence's asking you to look for him and when you turned up at the cottage to meet Anton and Patti. Can you tell us exactly where you went?"

Percy's smile faded.

"Not in so many words, but I could show you. I walked round the island looking for likely places where Gordon might have gone."

"But not the waste land where you eventually found him?"

"No."

"Even though that was adjacent to the area where he'd been putting up fairy lights earlier?"

"I . . . No. I didn't think of that."

"And even though you said you heard 'strange noises' coming from there. You were out looking for Mr Bemrose, yet when you heard a strange sound, you didn't connect it with the fact that he had disappeared? In fact, you thought it so unimportant that you carried on to the cottage to have a drink with Anton and Patti."

"I suppose it does sound odd when you put it like that. But, to be honest, I wasn't worried about Gordon – not until we found him, that is. He's always been a tricky character and totally governed by fixing his eye to the main chance. I thought Isobel was fussing unnecessarily – that he'd show up when it suited him."

"He'd been assaulted – given a 'pasting', as you put it. Why didn't you call the police?"

"I don't think any of us thought of it. Well, I suppose Patti must have. But he was being so obstreperous – our main aim was to get him back to the house. And then he insisted that the evening must carry on as planned."

Tim nodded curtly. He allowed a strained silence to elapse. Percy was trying to remain calm, but he looked as if he was on the back foot now.

"And later, when you'd found him and things were more or less back to normal – everyone had had dinner and the evening's events had started – there was a power cut. According to Patti, you were the first to take control, organising torches and preventing panic."

Percy relaxed again. He gave a 'what can you do' shrug.

"To be honest, there was no-one else. They were a pretty hopeless bunch when it came to practical stuff."

Tim noted that Percy had said "to be honest" twice in the space of a few minutes.

"Is that the secret of your success? Do you manage the practicalities of your relationship with Mr Greenweal?"

Percy was flummoxed.

"Yes, if you must know. But I don't see why . . ."

"Let's go back to the power cut. You were pretty quick off the mark to volunteer to go down to the cellar. Why was that?"

Percy shrugged again.

"Just helping out. I wanted to get the show back on the road as soon as possible. And Gordon wasn't really up to it – Patti didn't think so, either."

"So while they were in the cellar, you went back to the ballroom to wait with the others?"

"Yes."

"Did anything happen there? Did anyone say anything you found strange?"

"That depends on what you mean by 'strange'. The whole evening was pretty strange. Colin Franklin came in with Victor le Grange after the power cut. Le Grange told us some cock-and-bull story about wanting to return Amelia Baker's phone. It was obvious he'd intended to spend the night with her. Somebody mugged him in the darkness. He wasn't badly hurt – he made the most of it to cover up the fact that he'd been found out."

"Another assault – yet still you didn't call the police? Even though you'd cast yourself as the 'practical one'?

"Couldn't, by that stage. No-one could get a signal."

"Colin Franklin went out again, didn't he, to continue his search for Montagu Sykes and Richard Renwick? Where were you while he was doing that?"

"I stayed with the others. All of the time."

"And aside from Dr le Grange's somewhat dramatic reappearance, nothing unremarkable happened?"

"No, I wouldn't say so."

"Colin eventually found Montagu and Richard, didn't he? Can you remember the time when he brought them back?"

"Not the exact time, no, but it was just after the lights went back on again. Around 9 p.m., I'd guess."

"But you still couldn't get a mobile signal?"

"No, I don't think so."

"Did you try?"

"I can't remember. Somehow, we all agreed to carry on with the evening as planned, only later than planned, of course."

"Please think very carefully, Mr Forsyth, about what happened next, because so far no-one has been able to tell us."

"Not even Patti? I thought you were using her story as your gold standard."

Rather unwisely, Percy Forsyth was smirking.

"Miss Gardner can't remember much about events after the performance started."

"Really? Saintly Patti? You do surprise me!" Again the smirk.

"I'm not sure what you mean by that, but if you can yourself remember the sequence of events, we'd be grateful if you would describe them to us."

"Not much to tell, really. The performance went ahead. It was a truncated version of *Arsenic and Old Lace*. The acting, aside from Anton's, was as atrocious as we'd expected. Gordon's big surprise, that he would himself be 'killed' on set to provide clues for the whodunnit exercise the next day, turned into a bit of a damp squib after all that had happened. A bit too close to home, I supposed."

"By that you mean it was no longer amusing, now that several people had actually been attacked?"

"Yes."

"And then what? What happened after the performance?"

"We tried to call for taxis for the amateurs – we certainly couldn't get a signal at that point – and it was decided they should stay the night. I went with Isobel to find bedding for them all. Everyone else went to bed. I spent some time helping to make up their beds and then I went to bed, too."

"Did Mrs Lawrence go to bed?"

"I don't know. I think she went home. She does have a room here that she uses sometimes, but she'd said she was not planning to stay. I don't know why. She lives very close to here."

"And Victor le Grange?"

"What about him?"

"Did he spend the night in the ballroom with the actors?"

Percy Forsyth rolled his eyes.

"What do you think?"

"Are you saying he spent the night with Miss Baker, in the cottage she shared with Miss Westerman?"

"I don't know that for sure. But he certainly wasn't in the ballroom when we were making up the beds . . . and he's still here now, isn't he?"

"Indeed. So you went to bed. Did you sleep well?"

"Reasonably well."

"Nothing woke you up in the night?"

"Not that I can recall."

"What about Mr Greenweal?"

"He had a bit of a disturbed night. He'd had more to drink than I had."

"How do you know he had a rough night, if you were able to sleep yourself?"

Percy Forsyth grinned.

"He told me so this morning. Not one to hold back on telling you, is Anton, if things aren't going smoothly for him."

"So when you woke up, you weren't suffering from the headache and nausea that seem to have afflicted everyone else?"

"No. I didn't have all that much to drink, actually. I slept heavily, but when I got up I felt fine. Patti and I were the first to surface."

"What time did you get up?"

"I don't know. Not long before I saw Patti."

"You met Patti outside the ballroom?"

"Yes. She was feeling a bit groggy. She didn't relish going into the ballroom – I think she knew it would be a bit squalid. So I went in with her."

"What happened then?"

"I suggested that it was time everyone woke up. Eventually they started moving, all but Montagu Sykes. One of the girls – Avril, I think, uncovered his face and his head lolled to one side. Patti immediately realised he was dead."

"So she said. She also said you mainly stayed with the actors after that. Did you at any point go to any other part of the building?"

"Only the kitchen, to make tea."

"Did you go upstairs?"

"No." Percy looked Tim directly in the eye. "I hadn't been upstairs since Anton and I moved our stuff out from our room and down to the cottage the day before."

"I see. That's all I want to ask you, for now."

"Can I ask a question?"

"Of course."

"Why the grilling? I'm not under oath."

Tim gave him a long look.

"We're just collecting statements at present," he said. "Yours will be given to you to approve and sign. You're right, you're not under oath; but, if you sign the statement, you're agreeing that it's true. If it's later established that you've been lying, naturally that compromises you."

Percy Forsyth got to his feet.

"I can go then, can I?"

"Yes, but please don't leave the premises yet. We'll tell you as soon as that's possible."

CHAPTER 64

ANDY AND JULIET had finished their interviews.
Juliet came to find Tim as he and Ricky were taking
a break.

"I don't think we can do much more here now, do you?
Shall we let them all go home?"

Tim sighed.

"You're probably right. The interviews have been disappointing, in a way. They haven't thrown up any discrepancies.
And we've discovered more possible motives than we have
crimes, but no-one really stands out as a suspect. If we let
them go, we'll first have to make sure they've all given us their
correct contact details and notify us if they want to spend
the night away from home; and tell them they can't leave the
country . . . and all the rest of it."

"Andy and I will take care of that. Then is it all right if we
go, too, and let Forensics get on with their job?"

"Not like you to be in such a hurry to get away," said Tim,
meaningfully, "but yes, you can. I've asked Peterborough to
send a SOCO team. It would be awkward for Patti's team to
do it. Probably in breach of some rule or other, too."

"Patti is free to go home, as well?"

"Certainly. No-one can stay here, that's for sure. What's
the matter, Ricky?" Ricky MacFadyen had just grabbed at the
sleeve of his jacket.

"We haven't interviewed Mrs Lawrence yet," he said.

307

"Christ, how could I have forgotten that? No offence, Ricky, but would you mind if Juliet helps me with her? I think she might be quite a tough nut to crack."

"Sure," said Ricky, wryly, "I know when I'm outclassed."

"Really, Tim, what a put-down! And none of us has cracked any tough nuts today. As you said, we haven't got very far at all. I really think Ricky should do it."

"Well, I'd like you to do it," said Tim, his tone dangerous.

"Yes, sir," said Juliet.

Tim listened for but could not detect for certain a twang of irony in her voice. "Andy and Ricky, will you go and talk to everyone we've interviewed? Tell them the conditions on which we're letting them go?"

After they'd departed, Tim was gentler with Juliet.

"I'm sorry if you don't want to stay. I genuinely need your help with Mrs Lawrence. You'll be able to pick up stuff that none of the rest of us is likely to. You've got the best antennae."

"It's not so much that I don't want to stay - I need to see Sally."

"Who?"

"Sally, the dog I rescued yesterday. The one who'd been injured hare coursing. The vet amputated one of her forelegs last night. I've seen her briefly today, but I promised him I'd go back again."

"I see. Was that the vet you were talking to earlier?"

"No, it was Jake. He's going to help with Sally, too."

Tim suppressed a smile. Juliet rarely talked about Jake - Tim and Katrin were bursting to know more - but Katrin had long ago decided that Jake was a 'good thing', which was all the endorsement Tim needed. He waited for a couple of seconds, but Juliet didn't volunteer any more information.

"Right, let's get on with this, then. We'll push through it as fast as we can."

Isobel Lawrence may have shown signs of emotion earlier in the day, but by the time she came to be interviewed her composure was icily assured. She stood silently, pulling herself up to her full height as she entered the interview room and waited to be invited to take a seat; when one was offered, she adopted the pose of a Victorian high society matron and sat with her back absolutely straight, her ankles neatly crossed beneath her chair.

"Mrs Lawrence, thank you for waiting," Tim said. She inclined her head graciously. "And I'm sorry for your loss. You must have known Mr Bemrose for a long time?"

"Quite a long time. About twelve years, I think."

"Did you know him before he bought the island – Holyrood, as he called it?"

"Yes, but not well." She paused. "Although I've come to realise no-one knew Gordon all that well."

"He and others generally referred to you as his 'housekeeper'. What did that involve? Can you tell us what the employment arrangements between you were?"

"It's a part-time job. He has a regular cleaner and other cleaning staff when the cottages are in use. I supervise them, and I do the catering when he has visitors. I've helped him with choosing furniture and decorations sometimes, too, but he only listens when it suits him."

"I'm a bit puzzled now. You say 'when the cottages are in use' and 'when he has visitors', but I'd understood this to be the first crime weekend he'd organised. He called it an 'introductory offer', didn't he?"

Isobel Lawrence's expression became an inimitable mixture of amusement and disapproval.

"This is the first crime weekend. I can't count how many different projects Gordon has tried since I first worked here – most of them business ventures involving cajoling other people to put up the cash. My job is – was – to see they were properly entertained and looked after. Mostly they stay – stayed – in the house, but sometimes in the cottages. Of course, until recently he only owned two of the cottages. The other two – the ones that belonged to Mr Hicks and Mrs Shennan – have only just been renovated."

"What kind of business ventures were they?"

She gave a short, harsh laugh.

"All kinds. I don't know the details – Gordon didn't confide in me. Naturally I caught snippets of conversation. Mushroom farming was one idea he had. It came to nothing when the person he asked to be his partner ran off with some cash. That's why I remember it – it was unusual for someone to get one over on Gordon. And he had some shares in a greyhound track. It wasn't local – Harlow, I think – but the owner came here once. But there were dozens of these projects. I've no idea how successful they were business-wise, but Gordon always tired of them and moved on. That's just how he was. I was pretty sceptical about these crime weekends, I can tell you. They need so much work upfront and obviously it takes time to build a reputation. Though, to give Gordon his due, he's worked hard at the crime thing. Perhaps he'd found something that suited him at last. That would be ironical, wouldn't it?"

She turned shrewd eyes on Tim. He caught a spark of something glinting through the wisdom – malice? – before she dropped her gaze.

"You're making it clear you didn't approve of Mr Bemrose's activities. May I ask why you decided to work for him – and to stay for such a long time?"

"I . . . it was convenient," she said, sinking her head lower. She clasped her hands together in her lap.

"We've already found out that Gordon Bemrose was a man who liked to exert pressure on others to do what he wanted them to do. Did he have some kind of hold over you?"

"No!" The answer came too quickly.

"Well," said Tim, after a short pause, "as I've just said, we know Gordon took advantage when he could. We also know he had enemies. To your knowledge, was there anyone who disliked him enough to want to kill him?"

Mrs Lawrence unclasped her hands and put her right hand to her forehead.

"A difficult question to answer," she said. "Personally, I don't think rational people ever kill others. But who's to say how rational someone can be if someone else persistently goads them, or threatens them with exposure, say." She still wasn't looking at Tim directly.

"That's a very interesting observation. Is that what Gordon was doing? Goading people? Blackmailing them, perhaps?"

She flicked a glance at Juliet and looked away again.

"I was merely speaking hypothetically," she said, her voice dull. "As I've told you, I really have no idea what Gordon was getting up to."

"Can you account for your movements yesterday afternoon and evening?"

"Of course: more than anyone else, I should think. I was either in the kitchen, the dining-room, or the ballroom all evening, mostly with others present. At intervals I spent a few minutes on my own earlier in the evening, when I was preparing food, but if I'd been somewhere else the food wouldn't have been ready, would it?"

"No, I suppose not," said Tim. Isobel Lawrence was the last person he suspected of carrying out the attacks. His question had been a formality, a bland lead in to what he really wanted to ask her.

"You were cooking, fetching and carrying all evening, looking after others all the time. You must have been exhausted when it was finally over?"

"Looking after others on such occasions is my job. I don't find it particularly tiring. Like everyone else there, I suppose, I could have done without the histrionics."

"Do you mean the attacks?"

"Yes, the attacks, and all the rest of it. Anton behaving like a spoilt child and the appalling Dack woman getting drunk. And that embarrassing travesty of a play. I could go on. I never knew what to expect when Gordon had one of his do's, but he certainly surpassed himself this time."

"You have a room here, I understand?"

"I have stayed here on occasion, yes. I'm not sure that Gordon would have thought of it as 'my' room."

"But not last night?"

"No. I'd decided not to."

"Why was that?"

"I don't know. Perhaps I had an inkling that I'd have had enough by the end of the evening."

"You didn't reconsider when it grew so late? It was very foggy outside, too. Not inviting."

"It did cross my mind that perhaps I should stay. But it was too late by then – I had brought no extra clothes.

I wouldn't have been able to make myself look presentable today - not to the standard I've set myself. I pride myself on my professionalism."

"Yes, I can see that. So you were the only person who was here last night who actually left the island?"

"I don't know the answer to that, Detective Inspector," Isobel Lawrence said drily. "I can only tell you that I certainly did leave the island myself. I'd say that makes me less of a suspect than anyone else, wouldn't you?"

Tim nodded encouragingly, though he considered the observation an odd one.

"How did you get home?"

"I walked. It isn't far. I have a flat in Cradge Bank. It's only just over the river."

"Can you tell us roughly what time you returned this morning?"

"It was later than I intended. I overslept, which is unheard of for me. I knew the breakfasts would be late. Fortunately for me, everyone else seemed to have overslept as well. I went straight to the kitchen."

"What did you do next? Did you get on with preparing breakfast?"

"I . . . I was going to. I decided to take Gordon a cup of tea first. I wanted to see if he was all right after all that had happened yesterday evening. He's - he was - strong, but he should have agreed to see a doctor. And he was so keen on making the crime weekend a success, I thought it strange that he, of all people, wasn't already up."

"So you took the tea up to his room. Did you knock on the door?"

"Yes, I knocked and waited for a moment; then I went in."

"What did you see?"

"I saw that the bed had been overturned. The mattress was on top of the bedclothes and they'd all been pulled off on to the floor. I put down the tea and went to lift up the mattress. I was trying to drag it back on to the bed. That was when I saw . . . the knife. I recognised it: it came from the kitchen. It had been plunged deep into Gordon's back." She had hesitated only once, before mentioning the knife. Otherwise, she could have been reading from some bland and turgid report. She'd raised her head now and was staring into the middle distance. Tim scrutinised her face. Mask-like, it showed no emotion, except that there was no colour in her cheeks; her complexion was sheet-white.

"Wow!" said Juliet, after Mrs Lawrence had gone.

"Wow, indeed. What did you make of that?"

"I think she was holding a lot back, but sticking to the truth as closely as possible."

"That's what a good liar does."

"I know. But I think she did tell some lies – she was too quick off the mark to deny that Gordon Bemrose had a hold over her; and I think she knows more about his dodgy deals than she's letting on. And her account of how she found him was bloodless."

"Do you think she liked him?"

"I'm not sure. Not on the face of it, no. Yet it's hard to believe that a woman like her would put up with working for a man she didn't like for twelve years, even if he did have something on her. She'd have found a way out."

"Did she kill him?"

"I don't think so. But I've got a feeling that if she'd been more open, she'd have led us to the person who did."

CHAPTER 65

JULIET HAD GONE. So had Andy and Ricky. As far as Tim knew, so had the guests and all the others who had been taking part in the crime weekend, including Anton and Percy, Patti and Mrs Lawrence. The team of SOCOs had arrived while he and Juliet were talking to Mrs Lawrence; Ricky had shown them the lay-out of the house and the places where the two corpses had been found.

Tim decided to make another tour of the house before returning home himself. His own house was barely a mile away – it would take him only a few minutes to get home – but this place seemed to exist in a parallel universe. He thought he might make more sense of it if he could explore alone – well, as alone as it was possible to be now the SOCOs had started their labours.

The ballroom was still a chaos of discarded blankets and scattered cups. Nothing new to interest him there. One of the SOCOs was in the kitchen, boxing up the cups and glasses that had been stacked there for testing. Some blood-stained swabs nestled in a plastic evidence bag. He was looking forward to finding out what evidence all these items might yield; but there was nothing else there to interest him.

Colin and Margarett Franklin's room looked as if it had been prepared for the next guest. It was scrupulously tidy, the other bedding folded neatly on top of the quilt. Margarett had evidently made good use of the time they'd been cooped up in there.

Tim went upstairs. As he'd expected, there were more SOCOs in Gordon's room, going over every inch of the carpet minutely, bagging every tiny item they discovered. He left them to it. As on his first visit, the room didn't 'talk' to him.

Patti's room, further down the corridor, had been left untidy. There was an unpleasant odour. He located its source: there was a balled-up dress close to the bed which smelt rank. Tim left it where it was, making a mental note to tell one of the SOCOs to bag it, though he was sure they'd find it.

There was another SOCO in the bathroom. She was working through the contents of a bathroom cupboard, but she sat back on her heels and gave Tim a grin when she saw him.

"Found anything in here?" he asked.

"There's this," she replied, holding up an evidence bag. A knife had been slotted into it diagonally, its slim blade glinting through the plastic.

"Interesting, but it's not the murder weapon," said Tim. "The killer didn't trouble to remove that from the victim."

His words disappointed her.

"It still might tell us something," she said, brightly. "It's an odd place to store it: it's clearly a kitchen knife. We can test it for prints; or don't you think it's worth it?"

"You're right, of course it's worth it. I didn't mean to put you off."

He moved back out into the corridor, passing Gordon's room again, and was about to hit the stairs when he noticed the closed door between it and Patti's room. It led to the room Mrs Lawrence used when she stayed the night, the room she'd been quite adamant was not 'hers'. He opened the door and went in.

The curtains were closed, but he could see this room was tidy, too, almost clinically so. There was an empty water carafe and a glass on the bedside cupboard and a miniature tray, presumably intended to hold small change and jewellery, on the dressing table. Otherwise it was bare: there was nothing to indicate that someone had tried to stamp it with their personality.

Tim was turning to leave this room when accidentally he focused on something that seemed out of place, a minor thing, but possibly of significance: the bedspread had been ruffled. On the side of the bed nearest the door, it was a good three inches from the ground. He walked round the bed to the other side, where he saw that it slightly trailed the floor. Mrs Lawrence was nothing if not precise: he doubted she would have made the bed in such a sloppy way. Leaning over, he yanked back the cover to reveal that the pillow had not been plumped up. It still bore the unmistakeable indent of someone's head. Had Mrs Lawrence spent the night at Holyrood, after all? If so, why had she denied it so vigorously and why had she had such a half-hearted stab at making the bed? She might have left it like that on an earlier occasion, but he doubted it. He'd need to make sure the SOCOs bagged the pillow, too. He was pondering the significance of his discovery as he descended the stairs. He hadn't been out to the cottages yet, but first he wanted to take a look at the sitting-room again.

A horrible stench assailed his nostrils. One of the SOCOs, a man, was walking towards him, carrying a square plastic box. He was wearing a face mask. The smell was coming from the box. Putting his hand over his nose and mouth, Tim peered into it. All he could see was a large black bin-liner, from which some foul liquid was seeping.

"What in God's name have you got there?" he demanded to know.

"No idea, Chief," the SOCO replied cheerfully. "It's the decomposing remains of something."

"Human?"

"I don't think so. From the size and shape of it, I'd say it was an animal. Can't think why it had been left down there." The man jerked his head over his shoulder in the direction of the cellar. The cellar door was standing open. "Funny, isn't it?"

"Very strange. Whatever you've got there needs testing."

"I know. You don't think I'm carting this around for fun, do you?"

The man's tone irked Tim slightly, but he let the comment pass. He needed some fresh air. He postponed his visit to the sitting-room and followed the SOCO outside.

He was astonished to see Ava Dack and Lizzie Fox standing disconsolately in the drive, both huddled into their coats, broad scarves tucked around their necks. Tim went over to talk to them.

"Mrs Dack! Mrs Fox! You're still here."

"You don't need to tell us that," said Ava. "We'd rather be anywhere else just now – litererally! We've got to wait for our lift, haven't we? Reggie and Jackson wasn't expecting to have to fetch us today and they're taking their time about it."

"If it helps, I can arrange for you to go home in a police car."

Ava curled her lip. She was about to retort when Lizzie cut in.

"I think they're here now. A car's just been stopped by those two coppers on the gate." She was pointing with her finger. Ava and Tim followed her line of sight and saw Giash Chakrabati bending down to say something through the open window of a gleaming black 4 x 4. The conversation was brief. Giash straightened up and stepped back smartly as the car revved suddenly and shot past him on to the gravel drive. Its driver pulled up beside Ava and Lizzie.

"Hello, Reg, where's Jackson?" said Ava.

"He's finishing up some business. We'll go back for him," said the squarely-built, red-faced man who was clambering inelegantly out of the car. "Bloody nuisance, you two wanting picking up today," he added. "We haven't finished what we've got to do yet, not by half." His eye fell on Tim and rested for a beat. Tim felt himself being sized up.

"You one of the geezers who organised this do?" Reggie asked.

"No, Reg, 'e's a copper. I thought you'd be able to see that. You always say you can smell 'em a mile . . . ."

"That's enough, Ava. Afternoon," he added, tossing the word in Tim's direction. "If it's all the same to you, we need to push off. As I've said, we've got things to do."

"Be my guest," said Tim mildly. "Mrs Dack and Mrs Fox will be the last to leave. I was surprised when I came out just now to find them still here. I'm DI Yates, by the way."

Reg Dack didn't answer him. It was true he'd already explained that he was in a hurry, but he now seized Ava's and Lizzie's suitcases like a man possessed and chucked them into the back of the 4 x 4. He yanked open one of the rear doors for Lizzie and indicated to her to get in with a toss of his head in the general direction of the back seat. Ava was already scrambling into the front passenger seat after a small tussle between her kitten heels and the gravel. Reg Dack heaved himself into the driver's seat and reversed smartly, just stopping at the spot where Giash Chakrabati was still standing. He turned the car to face the road and he and the two ladies disappeared smartly. The vehicle could be heard roaring along Cowbit High Bank.

Giash walked back to meet Tim.

"Strange character!" he said.

"Sure was," said Tim. "He damned near knocked you over. He reminds me of . . . " Tim paused.

"Reminds you of what, boss?" Giash prompted. "I don't think he comes from round here."

"I don't think he does, either. He reminds me of someone I arrested once when I was a young copper in London. I'm trying to remember his name. He got off, whoever he was – I don't think the case was even brought to court. Really unpleasant character. His name'll come to me. It could even have been him," Tim added. "The bloke I'm thinking about, I mean."

"Well, that guy's name's Reg Dack," said Giash.

"It is now," said Tim meaningfully.

CHAPTER 66

IT WAS 6.30 p.m. Juliet desperately wanted to see Sally again. She scrutinised her watch as if it could give her permission, or perhaps make time go backwards an hour or two. In her heart, she knew she shouldn't disturb the Trawford family again so late on a Saturday. Instead, but feeling wistful, she headed for the children's home.

Although it was dark, Jake was outside, retrieving scattered footballs and some portable goal posts. He turned towards the sound of her car as he heard the gates open, knowing immediately who it was, because only a handful of people had key-cards to the gate. He hurried towards it as she reversed neatly into a parking space.

"Juliet! Great to see you. I'd given up hoping that you'd be able to come today. I thought if you could get away at all, you'd make a beeline for the vet's."

She laughed as he kissed her.

"Don't think I wasn't tempted!"

"Come inside and have some tea. And something to eat. You must be starving."

He was right: she was hungry as well as tired. It hadn't hit her until he mentioned it. She'd eaten nothing since the croissant he'd given her that morning. As she followed him into his flat and sank down on his shabby old sofa, she reflected that perhaps she did like to be cosseted, especially after the sort of day she'd just had.

"Tea or a glass of wine?"

"Oh, tea first," she said. "Perhaps some wine later."

"Staying the night?" he asked, with studied casualness.

"Oh, I don't . . . " She stopped herself from completing the sentence. She would certainly be working tomorrow and she kept no clothes at Jake's; but she could go back to her flat early in the clothes she was wearing and change. "Yes," she said, leaning back and closing her eyes. "That would be lovely."

She had almost drifted into sleep when Jake brought the tea.

"The dog's great," he said.

"I'm so glad you took to her. Was she still shaky when you saw her?"

"I guess so. Perhaps a bit more confident than when you saw her. She tried to stand while I was there. Trawford seemed pleased with her progress."

"Yes, he's . . ."

"Something very strange happened, though."

"Oh? At the vet's, you mean?"

"No. When I was driving back here afterwards. On that field where the road curves as it leaves Spalding and heads for Pode Hole. There used to be an orchard there, but it was very old. The trees were cut down last winter. There's a big expanse of open land there now. I saw three or four vehicles parked on it - large vehicles, SUVs and jeeps - and then, running across the field towards the road, a couple of greyhounds and a dog just like Sally. Another Saluki! Extraordinary, isn't it? I'd never even heard of the breed until yesterday and now I've seen two in the same day."

Juliet sat bolt upright, spilling some tea into her lap.

"Careful!" said Jake gently. "Is something wrong?"

"Don't you see, Jake? You must have seen them!"

"Seen who? I'm sorry, I've lost the plot here." Jake was bewildered and unhappy.

"The hare coursers. That must have been them. Most probably the ones who owned Sally, but, if not, some others."

"Oh, God! I should have been more with it. I'm sure you're right. I should have called you, shouldn't I?"

"Yes," said Juliet, aware that she was being mean. "But although it's too late to catch them this time, there may be some clues in that field." She was already standing. She scooped up her coat from the back of the sofa.

"You don't mean you're going to search it now!"

"That's exactly what I mean. I'm determined to catch these people, and make sure they're punished. I . . . "

"Juliet, stop it! Stop it now and listen to me. If they've dropped anything in that field, it will still be there tomorrow. Who do you think is going to go out there on a night like this and destroy the evidence? And even more to the point, what do you think you're going to find, in the pitch black and cold? The most likely outcome is that you'll catch pneumonia."

It was the first time he'd raised his voice to her. To his horror as well as her own, she burst into tears. She fell back on to the sofa. Jake went to sit beside her. He took her hand.

"I'm right there with you, you know. One hundred per cent. For your own sake, you need to try to be a bit more rational about this."

"I know. I'm sorry. And it's not your fault you didn't think to call me. To tell you the truth, it's highly unlikely that Tim would have let me leave the murder investigation. He might have been able to send some uniforms, but they wouldn't have got there in time to arrest anyone. And we're going to be overstretched now, so he wouldn't have given it priority."

"I'll come with you to the field first thing tomorrow, if you like. As soon as it's light. I can show you where I saw the vehicles and we can search the area ourselves."

"Aren't you on duty this weekend?"

"Yes, but there'll be someone here to supervise the breakfasts. As long as I can get back by nine, it should be possible."

"Tim and I have arranged to meet at nine to discuss today's interviews."

"Great, that fits, then."

"I'll need to fit in picking up some clothes to wear tomorrow."

"We can go together to fetch them before it's light. You'll just have to be careful not to get too grubby in the field afterwards."

Juliet smiled.

"I doubt if Tim'll notice if I do."

"Good. Now can we get on with enjoying our evening? What would you like to eat?"

CHAPTER 67

DORA WESTERMAN LET herself into her relatively nondescript flat in the relatively nondescript town of Newark. She lugged her suitcase through the door and abandoned it in the tiny hall. Briskly, she moved into the kitchen-diner and filled the kettle before taking off her coat. She made herself tea – in a proper brown earthenware pot, not by dunking a tea-bag – and sat down to relish it in her outsize single armchair. The events of the last thirty-six hours had told on her: she was exhausted, but jubilant. She held up her teacup to the framed photo that stood on the small occasional table by her side. "Cheers, Auntie Joan!" she said.

Colin and Margarett Franklin were still on the road, driving back to their home in Kent. A silence as thick as the fog, which was descending again, built a wedge between them. Colin stared ferociously at the road; Margarett looked out of the passenger window, her head turned away from him. When they'd been driving for two hours, he'd had enough.

"For God's sake," he said, "what's bugging you now?"

Slowly she moved her head and leaned closer to him.

"Look at me!" she said.

"I can't. I'm driving. There'll be an acci . . . "

"Look at me, Colin!" she shrieked.

Half-heartedly, he flicked his gaze sideways to meet her eye, before fixing it on the road again.

"Did you do it?" she demanded. "Did you kill the bastard?"

Colin didn't reply. The crushing silence descended upon them again.

Richard Renwick rather enjoyed seeing the expression on his mother-in-law's face as he and Sonia walked through their own front door.

"What's happened?" she asked, twisting the tea-towel she was holding in nervous hands. Sounds of a gameshow could be heard coming from the sitting-room. The children were clearly watching TV. She closed the door on them.

"Quite a lot," said Richard, grinning. "You wouldn't believe the half of it. Sonia'll tell you. I need to hit the phone now, to find us a nice hotel for the next couple of days. All right if we ask you to stay until Tuesday? We'll come back on Monday evening."

"Yes, but . . . "

"It's all right, Mum," said Sonia. "Come into the kitchen and I'll explain."

Anton and Percy had ridden their motorbike to Anton's house at Metheringham. It was cold inside; the old stone flags became relentlessly damp and chilly after even a few hours without heating. Percy set about building a pyramid of sticks and newspaper and some logs in the grate of the inglenook fireplace, while Anton busied himself making hot Scotch toddies. He placed a cut glass tumbler containing a generous measure of tawny liquid on the hearth beside Percy, who was just putting a match to his creation. The paper burst into flames, the sticks igniting also, and one of the logs caught soon afterwards. Percy took the glass and sprawled on the hearthrug, propping himself up with one elbow, while Anton stretched himself out on the sofa.

"Your health!" said Percy, raising the glass in mock

solemnity. "And here's to the shade of good old Uncle Gordon!"

"That's very wicked of you!" said Anton.

As if they were a couple of teenagers, they both collapsed into giggles.

Amelia Baker had declined Victor le Grange's offer of a lift back to London and had instead accompanied Dora Westerman to the railway station in Spalding. Dora had wanted to walk, but Amelia had insisted on paying for a taxi. They had been instructed by PC Chakrabati to ask its driver to pick them up on Little London Bridge. The taxi had been a good idea, because Amelia and Dora had just managed to catch the 16.22 train to Peterborough, where she had boarded for King's Cross, leaving Dora waiting on the platform for her own train. Dora didn't disclose her destination and Amelia didn't ask. She had been bound up in her own feelings, a mixture of shame, misery and despair. She'd begun to doubt Victor when he'd been stupid enough to get himself mugged the previous evening – she still didn't know why he'd been outside – but she'd allow him to sleep with her nevertheless, mainly because, if she was honest with herself, everyone else had seemed to expect it. But the craven way in which he'd begged the police not to tell his wife where he'd spent the night destroyed every last vestige of faith she'd had in him. He was a chancer and a womaniser who exploited his students. It was only because it would shame her even more that she'd decided not to report him to the university authorities.

Her parting from Dora had been restrained, but cordial. She felt that Dora understood; and she was profoundly grateful to her for not intruding on her thoughts with small talk.

Dora asked for her telephone number and said she would call next day, to see if she was all right.

Patti went straight to her childhood home, to which she'd just moved back after years of independence. One of her mother's neighbours, a young mother called Jenny Edwards, had offered to keep an eye on her while Patti was away. Patti let herself into the house, which seemed strangely quiet and cold. She went from room to room downstairs, but there was no sign of her mother. Fearing the worst, she was about to go upstairs to search the bedrooms when Jenny tapped on the door and her mother walked in, Jenny following behind her.

"Hello, we didn't expect you back until tomorrow!" said Jenny. She was a plump, cheerful thirty-year-old. Although sometimes irked by her propensity to gossip, Patti liked her tremendously.

"I came back early. Have you been out somewhere?"

"No, but your Mum told me this morning that she was scared of being on her own, so she's been with me all day. I was going to make a bed up for her, but now you're here I guess she can come home again?"

"Yes, of course." Patti was bewildered. Her mother had been a widow for many years and never complained about being alone before.

"She's had her tea," Jenny continued. "I'll just leave you to it, shall I?"

"Yes – thank you," Patti called belatedly after Jenny's retreating form. The door closed behind her.

"What's the matter, Mum? You're not usually afraid of being on your own."

Her mother seemed brighter than usual. The day spent with the Edwards family had been good for her.

"I know," she said. "But I had such horrible dreams last night, they really frightened me, they were so real. I thought I saw you sticking a knife into somebody. I think it was you – you looked shadowy. Jenny was really nice to me when I told her about it this morning. I'm sorry, I know it was stupid. I'm glad you're here now, though."

It didn't occur to her mother to ask Patti why she was back early and she volunteered no explanation. And Patti was shocked to the core by what she'd just heard.

Isobel Lawrence had returned to the maisonette she shared with her brother. Her brother was out and had left the kitchen in a mess, but for once Isobel hadn't the energy to tackle it. She sank on to one of the two wooden wheelback chairs at the kitchen table and buried her face in her hands. She was weeping bitterly.

CHAPTER 68

JULIET AND JAKE were up and eating breakfast – croissants again – before 6.30 on Sunday morning. By just after seven, they had left the children's home in separate cars and both dropped by Juliet's flat. She changed into a shirt and jacket, tailored trousers and ankle boots. Jake then drove to the field where he had seen the greyhounds and the Saluki, Juliet following. Juliet put on a knee-length parka and exchanged her ankle boots for wellingtons. Jake was already dressed in a cagoule and wellies.

The field was remote. There were no houses within sight of it and no street lights nearby. The sun should have been rising about the time they arrived, but the morning was getting off to a sluggish start, the sky obscured by cloud, and visibility was poor. There hadn't been much rain recently, but underfoot it was sticky. Their wellingtons were soon caked with dark Fenland mud. Jake had brought a powerful torch, which he shone on the ground. Juliet was also carrying a torch.

"Be careful you don't trip; some of the tree roots from the orchard haven't been dug up properly."

"It's a huge field," said Juliet. "It will take hours to cover all of it."

"Obviously we can't search it all now. I'll take you to the place where the vehicles were. If we find something there, you'll be able to send in some coppers to work through the rest of it, won't you?"

"I guess," said Juliet doubtfully. "If Tim agrees it's a priority. We're going to be over-stretched now we've got this murder case to solve. Even more so, if it turns out to be two murders."

"I thought you said the actor guy died of natural causes."

"He may have done. That's the official story, anyway. But as Tim always says, coincidences are suspicious. He could have been murdered; and it's more than possible that someone killed him by accident."

"I'm baffled!"

"Don't bother about it. I shouldn't have told you, anyway. Sorry, I didn't mean to sound so abrupt!" Juliet added. She couldn't see Jake's face properly, but she'd sounded more graceless than she'd intended and something about the way his body stiffened told her that the comment had hurt him.

He trudged on beside her for a while, still shining the torch at their feet until they were about a third of the way across the field. He stopped suddenly, at a place where there was a dip in the ground.

"This is where the vehicles were." He swooped the torch round in a circle. "You can see the tyre-marks quite clearly." Wide tyre-marks had gouged deep imprints into the mud.

"Several vehicles," she said. "And some dogshit."

"Well, that doesn't prove anything, and I'm certainly not going to help you scrape it up, even though you do have some evidence bags with you." Jake laughed. "Though I suppose it's a task I'm going to have to get used to soon enough." Juliet's heart went out to him; this casual remark made her doubly ashamed of her earlier brusqueness. She wondered why she snapped at him so frequently; she was much more considerate to everyone else, even people she didn't particularly like.

"What exactly are we looking for?" Jake continued.

"Well, I can't be absolutely exact, but the tyre tracks are a good start. The light's terrible, but I'll try to take photos of them with my phone. If we know the make of the vehicles it will help to track down suspects. And I'll ask Tim if he can send someone to take some better pictures than I can, and maybe some casts. He's sure to agree to that, even if we can't spare enough people for a fingertip search. And – this is going to sound really nasty – a dead hare, one that's been ragged to death, would be the clincher, to prove that whoever was here had been out coursing. The hare might be difficult to find, though. The one in Campain's Lane had crawled to the edge of the field there."

"We've got another hour. The light is bound to improve, but take some photos now and we'll come back for more before we leave. There's time for us to walk round the whole perimeter of the field, if we go in opposite directions. What else should I be looking for?"

"Anything that might help to identify the bastards: something that's been dropped or discarded recently, even if it seems quite ordinary. Empty drinks cans, cigarette packets, fag-ends or matches, though they're likely to have been ground into the mud. Here, take some evidence bags with you. And latex gloves."

"Your torch working?"

"Yes." Juliet switched it on.

"Take care," Jake said, "and if anyone dubious comes near you, scream as loud as you can!"

Juliet bit back another retort. Did he think she was helpless? She knew more about self-defence than he did.

"You, too!" she said lightly. Quickly, she kissed his cheek. "Thanks for doing this, Jake. I'm really grateful."

"Whatever it takes. If the only way of being with you is in a god-forsaken field in winter, the god-forsaken field it is!"

Juliet fervently hoped he wouldn't say more. He didn't, but instead turned and began to tramp away from her, walking slowly and circling his torch over the bank of the dyke that edged the field as he went. She looked back at him for a moment before she began her own march in the opposite direction.

Forty-five minutes later, they met at the middle of the far edge of the field, which was bounded on that side by a fence. The sun had risen properly now, though the daylight was grey and soupy.

"Hi. All good?" he called as he approached.

"Yep. You? Did you find anything?"

"Not much. I've bagged what I found, but I think it's all far too old or irrelevant. Empty crisp packets and chocolate wrappers that have faded and a child's sock. And this," he added mischievously. He fished in his pocket and pulled out a clear plastic evidence bag which he passed to her. Juliet took it, smoothing the plastic to get a better look at what was inside.

"It looks like a thick rubber ring," she said, mystified.

"That's exactly what it is. It's a castrating ring, for a ram," said Jake. "I thought you might not have seen one before."

"Ugh!" Juliet handed it back. "I haven't. It looks cruel."

"Apparently it isn't: it's supposed to be the most humane way of doing it. Interesting, anyway, but unlikely to have been dropped by someone coursing hares. Did you have any more luck than me?"

"Nothing at all. All I found were some shards of pottery that had obviously been lying in the soil for years. I didn't bother to bag them."

"Oh, well, we tried. The quickest way back to the cars is straight across the field from here. We can see where we're going now. It's a bit of a quagmire in the middle, but we're both wearing wellies; and we're dead opposite the tyre tracks. You'll be able to take better photos of them when we reach them."

"Fine," said Juliet shortly. She had the distinct feeling she was being managed; she was trying not to resent it.

Jake didn't react. He linked his arm in hers and they plodded across the field together until they reached the "quagmire".

"We can walk round it," said Juliet. "Going straight through will be risky: we're likely to get stuck."

"OK, but just let me get that first."

"Get what?" Juliet had gently disengaged her arm and was heading to the left of the mud patch. She looked towards where Jake was pointing. Something bright red was sticking up in the slime.

"I don't think it's . . ." Juliet began, but Jake was already wading towards the object. The mud was deep, already halfway up his wellingtons. Juliet stood still and watched. Jake continued to squelch through the mud. A couple of paces away from his quarry, he overbalanced and fell sideways, submerging his right side and arm in the ooze. He succeeded in standing upright without tumbling face-first into the mire. Once he'd regained his balance Juliet saw that the red thing had disappeared, dislodged by his movements.

"Bugger!" he shouted. "I'll have to fish around for it now."

"Just leave it, Jake," she called. "It's not worth the risk!"

"I've not come through all this shit to give up now," he yelled back. He plunged his soiled arm into the morass and thrashed it about. "Gotcher!" he shouted triumphantly. He inspected the item he was holding. It was now covered completely in black mud, but it could plainly be identified as a woman's shoe.

"Oh," he said, disappointed. "It's a shoe – a female shoe. I don't think it can have been left here by the hare coursers, do you? Shall I throw it back?"

Juliet was about to agree when a detail from one of the interviews she'd conducted at Holyrood House flashed through her head.

"No, don't throw it back, Jake! Bring it here! I think you may have found something very important indeed!"

CHAPTER 69

TIM WAS PACING up and down his office when Juliet knocked and entered without waiting for him to respond. She was carrying the shoe in an evidence bag. She'd rubbed away some of the dirt to reveal its colour without cleaning it properly. There was a slim chance it might hold further clues, despite its mud-bath.

Juliet was excited. She held up the evidence bag.

"Tim, look what I've found! It's a red Christian Louboutin shoe. I think it must be . . . " she stopped mid-sentence. "Tim, what's wrong?"

She'd been working with Tim for almost a decade and had experienced his every kind of mood – humorous, playful, angry, sardonic, sad, stressed, whatever – but she'd never seen him look as miserable as he did at this moment. Not just miserable: crushed.

He turned his head to look at her, moving in slow motion, as if the effort were too great.

"Juliet. What did you say?"

"I'll tell you in a minute. What's the matter? Are you ill?"

"No. No, I'm not ill." Tim smoothed his forehead with one hand. "I've got some results back on the fingerprints that were taken yesterday. There's a match."

"That's a good thing, isn't it?" Juliet said carefully.

"You'd think so," said Tim, "wouldn't you?" He wiped his forehead again.

"Tim, stop being cryptic and tell me what this is about. What is it that's upsetting you? And sit down, for God's sake."

Tim sank into one of the chairs arranged round the small table he used for informal meetings. Juliet took one of the others.

"Do you remember . . . no, I don't think you were there . . . I think you'd already gone home . . . yesterday afternoon I took a final look round Holyrood House. One of the SOCOs was in the upstairs bathroom. She'd just found a knife in there and bagged it."

"You're right, I didn't know about that. Is that where the fingerprint was found - the one with the match?"

Tim nodded.

"And?"

He swallowed. "The match is with Patti's fingerprints. The knife had been hidden in a bathroom cupboard, behind some other items."

Juliet paused to consider.

"It wasn't the murder weapon, though, was it? The knife that killed Gordon Bemrose was left sticking in his back."

"I know. But both that knife and the one in the bathroom were taken from the knife block in the kitchen. Isobel Lawrence was quite clear they were both there on Friday, although she couldn't say exactly when they went missing. It's hard to believe they were taken by different people. As far as we know, only Patti and Gordon Bemrose spent the night upstairs in the house on Friday night. Patti could have taken both knives, hidden them in the bathroom and then decided on the bigger one to kill Gordon during the night."

"Were there any prints on that knife? The murder weapon, I mean?"

"No. It had been wiped – or the murderer was wearing gloves."

Juliet was silent for some moments, her thoughts spinning.

"Patti's a forensic scientist. If she'd committed a murder, she'd never have incriminated herself by leaving her prints."

"I know she wouldn't usually. But it's highly probable that everyone there, including Patti, was drugged with something. If she killed Bemrose during the night, still in a drugged state, instinct would have told her to wipe the murder knife, but she might have forgotten about the other one."

"She'd have needed a pretty strong motive to kill her own uncle."

As she spoke, Juliet remembered Patti's unconvincing denial when Tim had asked her if she had a reason for wanting Gordon Bemrose dead.

"She may have had one. I thought she was holding something back when I asked her if she had a reason for wanting him dead. You noticed it, too."

"Yes, you're right. But we still only have circumstantial evidence on her. There's no proof that she went into Bemrose's room."

Tim suddenly regained his energy.

"Come off it, Juliet, do you really think that? If it was anyone else except Patti, would you be making excuses for them?"

"I guess not." Juliet gave Tim a keen look. "So what are you going to do?"

"We're going to have to pursue it and, if she hasn't a convincing explanation, we'll have to arrest her and charge her. She remains a suspect, like all the others."

"And remand her in custody?"

"That's not for us to decide. It's likely a judge will let her have bail. She'll be suspended from work, of course."

"I'm sorry to ask you this, Tim, but you'll understand why. I've often noticed the tension between you and Patti – I think we all have. Do you have some kind of . . . special relationship with her?"

"It's fine to ask; and the answer is no, not now. She was my girlfriend when I first came here. Before I knew Katrin – we split up a few months before Katrin and I met. It was my decision more than Patti's. She took it hard."

"I see. Thank you," said Juliet tautly.

"But what?"

"It's up to you, Tim. But if it does become necessary, perhaps you shouldn't be directly involved in charging her. Even if the relationship is over."

"It's not just over, it's ancient history. Besides, everyone here knows Patti – everyone has some kind of relationship with her, as a colleague or a friend. Much as I'd like to pass the job on to someone else, I think it should be my responsibility."

"Hmm." Juliet was doubtful. "Do you want me to come with you?"

"That would be great." Tim paused. "I'd better let Thornton know first. He'll be furious if I don't tell him . . . and he'll have to manage the Press. They're going to have a field day when they find out about this."

Superintendent Thornton was already annoyed about the murder(s) and the likely effect on both his force's crime-solving record and his budget, not to mention the fact that he had had to show up for work on Sunday as well as Saturday. (His original plan had been to coast through Saturday morning, taking it as an official working day, support the cadets' football match in the afternoon and claim a handy lieu day closer to Christmas.) Tim was now standing in front of him with the unwelcome news that Patricia Gardner had become a significant suspect. He steepled his fingers and glared at Tim through the pink prism he had created.

"I'm quite furious about this, Yates, quite furious. I want you to know that. You could hardly have revealed to me anything more inconvenient."

"I know, sir. I feel the same way myself . . . "

"I suppose there is absolutely no doubt whatsoever?"

"None at all about the fingerprint match; naturally there's doubt that she committed the murder. That's for us to follow up. And if we aren't able to convince the CPS, they'll throw the case out and it won't even come to court. But, as I've explained, the evidence against her is quite compelling."

"Mainly circumstantial, though, as you have already pointed out."

"Yes, sir, but . . . "

"I know what you're going to say, Yates. You're going to say that if it wasn't anyone else – that is, anyone not connected with this police force – I would be only too pleased for you to charge them so early in the investigation."

"Well, I . . . "

The Superintendent sighed heavily.

"And I suppose you're right, Yates. If you're not right, you'll have to live with the consequences. It won't make you popular with your colleagues, you know. And you'd better work on every step of it according to the book. The Chief Constable won't be pleased if you fuck up and Gardner sues for compensation."

"I know that, sir," said Tim, noting that Patti had already become a mere surname in his boss's vocabulary.

"Very well, Yates, you are authorised to get on with it. On your own head be it. And be sure to take DS Armstrong with you."

"How was it?" Juliet asked, who was waiting for Tim in his office.

"Much as I expected. We're ok to go forward, even to the point of arrest if we think it's justified. He wants you to come with me. If the prosecution is successful, he'll take the credit. If it fails, we're on our own."

"Did he say that?!"

"Not in so many words, but it's what he meant."

CHAPTER 70

"**A**RE YOU STILL sure you want to do this?" Juliet said to Tim as they drew up outside Patti's house. "We could call a squad car and get a uniform to come in with me. They'd be here in ten minutes."

Tim's face was ashen.

"No, I've told you, I want to do it. Patti'll take it better from me."

"Are you sure about that?"

Tim didn't answer. He got out of the car. Juliet followed him.

He'd visited this house many times during their romance, although she hadn't lived here then. She'd moved into a flat in Holbeach some time before he met her, when her father was still alive. Tim had barely known her father; he'd died in a car accident shortly after Patti first introduced them. The accident had transformed Sheila Gardner overnight from a cheerful, competent woman in late middle age to a fretful, uncertain elderly lady whose grip on reality had weakened visibly. Patti had wanted to move back to the family home immediately, but Tim had persuaded her to wait and see if her mother's mental state improved. He'd argued that Patti wouldn't be doing Mrs Gardner any favours by undermining her independence, but Patti was quite aware the real reason was his unspoken fear that her mother's perpetual presence would put a dampener on their relationship. Patti had sold the flat and returned to look after her mother quite recently.

Untypically, Tim had rehearsed what he was going to say to Patti; but it hadn't occurred to him that Sheila Gardner might answer the door. She looked blank for a moment before grasping both his arms and planting a kiss on his cheek.

"Tim! How lovely to see you. It seems an age since you last came. I don't know if Patricia's ready – is she expecting you? I'll just tell her you're here. Who's this?" she added, looking past him at Juliet and frowning slightly.

"Sheila, I . . . "

"I'm DS Armstrong," said Juliet firmly. "Hello, Mrs Gardner. I'm afraid this isn't a social call."

"Who is it, Mum?" Patti appeared beside her mother. She paused just for a second. "Oh, hi, Tim. And Juliet. Do you want to come in?" She put her arm round her mother's waist and led her away from the door. "I'll just settle Mum in the kitchen. Go through into the sitting-room. I'll be with you in a minute."

Tim turned into the stuffy little front room, which was just as he remembered it. The furniture was very seventies and predominantly brown. The shag pile carpet had seen better days. Juliet perched uncomfortably on a spindly-legged two-seater settee. Tim remained standing.

"Sorry about that," said Patti brightly as she entered the room. "Mum gets a bit confused these days. She'll probably stay where she is – I've settled her with a book, but if she does come in here, please don't tell her about Uncle Gordon. She won't be able to take it in properly, but it's bound to upset her. Is there something we didn't cover yesterday? And can I get you a hot drink?"

Tim gave Juliet a stricken look.

Rising to her feet, Juliet immediately said, "As I've just told your mother, this isn't a social visit."

Patti immediately sat down, putting her hands over her face. "Go on," she said.

"Patti, we have to tell you that your fingerprints have been found on a knife at Holyrood House. We need to ask you how they came to be there."

"If you mean the knife in the bathroom, I found it when I was looking for some toiletries. I put it back. It wasn't the murder weapon. Of course it had my prints on it."

Tim, regaining his composure, patiently pressed forward. "That's our problem, Patti: both that and the murder weapon came from the same place in the kitchen; your prints are on one, whilst the knife used in the killing was wiped clean. Did you wipe it?"

The unasked question hung in the air. Patti looked ashen. What she said next defied Juliet's rational expectations of, possibly, a matter-of-fact explanation or an icy rebuttal or even an emotional outburst. "Do you know," she said, the slightest inflection of curiosity colouring her otherwise flat voice, "I have actually been wondering whether I did it. And the strange thing is, I don't know. I really don't know! That's not much of a defence, is it, DI Yates?" She gave Tim an ironic look and smiled.

"I can barely believe that it has come to this, Patti, but, as this is your response, you leave me with no option but to charge you." Tim's own voice was strangled. "Patricia Gardner, I am arresting you for the murder of Gordon Bemrose. You do not have to say anything. But it may harm your defence if you do not mention when questioned something which you later rely on in court. Anything you do say may be given in evidence." Patti's only response was to put her hands once again over her face. "And I strongly advise you," continued Tim, "to say nothing further until your lawyer is present."

"Ok. That's good advice. Are you taking me to the station?"

"Yes," said Juliet. "Will your mother be all right?"

"I'll ask the neighbour to look in on her. She may invite her to spend the night next door, if I say I'm not coming back. I won't be coming back, will I?"

"Not tonight," said Juliet. "You'll be in court tomorrow. After that, we'll have to see. The judge might let you have bail."

CHAPTER 71

PATTI'S SOLICITOR WAS Jean Rook, a powerful and intelligent feminist for whom Tim had a great deal of respect. He and Juliet both attended the preliminary hearing at Lincoln Crown Court, where Ms Rook spoke eloquently of Patti's commitment to her mentally frail mother and assured Mr Justice Ellison that she was not a danger to the community. Tim agreed it was not in the public interest to remand her in custody and that she should be granted police bail to facilitate further questioning. The judge ordered Patti to surrender her passport and report to Spalding police station three times a week; he did not impose a curfew.

Patti's reaction was tranquil, if not resigned. After the hearing, she allowed Jean Rook to lead her away to a taxi. Tim and Juliet left the court at the same time. He had decided not to try to talk to Patti or her lawyer himself, but before she followed Patti into the taxi, Jean Rook turned and said to Tim, "I'll be in touch, DI Yates. The sooner we can meet, the better. Don't you agree?" Her dark eyes were shining.

"Indeed," said Tim, stepping back on to the pavement. He had been gratified to find no reporters present. There had been no public announcements about the murder yet; evidently Gordon Bemrose's weekend 'guests' had all kept their mouths shut. Tim knew this situation couldn't last, but, for Patti's sake, he was glad she hadn't had to face a media scrum.

"I'll bring the car round," said Juliet. "What now?"

"I'm not sure," said Tim. "I think we need to go back to the station and wait for the forensics, chivvy the labs if necessary. We've by no means got to the bottom of this. Regardless of whether she killed Gordon Bemrose, Patti couldn't have been responsible for all the assaults."

"She could have been Gordon Bemrose's attacker on both the occasions he was assaulted – outside the house on the waste ground and then in the cellar."

"True. But she couldn't have attacked Victor le Grange or Sykes or Renwick. All the statements corroborate that she was in the house when those assaults happened. Even if Patti is guilty of Bemrose's murder, someone else was up to no good that night."

"What about the shoe?"

"I'd forgotten the shoe. Are you sure it belongs to Lizzie Fox?"

"Not one hundred per cent sure, no. We need to ask her if it's hers. But there won't have been many people in Spalding wearing red peep-toed Christian Louboutins last Friday."

"I suppose not. What do you think? That she was attacked as well as the others, even though she thought she'd tripped, and the shoe was taken as some kind of trophy?"

"I haven't got as far as working it out. It's possible someone was hare coursing in the spot where the shoe was found. What if the recent spate of hare coursing is linked to this case?"

"I wish! It's a neat idea, but probably a bit too neat. I know you want to catch the hare coursers, but they're going to have to be put on the back burner until the Holyrood House stuff is cleared up. And I doubt the crime weekend was a cover for a secret hare-coursing meeting."

"Let's go and see Lizzie Fox and ask if it's her shoe. I want to see her reaction."

Tim looked at his watch. It was just after 11.30.

"She lives in Essex, doesn't she? It's going to take more than two hours to get there. And I want to go back to the station to see if any results have come in."

"We'd need to go to the station anyway, to pick up the shoe. If the results aren't in, will you come to Essex with me?"

Tim sighed.

"I suppose so. It'll be better than putting up with the general gloom that's hanging over the place. I'm not exactly flavour of the month for charging Patti, am I?"

Juliet smiled wryly. The involuntary action tightened the scar on her face. She smoothed it with her hand. She'd hardly thought about it – or the impending operation – for the past two days.

"Do you really think Patti did it, Tim?"

"I don't know. I'm as confused as she appears to be. If she killed Gordon Bemrose in some kind of fugue-like state, which is what I think she's suggesting, she's going to find it hard to convince a judge. There's been a spate of defences based on that recently."

"Convincing a jury might be easier, if they haven't heard of the other cases."

"Agreed, but the judge could direct them to ignore it. In my experience, judges prefer simple verdicts: innocent or guilty, none of this messy mitigation stuff."

Andy Carstairs was sitting morosely at his desk when Tim and Juliet appeared in the open plan area. His loyalty to Tim was unshakeable, but he was puzzled. Patti seemed to him to be the last person ever to commit a murder and, like Juliet, he found it incomprehensible that she would leave forensic evidence at the scene. He didn't know whether the e-mail he'd just received would help Patti's case or not.

"Any news from the labs?" Tim asked.

"Some. There were traces of flunitrazepam in the cups and glasses sent for testing; and small amounts in some of the urine samples taken from those who stayed at Holyrood House Friday evening."

"Rohypnol, in other words."

"Yep."

"Anything else?"

"Professor Salkeld is going to do full autopsies on both Gordon Bemrose and Montagu Sykes tomorrow and won't commit to stating the cause of death until then. But he already has samples that suggest Sykes had taken a massive dose of flunitrazepam."

"Enough to kill him?"

"I think that's what the Professor's saying. Without actually saying it, if you see what I mean."

"Did anyone test clear?"

"Not entirely clear. Small traces only in the urine of the housekeeper, Mrs Lawrence . . . and Percy Forsyth, too. But the path lab's sent the results with the usual warning: the drug leaves some people's systems more quickly than others, tests can be inaccurate, etcetera, etcetera. What I don't understand is what any of this has to do with Patti. Why would she want to drug a houseful of people?"

"The obvious answer would be so that she could commit the murder without fear of being disturbed. What were her own test results like?"

Andy turned back to his computer screen.

"Similar to some of the others, the other women in particular. Not light."

"She'd have been taking a risk, then, if she drank it knowing it would make her sleep heavily. She'd have no guarantee she could wake up and commit the murder, could she?" said Juliet.

"No. On the other hand, if she did wake up, she could have killed him while she was in a fugue."

"Someone managed to get their hands on a lot of flunitrazepam. Would Patti have been able to do that?"

"As a forensic scientist, she'd stand more chance than the average person. She'd need a permit, though, as well as a good reason for wanting it; and she certainly wouldn't be able to get hold of a large quantity all in one go."

"We can check her lab records," said Juliet.

"Yes, get someone to do that, will you? But it still doesn't add up. Whoever wanted all the people staying in that house last Friday to be incapacitated must have needed to take advantage of the opportunity offered by the crime weekend – they thought it their best chance of killing Bemrose. Patti was his niece. She'd have had other opportunities. Why would she run that risk?"

"You've already answered that – the more suspects, the better her chance of getting away with it." Juliet turned red as she spoke. She was playing devil's advocate: she couldn't imagine Patti plotting evil.

"We already know there were several people there who held grudges against Gordon. Perhaps some of the others did, too."

"Or he was killed by one of the ones who said they wanted to kill him," said Andy. "What do they call it? Hiding in plain sight?"

"We still don't have a motive for Patti, either," said Juliet.

"We'll be interviewing Patti again . . . and soon," said Tim. "Jean Rook is expecting us to – in fact, she seems to be spoiling for a fight, which doesn't surprise me. But we need to talk to all the others again, too. Juliet, can you draw up a schedule? Everyone by the end of this week, if we can manage it."

"Do you want them to come here, or will we visit them?"

"Unless they can't get here for some reason, ask them to come here. We can fit more in that way." Tim thought for a second. "With just one exception. Lizzie Fox. Your idea of calling on her is a good one. Let's get her on the hop if we can. I want to hear what she has to say about that shoe and where it was found."

"Today?"

"Yes, today. Get in touch with the others before we leave – concentrate on the crime weekend guests for now. We'll fit the locals in around them. Andy can help you."

CHAPTER 72

LIZZIE AND JACKSON Fox lived in a gated estate development in Brentwood. A noticeably thuggish porter was sitting in a kind of sentry-box by the barrier at its perimeter wall. He came out of his sentry-box, gesturing, and tried to send them packing until Tim showed him his ID card, whereupon he grudgingly let them through the barrier, incensed that Tim would not tell him which house they wanted to visit. Tim had the distinct feeling that unofficially the man's role extended well beyond protecting the residents' properties.

The Fox house was an 'executive' property, with an extensive frontage decorated with Grecian pillars painted brilliant white. The porter must have been watching on CCTV and warned the Foxes, because while Tim was still parking in the street a man came hurrying out of the house. He was about to get into one of several vehicles parked in the house's turning-circle – a red Mazda pick-up – when Tim handed his car-keys to Juliet, nipped quickly out of his car and walked briskly up the drive to greet him. Juliet locked the car and followed.

"Mr Fox?" he said affably.

"Who wants to know? I'm in a bit of a hurry." The voice, and even more the turn of phrase, seemed familiar to Tim.

"DI Yates. South Lincs Police." Tim flashed his ID card. "I've come to see your wife."

"Oh, yes. It's about that death in Spalding, isn't it?" Jackson Fox sounded relieved. "Bad luck, that was, especially for Lizzie and Ava. Spoilt their weekend. Well, she's in, if you knock. Like I said, I need to get a move on. Got to see a man about a dog." He cackled nervously. Listening to him, Tim was convinced he'd met him before.

Juliet had caught them up. Jackson Fox sidled past her and climbed into his Mazda. He reversed down the drive with more rapidity than caution.

"Have you seen him before?" Tim whispered to Juliet.

Juliet glanced back at the vehicle, which was now heading fast towards the porter's gate, unquestionably breaking the estate speed limit of 20 mph.

"No, I don't think so," she said. "He's a typical Essex type, isn't he? I've met plenty like him; but he doesn't ring any particular bells."

Tim knew Juliet's memory could be relied on. The bloke was ancient history, then.

"I'm pretty certain I know him – or did know him, once. If you don't recognise him, it must be from way back when; my time in London, probably. Anyway, let's get on with this, shall we?"

"Yes. Don't forget you promised to let me do the talking."

Tim rang the doorbell. Lizzie Fox opened the door immediately; she must have been standing just on the other side of it. Lizzie was dressed in a leopard-print 'onesie' with wide-fitting trousers. She was holding an outsize ballon glass.

"Mr Yates, come in." Lizzie peered round the lintel. "Oh, and you've brought your lady friend, too. Well, come in, both of you. I was just having a little gin and tonic. Can I get you one?"

"No, thank you, Mrs Fox, we're both on duty."

"Oh, yes, but what's a little drinkie between friends?"

She winked at Juliet. "Anyway, it's this way. Just follow me." She meandered off down the hall, her leather mules slapping against the soles of her feet.

Tim and Juliet followed. The hall floor was covered in a rather restrained, if very thick, biscuit-coloured carpet, but restraint had been thrown to the winds when the sitting-room into which she led them had been decorated. Both the carpet and the furniture, which consisted mainly of several groups of armchairs and sofas, were a penetrating shade of mauve and the walls were dark purple. The room itself was about the size of a football pitch. A massive china cheetah was stationed on each side of the fireplace, the surrounds of which had been embossed with motifs drawn from fake mediaeval heraldry.

Lizzie threw off the mules and ensconced herself in one of the armchairs set in an alcove made by a bay window, tucking her feet under her. She took a sip of her gin.

"Well," she said. "This *is* nice. I knew you was going to speak to us again, but I thought I'd have to come to your police station. Shall I get Ava to come round? She don't live too far away. She *will* be pleased to see you."

Juliet turned away her head to hide a smile. It was the most fulsome reception she'd received from a member of the public in years. Clearly Lizzie extended the same hostess style towards everyone who visited her at home, without discrimination.

"Thanks for asking, but we don't want to see Mrs Dack today," Tim said quickly. "We'll probably ask her to come to the station later in the week."

Lizzie pulled out her feet from under her and sat up straighter in the chair. She set the glass of gin down on the small table beside her. Her demeanour had changed.

She ditched the hostess welcome and the syrupy voice in a heartbeat.

"Oh, yes?" she said. "Privileged, then, am I? Just what *do* you want?"

"It's nothing to worry about, Mrs Fox," said Juliet. "We just want to ask you a few questions."

"I've heard that one before, an' all." Lizzie eyeballed Tim. "Well, you'd better get on with it, then," she added, seeing he wasn't impressed.

"You had a nasty fall when you were outside in the dark at Holyrood House, didn't you?" said Juliet. "I'm sorry we didn't enquire into it more closely when we interviewed you."

Lizzie began to relax again.

"Ah, well, you 'ad other things on your minds," said Lizzie magnanimously.

"You said you tripped and fell because you saw someone who frightened you. Are you quite sure he didn't attack you? As you know, several other people were attacked on Friday evening."

"What? No." Lizzie wriggled her toes into the carpet pile. "Just me own stupidity. I shouldn't 'ave worn me Labootins outside in the dark there. I couldn't see where I was going. Came a real cropper, I did. Me leg was bleeding."

"Did you get it checked out by a doctor?"

"Nah – I'm tougher than that. I've got a real rainbow bruise, though – see!"

Lizzie rolled up the right leg of her onesie. She showed off a large scab below the knee and several bruises in the purple stage of recovery.

"That does look nasty," said Juliet. "I believe you said you lost one of your shoes as a result of the fall – or Mrs Dack told me, I can't quite remember. Was it one of the Louboutins you just mentioned?"

"Yeah, lovely shoes they was, too. Jackson only give them to me a couple of weeks ago."

"Was it the one from the leg you injured?"

"Yes," said Lizzie.

"We think we may have found the shoe."

"Really?" Although Juliet hadn't mentioned the state it was in, Lizzie didn't exactly sound delighted.

"Yes. Is this it?" Juliet produced an evidence bag. Inside was the shoe Jake had found in the field, now tested for prints (none could be detected) and cleaned up enough to be recognisable.

"Yes, that's it," said Lizzie dully. "Look at the state of it, though."

"I know. It doesn't look as if you'll be wearing it again. The funny thing is, though, we didn't find it in the grounds of Holyrood House."

Lizzie frowned. "Oh? Where was it, then?"

"We found it in a field a few miles outside Spalding. Can you tell us how it got there?"

"No, sorry, I haven't got a clue. Perhaps whoever it was what was lurking about that night took it."

"And then threw it away in the field?"

"I suppose so. Doesn't make much sense, does it?"

"No," said Juliet, "it doesn't. Well, thank you for your time, Mrs Fox. Is it all right if we keep the shoe – for now?"

"Be my guest – but is that all? You come all this way to ask me about that shoe?"

"And to see how you are," said Tim smoothly. "We wanted to check that you weren't suffering from shock.

It can come quite a while after a traumatic injury, you know."

"Yes, well – thank you. Grateful, I'm sure," said Lizzie, getting out of her chair again and straightening the onesie. "I'd best show you out, then, 'adn't I?"

As they reached the door, Tim turned to her again. "You said in your statement you didn't recognise the man you saw. You gave us no description of him, except that he looked 'furious' and frightened you. Can you give us anything more specific?"

"Can't say I can. I was too shook up."

"And you're quite sure you didn't know him?"

"No – I mean yes. I didn't know him from Adam."

"Thank you," Tim said again. Lizzie shut the door on them smartly as soon as they had crossed the threshold.

They drove slowly past the truculent porter. He gave them a mock salute as he raised the barrier for them.

Tim carried on for a short distance until they were out of sight of the compound, then pulled to the side of the road.

"Well," he said. "What did you make of that?"

"She's lying," said Juliet, with certainty.

"I don't doubt that – she probably doesn't know what the truth is. But where's your proof?"

"It's the wrong foot," said Juliet. "The shoe. The one we have is for the left foot. She hurt her right leg and she said she lost the shoe from the leg that she injured."

"So you didn't find the shoe she lost when she fell over?"

"No. That's probably still at Holyrood House somewhere. Or maybe someone did take it – but in that case, as far as we know, they've still got it."

"But if Lizzie had the left shoe on Friday night, she must either have given it to someone who subsequently dumped it, or . . . "

" . . .or she was in that field herself at some point after she left Holyrood House. Take your pick," said Juliet.

"Why didn't you confront her with it?"

"I didn't want to make her suspicious – at least, no more than she was already. Did you see how she sat up when we said Ava would have to come to the station to be questioned? We haven't interviewed Ava yet – I think we should see if her story still matches Lizzie's, if we scrutinise it a bit more."

"O-kay," said Tim slowly. "Are we done here, then?"

Juliet was about to reply when he struck the side of the steering wheel with the flat of his hand.

"I've just remembered where I saw him before," he said.

"Who? Jackson Fox?"

"Yes, but he wasn't called that then. I can't remember what name he was using, but I can find out. It was when I was working for the Met. He was involved in a dog-track scam. We arrested one of his mates, as well. Ten to one that's the bloke who now calls himself Reggie Dack."

"The bloke who was in a tearing hurry to get away when he picked up Ava and Lizzie on Saturday?"

"Now we know why! He probably recognised me. This could be our breakthrough. They'd both better have watertight alibis for where they were last Friday night."

Juliet was thinking about something else.

"By dog-track, do you mean greyhounds?"

CHAPTER 73

JEAN ROOK AND Patti arrived at the police station at 9.50 a.m. the following day, ten minutes before the time scheduled for Patti's first interview with the solicitor present. Superintendent Thornton had warned his staff not to engage Patti in social conversation. Most had found something pressing to do elsewhere or disappeared to the canteen.

Thornton himself came to meet them and escorted them to the interview room. He had wanted to conduct the interview himself, but Tim had pointed out that if Jean Rook were to make a complaint about the way Patti was being interviewed, Thornton would then not be able to step in, which would mean finding someone from elsewhere in the South Lincs force to take over.

"Do you think that Rook woman is likely to complain, then, Yates?"

"I wouldn't put it past her. She'll do anything to get Patti off."

The Superintendent muttered something. To Tim it sounded like "a not undesirable outcome", but it was hard to believe Thornton would have said this. More loudly, Superintendent Thornton continued: "All right, Yates, you and DS Armstrong can do the interview. But I want Armstrong to lead it. Is that understood?"

"Yes, sir," said Tim. "Any particular reason?"

Thornton shot him an evil look.

"It's a question of tact, Yates. If tact is needed to stop Ms Rook making a fuss, I know we can rely on DS Armstrong to exercise it."

His unspoken opinion of Tim's and Juliet's respective interviewing methods was left hanging in the air.

Tim and Juliet were therefore already seated in the interview room when Superintendent Thornton ushered in Patti and Jean Rook. He hovered in the doorway for a few seconds. Jean Rook looked at him quizzically. He cleared his throat.

"I'll be in my office if anyone needs me," he said, shutting the door behind him.

Jean Rook began speaking before Tim could even explain use of the tape and how they would proceed.

"Let's not pretend this is easy for any of us, DI Yates, especially for my client. We're in an unusual situation here, although it isn't unique for police officers sometimes to bring charges against their colleagues. You should know that, to prepare for this, I've made a study of such cases. If I'm not entirely satisfied that this interview is being conducted correctly and without any bias either for or against Ms Gardner caused by the fact she is your colleague, I will insist that an interviewing team is brought in from elsewhere."

Tm looked at Patti. She was pale but composed, her hands folded in her lap. She was dressed in a light blue jumper and a navy herringbone skirt. Blue had always been her favourite colour.

"DS Armstrong will lead the interview," Tim said. "She will conduct it as impartially as if she had never met Ms Gardner before today. The interview will be taped, in accordance with standard police procedure. I will tell everyone when I turn on the tape . . . and if I turn it off. DS Armstrong will caution Ms Gardner again before she begins. Ms Gardner is familiar with the procedure."

Jean Rook looked at Patti, who nodded agreement.

"Very well," said Tim. "I am going to turn on the tape now. Present in the room are Ms Patricia Gardner, MS Jean Rook, DS Armstrong and myself, DI Yates . . . "

Juliet took Patti through every detail of the statement she had given about the Friday afternoon at Holyrood House, asking her each time if she wanted to change what she had said in any way. Each time Patti said she stood by her statement and had nothing to add.

"Now we come to the incident outside, after you'd called in for a glass of wine at the cottage where your cousin was staying. You said that you and your cousin and Percy Forsyth found Gordon Bemrose tied up on some waste land at the end of the row of cottages. It transpired that he had been assaulted."

"That's correct."

Juliet paused. Jean Rook was staring at her, almost willing her to put a foot wrong. Juliet chose her words with care.

"According to your statement, you went to the cottage alone? No-one saw you leave Holyrood House?"

"That's correct," Patti said again.

"Did you see anyone at all before Anton Greenweal opened the door?"

"No. I thought I heard a noise, but I couldn't be sure. The main road isn't far away and the fog plays tricks with sounds."

"You say in your statement you didn't think the noise was worth investigating?"

"No, I didn't. For the reason I've just given you."

"If I may ask you a hypothetical question - I emphasise

that I'm suggesting a theory, not presenting you with a fact – did you have the opportunity to assault Gordon Bemrose between leaving Holyrood House and your arrival at Anton Greenweal's cottage?"

"Don't answer that," Jean Rook said quickly. "We don't want to deal in hypotheses, DS Armstrong. We'd much prefer to stick to the facts."

Juliet turned to Patti.

"That's right, I'd rather not speculate," she said, her eyes downcast.

"All right," said Juliet.

They ploughed on through Patti's statement until they reached the account of the assault on Gordon in the cellar.

"You were alone with Mr Bemrose in the cellar?"

"As far as I knew. After he was attacked, I thought I saw someone else there, hiding in the shadows."

"That's not in your statement."

"No. And I admit I had forgotten about it. Gordon was scared and although he insisted he hadn't been attacked I could see that he had. That wound in his neck couldn't have been caused by a fall. I was scared, too – all either of us wanted to do was get out of there, once he'd fixed the lights. And after that, there was so much else going on that I didn't think about it again."

"You didn't think about it, or, on reflection, you've now thought it advisable to explain how Mr Bemrose could have been attacked in the cellar by someone other than yourself?"

Jean Rook got to her feet.

"DI Yates," she said, "as the senior officer here, I appeal to you. Your sergeant has introduced hypothesis again. I say again, and as forcefully as I can, that my client will not answer questions based on notions or theories."

"All right," said Tim. "DS Armstrong won't do it again. Would you like the question to be wiped from the tape?"

"No, please leave it," the solicitor said tautly. She looked at her watch. "This interview has been in progress for almost two hours now. I suggest we take a break. And I'd like a few minutes alone with my client."

"We'll send in some more tea," Tim said. "You both know where the toilets are."

"I'm sorry about the hypothesis thing," Juliet said to Tim as they headed towards the canteen. "I thought it was better than asking her direct if she'd beaten up Gordon Bemrose."

"It *was* better. And although Gordon was a pretty solid guy, Patti could have done it – she's a dab hand at martial arts." He paused to think for a moment. Although Patti had been charged on circumstantial evidence only, the more he thought about it, the more he thought she must be guilty. If Jean Rook thought the same, she'd be planning to get a different force to interview Patti if she possibly could.

"Jean Rook's going to say today's interview can't last much longer now. You need to get your main questions in before she decides to close it down."

They returned to the interview room. Jean Rook and Patti weren't talking to each other when they went in; they were sitting in silence, tranquilly drinking tea. Tim thought he detected a spirit of resolve in Patti that hadn't been there before.

"I think we've talked about the events of last Friday enough for now," Juliet said, after they'd been through the preliminaries. "I'd like to refer you to DI Yates's question towards the end of your previous interview, when he asked if you had any reason for wanting Gordon Bemrose dead. You hesitated before you answered no. Neither DI Yates nor I found your denial very convincing."

"That's surely a matter for you and DI Yates," said Jean Rook, "since you obtained an answer. My client . . . "

"No," said Patti. "It's all right. I want to tell them. It's going to come out anyway, when Gordon's estate is probated. But I'd like to say first it was a reason for disliking him, though, not for killing him."

"Go on," said Tim, forgetting that Juliet was supposed to be taking the lead.

"You've seen my mother," Patti said, addressing herself to him. "She has dementia. It's not very far advanced yet, but we have reached the stage where she can't be left on her own for long. We haven't told anyone else yet. She's managed to run up a huge credit card bill – for more than £10,000. Gordon lent me the money, on condition that if I hadn't paid him back after six months, he'd start charging interest, at quite an exorbitant rate."

"If your mother has dementia, you'd have stood a good chance of having the bill waived. The credit card company was at fault for setting such a high limit on her account."

"I know that, but it would have meant admitting she has dementia, and she's still aware enough of what's going on for that to have humiliated her hugely. I was afraid it would send her into an even steeper decline."

"Did Gordon know about the dementia?"

"No, and she wouldn't have wanted me to tell him. And Gordon enjoyed hanging it over my head when he wanted me to do him the favour of helping with his crime weekend. That's the way he operates. That's how he persuaded Anton to help, too. Anton owes him much more . . . " She stopped suddenly.

"Please go on. How much does Anton owe him?"

"I think that's a matter for you to take up with Mr Greenweal," said Jean Rook stiffly. "My client is getting tired. We should conclude this interview now."

"God, this is confusing," said Tim, after Patti and Jean Rook had gone. "First I thought she was probably guilty, but towards the end of the interview I was almost convinced she wasn't. I'm surprised at her poor judgment over the credit card business, though."

"You can understand that she wanted to protect her mother. What about Anton Greenweal? As Patti inadvertently told us, he had more reason for killing Gordon than she did."

"I'm far from convinced it was Greenweal. He just doesn't have the stomach for a knife crime. But we'll have to ask him about the money."

CHAPTER 74

ANDY HELPED JULIET schedule interviews over the next two days. Tim had worked out a kind of reverse priority list, by calculating who, besides Patti, was most likely to have been capable of the murder(s) and the assaults. He was trying to keep an open mind on whether the murderer was also responsible for the assaults, or whether the assailant was someone else. There might even have been more than one assailant; and, at a push - for he didn't yet have conclusive proof that Sykes was murdered - two murderers.

Least likely on his list were any of the amateur actors, followed by Richard and Sonia Renwick, who seemed to have wandered from one nightmare to another by accident, and Victor le Grange and Amelia Baker, who had almost undoubtedly used the crime event as cover for a dirty weekend. After some hesitation, he placed Dora Westerman next lowest. She'd admitted to wanting to kill Gordon, but he doubted she could have plunged the knife into his back with such force; and she was certainly not guilty of the assaults. Margarett Franklin came next. She was a younger, more powerful woman than Dora and therefore more capable of wielding the knife, but somehow he doubted she had it in her to kill, despite her distress and anger over her daughter's death. And she couldn't have been responsible for any of the assaults except, at a pinch, the first attack on Gordon. Given her nervous disposition, he just couldn't imagine her lurking in the pitch-black darkness, waiting for Gordon to come past.

Ava Dack and Lizzie Fox were guilty of something, but he doubted it was murder. Tim suspected they'd been operating a scam either with or on behalf of their husbands. He knew he'd have to get to the bottom of what they were up to, but that would hinder, rather than help, the murder investigation: it simply meant he'd have to divert precious time away from catching the killer.

Colin Franklin was a likely suspect: he was strong enough to have murdered Gordon and outspoken in his regret that someone else had got there first. He'd been outside or un-accounted for during each of the attacks, except the one in the cellar; and at a stretch he could have been responsible for that, too: he'd moved around so much that evening that it was unlikely anyone could provide chapter and verse about where he'd been at any exact time.

That left the four people best known to Gordon: Patti; Anton Greenweal and Percy Forsyth; and Mrs Lawrence. Tim didn't need reminding that most murders were committed by people familiar with the victim. Patti was still his prime suspect, though his doubt of her guilt was increasing. He was convinced Anton was incapable of such a crime. That left Percy Forsyth and Mrs Lawrence. Tim had a hunch there was more to understand about Mrs Lawrence's relationship with Gordon than she'd disclosed, but she had cast-iron alibis for all the times at which the assaults had taken place. If she could also prove that she hadn't spent the night at Holyrood House, as she claimed, she was in the clear.

Percy Forsyth was another matter. Tim suspected he was capable of the attacks, but pinning all but the first of the assaults on him would be difficult. There was, however, only Anton's word for it that they had both spent the night in the cottage; and Percy was familiar with the geography of Holyrood House. Tim decided they would interview Percy last. And then Patti again.

He scribbled some notes about interview order for Juliet and she and Andy hit the phones. They spent most of the rest of the day compiling the schedule, filling in gaps with the thespians, all of whom seemed to be available on any day at any time. The schedule was as complete as they could make it when she took it back to Tim.

"Great, thanks, Juliet," he said, casting his eye over it. "But you've put Isobel Lawrence right at the end and I can't see Amelia Baker on it at all."

"Mrs Lawrence's brother's been having seizures, apparently. She's taking him to Nottingham for some tests. They're going to keep him in overnight and she'll stay with him, but she says she can get back for the end of the second day we're interviewing. She's been waiting a long time for the appointment. I didn't think you'd want me to ask her to cancel it."

"No, that's fine. I don't really mind when we see her. What about Amelia Baker?"

"I only spoke to her flatmate. Amelia's gone to Amsterdam for a few days, to a Christmas fair. We have her mobile number – do you want me to ask her to come back?"

"Stupid girl! We told her not to leave the country or go anywhere we couldn't get hold of her. Still, I doubt if what she has to say is vital; it's not worth making her cut short her break. Probably needs it after the way that little shit treated her. I take it you managed to reach him?"

"Victor le Grange, you mean? Yes, at his office. He was

whispering into the phone and kept the call as short as he could. I've scheduled him for the middle of the day tomorrow so he can get here and back without having to explain himself. He'll be back in London in time to go home in the evening as usual."

"You're too nice, Juliet. He's such a craven little sod, I'd love to put him in an awkward situation, give his wife a hint of what he's been up to. Still, I don't suppose it would help us much."

"He's the sort of person who would file a complaint for lack of respect for his privacy."

"You're right. Thanks again for this." Tim waved the schedule at her. "Professor Salkeld rang while you were working on it. Cause of death for Gordon Bemrose was penetration of the heart by a large kitchen knife. No surprises there, but there was one interesting feature: Bemrose had a brain tumour. Probably inoperable, according to the professor, but unlikely yet to have caused him pain, so we don't know whether he knew about it or not. Cause of death for Montagu Sykes: a massive dose of flunitrazepam. Far more, apparently, than it's likely he would have consumed from drinking from the cups and glasses that we tested."

"So, are we looking at two murders?"

"I think so. And possibly two murderers, too, one of whom may or may not have been Patti. And one or several assailants. Or indeed, one person who managed to carry out the whole sorry lot. But then it wouldn't have been Patti."

Tim was speaking with a put-on, archly lugubrious voice. Even so, Juliet detected a strong undercurrent of despair. In truth, and despite Patti's arrest, they had made little progress since they had first been called to the crime scene.

CHAPTER 75

Iᴛ ᴡᴀs Tᴜᴇsᴅᴀʏ and Tim and Juliet were ploughing through interviews. Tim had considered – and rejected – the idea of working in two teams of two with Andy and Ricky; he decided it was probably best if he and Juliet carried out all the interviews this time. It would be easier for them to spot any discrepancies if they examined everyone. In the event, Superintendent Thornton commandeered Andy and Ricky shortly afterwards. The Chief Constable had called him again about apprehending the hare coursers. It had been a short call in every sense of the word and it rattled Thornton considerably; having himself insisted that the hare coursing be put on a back burner after the murders, the Superintendent was now trying to blame Andy for the lack of progress that had been made. Belatedly, Andy and Ricky had been packed off to the field where Juliet and Jake had found the tyre marks, to take casts.

Richard and Sonia Renwick, interviewed together this time, recited practically verbatim the same account of their Friday night at Holyrood House as they had on the previous occasion. There was nothing fresh to be gleaned from their interview, except that they were clearly getting on much better with each other than they'd seemed to previously.

"We really must get back to work soon," said Richard mischievously as they were preparing to leave. "We took yesterday off, as well as last Friday. There's a lot to get on with now."

"You're a writer, aren't you?" Tim asked politely.

"Yes, he is." Sonia Renwick almost simpered. "And he's had a wonderful idea for a new play. His agent's very excited about it. It could make him famous."

"Oh?" said Tim, striving to show interest. "Congratulations. And thank you very much for coming at such short notice."

"Well, just let us know if you need us again," Sonia chirruped.

"I've got a horrible feeling I know what he's planning to write about," said Juliet, after they'd gone.

"What? Oh, I see what you mean," said Tim. "Well, if he doesn't write about it, someone else will. I guess he'll tell as good a yarn as someone who wasn't there. Just as long as he doesn't try to publish anything before the trial . . . if there is a trial."

The desk sergeant sent a message to say that Dora Westerman had been delayed because the train she'd meant to catch had been cancelled. This suited Victor le Grange, now invited to take her slot in the schedule; he had arrived at the same time as the Renwicks and had been pacing up and down Interview Room 2 ever since.

"May I impress on you how important it is that this is kept confidential," he said as soon as he saw Juliet and Tim. "It's not just my wife that concerns me: it's my employer, too. I could lose my job if it gets out about Amelia . . . and, anyway, it was all much more innocent than it looked," he said emphatically. He glared at them with bloodshot eyes.

"I'm certain it was, Dr le Grange," said Tim. "I assure you, our lips are sealed. I should warn you, though, there's nothing we can do about it if you're called as a witness in court."

"But I don't know anything!" Le Grange wailed. "Nothing.

Nada. I went to that place to drop Amelia off and foolishly stayed longer than I should have done. Then I was mugged and spent the rest of the evening with everyone else, in that so-called 'theatre'. I had to stay the night because of my injuries, and because it had got so late by the time the electricity came on again. I slept in the sitting-room in Amelia's cottage, which she and Miss Westerman kindly allowed, and we woke up the next day to discover Bemrose had been murdered. That's all I know."

His story sounded rehearsed, as if it had been prepared for someone unlikely to believe it – his wife, probably.

"Yes, I'm sure all that is true, Dr le Grange. Now, could we focus on the mugging. You said before you weren't certain you *were* mugged, but you now seem to have decided that you were. Did you see or hear anything or anyone between the time you left the cottage and the time you were attacked? I realise we're only talking about a few seconds."

"No, all I remember is that it was bloody dark and then that black chap was standing over me. Come to think of it, it could have been him, couldn't it? Who mugged me, I mean?"

Tim sighed.

"I wouldn't insinuate that Mr Franklin attacked you unless you have some evidence. Guesswork isn't going to help us."

Le Grange lapsed into a mutinous silence. It was obvious they'd get no further with him.

Dora Westerman had still not arrived. Tim and Juliet therefore had time for lunch. Immediately afterwards, Avril Spearman arrived, with a plain and forbidding woman in tow. Like all the witnesses, Avril had been told she could be accompanied by someone if she wished. It was apparent, however, that little chemistry existed between her and this woman.

"Good afternoon," said the woman. "I'm Janice Pell. Avril's probation officer."

"Thank you for coming with Avril," said Tim, ushering them into the interview room.

"It wasn't my idea," said Avril passionately. "Showing me up proper, this is. And I ain't done nothink wrong. I was told to join the acting as part of me community service. It's not my fault if that old guy got himself topped, is it? Can you tell 'er," she jerked her head in Ms Pell's direction, "that I didn't do owt?"

Juliet smiled sympathetically at Avril, in part to hide her amusement. She liked Avril a lot more than Janice Pell, who had seated herself as far from the teenager as she could and was wearing an expression of extreme distaste. It was hard to believe her capable of achieving any kind of rapport with those under her supervision.

"Avril has been extremely helpful," Juliet said. "We have no reason at all to believe that she was responsible for any of the crimes that took place at Holyrood House last Friday. We've just asked her back today to go over her statement again, see if there's anything that she missed. It's not unusual for witnesses to recall facts they didn't mention when they were first interviewed or mention something that later strikes them as more important than they'd first thought."

"I daresay," said Janice Pell. She sniffed and looked at Juliet accusingly. "Just one thing, DS Armstrong – can you tell me whether Avril indulged in alcohol on the occasion we are discussing?"

"What a cow!" Tim said, after they'd gone. "Avril's probably broken the conditions of her probation by drinking and that Pell woman will make her pay for it. But I wouldn't say Avril's a suspect, would you?"

Several of Montagu Sykes's elderly amateur actors took up the rest of the afternoon. Tim had barely seen them during the weekend interview sessions at Holyrood House and therefore hadn't realised how senile some of them were. All claimed to have spent the whole of their time on the island in the ballroom, but they exhibited varying degrees of confusion when asked to give further details.

Wright, who seemed to be the most decrepit of them all, kept going on about "Wally Potts's lad", maintaining that you couldn't trust Wally as far as you could throw him and the lad was probably tarred with the same brush. He repeated this so many times that Tim eventually lost patience. Juliet was kinder to the old man and made sure he was given tea and biscuits before he went home, but she was just as mystified as Tim about what he was trying to tell them.

He was succeeded by George Thomson, who began his interview in a perfectly lucid way and then also began to talk in riddles. It was after Tim had pressed him to say whether he had really spent all the time in the ballroom or perhaps visited other parts of the house, however briefly, that George began to discuss his health issues.

"I've an enlarged prostate, see, and it means I have to go quite frequently," said George, addressing himself squarely to Tim and ignoring Juliet. "I was worried about it, like, with me being Freddy. I didn't want owt to happen while I was on the stage. They showed me where the lav was, though, and I went first off and then several more times. Of course, I were only pretending to be Freddy. But on one of my trips to the toilet I see the real one."

"I'm not sure I follow," said Tim curtly. "The real one what?"

"The real Freddy, of course, like I said." George lay a great deal of emphasis on his last three words. Juliet could see he was becoming agitated.

"We're sorry, George," she said apologetically. "We've seen a lot of people today and we're getting a bit tired. Could you explain what you mean by 'the real Freddy?'"

George puffed out his cheeks.

"It's like I said . . . "

"Yes, we understand what you said." Juliet butted in before Tim showed his impatience and shut the old man up altogether. "You were the Freddy in the play. You're not the 'real' Freddy. Your name is George. So, who is the real Freddy? Was it someone you saw at Holyrood House?"

"Seen 'im around quite a bit, I have," said George defensively. "Yes, 'e was there. Talking to the 'ousekeeper lady. And Monty was there, too."

"Did you speak to any of them?"

"No, I don't think they saw me. I wasn't about to go butting in."

Juliet tried to draw him out further, but George could only repeat the same few sentences again. When asked to describe the other Freddy, he merely looked blank.

"Do you think there was anything in that?" Tim asked Juliet, after George had gone.

"I don't know. Nothing that would stand up in court. And George should have had a responsible adult with him: if we'd known how fragile he is - mentally, I mean - I think we'd have thought twice about interviewing him on his own."

"We'll have to discount what he said, in other words," said Tim. "All right. In with the next one."

They toiled on for the rest of the afternoon without making any headway. Vicky's was the last interview that day. Either she wasn't on probation or she'd managed to keep her probation officer out of it. "Dunno" was her answer to almost every question she was asked. After a few minutes Tim allowed her to leave.

"Let's call it a day," said Tim wearily, after Vicky's departure. "It doesn't look as if Dora Westerman's going to show up and quite frankly I've had enough."

"I'll call her tomorrow," said Juliet. "It sounds as if she was genuinely delayed. And I would like to go now myself, if that's ok with you. I want to call in at the vet's to see how Sally is."

Juliet was barely out of the door when Tim's phone rang.

"Are you sure?" he said. "Yes, that is very helpful. Thank you."

He put down the phone. The remains of the animal found in the plastic sack in Gordon Bemrose's cellar had been analysed. It was a Saluki. Tim wasn't in the habit of talking to himself, but on this occasion he spoke his thoughts aloud. It made them seem more feasible.

"So that was one of your scams, was it, Gordon? Hare coursing. Perhaps Juliet was right – the two cases are linked."

Tim shovelled the transcripts of all the interviews into his briefcase and prepared to leave the police station. He was out on the forecourt, flicking the remote to unlock his car, when he heard someone call his name. He turned to see Dora Westerman approaching him.

"DI Yates, I'm so sorry I'm late. The trains have been a nightmare!"

"Miss Westerman, we thought you weren't able to get here today! I'm sorry, but DS Armstrong has left the station now. We need to do the interviews together. Can you come back tomorrow?"

Dora Westerman stiffened. It was impossible not to observe the steely glint in her eye.

"DI Yates, I have just spent more than six hours travelling and waiting endlessly for trains because I thought it was important to keep your appointment. Are you suggesting that I should now try the same journey in reverse and then again tomorrow? I doubt very much that I'll be able to get home this evening, in any case."

Tim scanned the horizon as if for inspiration, or Juliet's miraculous return. He was relieved to see Verity Tandy emerging from the station. At the present moment no-one except Juliet could have put in a more welcome appearance.

"PC Tandy! Could you come over here for a moment?"

Verity Tandy gave Dora a friendly smile as she walked towards them.

"Hello," she said, "we met last Saturday, if you remember? At Holyrood House?"

"PC Tandy, we'd hoped to interview Miss Westerman again today, but unfortunately she was delayed. Could you find some accommodation for her tonight, so she doesn't have a wasted journey?"

"Sure," said Verity. "There are several small hotels and boarding houses we use round here. Let me make a few calls. Then I'll give you a lift, if you like."

"Nowhere fancy, mind," Dora said.

Tim had thanked Verity, arranged with Dora Westerman to come to the station at noon the next day and gratefully said goodbye to both women before it struck him that Dora was carrying a very large bucket bag. Had she meant to stay overnight all along?

CHAPTER 76

IF TIM AND Juliet had been struck by the new-found amity that had broken out between the Renwicks, they were even more surprised by the open hostility Margarett and Colin Franklin now showed towards each other.

They'd invited the Franklins, Like the Renwicks, to be interviewed together to review their statements. They started with Colin Franklin's statement, which was the longest of those taken at Holyrood House. Colin had certainly been active that evening.

"Mrs Franklin wasn't feeling too well, so you took her tea to your room and then you went out for a walk. Where did you go? Did you leave the island?"

"No. I wanted to explore it - see what it was like."

"In the dark?"

"He just wanted to get away from me for a while," Margarett said dourly.

"Had you been to the island before? You said your daughter worked for Gordon Bemrose."

"Margarett and I went to look at the room a few weeks ago. We didn't see the island when Cicely worked for Bemrose. She didn't work on the island - she was working in one of his other businesses."

"No, she only died on the island, that's all; or rather, in the river. She drowned herself, DI Yates, because of that man," said Margarett, glaring at Tim as if he could have prevented it.

Tim ignored her. This was the first he'd heard of the Franklins' prior visit.

"The other guests appear not to have visited in advance. Why did you?"

"Like I said, to see the room. Margarett said she couldn't stand to be in one of the cottages. They're too close to the river. So we came to see what the guest room in the house was like and made sure we got it."

"Mrs Lawrence told us your shoes were filthy when you went to the drinks reception. You had to change them for trainers."

"That's right. I should have changed my shoes before. Margarett did tell me they were muddy. I forgot."

"Were they muddy because you'd been walking – or hanging around – on the piece of waste ground where Gordon Bemrose was first attacked?"

"I don't know where I went. The whole place was muddy, apart from the footpath. I didn't see anyone while I was out – not Gordon or anyone else."

Tim thought he detected a note of defensiveness creeping into Franklin's voice.

"What about when you found Victor le Grange after he'd been mugged? Did you see anyone then?"

"No. I didn't hear anything, neither."

"Mr le Grange has suggested – I must emphasise he is only speculating – that you might have jumped him before pretending to rescue him."

Colin Franklin curled his lip in a sneer.

"What would I waste my time on the likes of him? A jumped-up ponce cheating on his wife with one of his students."

Tim let the comment hang in the air for a moment.

"According to your statement, you got him back on his feet and took him into the ballroom, where everyone else was; and then, some time later, you went out again. You were a very busy man that evening. Almost every time someone went missing, it was you who did the searching. Why was that?"

"There was barely a proper man in the whole place. The only other bloke I'd give the time of day to was Percy Forsyth. We agreed he ought to stay with the others, to stop them getting hysterical, like." Colin glared at his wife as he spoke.

"Oh, I suppose you mean me by that, do you? 'Given to hysteria – a bit weak in the head'?"

"Mrs Franklin, if you don't stop these interjections, I'm going to have to ask you to wait somewhere else until we come to your own statement. Your comments aren't helpful – in fact, they're very distracting."

The interview ground on. Tim and Juliet examined each of their statements minutely, sometimes spending several minutes on a single sentence, while the Franklins jibed at each other with just enough restraint not to make him eject one of them from the room. At the end of the interview, which long overshot the time they'd allocated to it, Tim and Juliet were exhausted but had made no significant breakthrough.

They'd decided to ask Lizzie to attend again as well as Ava. Both had been waiting with the desk sergeant for some time, as she informed Juliet when she arrived to ask if she should show them in.

"I'll be glad to get rid of those two – if they're not moaning about having to wait, they're shrieking with laugher about something. I'd rather be dealing with a couple of drunks."

It was on the tip of Tim's tongue to say she probably was

dealing with two drunks, but he stopped himself in time. It could only complicate matters further. The observation did, however, prompt him to ask Ava how they'd travelled to Spalding.

"I took Reggie's four by four, didn't I? Flat refused to bring us hisself and so I said to 'im you needn't think I'm driving all that way in that pisspot little Yaris." Lizzie giggled. Tim was again reminded that he needed to find out the real names of the two men who called themselves Reggie Dack and Jackson Fox.

Juliet turned to speak to him.

"DI Yates, could I have a word?"

Tim was immediately apprehensive. He knew Juliet wouldn't interrupt the interview schedule without a good reason.

"Certainly. Ladies, help yourselves to tea. We won't be gone for long."

Juliet went into the small kitchen near the interview room. Tim followed.

"If they've come in Reggie Dack's four by four, it may be the vehicle Jake saw in the field where we found the shoe. There may be soil samples still trapped in the tread of the tyres – the field was very muddy. At any rate we could have someone take an impression of the tyres while we're interviewing."

"You're right. It's a pity Andy and Ricky are both out."

"I saw Giash Chakrabati earlier. Perhaps ask him?"

"Yes. See if you can find him, will you, while I go back to the two ladies. And get him to check on the registered owner. I doubt the vehicle's been stolen, but you never know."

"I think I'd better go back to them while you find Giash, don't you? I wouldn't put anything past them."

"What? Oh, you mean they might say I attacked them. You must be joking! Those two could eat me for breakfast."

"Precisely," said Juliet.

Ava's memory of the whole Friday night was hazy, but since everyone else who'd been present had said she was drunk, Tim didn't think her foggy recollections were a sham. Lizzie tied herself up in knots when they again asked her about the shoe, telling her this time it was the left shoe, not the right, that had been found. Ava came to her defence.

"I expect she was confused," she said indignantly. "Just had a nasty fall, din't she? For all we know she might of put the left shoe on the right foot and not realised."

"God!" said Tim, after they'd gone. "I hope Giash got the tyre samples, all right. He should have had plenty of time to do it, anyway. Dora Westerman'll be a breeze after those two."

"I wonder what she's been doing this morning?"

"Just kicking her heels, I suppose."

"It occurred to me when you were asking the Franklins why they'd visited Holyrood House before the crime weekend: Dora Westerman must have been there before, too. Lots of times, if what she told us about her aunt was true."

"You mean, she knew her way around the island?"

"She knew her way round her aunt's cottage. I doubt if she'd been in the main house, unless she was on friendlier terms with the people who lived there before than she was with Gordon. I was thinking more about whom she might have met on the island, besides Gordon."

"You can ask her," said Tim.

CHAPTER 77

JULIET WENT DOWN to meet Dora Westerman to escort her to the interview room while Tim made a quick call to Giash Chakrabati.

"Did you get the tyre samples?"

"Yes," said Giash. "What do you want me to do with them?"

"They need sending to the lab with some samples that DC Carstairs is collecting. DC MacFadyen is with him. They'll know what to put on the requisition form." Tim looked at his watch. "They should be back any time now. You wouldn't have time to wait for them, would you?"

"I think they might be here already. I caught a glimpse of DC MacFadyen going into the canteen."

"That figures," said Tim. "See if you can find them, will you?"

There was a tap at the door. Juliet was peering through the glass window. Tim waved her in. Juliet stepped aside after she'd opened the door, to allow Dora Westerman to precede her. Tim was surprised to see Amelia Baker following in Dora's wake. Juliet shut the door.

"Miss Baker! I thought you were abroad somewhere."

"I was, but my flatmate got it wrong. My flight back was yesterday, not tomorrow, as she said. When I heard you wanted to see me again, I thought I'd better come as soon as I could. Dora told me when her interview was and I thought it might help you if I came at the same time, since we shared the cottage." She paused and swallowed. "Is Victor - Dr le Grange - coming today?"

"No, we saw him yesterday," said Tim. His mind was working overtime. The earliest Dora Westerman could have told Amelia the time of her interview was when he'd agreed it with her yesterday evening. He supposed that was time enough for Amelia to make travel arrangements. But why did they both seem so keen on being interviewed together?

"You can do us separately, if you like," Dora Westerman said, as if reading his mind.

"Together is fine," said Tim. "We want to go through the statements we took at the weekend, in case anyone has anything to add." And now that Amelia's here as well, it's unlikely Juliet and I will get any lunch, unless we work through them double quickly, he added silently. But Amelia had been besotted with le Grange last Friday and not paying attention - it was unlikely she would have anything of interest to tell them. Tim gave her an avuncular smile, to which she responded with such a direct stare that he was shamed into seeing more to her than he'd realised.

Amelia and Dora were seated side by side. They seemed very comfortable in each other's company.

"Will you start, or shall I?" said Dora.

"You go first."

Dora folded her hands in her lap and began. Her story was lucid and coherent; she told it as if she were a librarian addressing a group of school children.

"You see, DI Yates, we have compared notes. We both saw something strange - aside from the other very strange things that were going on in that house that night. Separately, what we saw made no sense, but, when we put the details together, they seemed to fit like pieces of a jigsaw puzzle. I should warn you, though, that we don't have all the pieces."

"Go on," said Tim. He would have been enjoying this if he didn't have so much else to worry about.

"Last Friday afternoon, when I sat by the sitting-room window while we were having drinks, I thought I heard a motor – not a motor car, the sound of a boat on the river. I was trying to look out of the window, but it was pretty murky outside – it was foggy, as you know, and dusk had fallen. I stared across the river, but I couldn't see anything. And then Mrs Lawrence insisted that the curtains should be drawn. She was quite abrupt about it. I thought it was odd, but I supposed her brusqueness was easily explained – the poor woman was obviously overworked and trying to attend to everyone. I thought no more about it at the time – not even when you first interviewed me. But that was before I'd talked to Amelia."

She smiled at Amelia Baker.

"I was late for dinner," Amelia Baker continued. "Victor was fussing about this and that. One minute he was going to shut himself up in the double bedroom and not come out until he went home on the Saturday evening; the next he didn't want to stay at all. He said he'd be sure to be discovered – he had some idea that he'd met Richard Renwick before – and then his wife would find out. He was annoyed that the Renwicks had seen him. I was having serious doubts about him. I'd really looked up to him until then, but he was being so self-centred, and at the same time so cowardly, that I was beginning to think I'd made a huge mistake. I know everyone else thought I was making a fool of myself."

"I didn't," said Dora forcefully. "I know his type. It's easy to get caught out."

"Eventually we agreed that he'd think up some excuse for why he hadn't gone home after he dropped me off and pretend that when he did try to leave, he'd been mugged. Then he could stay in the cottage overnight, as we'd planned, and hang around on Saturday with a story that everyone on the island could believe, while, with his wife, sticking to the story he'd told her that he was at a symposium in Lincoln. He'd always intended to go home on Saturday evening. I agreed to spend Saturday morning with him – I thought we could go for a look round the town."

"So he *pretended* to be mugged?" said Tim.

"I don't know. I doubt he's a good enough actor. I think the attack was real."

"Poetic justice," Dora murmured.

"Because of arguing with Victor, I was late for dinner," Amelia continued, "As I came past the dining-room I could hear Mrs Lawrence and someone else making plans for the Saturday morning. I hadn't read the schedule for the weekend properly, but when I heard the boat trip being discussed I stayed to listen. It dawned on me that if I missed the boat trip, I wouldn't be able to join in the whodunnit session that evening."

"Did that matter to you?" asked Juliet.

"Yes. Believe it or not, I wasn't just there for a dirty weekend with Victor. That was his idea and came afterwards – I should never have agreed to it. I'm making a study of crime fiction and its spin-offs. The weekend was genuinely important to me. I was there to see what a crime weekend was like, and, more particularly, to watch the people involved."

387

"Very usefully for you, DI Yates," added Dora.

"Why did you want to watch the others?"

"I wanted to understand what made them tick – why people would spend so much time and money on such a thing."

"Like sociologists make studies of pigeon fanciers or of people who keep on going to the same holiday camp year after year?" said Juliet.

"Exactly," Amelia agreed. "But I didn't want to get caught eavesdropping. After I'd learnt about the boat trip, I carried on along the corridor. Montagu Sykes went past me."

"Did you see anyone else?"

"Yes. Percy Forsyth. He'd been upstairs – he was at the other end of the corridor. I don't think he saw me. Then one of those old men Montagu said were actors came out through the ballroom door. He was desperate to find the toilet. I went with him to look for it."

"You were late for dinner, though, weren't you? Even though at the time you're speaking of the other guests had yet to arrive?"

"Yes. I waited for the old man to come out of the toilet. He seemed so confused, I didn't think he'd find his way back to the others alone."

"Can you remember his name?"

"Yes, it was George."

"Thank you. Is there anything else you didn't put in your statement, that you want to tell us now?"

"Just one other thing. After the power-cut, when Colin Franklin brought in Montagu Sykes and Richard Renwick from outside, Percy told Gordon Bemrose to offer everyone a drink. Percy was taking Richard Renwick to his cottage to have a shower because Richard was nervous about going outside again on his own. Mrs Lawrence was asked to get the drinks. When she came back with them, I saw her hand Montagu a flask."

"Do you know how she came to have it in her possession?"

"I do!" said Dora. "I saw Percy ask Montagu for it shortly after they came into the hall."

"He must have left it in the kitchen on his way to Richard Renwick's cottage," Amelia added.

"So . . . what are you suggesting?" Tim asked.

"Poison!" cried Dora Westerman triumphantly. "We think Mr Sykes was poisoned. By whatever was in the flask."

Juliet thought this was a brilliant guess, considering neither of the women knew about the Rohypnol. Aloud she said. "That's an ingenious idea, if it's correct. But there's one thing that puzzles me . . ."

"Oh?" said Amelia, immediately on her guard.

"The things you've told us are obviously important. Too important for them not to have seemed significant, or to have slipped your minds, when you were first interviewed. And certainly remarkable once you'd compared notes and, as you put it, fitted together some of the pieces of the jigsaw. I'd like to suggest to you both that you agreed not to mention what you've just told us. Did something happen between last Saturday and now to make you change your minds?"

Amelia looked at Dora. Juliet saw several different expressions flit across Dora's face in quick succession.

"You're very clever," she said at last.

"Well?" said Tim.

"I think I've made my feelings about Gordon Bemrose very clear, DI Yates. He deserved to die and no death was too horrible for him, as far as I was concerned. But Montagu

Sykes was different. He was just an innocent victim who got in the way. To kill him was an outrage. It made us see that the murderer would stop at nothing. There might be other murders."

"You agreed with this?" Juliet asked Amelia.

"I . . . yes. Dora showed me what kind of person Gordon Bemrose was. Manipulative, trampling on others' feelings to get his own way. Like Victor."

"Amelia hasn't done anything wrong. She'd never have identified the killer from what she knew."

"So what did you know, Miss Westerman? What makes you so sure you know who the killer is?"

CHAPTER 78

T HEY HAD NOT expected Isobel Lawrence to show up, but immediately Verity Tandy came down with Dora Westerman and Amelia Baker to sign them out the desk sergeant called Juliet to say she was waiting to see them. Looking at her watch, Juliet saw that if Mrs Lawrence had arrived punctually, they had kept her waiting some time. She must have nerves of steel!

She'd been shown into Interview Room 2. When Tim and Juliet entered the room, she was sitting stiffly upright on her chair, her hands folded in her lap. As when they first met her, she was dressed almost entirely in black, the block ebony of her dress relieved only by a narrow cream lace collar. Her face was very pale, but otherwise she seemed composed. She half stood when she saw them, until she read Tim's quick gesture that she should keep her seat.

"Mrs Lawrence," he said. "Thank you for coming."

"You sound surprised, DI Yates," she said drily. "Did you think I wouldn't keep your appointment?"

"It had crossed our minds," Tim replied. "We know Miss Westerman came to see you this morning."

"Yes; clever of her, wasn't it, to build up a picture of what had happened? I'm not altogether surprised – she made a good impression on me on the occasions she visited her aunt. But I must admit I under-estimated that silly girl. According to Dora, they worked it out together. I'd never have believed that girl had it in her. Was it because Dora told you she'd called on me that you thought I wouldn't come?"

Tim nodded. "I must tell you at this point that you are entitled to have a lawyer present before you say any more."

"There'll be time for that later. I'm quite happy to talk to you now. It was sweet of Dora to want to warn me, but I'd already made my plans. I couldn't let your colleague take the rap for murder when I knew she wasn't guilty. I've spirited Fred away. I think it's very unlikely you'll find him."

"Hence your excuse that you'd taken him to see a specialist in epilepsy?" said Juliet.

Isobel Lawrence's face flushed red. Her mouth was working. The passionate emotion roiling beneath her calm exterior suddenly showed itself.

"Oh, Fred's an epileptic, all right," she said grimly. "He had Gordon Bemrose to thank for that. Gordon hit him with an iron bar when he was a young man. That's when the fits started." Tim noticed her voice was losing its polish. She had quite a strong Lincolnshire accent when she wasn't playing the part of the lady housekeeper.

"But he – and you – must have borne him a grudge ever since," said Juliet. "Why did Fred decide to kill him now? And why did you work for Gordon all those years? Why not just take Fred away somewhere?"

"Poverty," Isobel Lawrence said simply. "And in my case, stupidity, too. I was widowed very young – my husband was an RAF serviceman who died in an accident – and I suppose I fell for Gordon on the rebound. He treated me very well at first, but Fred saw through him – he found out that Gordon always had several women on the go. He challenged Gordon and Gordon lost his temper and hit him. Afterwards he made us hush it up by paying Fred's medical bills. Gordon gave Fred a monthly allowance – it more than covered the bills. Fred needed the extra – the work he gets from running that launch doesn't bring in much money and he can't hold down a more regular job. Gordon being Gordon, there was another twist to the bargain – he said he'd only keep on with the allowance if I agreed to work for him, too, as his 'housekeeper', whenever he needed one. So I was trapped. Funny, isn't it, that Gordon got through God knows how many women since I first met him and I was still there?" She gave a bitter little laugh.

"That still doesn't answer DS Armstrong's question," said Tim. "Why now? You and Fred must have had dozens of opportunities to top Gordon if you'd wanted to."

"Dozens," she echoed dully. "Yes, dozens, DI Yates, but I think you're missing the point: we didn't intend to 'top' Gordon, as you put it. I've told you, we were both trapped in relationships with him. There was no way out, because if I didn't carry on working for Gordon, he would stop Fred's allowance. Believe me, when the crime weekend started last Friday I had no idea that Gordon would be dead at the end of it. Neither did Fred."

"So what happened?"

"It took me some time to piece that together myself. I got there before Dora and Amelia Baker, but only because eventually I managed to get some sense out of Fred – he was just gibbering at first – and then I remembered something Percy had said quite casually when I made breakfast for him and Anton late on Friday morning."

"Which was?"

"They were joking – well, Percy was joking, Anton was moaning – about why they were there. It was typical of

Gordon – he'd pushed Anton into acting for him because Anton owed him some money. Quite a lot of money, from what they were saying. And then Percy said something about killing the golden goose before it stopped laying the eggs."

"Can you remember his exact words?"

"I can try. I think it was, 'We'll have to think about killing our golden goose before he lays his eggs elsewhere.'"

"What did you think he meant by that?"

"Quite honestly, I was too busy to think about it at all at the time. I liked Percy, but he and Anton – especially Anton – were full of nonsense and always made quite a lot of work. I did have a soft spot for Percy, though. Poor judgment, obviously."

Tim looked at Juliet. Evidently Dora Westerman and Amelia Baker had correctly identified Fred Sharman as Gordon Bemrose's murderer, so they'd been unsurprised by Isobel's confession, but she was introducing a new dimension to the investigation now. She saw that she'd dropped a bombshell and gave Tim another of her sardonic smiles.

"Blame is a hard thing to apportion, isn't it DI Yates? In your job, you must frequently find it to be so."

Tim was about to say that this wasn't one of the more common problems he encountered – that murder cases were usually pretty cut-and-dried – when Juliet cut in.

"That's a fascinating observation, Mrs Lawrence. Could you explain what you mean?"

"Percy talked Fred into killing Gordon. He told him Gordon was changing his will. Percy didn't know the exact arrangement we had with Gordon, but he guessed Fred was financially dependent on him. He panicked Fred into the murder. I honestly had no idea about it until the early hours of

Saturday morning. When I got home to our flat, Fred wasn't there; and when he did come in, he was covered in blood and in a terrible state. It took me the rest of the night to get him cleaned up and tell me what had happened."

"Did he hide in the room that you used when you stayed at Holyrood House?"

"Yes. How did you know that?"

Tim waved his hand. He was anxious not to slow the momentum of the dialogue.

"Did you genuinely decide you'd prefer not to stay the night yourself? A cynic might say you were paving the way for Fred to commit murder."

"Do you believe I would have let Fred kill Gordon if I'd known about it? Yes, I did 'genuinely' decide to go home. I thought it would be better for Fred if I saw him in the morning, particularly as he was taking the boat out. And I did want to get away from the guests for a few hours – when I put that in my statement, it was the truth. It was Percy who 'paved the way'. He struck lucky when the husbands of those two old tarts cancelled. He realised that if he could get Anton to persuade Gordon to let them have the free cottage, only Gordon and Ms Gardner would be sleeping on the first floor of the house."

Tim nodded. And, he added silently, he was lucky again when Patti found and touched that knife in the bathroom. Percy must have taken both knives from the block in the kitchen and left them in the bathroom cupboard for Fred.

"But Fred didn't kill Montagu Sykes," Isobel said suddenly. "And he didn't attack Gordon when he was outside, or the academic bloke. Believe me, I've been through it with him time and again. He admits to tying up Monty and Mr

Renwick. He says that after Percy had talked to him, he told him to take the boat round the other side of the island and come back later. When he did come back, he saw them just before the power-cut and then bumped into them after it happened. He didn't recognise Monty – he was wearing that American policeman's outfit and I think Fred got confused and thought he'd be arrested. So he tripped them and tied them up. He's quite positive that's all he did – besides kill Gordon, of course."

"Mrs Lawrence," said Tim, "you must tell us where Fred is now. I'm quite sure you've told us the truth and Fred has told you the truth. He's more likely to be charged with manslaughter than murder; and it's possible he won't be given a custodial sentence at all, given the circumstances. From what you've told us of his health, you may be putting him in danger by helping him to hide."

"I'll . . . think about it. I suppose I shall be charged, too?"

"You'll probably be charged with aiding and abetting Fred, or being an accessory after the fact. The charges are likely to be dropped if you hand him in."

"I've said I'll think about it. I'll decide on what's best for Fred. I'm not too worried about myself. One more thing I will say: Percy's dangerous. If I were you, I'd be worried about what he might do to Anton."

CHAPTER 79

ISOBEL LAWRENCE WAS detained at the police station until a solicitor could be found to represent her, when Tim and Juliet would ask her to give her statement again, under caution.

"I don't doubt that she'll both co-operate and stick to the statement," said Tim. "If she's telling the truth, Dora and Amelia are probably right about how Sykes died. They believe Percy Forsyth put something in Sykes's hip-flask. It squares with the path lab results – that Sykes died of a massive dose of flunitrazepam."

"It could be difficult to prove it was Percy who put it there."

"Maybe. In any case, it's time we paid Mr Forsyth-Jones – or Norman Potts, take your pick – a visit."

"Do you think Isobel Lawrence is being alarmist when she says Anton Greenweal might be in danger?"

"Percy's a sponger. As long as Anton's keeping him, he should be ok. Unless he's the beneficiary of Anton's own will, that is. But anyone who's murdered once might acquire the taste for blood."

"If the information we have is correct, technically Percy's not a murderer."

"A judge and jury might think differently. Besides, he is if he murdered Sykes. Let's . . ."

"Excuse me, DI Yates."

Tim turned to see Giash Chakrabati standing beside him.

"The four by four you asked me to check out: it's registered to a Mr Roy Dadd."

"Roy Dadd!" Tim exclaimed. "I can't believe I forgot his name! Still kept the initials, then – Reggie Dack now, and another twenty RDs to be taken into account along the way, unless I'm very much mistaken."

"Who is he?" asked Juliet.

"Started off as a small time crook, then got into a bigger league by fixing greyhound races. We tried to prosecute him for that when I was in the Met, but we couldn't make it stick. I seem to remember that, some time later, after I'd left the Met, he was done for dog-fighting and served time. We can look him up."

"Sounds the sort of character who'd run a hare-coursing outfit?"

"You bet! But we'll wait until we get the results from those tyre tracks before we try to nab him. He's a slippery character – he's got away with far more than we've managed to pin on him. And he'll be able to afford a good lawyer. For now, we need to catch Mr Forsyth before he disappears."

CHAPTER 80

"LOVELY HOUSE!" SAID Juliet, as she and Tim drew up outside Metheringham Manor. "Should we have got a warrant?"

"There wasn't time," said Tim. "We'll do that next, unless Mr Forsyth is very good at convincing us he's innocent."

As they approached the house, they could hear shouting. By the time they'd reached the front door, which was standing slightly ajar, two distinctive voices could be discerned. Percy and Anton were having a row.

"At least he hasn't killed Anton!" said Tim. He yanked at the massive bell-pull to one side of the door. A rich tolling peal resonated deep within the house, but the shouting didn't abate. The sounds of a scuffle could also be heard. Tim rang the bell again, but no-one appeared. The shouting grew louder and more vicious.

"I'm going in," he said. "Call for back-up."

Following the noise, Tim found himself in a long, high-ceilinged room with a massive fireplace. The two men were rolling on the floor, fighting savagely. Or rather, one of them was savagely attacking the other, at present trying to bang his head on the stone flags. Tim waited a few seconds while his eyes adjusted to the gloomy light and launched himself at the assailant, hauling him off his victim.

Percy Forsyth-Jones rolled sideways and heaved himself laboriously into a sitting position. His face was covered in scratches and the flesh around one of his eyes was already swelling alarmingly. He saw Tim and immediately took stock of the situation. Tim had pinioned Anton's arms behind his back, so he couldn't see who was restraining him.

"Let me go, you stupid fucker, whoever you are. I'll fucking swing for him!"

"DI Yates! Thank God you've come! I'm certain he would have killed me," said Percy in subdued but modulated tones. "Anton, I think you'd better make a clean breast of it."

Anton Greenweal stood stock still for a moment, evidently shocked when he heard Tim's name. Then he started struggling again.

"Oh, I see what you're up to!" he spat. "Trying to lay it all on me, now, are you? Well, I'll make sure you go down for just as long as I do!"

Percy rose slowly to his feet and sank into one of the outsize armchairs that stood in front of the hearth.

"The thing is, DI Yates, this is a family matter and I should never have allowed myself to get involved. Dear Anton discovered that his uncle was going to alter his will and leave everything to some mystery man he said he'd wronged. It wasn't at all like Gordon to show remorse – and come to think of it, I wouldn't be surprised if he wasn't having Anton on – but Anton in his wisdom decided to take it seriously. He asked me to help to do the old bastard in before he had a chance to see his lawyer."

"So you thought it would be a good idea to involve Fred Sharman, get him to do your dirty work?"

"I didn't say that, I . . . "

By the time back-up had arrived, Percy and Anton had each accused the other of plotting the murder, each providing so many details that it was clear they were accomplices.

"Easiest charge I've ever made," said Tim to Juliet afterwards.

"The prosecution and defence teams are both going to have fun," said Juliet. "How will they ever disentangle exactly who was responsible for what?"

"Not our affair," said Tim. "I won't lose any sleep over it, as long as Fred Sharman gets off."

CHAPTER 81

Two DAYS LATER, Tim and Juliet were knocking on Roy Dadd's front door. It was just after 7 a.m. Roy was not expecting them – Tim knew he would have made himself scarce if he'd had prior notice – and he was still in bed when Tim banged on the door.

He banged several times to no avail before he resorted to yelling as loud as he could "Mr Dadd! Open up! Police!"

Roy Dadd came thundering down the stairs and flung wide the door.

"What the fuck do you want? This is a good neighbour'ood." Roy peered discreetly to his left and right.

"Oh, gone all respectable, have you, Roy?" Tim held out his identity card. "DI Yates, South Lincs Police, and this is DS Armstrong. Can we come in?"

Dadd looked at the card and then scrutinised Tim's face.

"Seen you before, 'aven't I?" he said.

"That's right, Roy. Kempton race-track. Ring any bells?"

Roy Dadd scowled.

"That was a long time ago. And I got off – I was innocent, like. But you'd better come in."

Once they were inside the house and Dadd had ushered them unwillingly into his kitchen, he put on a show of bravado, but both Tim and Juliet could see he was nervous. He was fiddling with the belt on his dressing-gown.

"What's this all about, then?"

Tim produced three sets of photographs, one of the tyre tracks in the field and two of the plaster casts taken from the field and Dadd's four by four.

"We have reason to believe these tracks were made by the tyres on your car," he said, indicating the field photograph. "We took a plaster cast of them: it's identical to casts we also took from an imprint of your tyres when your wife was helping us with our enquiries earlier this week."

"Stupid bitch," Dadd muttered. "Why couldn't she bring her own car?" Then he looked relieved. "It's all paid up square and taxed," he said, "I've got the papers to prove it. It in't stolen."

"No, we know that, Mr Dadd," said Juliet. "It's the location of the tracks that concerns us."

"Why, where was that then?" Dadd looked worried again. "Look, I seen the news last night. I know you charged that woman with 'is murder and you couldn't make it stick. But it wan't me, honest! I just wanted to put the wind up 'im."

Tim couldn't believe his ears. Was he going to get two unsolicited confessions in the same week?

"Are you referring to the death of Gordon Bemrose?"

"Like I said, I wanted to put the fear of God in 'im. So Jacko and I jumps 'im and ties 'im up . . ."

Tim was thinking quickly, trying to visualise the Holyrood House statements that described the first attack on Gordon Bemrose.

"You did more than tie him up. Didn't you wrap him in plastic? Were you intending to take him somewhere?"

"We din't want to do 'im any real 'arm," Dadd said again, guilt written all over his face. "In any case, there was too many people about, so we 'ung around for a while and jumped 'im again. Only then we saw we'd got the wrong bloke and we scarpered, see?"

Tim did see. He saw that, based on the rest of the evidence, Dadd was telling the truth, but was terrified they wouldn't believe him. It gave them a supreme advantage. Tim looked as sceptical as he possibly could.

"Hmm. So why did you want to 'teach him a lesson'?"

"'E took my dog, din't 'e? Oh, 'e pretended 'e din't know where 'e'd gone, but I knew better. Sold 'im to someone, most like. 'E'd have fetched a lot. Ten grand, maybe."

Juliet thought of Sally and then the remains of the Saluki they'd found in Gordon Bemrose's cellar.

"Are you sure the dog was a male?" she asked.

Dadd looked puzzled for a second and let out a phlegmy cackle.

"Yeah. You fink I don't know the difference?"

"What breed of dog was it, Mr Dadd?" Juliet's tone was stony.

"A Salewki, innit? Why d'you want to know?"

Tim looked at Juliet and chuckled inwardly. Roy Dadd was about to get the grilling of his life. Juliet was on a mission now. No-one had yet been sentenced for more than six months for hare coursing, but he knew she'd do her best to gather enough evidence to double that figure; and she'd make damn sure that Dadd was kept away from dogs for the rest of his life.

"Reggie!" issued a plaintive voice from the stairwell. "Reggie, why you up so early? You got someone down there with you?"

404

CHAPTER 82

SUPERINTENDENT THORNTON WAS in an excellent mood. He'd just taken a call from the Chief Constable, who had congratulated him for solving a 'complex murder case' and cracking the latest spate of hare coursing with 'the minimum of resources and fuss'. Thornton could see promotion racing up in the wing mirrors. He might even get a Commendation.

Patti had attended an interview for a lecturing post on the King's Lynn campus of the College of West Anglia. She knew she'd given a good performance, but she was still astonished when she received the phone call offering her the job. Despite the difficulties she would still face in caring for her mother, she felt her luck had changed at last. She'd been a fool to hanker after Tim for all those years: she would put their relationship firmly behind her now and start a new chapter in her life.

Tim and Juliet were enjoying a celebratory drink in the White Hart.

"Gordon Bemrose's solicitor was in touch today," said Tim. "Apparently it was his intention to change his will by leaving everything to Fred Sharman. But he didn't get the chance to finalise it – the old will is still in place."

"Who are the beneficiaries, then?"

"There's a lot of debt, so the solicitor doubts anyone will get very much. Anton is one of the named beneficiaries, but if he's convicted he'll be disqualified. Fred's another, but the same goes for him, unless the judge directs that he isn't fit to plead. The others are Isobel Lawrence and Patti."

"I hope Patti gets something, after all she's been through."

"So do I," said Tim thoughtfully.

"Did you see her before she left?"

"No. She told Thornton she didn't want any kind of official goodbye – that it would be best to slip away unnoticed."

"She may have been unnoticed when she went, but I've a hunch we're all going to miss her. She'll take a lot of replacing. What did Superintendent Thornton say about it?"

"What you might have expected. He was 'glad we'd handled her arrest *sensitively*. Otherwise that Rook woman would be trying to get compensation for her.'"

Juliet snorted.

"Is that all?"

"Yes. As I said, just what you'd expect."

"There's one thing that's still puzzling me."

"Only one?" Tim grinned. Juliet ignored him and continued.

"Gordon was wounded in the cellar. In the throat. We still don't know who did that."

"You're right. We don't. And it could have been Patti, but I doubt it. I'd put my money on Colin Franklin. He was here, there and everywhere that evening. He had both the opportunity and the motive. And it could explain why he and his wife weren't getting on when we saw them again. She may have known – or suspected something."

"But how did he get into the cellar? The door was locked."

"There was a spare set of keys hanging in the kitchen, for all the locks in the house as well as the cottages. He could have borrowed those and put them back. But it was a really naff lock. A practical bloke like him could have picked it with a bit of wire."

Juliet had received the date of her final operation. It was still six weeks away, but she'd agreed with Jake they should move into the cottage now to sort out as much as they could and make sure Sally was settled there. Sally, with the help of a canine tripod specialist, was continuing to make good progress.

One hurdle remained: Jake's promise to his Aunt Emily to introduce Juliet to her. Juliet was astonished at how nervous she felt about this meeting – like a 1960s girlfriend being introduced to her boyfriend's parents for the first time, she thought, mustering as much irony as she could. She was convinced that Emily would dislike her because she hadn't committed to marrying Jake; and she was always self-conscious about her disfigurement when she met someone new.

They arrived at Aunt Emily's flat in the sheltered accommodation complex late one Saturday afternoon. Aunt Emily was waiting with tea and cake, but when they went in, she barely looked at Juliet. She had eyes only for the Saluki.

"Oh, what a beautiful dog!" she said.

ACKNOWLEDGEMENTS

ONCE AGAIN, I feel I must begin by saying once more how much I owe to Chris and Jen Hamilton-Emery for their unconditional support for and encouragement of all the DI Yates novels. The jacket which Chris has designed for *Chasing Hares* is particularly inspired! I'd also like to thank others who contribute to my own and Salt's many successes, especially Emma Dowson, who seems to cram thirty-six hours into every working day!

As I've said before, the Yates novels would be nothing without their readers. With great sincerity I'd like to thank all of you, including those whom I've actually met, those of you who have taken the trouble to 'meet' me or review my books with such generosity on my blog or on social networks, and everyone who has bought or borrowed my books to read. You are a constant source of inspiration to me.

Equally important is the growing list of booksellers and librarians who support my novels. You are too many to name, so please don't be offended if I have missed you out. Among booksellers I owe very special thanks to Sam Buckley and her reading groups at Bookmark in Spalding, who have followed DI Yates from 'birth' and Tim Walker and Jenny Pugh of Walker Books in Stamford, who always welcome me with generous hospitality for a signing session in the run-up to Christmas. I'd also like to say a big thank you to the proprietors of some of the non-traditional venues who have offered me events: the wonderful evening hosted by the micro-brewery at Pendrill Court in Papworth, Cambridgeshire, particularly stands out. On behalf of all writers, booksellers and readers, I'd like to add a special thank-you to Tim Godfray, the long-time CEO of the Booksellers Association, who retires this year, for the monumental support he has given us all for almost half a century.

Among librarians, Sharman Morriss, the librarian at Spalding Public Library, and Alison Cassels, at Wakefield One, have worked far harder for me than I could have had any right to expect. As well as hosting some memorable events for me in Spalding, Sharman has promoted my books among her colleagues in the rest of the county. Jane Barber and her colleagues at Stamford Library and Louise Jones and her colleagues at Lincoln Library arranged hugely successful events for me earlier this year

I'd also like to thank Carla Greene, at BBC Radio Lincolnshire and Elise Harrington, of Lincoln City Radio, whose dynamic interviews have attracted large numbers of new Yates readers, especially in Lincolnshire.

There are many other people whom I ought to thank here. As always, it's impossible to mention everyone, but I must pay tribute to those staunch friends who wait impatiently for the next book to come out and always promote it with enthusiasm, especially Madelaine and Marc and Anthony and Marcus, to whom this book is dedicated; Pamela and Robert, who provide support in so many forms that it is impossible to list them all; Sally, who always welcomes me when I'm feeling frazzled in London; and Ruth and Peter Cropley, the present owners of Sausage Hall, the third Yates novel, who I hope will also be pleased with the ninth!

The members of my family continue to provide great support, each in his or her own inimitable way. Once again James and Annika have worked meticulously through the final draft, picking up grammatical inaccuracies and other minor inconsistencies with hawk-like precision, and assiduously checking on my behalf details which I always seem to get wrong, even though I have checked them myself and was convinced I was right! Emma, who is now at school, continues to develop as a wordsmith and I am learning much from her clear-eyed view of the world and impeccable approach to logic.

Chris offers appreciation in his own measured, slightly barbed way, often sending it from far-flung places – and it is gratifying to know that the books have accompanied him on many otherwise tedious and often fraught journeys.

My very sincere thanks, love and best wishes to you all.

CHRISTINA JAMES

ALSO BY CHRISTINA JAMES

In the Family (978-1-907773-24-2)

Almost Love (978-1-907773-46-4)

Sausage Hall (978-1-907773-82-2)

The Crossing (978-1-78463-041-6)

Rooted in Dishonour (978-1-78463-089-8)

Fair of Face (978-1-78463-108-6)

Gentleman Jack (978-1-78463-134-5)

NEW FICTION FROM SALT

ELEANOR ANSTRUTHER
A Perfect Explanation (978-1-78463-164-2)

NEIL CAMPBELL
Lanyards (978-1-78463-170-3)

MARK CAREW
Magnus (978-1-78463-204-5)

ANDREW COWAN
Your Fault (978-1-78463-180-2)

AMANTHI HARRIS
Beautiful Place (978-1-78463-193-2)

S. A. HARRIS
Haverscroft (978-1-78463-200-7)

CHRISTINA JAMES
Chasing Hares (978-1-78463-189-5)

NEW FICTION FROM SALT

VESNA MAIN
Good Day? (978-1-78463-191-8)

SIMON OKOTIE
After Absalon (978-1-78463-166-6)

TREVOR MARK THOMAS
The Bothy (978-1-78463-160-4)

TIM VINE
The Electric Dwarf (978-1-78463-172-7)

MICHAEL WALTERS
The Complex (978-1-78463-162-8)

GUY WARE
The Faculty of Indifference (978-1-78463-176-5)

MEIKE ZIERVOGEL
Flotsam (978-1-78463-178-9)

NEW POETRY FROM SALT

AMIT CHAUDHURI
Sweet Shop (978-1-78463-182-6)

DAVID BRIGGS
Cracked Skull Cinema (978-1-78463-207-6)

PETER DANIELS
My Tin Watermelon (978-1-78463-209-0)

MATTHEW HAIGH
Death Magazine (978-1-78463-206-9)

ANDREW McDONNELL
The Somnambulist Cookbook (978-1-78463-199-4)

ELEANOR REES
The Well at Winter Solstice (978-1-78463-184-0)

TONY WILLIAMS
Hawthorn City (978-1-78463-212-0)

This book has been typeset by
SALT PUBLISHING LIMITED
using Neacademia, a font designed by Sergei Egorov
for the Rosetta Type Foundry in the Czech Republic. It
is manufactured using Holmen Book Cream 70gsm, a
Forest Stewardship Council™ certified paper from the
Hallsta Paper Mill in Sweden. It was printed and bound
by Clays Limited in Bungay, Suffolk, Great Britain.

CROMER
GREAT BRITAIN
MMXIX